Books by April Wilson

McIntyre Security, Inc. Bodyguard Series

Vulnerable

Fearless

Shane (a novella)

Broken

Shattered

Imperfect

Ruined

Hostage

Redeemed

Marry Me (a novella)

Snowbound (a novella)

Regret

With This Ring (a novella)

Collateral Damage

Special Delivery

McIntyre Search and Rescue Series

Search and Rescue

Lost and Found

McIntyre Protector Series

Finding Layla

Damaged Goods

A Tyler Jamison Novel:

Somebody to Love

Somebody to Hold

Somebody to Cherish

A British Billionaire Romance:

Charmed (co-written with Laura Riley)

Audiobooks by April Wilson

For links to my audiobooks, please visit my website:
www.aprilwilsonauthor.com/audiobooks

Fearless

McIntyre Security Bodyguard Series
Book 2

By

April Wilson

Cover by Steamy Designs
Photography by Eric McKinney/6:12 Photography
Model: David W

Visit www.aprilwilsonwrites.com to sign up for the author's e-mail newsletter to be notified about upcoming releases.

ISBN-13: 978-1530879465
ISBN-10: 1530879469

Published in the United States of America
First Printing April 2016

To my darling daughter, Chloe.

To my sister and BFF, Lori.

And to all the wonderful people around the world who read my first novel, *Vulnerable*. You made my dream come true.

1

I am *so* not a morning person. But still, I can't help rousing from a deep sleep when I feel a warm finger skimming up and down my naked spine. The finger morphs into a warm hand that slips down and cups my butt cheek, giving it a light squeeze. The pleasure is so intense I moan and snuggle deeper into my pillow.

It's way too early for coherent thought. I know this because it's still pitch black outside our bedroom window. As usual, someone's up awfully early. He's like a furnace, and the delicious heat of his big body radiates outward, sinking into my bones. I press back against him, soaking in his warmth and loving the feel of his bare skin against mine.

For crying out loud, it's not even dawn yet, and I'm still sleepy. I groan in objection. "Shane, it's too early. Go back to sleep."

He chuckles at the plaintive tone of my voice. I think he takes sadistic pleasure in waking me up early.

"I can't," he says, moving my hair off my shoulder so he can press tiny, nibbling kisses there. "I have to work, sweetheart."

"No, you don't. You're the boss." He's not just the boss, he's the CEO. Surely that gives him some leeway.

"I just wanted to say good morning properly," he whispers, his warm breath washing over the shell of my ear, ruffling my hair and sending a shiver down my spine. "Before I head to the office."

The office he's referring to is the one here at the house. For the past two months, since I was released from the hospital after suffering a horrible beating by one of the students at the medical school library where I worked, Shane's been working mostly from his satellite office here at his Kenilworth estate, instead of from his downtown office high rise.

"No," I groan, burrowing closer. "Don't go."

I can feel the vibration of his quiet laugh. His lips are in my hair and he whispers to me—something he knows I find arousing. "I have to. I have a conference call in twenty minutes with the director of the UK office."

I turn to face him, gazing up into his beautiful blue eyes. His short brown hair is sticking up in tufts, and I reach up to smooth one down. "But it's so early."

"Not in the UK, it isn't. It's mid-morning their time. How about lunch today? Can you fit me into your busy schedule?"

I laugh because I don't have any sort of schedule these days. Since getting out of the hospital, I haven't gone back to work yet. I've been in recuperation mode, giving my bruised ribs time to heal, the bruises on my face time to fade, my broken left arm time to mend. I'm fine now for the most part, and I really do need to get back to some sort of schedule. We've had this discussion before, and it's never gone well. But since he's in such a good mood, I think I'll try again. "It's time for me to go back to work."

A shadow dims his expression, and I know he's thinking of the assault. Just two months ago, I was attacked in my office and nearly killed. I haven't been back to the campus since. And Shane's made it perfectly clear that he doesn't want me to go back at all.

With the tip of his index finger, he gently traces the shadowed remnant of a bruise on the edge of my cheek. "Your bruises are nearly gone." His hand comes up and brushes my hair back from my face, tucking the tousled strands behind my ear. "You don't need to go back to work, sweetheart. I'd rather you didn't."

"I can't sit around here all day, being waited on hand and foot. It's driving me crazy. I have to do something productive." Besides, my car payment and student loan aren't going to pay themselves. Shane deposited a large sum of money into my bank account to cover my bills while I'm out on medical leave, but I can't just keep taking his money.

He strokes my cheek. "Honey, if it's about money—"

"It's not just the money."

Shane's got millions tucked away in cash, real estate, and technology patents. And his security services company—McIntyre Security, Inc.—is a privately held company worth several billion dollars. For him, money is no object. But for me, it is. I need to know I'm earning my own way.

I've been living in the lap of luxury for two months now, and it's not all it's cracked up to be. I'm the daughter of a retired kindergarten teacher —essentially raised by a single parent, since my dad died in the line of duty as a police officer when I was an infant. Mom and I were comfortable enough, but we didn't live a lavish lifestyle. Now, I live in a house that has its own staff, including a housekeeper, a groundskeeper, and full-time security.

Shane's housekeeper, Elly, manages all the cooking, cleaning, and laundry with a small staff. She treats me like I'm the lady of the house. She's a wonderful woman, and I absolutely adore her, but she won't let me lift a finger around here.

It's just not my style. I want to be out in the world, doing something to pay my own way. If I'm not going to go back to my job at the library, then I need to find something else.

What I really want to do is become involved in running Clancy's. I still can't believe Shane bought me a bookstore—and not just any bookstore, but one of the largest independent bookstores in the country! He bought me my *happy place*, and it must have cost him a small fortune. The building is located in the heart of downtown Chicago, on N. Michigan Avenue, the global tourist magnet of the Midwest.

I decide to test the waters. "I've been thinking about getting involved in running the bookstore."

"Good idea."

I know he likes this option better than me returning to work at the medical school library. He has greater control over security at the bookstore than he does at a sprawling college campus.

Shane rolls me to my back and leans down to kiss me, his lips warm and soft, languid, as he teases me awake. His hand comes up to frame the side of my face, his thumb stroking my throat. His touch is careful, gentle, as if he's afraid I might break into pieces. And that's the problem. He's been treating me like I'm made of spun glass ever since the assault.

I know it's partly because he blames himself for what happened. I appreciate the gallantry—I really do—but I wish he'd stop being quite so gallant. I want to feel his heat and his strength again. I want to feel him surging hotly inside me. It's been so long.

When I open my mouth under his lazy assault, he moans and

moves in for a deeper kiss. His tongue strokes mine gently, teasing me, and immediately I feel the blood heading south to pool between my legs, making me throb with need. What is it about this man? He can arouse me with just a simple touch.

I sigh as Shane pushes the bedding down to my waist, exposing my breasts to the cool morning air. I shiver, but whether it's from the cool air or from anticipation, I'm not sure. The nightlight on the bedside table next to me casts a dim, golden light on us.

I'm twenty-four years old and I sleep with a nightlight. I have for eighteen years, since the day I was abducted in my own front yard and spent twelve hours trussed up naked in a cold, dark cellar. The light helps keep the night terrors at bay.

The majority of my life has been colored by that horrendous night. I never saw the face of the man who grabbed me—his name is Howard Kline, and he's now a free man. Kline grabbed me from behind and threw me in the back of his work van, blindfolding me and taping my wrists and ankles so I couldn't move. I never saw anything. I only remember the sounds and the smells. I remember the sound of his voice, like crushed gravel. The smell of his foul breath and his unwashed body. The smell of clothes that hadn't been washed in a long time.

I learned later that he'd driven me out to the farm that he shared with his mother. He'd carried me down into a pitch black cellar and left me there, after cutting off my clothes. I remember the cold—my body was wracked with cold. I remember the smell of the damp earth, musty and moldy. I remember having to pee so badly it hurt, and I cried until I finally couldn't hold it any longer. I lay there all night it seemed, alone and afraid, crying for my mom, for my brother.

Sometime in the night, long after I'd run out of tears, the metal door to the cellar flung open and I heard the sound of boots thudding down the rickety wooden steps. Police officers stormed the little cellar, blinding me with their flashlights as they swept the room until they came to land on me.

My big brother, Tyler, was there first, pulling me into his strong arms. I remember him rocking me as another police officer cut the painful tape from my wrists and ankles. As I shuddered from the cold on my bare skin, Tyler removed his police jacket and wrapped me in it before carrying me out to a waiting ambulance. Those memories still haunt me. I hear that gravelly voice, and I smell his body odor and the musty earth. Sometimes I wake up screaming.

Shane looks up suddenly, his eyes on my face. "What is it?"

I smile and shake my head. "Nothing. I'm fine."

He frowns, and I know he's not fooled.

The faint glow from the nightlight is enough for him to make out my breasts in the early morning darkness. His big hand comes up to cup one of them, and he molds the small mound in his hand. He leans down and tongues the tip, causing my nipple to pucker instantly. When he flutters his tongue over the tight little bud, I feel an electrical charge course through my body, heading straight to my sex. I moan loudly as he draws my stiff, sensitive nipple into his mouth and sucks gently. With each warm, wet pull of his mouth on my nipple, I feel a corresponding softening between my legs. He's a master at seduction.

After paying rapt attention to my breast, Shane raises his head to look at me, a hopeful expression on his handsome face. His hand slips down to the hot, aching place between my legs, and his finger slips between my folds and rims my wet opening, teasing me mercilessly. "Yes?"

Already my insides are melting and my clitoris is throbbing. Of course he has to finish what he started, or I'll be a wreck all day, achy and needy and unable to think about anything else but his hot mouth on me. "You started this, so yeah, you'd better finish it."

That's all the invitation he needs. Shane comes up over me on all fours, caging me in—careful to keep his weight off me. I panic easily when I'm pinned down. He's learned just how much I can handle and when.

He bends down to kiss me, and I run my fingers through his hair, gripping the short strands and pulling him closer. I move my hands to cup his face, loving the feel of his short beard against my palms. We make slow love with our mouths, touching and licking and tasting each other until we're both breathing hard.

Eventually, he pulls his mouth away from mine and trails his lips along my jawline to the back of my ear, where he knows I'm extremely sensitive. At the feel of his lips teasing that tender spot, I clench my sex tightly around his finger, aching for a deeper, thicker penetration. I swear, he could make me come just by kissing me.

When he kisses and nibbles on a particularly tender spot, a shiver ripples through me. He knows exactly what he's doing, the fiend. He's made it his life's goal to learn all the ways to drive me wild.

His mouth skims down my throat, and he pauses to kiss my pulse point—another sensitive spot—just before slipping down to my left breast. He draws my nipple into his mouth and sucks on it until my hips are moving and I'm restless with aching need.

"Shane...." His name is little more than a breathy plea as I'm reduced to begging.

"Shh."

I'm pretty sure Shane lives to torment me. I run my hands across his firm shoulders and down his arms, tracing the well-defined contours of his biceps. He trains hard at all sorts of physical activity, including several forms of martial arts, and his body shows it. There's not an ounce of fat on him, and where my body is soft and yield-ing, his is unfailingly hard. I run my fingers along one of the scars on his chest—a souvenir bullet wound from his days in the Marine Corps—and down his ridged abdomen. As my fingers skate lightly past his belly, following his dark, narrow happy trail, I'm rewarded when he shudders.

"Patience, sweetheart," he says. His expression is tight, and I know he's far from unaffected.

I know exactly where he's headed when he starts to scoot down the bed. And although I'd prefer he let me shower first, I know he won't wait for that—he's far too single-minded once he's aroused.

He kisses his way down to my belly button, where he lingers for a moment, teasing the small indent with the tip of his tongue. I'm ticklish there, and he knows it. After trailing a smattering of kisses over the soft rise of my lower belly, he finally arrives at his destina-tion. He glances up at me then, his nostrils flaring as he undoubtedly detects the warm, earthy scent of my arousal. I'm wet already and, by the knowing expression on his face, I'm sure he can tell.

When he keeps going, my hands automatically go to his shoul-ders, resting there a little nervously. I'm still not used to such intense intimacy, and when his warm breath washes over the blonde curls between my legs, my thighs start shaking. My hands flex nervously on his shoulders, and I'm not sure if I want to draw him closer or push him away.

He nudges my legs wide apart with gentle, yet firm hands until he can wedge his shoulders between them, pinning them open. I feel so exposed, so vulnerable, when I'm spread open to him like this.

"It's okay, sweetheart. Relax," he says, as if reading my mind.

I suck in a breath as he pries open the lips of my sex. He flicks my clitoris with the stiff tip of his tongue, and I jump, crying out loudly.

My body bows off the mattress, and his arms sweep underneath my thighs to hold me open for his scrutiny.

Outside, the sun is just starting to rise over the towering trees, filling our bedroom with the pale glow of early morning light. Shane's oblivious to anything except what he's doing between my legs. He doesn't seem to be in any hurry.

I gasp when he sucks gently on my clit. "I thought you have to work!"

He chuckles. "They'll wait for me."

I laugh. Of course they'll wait. He's the boss. "Shane, please." He's teasing me, building up my desire, and I can't stand the suspense. I know what's coming—a mind-numbing, toe-curling orgasm that will leave me breathless—but waiting for it is driving me crazy.

His tongue is hot and wet as he strokes the length of my slit, licking slowly and sensuously, like a big cat, from my opening to my clit. My thighs are trembling uncontrollably and, out of desperation, I latch onto his hair. He's a master at this—a diabolically talented master—and I'm at his mercy.

I feel a finger push inside my opening, stroking me inside as his tongue gets serious. Slick with my arousal, his finger glides easily inside me as he touches and teases me. He brings some of that silky wetness up to bathe my clit, which tickles, and then he sinks that finger back inside me, curling it as he searches for the tender spot that makes me fall apart every single time.

I'm not sure which pleasure is greater—the feel of his strong tongue lashing my clit in tight little movements or his finger tormenting me deep inside. Either sensation is capable of setting off a stunning orgasm. Together, they are enough to make me lose my mind.

I grip his hair hard as I feel my orgasm ratcheting up with a vengeance, and a moment later, it detonates like a bomb inside me. The pleasure is so acutely intense I cry out loudly, unable to censor myself. My body bows off the mattress, but he holds my hips tethered to the bed as his tongue torments me through concentric waves of sensation. The pleasure is so exquisite, I'm reduced to whimpering. My God, I'm glad these walls are thick, because otherwise, half the household would be able to hear me.

Shane comes up beside me and wraps me in his strong arms, holding me close and rocking me through the residual tremors of my orgasm. I can smell myself, warm and earthy, on him, on his beard, and it's simultaneously titillating and mortifying. I don't think I'll ever get used to how comfortable he is with such raw intimacy. He's such a sexual animal, shamelessly taking everything he wants—every touch, every taste, every scent—and wallowing in it. But this is all still so new to me.

As the lingering tremors of my orgasm reverberate through me, I reach for his erection with my good hand. He's hard and smooth as stone against my palm, huge and pulsing in my grip. I squeeze him firmly, which I know he likes, and he groans. I'm hoping this time he'll let me pleasure him.

My optimism is short lived, though, when he gently removes my hand from his cock. "No, sweetheart."

I close my eyes and groan with frustration. "Shane!"

"No."

From the tone of his voice, I know it's futile to argue with him. We've been going around and around about this for weeks. After I was released from the hospital, he swore we wouldn't have sex again until I was fully recovered from the beating, and he's stuck obstinately to his pledge. Oh, he pleasures me frequently, daily in fact, but apparently that's not a violation of his vow. But he refuses to have intercourse with me or let me pleasure him. I think it's some kind of self-imposed punishment for what Andrew Morton did to me. No matter how many times I've told him otherwise, Shane blames himself for what happened.

"Shane, I'm fine," I tell him for the hundredth time. It's true. The bruises on my face, while still faintly visible, no longer hurt. My ribs have healed, and the fiberglass cast on my left arm is scheduled to come off tomorrow. "Really, I'm fine. Please, I want you—"

"I need to grab a quick shower before my call." He kisses me once more—the taste of my slick arousal on his lips a potent reminder of what he just did—then climbs off the bed and heads for our private bathroom.

For several long moments, I stare at the closed door to the bathroom, wondering what he's doing in there. I know he's hard as a rock because I felt the evidence in my hand. He has to be uncomfortable. His mind may be fully committed to this self-imposed celibacy, but I know his body isn't on board.

I can't help wondering if he takes care of it himself. Is he masturbating in the shower? Or is he taking a cold shower, hoping to kill the arousal he feels? Not only is he punishing himself, but he's punishing me. I need to feel him inside me again, thrusting deep and hard. I *ache* to feel him inside me.

I lay back in bed, my body soft and replete with satisfaction after the mind-blowing orgasm he just gave me. I can still feel the tingling between my legs, not to mention the wetness. I pull the covers up to my chin and wrap my arms around his pillow, snuggling back into our bed as post-orgasmic bliss flows through me.

My pleasure is marred, though, by the knowledge that he's suffering unnecessarily. I feel guilty wallowing in pleasure when I know he's denying himself the same.

My eyes are so heavy, I think I'll close them just for a few moments.

2

"Hey, Princess. You didn't come down to breakfast."

When I open my eyes, I'm blinded by the sunlight streaming through the balcony doors. Shane's sister Lia is sitting on the side of my bed, dressed in workout clothes—black boy shorts and a black sports bra. Her sleek muscles are toned and tanned from the summer sun.

I groan, feeling slightly hungover after having fallen back to sleep. "What time is it?"

"Eight-thirty. Time to rise and shine."

I nod, sitting up in bed. I must have fallen asleep while Shane was in the shower because I don't remember him coming out or getting dressed and leaving our suite.

"Since you missed breakfast, Elly sent up a plate for you. Voila! Breakfast in bed."

Lia hands me a covered plate, and I lift the lid to find my favorite breakfast underneath—pancakes and bacon. Elly spoils me rotten.

Elly serves a big buffet breakfast every morning in the dining room, and usually everyone in residence comes to eat. On any given day, that's usually a dozen people—including Shane's siblings, the household staff, and the security staff.

I feel guilty for missing it. "Did you see Shane at breakfast?"

"Just for a second," Lia says, stealing a strip of bacon off my plate. "Since you didn't come down, he filled up a plate and took it back to his office." She reaches out and ruffles my hair. "You should have come down. I missed you."

Lia's the silver lining that resulted from the assault. She is Shane's youngest of three sisters, and she works as a bodyguard at McIntyre Security. After I was released from the hospital, Shane assigned her as my primary bodyguard, which means she goes wherever I go. But more than that, she's become a close friend.

Lia makes this whole situation almost tolerable. Almost.

"I'm sorry I missed breakfast. I was awake when Shane got up, but I guess I fell back to sleep."

That's true of course. But it's not the whole truth. Sometimes I just can't face a table full of talkative people in the morning. I'm a bit of an introvert. And I'm still feeling guilty about Shane getting me off this morning, but not letting me return the favor. Something has to change, and soon.

Lia nudges my right arm—the one that isn't encased in a lime-green cast. "Hey, what's wrong? You look like someone kicked your puppy."

I give her a wry glance. "Your brother is what's wrong. He's driving me crazy."

She scoffs. "Tell me something I don't know. Shane's been an ass all summer. Ever since Andrew."

I don't want to think about Andrew right now. Every time I do, I picture him sitting in a straightjacket in a sterile room at the psychiatric hospital where he was sent by the judge who presided over my assault case. Andrew's young and probably scared to death. I can't help feeling sorry for him. And I know his parents are beside themselves over his incarceration. Yes, he nearly killed me, but I honestly don't think he meant to. He was just so angry at Shane, he lost it.

I have a sudden flashback to Andrew's boot coming at my face, and I flinch.

I force thoughts of Andrew out of my head. Remembering that day leads to dark, unpleasant memories I'd rather not relive. The last thing I need is more nightmares. The last thing *Shane* needs is for me to have more nightmares. No wonder he's punishing himself. Hearing me cry out in my sleep every night is a constant reminder of what happened.

I look at Lia. "Shane's avoiding me." I'm surprised at how much it hurts to admit that. "He works around the clock, so I hardly see him. He's up and gone from bed before the crack of dawn, and he waits until after I'm asleep to come to bed at night."

Lia frowns. "Beth—"

I shake my head because I don't want to hear any excuses for Shane's behavior. "It's driving me crazy. Sometimes I think about going home."

Now it's Lia's turn to shake her head. "You can't go back to the townhouse. It's not safe, and you know it. Besides, Shane would never allow it."

"It's not up to him." I glance out the balcony doors at the woods beyond the house. I don't want to leave this place. I just want things to go back to the way they were before the attack. I want Shane to stop punishing himself. "If I left, would you come with me?"

Lia crosses her arms over her ample chest. "As long as Howard Kline's still a free man, I'm your shadow. I go where you go."

I smile at Lia. While I haven't known her long, she's already become a close friend. And I don't have many of those.

She gives me a telling look. "You know why he's avoiding you, right?"

I shrug. I think I do, but I'm afraid to hear it, in case I'm wrong.

Lia rolls her bright blue eyes at me. "Because he's sexually frustrated."

Of course he is, but it's not from lack of trying on my part! "I've given him plenty of signals that I'm ready to resume—well, you know. But he refuses."

"*Sex*, Beth. You're allowed to say it. Anyway, give him some time. I remember what you looked like in that hospital bed, bloody and bruised. You looked like death warmed over. That's not an easy thing to forget. Especially not for someone like Shane, who thinks he's responsible for everyone he cares about—let alone the woman he loves. Just give him some time. Seeing you like that... it shook him. He's still not over it."

I sigh, wanting to change the subject before I start blubbering like a baby. I nod at her outfit. "Are you heading downstairs to work out?"

"Yeah. I came up here to check on you first."

"Can I come?"

"Sure, but it's just going to be me and Liam. Nothing exciting."

"I want to watch." It isn't doing me any good to hide away in my bedroom, feeling sorry for myself. "Just give me a few minutes to finish my breakfast and get cleaned up. I'll meet you downstairs."

* * *

I take the stairs down two flights to the lower level where the martial arts studio is located. Lia and her twin brother are warming up. While Lia's doing stretches on the mat, I watch Liam do a dozen pull-ups on a wall-mounted chin bar. His sculpted muscles flex and strain as he does his repetitions in rapid succession. From a purely objective perspective, I have to admit Lia's twin is all kinds of hot.

The twins are nothing alike. Yes, they're both muscular and fit, but that's where the resemblance ends. Lia is petite and curvy, with blonde hair and bright blue eyes like Shane's. Liam, on the other hand, is six feet tall, with a lean, ripped physique, broad shoulders, and brown hair and eyes. Liam works for McIntyre Security as a martial arts instructor. At twenty-two years of age, he already has an impressive record as an international martial arts champion. He's lethal.

"Hey, Beth," Liam says as he releases the bar and drops to his feet on the padded black mat. He's not even winded. "You here to watch?"

I grin at him, because I'm hoping I can do more than just watch this time. Ever since the assault, I've been wanting to learn self-defense, and Shane said I could once I was healed from my injuries. I figure I'm healed enough. "Can I join in?"

Liam gives me a quelling glance, which doesn't really surprise me. "No."

"Why not?"

He nods at my left arm in its full-length cast. "Isn't it kind of obvious?"

"But it's coming off tomorrow," I tell him. "And besides, Shane said I should learn self-defense."

"I know he did. But he's not going to let you train with a cast on your arm. I'm sorry. Maybe in a couple of months, when you're stronger."

I make myself comfortable on the black leather sofa situated beneath the picture window that overlooks the studio and watch the two youngest McIntyre siblings go through their paces. They knock the crap out of each other—kicking and punching and dodging blows that could fell a horse—and before long they're drenched in sweat. Lia has a bloody nose.

Even though Liam has mastered just about every type of martial art known to man, Lia can hold her own against her much bigger, more heavily muscled brother. Lia may be petite, but she's fast and unpredictable and tough as nails. She uses her speed and her small stature to her advantage. I've seen her flip guys twice her size.

I wish I was more like her. I wish I had her strength, her confidence. Maybe with some training, I can be more like her.

As I watch them going at it, I can't help thinking back to Andrew. I don't remember much about the attack—mostly I remember cowering on the floor as I shielded my head from his boot. I remember the fiery pain that shot up into my skull when one of the bones in my arm snapped like a dry twig. I can still hear the crack of the bone breaking.

Watching Lia and Liam spar stirs up memories better left forgotten, and soon the images from that day are playing over and over in my head in an endless loop. Before I know it, my heart's racing and I'm having trouble breathing. Hoping to circumvent an all-out panic attack, I jump up from the sofa and approach the mat, my throat tight.

"You have to show me something," I say, looking from one to the other. "Please."

If I could fight like they do, no one would ever be able to hurt me again.

Liam pauses as he turns to look at me, breathing hard, his hands on his hips. He frowns. "Beth."

"Please." And then the damned tears start, burning streaks down my face. "I'm sick and tired of being at the mercy of others. I want to be able to defend myself. I want to be able to fight back! Please, teach me something! Anything!"

"We could start her off slow," Lia says, glancing up at her brother. "Nothing too physical. Just some basic avoidance moves. Some footwork. That wouldn't kill her."

Liam shakes his head. "If Shane finds out, he'll kill me."

"Oh, hell, I'll do it," Lia says, glaring at her brother. She motions me forward. "Come on, Princess. Let's get your groove on."

I step eagerly onto the mat, and Lia directs me to stand facing her. Liam steps back, giving us room, and watches skeptically with his arms crossed over his muscled chest.

Lia positions herself in front of me. "Let's start with a basic avoidance move. If someone grabs your wrist"—and she demonstrates—"all you have to do is bring your elbow in like this"—another demonstration—"then twist your wrist to the side like this... and then bam! Here, I'll show you. Grab my wrist."

I grab Lia's left wrist with my right hand. In a slow and controlled move, she twists her wrist, bringing her elbow in, and effortlessly breaks my grip.

"Now, you try it," she says. She grabs my good hand, and I repeat what she did, breaking free of her grasp.

"That wasn't hard," I say.

"Try it again. This time, I won't make it so easy."

We repeat the move, but I have to put a little bit of muscle into it this time. Still, I manage to break Lia's hold without too much effort.

Lia cocks her head toward her brother. "Try it with Liam."

Liam steps onto the mat, shaking his head. "I'm going on record as saying I'm against this."

Lia laughs. "Liam, don't be such a freaking coward."

I stick my wrist out for him to grab. "Come on, Liam."

He gently clasps my wrist, and I easily twist free of his grasp. Too easily. He's barely going through the motions.

"I don't think you were really trying," I say, frowning. "Besides, this wouldn't have helped with Andrew. He came up from behind and grabbed me. What do I do then?"

Liam sighs as he makes a twirling motion with his finger. "Turn around."

I turn around, facing away from him.

Coming up from behind, he wraps his arms around me and pulls me securely against his hard chest, pinning me in place. "An attacker who grabs you from behind thinks he has you immobilized, but he doesn't. If you step to the outside—like this—you can hook your foot behind his knee, like this, and—"

"God damn it, Liam! Get your fucking hands off her!"

I flinch at the roar coming from the open doorway. I've never heard Shane yell like that before.

Lia turns to look at Shane. "Uh oh, Liam. I told you not to do that."

Liam releases me and gives his sister a blistering look.

I smile at Shane, hoping to defuse the situation. "I'm learning some self-defense moves."

Shane glares at his siblings as he walks into the studio, his expression hard. "Get out, both of you."

"Shane!" I say. "They were just showing me—"

"Out!" he yells, pointing at the door behind him. But his eyes are on me.

"I'll be right outside, Beth," Lia says as she follows Liam out the door. "Holler if you need me. I can take him."

I glance nervously through the picture window and see Lia standing in the hallway with a scowl on her face, watching me and Shane through the glass. Apparently, she takes her bodyguard responsibilities very seriously.

I glare at Shane. "You have no right—"

"The hell I don't!" He stalks toward me on the mat, and I take a step back. I can't help it; it's a reflex. He's never yelled at me before. At six-two, he can be very intimidating when he puts his mind to it—like right now.

"I just abandoned ten people on a trans-Atlantic conference call because I happen to glance at the video feed coming out of this room and saw my girlfriend—my *injured* girlfriend—engaging in martial arts training. With a broken arm!"

"I'm sorry about your conference call, but you didn't have to do that. Liam was just showing me—"

"You are in no shape for physical training, Beth!"

My heart is pounding now and I'm shaking. "Stop yelling at me!" He's so close, I have to crane my neck up to look into his face. His eyes are sharp and glittering with fire. I take a deep breath, trying to calm my racing heart. "Why are you so mad? You said you wanted me to learn self-defense."

"Not now! Not while you're recovering from a horrendous beating!"

"I'm fine, Shane." I take a deep breath and lower my voice in an attempt to calm him down. I've never seen him riled up this much before. "My ribs feel fine, and—" I raise my cast in the air—"this comes off tomorrow. I'm okay."

I'm momentarily distracted by the sight of Lia glaring at her brother through the viewing window. Shane looks back briefly, noticing we have a rapt audience, and then he turns back to face me, a scowl on his face. He takes a deep breath, and I get the feeling he's trying to rein himself in.

"What's gotten into you?" I say, propping my good hand on my hip. I'll be damned if I'm going to let him intimidate me.

Shane lays his hands on my shoulders and steers me backwards toward the locker room. I stumble off the edge of the mat, and he catches me.

"Where are we going?"

3

It's dark in the locker room, and immediately I tense up. Shane flips on a light switch.

"What is your problem?" I say, scowling at him.

I prop my good hand on my hip and do my best to look indignant, but it's hard to be taken seriously when your arm is wrapped in a fluorescent green cast. But I do my best to look pissed, because I am pissed.

He takes me by surprise when his hands come up to cradle my hot face. I gasp when he kisses me, his mouth ravenous on mine. Honestly, I didn't see that coming. I thought he was angry at me.

Encouraged by the sudden change in his demeanor, I take advantage of the situation and slip my tongue into his mouth. He groans, the sound loud and harsh in the quiet locker room. Now we're both kissing like we're starving for it, and I'm elated that he's letting himself go like this. He hasn't kissed me like this since—well, since before the assault.

He pulls me into his big body, which is hot as an inferno. I can feel his erection through his jeans, pressing insistently against my belly. His hand slips behind my head and he positions my mouth right where he wants it, so he can eat at me, his lips caressing and molding mine to his, his tongue stroking mine.

We drink each other in, inhaling our mutual sighs and absorbing the little sounds we both make. I can't help the whimper that escapes me, and he responds by clutching me even tighter. He draws my tongue into his mouth and sucks on it as he grinds his erection into my body.

Abruptly, Shane releases me and takes a step back, his chest heaving. I swear he looks shell-shocked. I nearly lose my balance, as I'd been leaning into him. He catches me and holds me at arm's length until he's sure I'm steady on my feet.

"I'm sorry I yelled," he says, running his fingers through his hair. "I wasn't yelling at *you*."

"It sure seemed like you were." Now I'm just plain mad at him, because he's already pulling away from me, both physically and emotionally. "You shouldn't have yelled at them either, Shane. They were just trying to help me. I asked them—I *begged* them—to teach me some self-defense moves."

He rubs his hand across his face, scrubbing his short beard, and exhales. "Beth, please. Wait a while, okay? You don't need to start training right now. Give yourself more time to heal."

I raise my left arm in the air, waving my cast in front of him. "I'm getting this off tomorrow, remember?"

"That's *if* the orthopedic doctor says it's ready to come off."

"Oh, it's ready to come off!" My anger is mounting. "If Dr. Meyer doesn't take it off tomorrow, I'll use a saw to take it off myself."

He grins at my empty threat, which only pisses me off more.

"Sorry," he says, reading my mood. He loses the smile.

I take a step toward him, closing the distance between us, and lay my good hand on the soft, faded cotton of his T-shirt, right over his pounding heart. "Shane."

Still breathing hard, he eyes me warily as if he's afraid of what I'm going to say. "What?"

I can't help noticing his blatantly obvious erection pressing against his jeans. My breath catches in my throat. I'm filled with a mixture of relief and anticipation, because I know he wants me.

He steps back, shaking his head. "I've got to get back to work, sweetheart." He lifts my hand and kisses it, as if that will soften the sting of his rejection. "No more self-defense lessons for the time being, okay?"

I'm tired of his evasiveness, so I pull my hand from his and reach up to cup the back of his neck. I pull his head down to mine and go up on my toes to reach his mouth.

"Beth—"

"Kiss me like you did a few minutes ago."

He shakes his head. "Sweetheart, no—"

"Yes."

He groans when I nudge his lips open with my own. His tongue sweeps across my upper lip as if he's tasting me. And then it sinks into my mouth, tangling with mine, stroking and caressing. For a moment, I think he'll give in.

But then he pulls back and gently extricates himself from my grasp. "I'm sorry, but I really have to get back. They're waiting on me."

"What good is being the CEO if you can't tell people to call you back later?"

He leans down and kisses my forehead, then steps out of my reach. "I'll see you at dinner tonight, all right?" He turns away and heads for the door.

"Shane, wait!"

He pauses mid-step, but doesn't look back. It hurts that he won't even look at me. I come up behind him and slip my good arm around his waist and lean into his back. He's solid and warm, and I breathe in his tantalizing male scent which stirs something deep inside me.

He stiffens, his muscles going rigid. "What?" He sounds annoyed. "I'm in a hurry, Beth."

Shane's dismissive words slice through me like a hot knife, searing me, and I swallow what I was about to say. I'm so out of my element here. Part of me wants to beg for his attention, but another part of me refuses to beg. Damn it, if he doesn't want to spend time with me—*be* with me—then I'm not going to grovel.

"Nothing," I say, letting my arm fall away from him. I step back and wipe my eyes with the back of my hand, glad that he's not looking at me. There's a deep, aching hole in my chest. "Go back to your meeting."

He turns partway, and I watch the muscles in his throat working as he swallows hard. He clears his throat. "I'll see you at dinner." His voice sounds as empty as I feel inside.

And then he walks away, without looking back once.

* * *

I follow in Shane's footsteps, feeling numb and confused. I know he wants me—his body's physical reaction made that abundantly clear. But I don't understand why he's putting this emotional distance between us. There has to be some way for me to get through to him.

I freeze when I hear heated voices in the hallway outside the martial arts studio.

"What the hell are you talking about?" Shane says, sounding gruff and impatient.

"Let me clue you in, *pal*." Lia sounds like she's on a roll. "You're being an ass."

"Mind your own business, Lia."

"Beth is my business. She's feeling pretty neglected these days, Shane. And if you don't get your head out of your ass, you're going to drive her away. She's already talking about going back to her townhouse."

I feel guilty for eavesdropping and am about to turn back when I'm stopped by Shane's angry retort.

"No way in hell!" he grates. "You can disabuse her of that notion right now."

"You can't keep her a prisoner here, Shane. If she wants to go, she can go."

There's a long silence, and I can just imagine Shane running his fingers through his hair—a habit when he's frustrated. When he finally speaks, his voice is low and subdued. "Has she been talking to Tyler?"

Shane and my brother have a tenuous relationship at best. Tyler is more like a father to me, and he finds it difficult to let Shane in. Tyler's also rather controlling, and that makes it even harder on him when he doesn't have a say in what I do. Shane knows that Tyler's tried before to talk me into staying with him at his Lincoln Park condo.

"He calls her every day, Shane. You know that."

"I mean about wanting to leave."

"I don't think she's said anything to Tyler yet about wanting to leave here. You'd know if she had. If she gives him the slightest hint that she's unhappy here and wants to leave, he'll beat down your front door so fast your head will swim."

Shane exhales. "Lia, try to distract her for just a little while longer. Once she sees the doctor tomorrow, and we find out if her arm is healed, I—" His voice trails off and I don't hear the end of that sentence. Then he says, "Go check on her, please. Make sure she's all right. I'm going back to my office."

"Shane—"

"Lia, just do it. Please."

4

Like a deer caught in a headlight, I'm standing frozen in place when Lia pops back into the studio.

She stops abruptly when she catches sight of me and frowns. "You heard that, didn't you?"

I nod, not bothering to pretend I wasn't eavesdropping. I heard so many things in the tone of Shane's voice, from impatience to anger to annoyance to resignation. I don't know what to think anymore. It feels like everything is unraveling around me.

I swallow against the painful lump in my throat. "Shane couldn't get away from me fast enough. He said he had to get back to his conference call, but I know that's bull."

Lia shrugs. "What can I say? My brother's an idiot. Hell, they're all idiots."

"He wouldn't even look at me, Lia." My knees feel weak and I'm more than a little nauseous, so I drop down onto the sofa before I fall down.

Lia squats in front of me and takes my good hand in hers, squeezing it tightly. "Listen to me, Beth. Shane's determined to punish himself for what Andrew did to you, and he's stubborn as hell in case you haven't figured that out yet."

I laugh, despite the tears clogging my throat. "I think I've figured that out. But what Andrew did wasn't Shane's fault. I've told him that over and over again."

"Wasn't it, though? Andrew attacked *you* to get back at Shane for humiliating him at the hospital benefit. To be perfectly honest, it is Shane's fault. He underestimated how messed up Andrew Morton is."

I shake my head. "But I don't blame him."

"I know you don't. But Shane does, and that's what matters."

"I don't know how to get through to him, Lia."

"I do," Lia says. "He expects you to stick around here and wait for him to work his shit out. Don't let him get away with it. Make him sweat a little."

"How?"

"Teach him not to take you for granted." Lia rises to her feet and pulls me up to mine. "Let's go on a road trip—just you and me. We'll go all Thelma and Louise on him. That'll shake him up, trust me."

The idea of a road trip has a lot of appeal. I haven't left the house in nearly six weeks, and I have a massive case of cabin fever.

Lia grins. "I'm serious. Let's bail, you and me. Girls' day out. We'll leave the knucklehead here to stew a bit."

"You mean sneak out? How can we do that with security watching every inch of the property?"

She eyes me. "Oh, ye of little faith. Just leave everything to me.

Let me shower and change, and then we'll sneak out. Shane won't know what hit him until we're long gone. Grab whatever you need and meet me at the front doors in twenty minutes."

* * *

I run back upstairs to collect my purse and phone from our suite. Then, so as not to attract a lot of attention, I head sedately down the second floor hallway, where I run into Elly. She's pushing a cart filled with clean towels for the suites.

Elly's dressed in a form-fitting pair of brown riding pants and a billowy, white embroidered top. Her lovely silver hair hangs down her back in a thick braid, and her oval face is softly wrinkled. Horses are her passion, and when she's not busy in the house, she's either in the barn or out riding in the pastures.

"Hi, Beth," she says, smiling.

My face heats up because I feel guilty for not coming down for breakfast this morning. "Hi, Elly. I'm sorry I overslept and missed breakfast this morning. Thanks for sending up a tray. It was delicious."

She immediately dismisses my thanks. "It was no trouble at all, darling. Shane said you didn't sleep well last night and to let you sleep in. Where are you off to?"

"Lia and I thought we'd... go outside... to get some fresh air." And now I feel even more guilt for lying to her.

"Since you're going out, I'll just tidy up your room now. Is there any laundry you'd like me to do for you?"

"None for me, thanks. I think Shane left some suits hanging on the back of the closet door that need to be sent out for cleaning."

She nods. "No problem. I'll get them. You girls have fun."

I resume walking toward the staircase, but she calls my name, bringing me up short. "Is there anything special you'd like for lunch today?"

Oh, crap. If our plan is successful, Lia and I won't be here for lunch.

I smile at her, compounding my sins. "No, nothing special," I say. "Whatever you were planning is fine."

"Okay, then. Have fun."

* * *

I finally make it down the main staircase to the foyer and wait for Lia by the front doors. My heart is pounding. The prospect of a girls' day out is thrilling, but I'm also terrified of getting caught.

The door to the business wing just across the foyer opens, and my heart practically stops. Fearing it's Shane about to come through the door, I plaster an innocent smile on my face. But it isn't Shane. It's Cooper. I heave a sigh of relief.

Cooper's dressed in jeans, a T-shirt, and scruffy brown boots—his usual attire. I don't think I've ever seen him in anything else. The only thing missing is the gun holster that's usually strapped to his chest. But the security here is so tight, he doesn't feel the need to walk around armed.

Cooper's in his early 50s and, for an older guy with trim gray hair and beard, he's pretty handsome. He is Shane's right-hand man and best friend. Since I met him, we've grown close—he's become like a father to me. And since I don't have a father, I could sure use one.

"Hey, kiddo." Cooper smiles at me. "How's it going?"

I drop the fake smile because I don't have to pretend with Cooper. He sees everything. I have no doubt he knows the score.

Cooper eyes the purse strap over my shoulder, but he doesn't comment on it. "How's your arm?"

"Good. I get the cast off tomorrow."

"Yeah, Shane told me. Glad to hear it." His eyes narrow. "You goin' somewhere, honey?"

I love Cooper, and I don't want to lie to him, but at the same time, I'm not completely sure how he'll react to our escape plan. If he raises the alarm, we're sunk.

Before I can respond, Lia walks into the foyer dressed in khaki cargo pants, a black tank top, and running shoes. Her pale blond hair is damp from a shower.

She smiles at Cooper. "Hey, Coop."

Cooper nods back at her. "You girls going somewhere?"

"You bet we are," Lia says, sounding more than a little defiant. "It's nice out. We're going for a walk."

"A walk? Beth needs a purse to go for a walk?" Cooper gives us his *I'm-not-an-idiot* look. He crosses his arms over his chest and frowns at Lia.

"Sure," Lia says. "She carries her inhaler in her purse." Lia's gaze flickers briefly up at the surveillance camera covering the front door before returning to Cooper. "Sometimes a girl just needs a break, you know what I'm saying?"

I hold my breath as a long look passes between Lia and Cooper. Cooper can make or break our escape plan with one word.

"Well, all right then," Cooper says, transferring his gaze to me. "You girls have a safe *walk*." He holds out his arms, and I step into his embrace, hugging him with my free arm. He leans down and drops a kiss on my forehead. "Be careful, kiddo."

Cooper releases me and steps back. "I'll buy you girls ten minutes," he says, keeping his voice low, "but that's it. Have fun and make it count."

As Cooper closes the front door behind us, I follow Lia at a brisk jog down the front steps and across the concrete drive to her black Jeep.

"Won't he get in trouble for this?" I say. "Shane's going to be mad if he finds out Cooper knew."

"Probably. But Cooper knows Shane's being an ass, and maybe he thinks you making a run for it might bring him to his senses."

I chuckle as I climb into the front passenger seat and buckle my seat belt. I haven't been this excited in a long time. And honestly, I don't care where we go or what we do. It just feels good to get away—assuming we can get away. "Won't we have trouble getting through the gates?"

"Not if Cooper keeps his word."

Sure enough, as soon as we approach the first of the two security checkpoints, the gate opens automatically and we breeze right through. Cooper must have told the security staff to let us pass. And the same thing happens at the second checkpoint. When we reach the main road, Lia turns left and heads south for Chicago.

I glance back as we pick up speed, half expecting to see a security team come chasing after us. "So, where are we going?"

Lia shrugs. "This is your show, Princess. Where do you want to go?"

I finally face forward and start to relax. "I don't know. There're so many things I'd like to do. How about we head downtown and play it by ear? I want to see Gabrielle. I'd love to go to Gino's for lunch, and I'd like to stop in at Clancy's."

I haven't seen Gabrielle in about a month now. With her busy work schedule at the restaurant, and with me living outside of the city now, we just haven't had a chance to get together. It's been hard on both of us. Texting and Skype just don't cut it. Before I moved in with Shane, she and I lived together for several years. There wasn't a day that went by that we didn't see each other. She was my only friend, really, before I met Shane and Lia and the rest of the McIntyre family. I miss her.

Lia chuckles. "I think we can manage that. Why don't you call Gabrielle and see if she's free for lunch? We'll swing by the apartment building and get her, and then we'll go grab pizza at Gino's. After that, we'll check out your bookstore." Lia smirks. "That should be fun."

I check the time and frown. "By the time we get to the city, it'll be the lunch hour rush. We'll never get into Gino's."

Lia chuckles as she pulls out her phone and makes a call. "Yeah, this is Lia McIntyre. I need a private table for three in 45 minutes. You got that? Thanks."

I grin from ear to ear as Lia ends the call. "Really? You can do that?"

"It's one of the perks of working for Shane. Hell, I don't mind dropping names and pulling a few strings."

Not five minutes after we left the estate grounds, my phone rings. I check the caller ID. "Crap."

Lia glances at me. "Who is it? Shane?"

I stare at his name and photo on my caller ID. "Yes."

"Don't answer it."

"What?"

"You heard me. Do. Not. Answer. It. You're letting him sweat, remember?"

I stare at Shane's image on my screen, my heart rate increasing with each peal of the ringtone. I'm torn. Part of me feels compelled to answer his call, but the other part of me is chicken and doesn't want the confrontation. The decision is taken out of my hands, however, when the call goes to voice mail.

A moment later my phone chimes and I sigh. "He left a voice message."

"Relax. He knows you're with me."

"He's probably pissed."

"Of course he is. That's the whole point. Thelma and Louise, remember?"

Lia's ringtone goes off next, but she doesn't even bother to look to see who it is. "Let him sweat."

But when my phone rings again, almost immediately after Lia's, I relent and accept the call. "Hello?"

"Where the hell are you going?" Shane doesn't even bother to temper his tone.

I swallow, determined not to be cowed. It's a free country. If I want to go out to lunch with my friends, I will. "Lia and I are going out for lunch. And then, maybe we'll stop by the bookstore."

"Tell Lia to turn that vehicle around right now and come back here."

"Shane—"

"Just do it."

"Shane, no." I take a deep breath and steel myself. I'm not turning back. "I need to get away for a while. I need... a break."

There's a long pause, and then he says, "A break from what? From me?"

I close my eyes at the pain I hear in his voice and take a steadying breath. "No, not from you. Well, maybe a little. Okay, yes. From you."

I hear a muffled curse, as if he'd covered the mouth piece with his hand. Then he's back. "Please, Beth, just come home. We'll talk. I know I've been an ass. Cooper just spent the past five minutes making sure I knew it. Please, come back."

"Shane, I really do need a break. I need to see Gabrielle. I need to be somewhere else for a while. Don't worry. I'm with Lia. We're going to have a girls' day out. It's long overdue."

There's a long silence over the phone. My heart's pounding so hard I'm sure he can hear it over the phone.

"Beth." He sounds oddly defeated, which makes me ache for him even more.

"Shane, don't. It's just a girls' day out, that's all. It's not a big deal. Please don't turn it into one."

He sighs. "Do you have your inhaler?"

"Of course."

"How long do you think you'll be gone? Will you be home for dinner?"

Now it's my turn to pause. I don't know how to answer him. At the moment, I just want to get away. I don't want to think about when I'm coming back. "I'm not sure. There are things I want to do downtown. We're going to eat and then stop by Clancy's. And after that... I'm just not sure."

Lia shoots me a look. "Tell him we'll be back when we're back."

There's another long silence and then, sounding resigned, Shane says, "All right. Please, come back soon."

"Don't worry. We'll be fine. I'll see you later, okay?"

After I tuck my phone back into my purse, Lia says, "Well, that didn't go so badly."

It didn't. So why, then, does my chest ache so badly?

$\boldsymbol{5}$

As we pull into the front drive of Shane's apartment building on Lake Shore Drive, I gaze up in awe at the towering glass and steel structure. Located in the heart of The Gold Coast, this building is one of the most prestigious properties in the city, and it never fails to amaze me that Shane owns the building. The *entire* building. That kind of wealth is hard for me to wrap my mind around. I guess I shouldn't be surprised—after all, he bought me a bookstore for no good reason... just because he knew how much I love that place.

Shane and Cooper share the penthouse floor, which is so huge I haven't even seen half of it yet. I think there are something like six bedroom suites in the penthouse, and only two are used on a regular basis. I think I've located four of them so far.

Shane's siblings come and go from the penthouse—it's like Grand

Central Station, but I wouldn't trade that for the world. As we pull up to the building, with its lush, two-story atrium lobby filled with live trees, I realize how much I've missed this place. I'd spent a couple of memorable nights here with Shane before the assault, and this place feels special to me now. In some ways, being here makes me feel closer to him even though we're miles apart.

Lia pulls into the secure underground parking garage and parks in her reserved spot near the bank of elevators. The plan is to leave the Jeep here and use cabs to move around in the city, since parking in downtown Chicago isn't easy. Using cabs is much more efficient.

We head up to Gabrielle's apartment, which is on the 48th floor. Shane has reserved the top five floors of the building for employees of his security company. Jake, Lia, and Liam all have apartments in this building.

When Shane moved me out of my townhouse for safety reasons—because of Howard Kline—he offered Gabrielle free use of an apartment in this building. I'm excited to see Gabrielle's apartment for myself. She gave me a video tour of it with her phone a couple of weeks ago, but that's not the same as seeing it for myself.

She answers the door as soon as we knock.

"Beth!" Gabrielle wraps her arms around me and squeezes tightly. "God, I've missed you!"

Gabrielle is more than just a friend—she's like the sister I always wished I'd had. When we lived in the townhouse, even though we worked very different schedules, we still found time for girls' nights in—curling up on the sofa to eat carry-out and ice cream and watch rom-coms and action movies.

And when I screamed bloody murder in the middle of the night, she always came running, without question, without recrimination. Half the time, she ended up spending the rest of the night sleeping with me in my bed, keeping me company and scaring away the boogie man. I owe her so much. I can never repay her for what she's done for me.

I'm so happy to see her, my eyes well up with tears. She's dressed in her white sous chef uniform, so she must be getting ready to head to Renaldo's, the upscale Italian restaurant where she works. Shane is friends with Peter Capelli, the owner of Renaldo's.

Just seeing Gabrielle's familiar face makes my throat tighten. She looks as gorgeous and vibrant as ever, with her long, curly red hair and freckled face. She's come out to Kenilworth to see me a few times in the past couple of months, but it's just not the same as being roommates.

Gabrielle looks at me and frowns. "What's wrong?"

I shake my head as I pull back. "Nothing's wrong. I'm just happy to see you."

She releases me, looking skeptical at my reply, and eyes my cast. "How's your arm?"

"Fine. The cast comes off tomorrow."

Gabrielle looks past me at Lia, and I realize they hardly know each other. They met briefly at the hospital, when Gabrielle and my mom came to visit me. They've seen each other a couple of times since then at Shane's estate, but for the most part, they're strangers.

"You guys know each other," I say, watching them size each other up. They're such opposites. Lia's petite and curvy, and Gabrielle's five-ten and willowy. They're as polar opposite as ice and fire sometimes.

"Hey, Gabe," Lia says as we follow Gabrielle into her apartment. Lia glances around the open floor plan, which I assume is very similar to her own apartment. "How do you like the place?"

Gabrielle grins. "Honestly, it's amazing! Come take a look at this view."

Gabrielle gives us a quick tour of her apartment, starting with the open living room with a gas fireplace and stone hearth, dining room, and gourmet kitchen—which is perfect given Gabrielle's promising career as a chef. The apartment is spacious and airy, and the exterior wall is all windows, with an incredible view of the lake. The floors are hardwood, and the color scheme is muted with soft, natural tones. She shows us the two bedrooms, each with its own private bath, and a small study with bookcases, a desk, and a laptop.

This apartment goes for a fortune on the open market, and neither she nor I could ever afford something like this on our own, even if we pooled our resources.

I'm surprised to see Gabrielle dressed in her restaurant uniform this early. She usually doesn't leave for work until late afternoon, as she works the very desirable evening dinner shift. "Are you going to work?"

"I have time to go to lunch with you guys, but then I have to get to the restaurant. One of the other sous-chefs is out sick today, and I'm filling in for him."

* * *

We arrive at my favorite Chicago pizza restaurant, Gino's, by taxi, and there's already a line out the door and down the sidewalk. In full bodyguard mode, Lia ushers both me and Gabrielle inside the restaurant, herding us like a mother hen with two chicks. She steers us through the waiting crowd right up to the host's podium.

"Lia McIntyre," she says to the young woman on duty.

The host signals a man standing just a few feet away, and he comes right over, three menus tucked into the crook of his arm.

"Right this way, ladies," he says, smiling graciously at us.

We follow him up the steps to the main dining room, which is abuzz with the chatter of contented diners and the clatter of silverware. He leads us across the dining room to a closed door on the other side, marked *Private*.

"Right in here, ladies," he says, opening the door for us and flipping the light switch. "Will this do?"

It's a small, unoccupied room with just a half-dozen tables. We follow him inside, and immediately the sound level drops to a manageable drone. We'll actually be able to hear ourselves talk in here.

"It's perfect," Lia says. "Thanks."

"My name's Jeff, and I'm the manager. Anthony will be your server. He'll be here shortly to take your food orders."

After taking our drink orders, Jeff the Manager leaves us alone, closing the door on his way out and shutting out the noise.

Gabrielle looks pointedly at me. "Now, tell me what's wrong."

I look into a pair of very familiar, and very determined, green eyes flecked with bits of gold and framed by thick cinnamon-colored lashes. Her peaches-and-cream complexion is dusted with tiny cinnamon-colored freckles. I smile and busy myself arranging my place setting. "Nothing's wrong."

"Beth, I know you. And I know when something's wrong. You hardly said two words on the ride over here. Now spill it."

I shrug. "I've just been a little emotional lately."

Gabrielle gasps. "Oh, my God, are you pregnant?"

"No!" I'm tempted to throw my napkin at her. "Jeez, Gabrielle!"

"It's Shane," Lia says, cutting to the chase. "He's being a dick."

I chuckle every time Lia calls him that.

Gabrielle frowns. "Shane? What did he do this time?"

Gabrielle's never been too sure about Shane, but for my sake, she's been willing to give him the benefit of the doubt. The thing is, she knew all along that Shane's company was providing me with protection from Kline, long before I found out. When Tyler, who was now a homicide detective, discovered that Howard Kline was being paroled early from prison, he hired McIntyre Security to protect me. Shane and Tyler had known each other professionally for years, although they didn't always see eye to eye. Tyler had confided in Gabrielle, telling her that he'd hired McIntyre Security and pulled her into the loop. When I suddenly started dating this supposedly random stranger I'd met late one Friday evening at the bookstore—Shane—she was hostile to him from the beginning because she knew he wasn't random or a stranger. And she knew full well he was essentially deceiving me by not disclosing the fact that his company had been hired to protect me from Howard Kline.

"It's more like what he hasn't done," Lia says, passing out the menus. "God, I'm so hungry I could eat a horse."

* * *

Our server—Anthony, a tall, painfully thin young man with short black hair and a black goatee—returns in record time with our drinks, and he leaves with our food order. We each order house salads and decide to share a deluxe, deep-dish pizza.

Once we're alone again, Gabrielle turns to me. "Now tell me, what's Shane done? Or rather, not done?"

I take a sip of my Coke, savoring the icy sweet burn. "He's... um..."

Lia sets down her bottle of dark ale. "He won't have sex with her."

Gabrielle looks confused. "You're kidding me? Why? Is he crazy?"

"Hell, yes, he's crazy," Lia says. "I mean, look at her." She flourishes a hand at me. "Who wouldn't want to have sex with Beth? Hell,

I'd do her."

I roll my eyes at Lia and blush. "He's...." How do I explain this without sounding like an idiot? *My boyfriend makes me come—repeatedly—but he won't let me return the favor.*

"He's punishing himself," Lia says as she checks an incoming message on her phone. She snickers.

"What?" I say.

She chuckles as she sends back a quick message. "Shane's pissed at me."

Gabrielle adds sugar and cream to her coffee and stirs. "Why is Shane punishing himself?"

I sigh. "He blames himself for what Andrew did." I pick up my phone. "Maybe I should text Shane and at least tell him where we are. He's probably worried."

"Don't bother," Lia says, setting down her phone. "He knows exactly where you are. He *always* knows exactly where you are."

Gabrielle frowns. "How?"

Lia shrugs. "He tracks her phone."

"He what!" Gabrielle cries.

I look at Lia. "He does?"

"Of course he does. Shane doesn't take any chances where you're concerned. There's a GPS chip embedded in your phone—I mean one Shane put there. There's also one in your purse and in all your shoes."

"That's just creepy, Beth," Gabrielle says, shaking her head. "You should toss your phone in the nearest trash can."

"She'd have to toss out her purse and shoes, too," Lia says. "It's hardly worth it."

I glance at my phone and have to fight a smile. I'm sure I should be outraged at the intrusion into my privacy, but I'm not. Quite the contrary. Maybe he's not ignoring me as much as I think he is.

Gabrielle scowls at me. "Quit smiling, Beth. It's not funny. It's downright creepy."

Halfway through lunch, Gabrielle glances at me. "Have you seen Tyler lately?"

I nod, unable to speak because my mouth is full of food.

"He stopped by the house for dinner earlier in the week," Lia says. "And he calls her every day. He's like a bad penny—he keeps showing up."

"He misses you," Gabrielle says to me. "He wants you to move in with him. Maybe you should give it some thought."

I'd be lying if I told Gabrielle I haven't considered it. "No. If you think Shane's controlling, you should try living with my brother. He's far worse. Besides, I have no intention of leaving Shane."

"Stalker-boy, you mean," Gabrielle says.

* * *

After we finish eating, Anthony and two bus boys come into our dining room. As the bus boys quickly whisk away our dirty plates, Anthony asks us if we'd like anything else.

"Just the check," Lia says. "We're done here."

"That won't be necessary, Ms. McIntyre," Anthony says. "Mr. McIntyre called and settled it over the phone."

Gabrielle rolls her eyes at me and Lia after Anthony leaves the room. "I told you he's a control freak," she says.

Lia chuckles. "At least Shane's subtle about it."

After we hug good-bye, and I promise to come spend a night with her in her apartment very soon, Gabrielle catches a taxi to Renaldo's. Lia and I walk over to N. Michigan Avenue and head toward Clancy's

Bookshop in hopes of walking off at least some of our carb-overload.

"Are you ready to face The Dragon Lady?" Lia says, smirking at me.

The Dragon Lady is Vanessa Markham, the general manager at Clancy's. That woman has certainly earned her nickname. If I had a nemesis, she'd be it.

"I don't think I have a choice."

6

I feel better than I have in days the moment I step through Clancy's front doors. The bookstore isn't simply my happy place now, it's *mine* period. As in, I own it. I glance around the huge, open store at the countless rows of books and merchandise filling two expansive floors, at the constant stream of customers, and I have trouble comprehending it all. It still hasn't fully sunk in that Shane actually purchased Clancy's for me two months ago. What in the world was he thinking? We'd only known each such a short while.

I always smile when I think back to the night we met right here in the bookstore. I was seated in one of the comfy chairs, reading an anthology of spanking stories on a Friday evening as was my habit. I admit it wasn't a very auspicious way to meet the man of my dreams.

I'll never forget his pick-up line. *Is that a good book?*

I was so utterly mortified, I wished for a hole to open up and swallow me right then and there.

When he first spoke, I lowered my gaze to my hands in my lap, desperately willing him to just go away. I'd made it my life's goal to avoid strangers, and here was this man—this gorgeous, blue-eyed man in a sexy dark suit and white dress shirt—trying to make small talk with *me*!

I tried to bolt, but he caught my hand and stopped me and convinced me to stay a little while longer. We ended up sitting at a window table in the bookstore cafe while he ate a sandwich and drank coffee, and I sipped a fruit smoothie. I still ended up bolting in a panic, but he didn't give up. Exactly one week later, he found me again, right here in Clancy's, and we went out on our first official date that evening.

My smile fades a bit when I think about how strained things are between us lately. He says all the right things, and he treats me like a queen. He spares no effort seeing to my needs in bed, but it's all one-sided. He won't accept any sexual pleasure for himself. And he's so damn stubborn! I have to find a way to break his control.

Lia and I are standing just inside the store where the new release tables are located. Off to the side is the customer service counter with four busy registers. A long line of customers has queued up to check out.

"Business certainly looks good," Lia murmurs into my ear. "I guess you won't go hungry."

I blush. "Well, if it is good, it's absolutely no thanks to me."

Since Shane presented me with the bookstore, I've only been here twice before today, and then only for short visits. I have yet to take an active role in the store—Shane asked me to wait until after I had healed. It's like my whole life was put on hold because of the attack. I'm tired of the inaction—of putting things off. I need to move forward, to get my life back on track.

Fortunately, Clancy's is in great shape with or without my involvement. I have absolutely no illusions that I'm needed here, because I'm not. When Shane bought this place, he kept the existing—and very experienced—management team and workforce in place.

There's a general manager—a woman in her early 30s named Vanessa Markham—and four assistant managers, plus an assortment of employees to take care of all the business operations, everything from accounting to human relations to purchasing to IT. There's also a beefed-up security team in place now, courtesy of Shane.

I imagine the employees would resent me coming in and having any say in how the business is run. Still, I'm curious about the bookstore, and I want to know more. I'm more than ready to learn whatever I need to learn so I can fit in here. This is my happy place, after all.

I catch sight of the general manager across the floor. She's eyeing me disapprovingly, a frown marring her lovely, oval face. Vanessa doesn't like me, and she makes no effort to hide that fact.

"Uh oh," Lia whispers. "Dragon Lady at two o'clock. Brace yourself. Here she comes."

"Shh!" I elbow Lia. Lia's the one who came up with the nickname for Vanessa. "Behave. I need to make a good impression."

"Why do you care? You own this place."

"Shh!" I smile at the approaching woman.

"Hello, Miss Jamison," Vanessa says, eyeing first me and then Lia. "What brings you here today?"

I respond to her cool, assessing gaze with my best friendly smile—at least I hope it's friendly. "Hi, Vanessa. Please, call me Beth. I was downtown today, and I thought I'd stop by."

I'm trying here, I really am. But the truth is, Vanessa scares the crap out of me. She has an MBA from the University of Chicago, and she's been managing Clancy's for nearly a decade. I suspect that Fred Clancy had given her the run of the place—carte blanche—and Vanessa resents a new owner coming in.

She's dressed to the nines, as usual. Today, she's wearing a classic, gray houndstooth skirt and jacket, with a cream silk shell blouse and a string of fat, luscious pearls. Her ash brown hair is neatly parted in the middle, and it hangs thick and perfectly straight past her shoulders. She's beautiful and perfect and cold as ice. She has a way of looking at me that makes me feel like I'm twelve years old again and in trouble with the principal for running in the halls.

"Well, enjoy your visit, Miss Jamison," Vanessa says, already turning away.

"Actually, Vanessa," Lia says, derailing the woman's abrupt departure. "Beth would like to see her office."

I shoot a sideways glance at Lia. *Office? What office? Lia!*

Vanessa's lips curve in a smile that definitely doesn't reach her whiskey-colored eyes. "I'm afraid Beth doesn't have an office."

Lia props her hands on her hips. "Try again, sister. Since this is *her* bookstore, I'm pretty sure she has an office."

I smile apologetically at Vanessa. "That's okay—"

"No, it's not okay," Lia says, and I can tell she's just getting warmed up. "Did Clancy have an office?"

"Well, yes, of course he did," Vanessa says, crossing her slender arms over her chest.

"Then I guess Clancy's old office belongs to Beth now, since she's the new owner. Take us to it."

* * *

We follow Vanessa up a wide curving staircase to the second floor, where the business offices are located off a side hallway that's closed off to the public. Lia and I follow Vanessa through a door marked *ADMINISTRATIVE OFFICE.*

"This is the main office," Vanessa says, motioning around the large room. There are a half dozen desks scattered throughout the room, all currently occupied by a half dozen curious employees, who are trying hard not to stare at me. On one wall is a massive shelving unit filled with hundreds of books, and there are boxes everywhere in various stages of unpacking. On the far side of the room is another door marked *PRIVATE.*

Lia scans the room. "Where was Clancy's office?"

Vanessa's lips flatten as she points toward the door marked *PRIVATE.* "Actually, I'm in his office now. As the general manager, I thought—"

"Well, you thought wrong," Lia says. "That is Beth's office now."

Vanessa glares at Lia, refusing to be cowed. "I doubt Beth will be here often enough to warrant having an office."

"Actually, I'd like to become involved in running the bookstore," I tell her. "I'd like to work here. But I don't need an office. You can keep it."

Vanessa crosses her arms again, and a slender, gold Rolex peeks out of her suit jacket sleeve. She eyes me sharply. "Do you have any management or business experience whatsoever?"

I feel a rush of heat sweep through me. "No."

"Did you take any business courses in college?"

"I—no."

"Do you have any retail experience? Fast food? Anything?"

I sigh. "Well, no."

Vanessa gives me a brittle smile. "And you think you're qualified to run a multi-million dollar business?"

My heart is hammering now, but I stand my ground. I'm not going to let her chase me off.

Lia pushes forward, stepping between us. "That's all irrelevant, Vanessa. This is Beth's business, and she can do whatever the hell she wants with it. If she wants to pass out free books on the street corner, that's her prerogative. Not yours."

Vanessa stiffens. "I doubt Mr. McIntyre—"

Lia steps forward, getting right in Vanessa's face, which isn't easy as Vanessa towers over Lia. "Don't you dare *Mr. McIntyre* me, Vanessa. I guarantee you he'll side with Beth. You can count on it."

"I'm willing to learn whatever I need to know," I say, hoping to defuse the tension. "I've been thinking about going back to school—"

"This isn't your personal playground, Beth," Vanessa says. "The livelihoods of twenty-two people depend on the success of this store. Just because you have a sugar daddy—"

Lia and I both gasp at Vanessa's audacity, and for a minute, I think I'm going to have to physically hold Lia back—that is until we're all distracted by a discrete cough—a deep, male cough.

"Excuse me, ladies."

Everyone in the room turns to look at the man standing in the open doorway. He's dressed casually in faded blue jeans, a button-down white Oxford shirt, and a navy windbreaker. He's a big guy, with shoulders and a chest that won't quit. He's built like a tank, very tall, with legs like tree trunks. He's huge! He has to be nearly six-four, and he ducks as he steps through the doorway.

He has short hair the color of dark chocolate and dark, perceptive eyes that are currently scanning the office. He's fit and muscular—and very good looking. Definitely ex-military. I've learned to recognize them on sight. And he's got to be carrying a concealed weapon strapped in a holster on his chest—wearing a windbreaker indoors in the summer is a dead giveaway.

"Who the hell are you?" Vanessa snaps, her slender hands going to her hips. "These are private offices. You shouldn't be in here."

Ignoring Vanessa, the man walks directly up to me and offers me his hand. "Ms. Jamison, I'm Mack Donovan, your new head of security here at Clancy's."

I glance at Lia for confirmation, and she nods. "Yeah, he's one of ours."

I have to crane my head up to look Mr. Donovan in the face. "Call me Beth, please."

Vanessa sputters with indignation. "I beg your pardon! I did not authorize any new hires—"

Mack smiles politely at Vanessa. "Begging your pardon, ma'am, but I report directly to Ms. Jamison. I don't need you to authorize anything."

Vanessa actually stamps her stilettoed foot. "On whose authority?"

Her perfectly made-up face is turning beet read, and I have to bite my lip to keep from smiling.

"I report to Ms. Jamison—Beth," Mack says, correcting himself. "Her authority is the only one that matters here."

"We'll see about that!" Vanessa storms through the door to her private office and slams it shut behind her.

For a moment, everyone in the room is silent, as if we're not quite sure the coast is clear.

Lia breaks the ice with a friendly wave to the half-dozen employees in the room who all look a little shell-shocked. "Hi, folks. In case you haven't figured it out yet, this is Beth Jamison. It's her signature on your paychecks, and that makes her your boss. So be nice to her."

Their gazes dart back and forth between me and Vanessa's closed office door. Eventually, they wave back, offering a weak "hi" in unison.

"Hi, everyone," I say, my face burning as I wave at their wary faces.

Lia nods, apparently satisfied. "All right, then. Good job, people. Now get back to work."

* * *

Lia flags down a cab in front of Clancy's. "Overall, I'd say that went well."

"Oh, my God!" I sink into the back seat of the hired SUV and buckle my seat belt. "That was a disaster."

"No, it wasn't. But you need to get rid of Vanessa. That woman annoys the hell outta me."

The cab driver looks back at us and sighs. "Where to, ladies? I don't have all day."

Lia glares at him. "Just drive."

"I can't just fire her!" I say, grabbing the door handle to stabilize myself as our taxi pulls abruptly into the heavy flow of downtown traffic. "I can't just waltz into Clancy's and start taking over. Vanessa may be a bitch, but she was right about one thing. I have absolutely no experience running a business. The last thing I want to do is go in there and screw things up."

I check the time on my phone, surprised to see it's nearly five o'clock. Where has the afternoon gone? Obviously, we're not going to make it back to Kenilworth in time for dinner.

Lia must be reading my mind. "Where to next, Princess? The day's not over."

Shane's probably wondering where I am. "I don't know."

"Want to head back to the house?"

"Not really." Suddenly, I have a pang to go *home*—to the townhouse I shared with Gabrielle in Hyde Park, at least until two months ago. I sink back into my seat. "I want to go home, Lia."

Lia looks at me like I'm crazy. "Home where? To your townhouse? And bring down the wrath of Shane? Are you kidding?"

I think of the townhouse and how simple life was there before I met Shane. Before I found out that Howard Kline was a free man again. I shudder when I think of Kline loose on the streets of Chicago. That man has stolen so much from me. A monster who preys on children should be locked up, not roaming the streets a free man. I was one of the lucky ones—I was rescued. But not everyone is so lucky.

"I guess that's not a very good idea," I say. "Where I don't want to go is back to Kenilworth. I just can't face Shane right now." My throat tightens up, and my eyes pool with unshed tears.

"Hey, it'll be all right." Lia reaches over to squeeze my hand. "Shane will eventually come to his senses and quit being a jerk. In the meantime, what do you say we go on the lam and stay out all night?"

"What did you have in mind?" I say.

"Let's go to the penthouse, order in some Thai food, and watch a movie on the big screen. We can even spend the night, if you want. We'll have a slumber party, just the two of us."

"Really?" That perks me right up. I'm just not ready to go back, so staying gone a little longer really appeals to me right now. And I love the penthouse.

"But what about this?" I say, raising my cast. "My appointment's in the morning."

Lia shrugs. "I'll take you."

While Lia gives the cab driver the address, I relax back into my seat with a heavy sigh. The longer I'm away from Shane, the more I miss him, and the lonelier I feel.

7

ust as Lia and I exit the private elevator in the penthouse foyer, my phone rings. "It's Shane."

Lia opens the door leading into the penthouse. "Don't answer it."

I give her a wry glance as I accept the call. "Hi, Shane." I make an effort to sound happy and upbeat, as if today's just any other day.

"Beth, where are you? It's getting late."

He sounds worried, and I feel a twinge of guilt for sneaking off the way I did. But then I remember he's bugging my phone and my other accessories. "I'm pretty sure you know exactly where I am. Lia told me you bugged my phone. Is that right?"

There's a moment of dead silence on the other end of the phone. Then, his voice very calm and even, he says, "Well, yes, I did. But it's for your own safety, sweetheart. I'm not trying to spy on you. I just want to keep you safe."

"Why didn't you tell me? You should at least tell me when you do crazy stuff like that."

He sighs. "Beth, when are you coming home?"

Home? Right now, Kenilworth doesn't feel much like home to me. I'd rather be here at the penthouse—where Shane and I spent some very memorable evenings together.

"I haven't decided yet," I say, feeling my resolve to stay away grow. "Lia and I are going to order in something to eat and watch a movie. And then, I think we're going to spend the night here."

Once more, there's silence on the phone, and I feel the bottom of my stomach drop, leaving me queasy. Clearly he isn't happy about my little announcement, and that stupid twinge of guilt returns.

"Beth, please. Come home. I don't want to sleep without you."

Hot tears well up in my eyes, and I swallow against a painful knot in my throat. All of a sudden, I feel very much alone. I miss Gabrielle, I miss my brother, and I haven't seen my mother in almost a month. But most of all, I miss Shane. I miss *my* Shane. I ache for *my* Shane. Not this Shane who's holding part of himself back from me.

"I can't." My voice breaks as I try in vain to hold myself together.

"Beth." I hear sudden movement and a heavy breath, and then the sound of a door closing quietly. His voice is low, practically dropping an octave. "Please, sweetheart, come home and we'll talk. I promise."

I wipe my eyes with the back of my hand and take a deep, steadying breath. The last thing I want is for him to pity me. "No, Shane. I need a break. I need some time away. To think."

"Think about what?" His voice takes on a sense of urgency. "Damn it, Beth, what's there to think about?"

"I need to go. I'm sorry, but Lia's waiting for me."

"Wait! When are you coming home?"

"I don't know, Shane. But it won't be tonight." A little bit of space is starting to sound pretty good right now.

"What about your doctor appointment in the morning?"

"Lia's taking me. I have to go now. Good night."

"All right." He sounds resigned, albeit unhappy. "Good night, honey. I hope you sleep well."

That's not an idle comment on his part. My sleep is haunted by monsters both old and new.

The phone line goes silent, and there's another long, painful pause before Shane finally disconnects the call.

I stare at the blank screen on my phone and wonder what's happening to us. And more importantly, how do we fix it?

* * *

I go through the motions with Lia, and Lia—sensing my mood—doesn't push me. We order in Thai food, which a security guard from the front lobby delivers to us. We take our cartons of food and some soft drinks and freshly made popcorn into the screening room and watch *Avatar* on a 20-foot, high-resolution movie screen. The movie is stunning on the huge screen with its kick-ass Dolby surround-sound system. But the budding romance between Jake Sully and Neytiri just makes me miss Shane that much more.

"I guess we could have picked a better movie," Lia says, when the film credits begin to roll. She looks at me. "A comedy or an action movie would have been better choices. Do you wanna do a double-feature? How about *Die Hard*? Something kick ass."

I shake my head. It's already after ten, and I'm exhausted. "I'm tired, Lia. I think I'll go to bed."

When we walk into the kitchen to dispose of our empty food

containers, we find Cooper pulling a beer out of the fridge. I'm not exactly surprised to see him here. He has a tendency to show up unexpectedly.

"Evenin', ladies," he says.

I detect a faint southern drawl in his voice. It comes through when he's tired or upset.

He holds up a bottle of beer. "Can I get either of you a drink?"

Lia hops up onto one of the barstools at the breakfast bar. "I'll have what you're having." She deftly catches the chilled bottle Cooper tosses her way.

He looks at me, his impassive expression giving away nothing. "How about you, kiddo?"

I don't think it's a coincidence that he's here. "Did Shane send you?"

Cooper nods. "He sent me to check up on you and report back." He wags the neck of his beer bottle at me. "He's worried. You've got him pretty freaked out, young lady."

Lia takes a swig of her beer. "Serves him right for being a douche bag."

Cooper frowns. "Cut him some slack, Lia. This is all new territory for him. He's trying, and he means well."

I'm glad Cooper's here. I walk right up to him, and he opens his arms wide. I step into his embrace and wrap my good arm around his waist as his arms close around me, careful of my cast. "I'm glad you're here," I say. "Thanks for helping us escape this morning."

Cooper gives me a gentle squeeze and a fatherly pat on my back. "No problem, kid."

A yawn signals an end to my evening. "I'm wiped, you guys. I'm going to bed."

"Good night, honey," Cooper says.

"Are you staying the night?" I ask him.

"Yep. That's the plan."

"Good."

Lia waves her beer bottle at me. "Sleep well, Princess. I'll see you in the morning."

As soon as I walk into Shane's private domain—his apartment within the apartment—hot tears well up and spill over. I've been holding it in all day, a basket case of frayed nerves, and now that I'm alone, I don't have to try to pretend everything's all right.

"Lights, twenty percent."

I walk over to the exterior wall, which is floor-to-ceiling glass, and look out. My bird's eye view of Lake Michigan to the left and the city to the right is magical, especially on a clear night like tonight. I can see lights twinkling on the lake as evening cruise ships make their way through the inky black water. The glass and stone skyscrapers to the right are lit up like Christmas trees. There's a helicopter making its way lazily across the night sky, and it seems almost close enough that I can reach out and touch it.

I glance across the room at the big bed and feel a pang of loneliness. This is the first time I'll be sleeping alone in this bed. In Shane's bed. It's also the first night we've slept apart since I came to live with him at his estate.

It wasn't that long ago that Shane and I made love for the first time right here in this room. I'd never thought I could trust a man enough to let him in the way I let Shane in. And despite our disastrous first attempt at sex that night—which ended with me in ugly hysterics—the night ended beautifully, thanks to Shane's patience and perseverance.

I look around the suite, which seems so large and empty without him here. Besides the sleeping area, there's a cozy living space with a sofa and coffee table, a stone hearth, a large flat-screen TV, a bar, and a small kitchen. I remember the first time Shane gave me whisky, and I smile at the memory of how I coughed and sputtered after tasting that awful stuff.

I can't help wondering what Shane's doing right now. Is he in bed? Still in his office?

After a quick trip to the bathroom, I raid Shane's closet for a T-shirt to sleep in, and then I climb into the huge bed and burrow beneath the soft bedding.

The last time I was in this bed was the night of the hospital charity benefit—the night Andrew accosted me on the dance floor. The night Shane put the fear of God into Andrew and warned him to stay away from me, or at least that's what he thought. Unfortunately, it hadn't worked out that way. A few days later was when Andrew took his anger and resentment out on me, and almost killed me in the process. Now he's locked up tight, and I can't help feeling sorry for him.

I don't bother with a nightlight tonight, because the chocolate-colored drapes are wide open and a full moon hangs fat and bright in the night sky. Coupled with the ambient light of the city at night, the moon provides plenty of illumination. I know it's ridiculous for someone my age to need a nightlight, but when it's dark, I'm bombarded with memories of that dank, dark cellar and the smell of damp earth and mold.

It all comes rushing back—the cold, the pitch black darkness, the helplessness of being tied up and left alone. The pain of an overfull bladder that I was loathe to release because even at six years of age, I knew I was too old to pee on myself. So, yeah, I'd rather suffer the embarrassment of needing a nightlight than go down memory lane.

I wrap my arms around Shane's pillow and wish it were him I was cuddling with instead. I try in vain to fall asleep, but it's difficult to do without the warm presence of his body against my back, and the reassurance of his strong arm across my waist, keeping me tucked close to him. It's amazing how quickly I've gotten used to sleeping with him—how much I depend on him now. I press my face into his pillow and when I detect a hint of his scent, my throat tightens painfully.

I'm not at all surprised when I hear a soft knock at the bedroom door. I wipe my damp cheeks on the sheet and clear my throat. "Come in."

Cooper has changed into a pair of old sweats and a faded Marine Corps T-shirt. "Hey, kiddo. Mind if I sit down for a minute?"

I pat the empty side of the mattress. "Have a seat."

He sits on the edge of the bed and turns to me, his expression somber. "All right, Beth. Talk to me."

I'm afraid if I say anything I'll start bawling like a baby, so I just shake my head.

Cooper frowns. "What's wrong, honey?"

"He's... he won't...." What in the world can I say? *Shane makes love to me, but he won't let me touch him. He makes me come until I can't see straight, but he won't let me give him pleasure.* "He's... holding himself back from me. Lia says it's because he's punishing himself over Andrew. But I'm afraid—" I stop midsentence, afraid to put my true fear into words.

"Afraid what?"

"What if he's changed his mind?"

"About what?"

"About me. About us."

Cooper shakes his head, scoffing at the idea. "Trust me, honey. Shane's so in love with you he can't see straight."

"He has a funny way of showing it."

"Lia's right. He's punishing himself."

"Then he's punishing both of us." Tears spill down my cheeks, and I brush them away.

"You have to understand where Shane's head is, honey. He's the protector. He's always been the protector, since he was a kid. He's always protected his younger siblings, and now he protects you. But in this case, he failed. He failed to protect you when you needed him the most, and he's having a hard time dealing with that."

"What happened wasn't his fault!"

Cooper shakes his head. "You'll never convince him of that, Beth. Don't waste your breath trying. No one's harder on Shane than he is himself."

"Then what do I do? How do I get through to him? Because right now, I feel like he's giving up on us."

"Do exactly what you did today. Throw him off balance, push him. Taking off like you did today had one hell of an effect on him. He's been pacing his office like a caged tiger since you left, snapping at everyone—including me. Of course I gave him plenty of reason to snap at me. I told him exactly how big an idiot he was. I'm surprised he hasn't shown up here before now."

Exhausted, both physically and emotionally, I lay my head on Shane's pillow as the tears resume, burning wet trails down my cheeks. What I wouldn't give to have Shane here in this bed with me now.

Cooper brushes my hair back from my face. "Hang in there, kiddo. He'll come to his senses eventually. You just gotta be patient."

8

I'm half-asleep when I feel the mattress dip down beside me. A moment later, a big, warm body presses up against me. He rolls me to my side, facing away from him, so that he can spoon behind me. His arm comes around my waist, and he tucks me in close.

I smile with relief when I feel his lips in my hair. "Shane?"

His chuckle is a low rumble against my back. "It had damn well better be me. Go back to sleep, sweetheart. I didn't mean to wake you."

"You didn't wake me. I can't sleep."

He squeezes me gently and kisses the back of my head. "Me neither. I missed you. I'm here now, so go to sleep."

I know I'm dreaming, because I normally wouldn't stand naked in broad daylight on the sidewalk in front of my townhouse, on display for the entire neighborhood to see. I shudder, feeling chilled to the bone as I look around to see if anyone's watching.

I notice a man standing on the street corner. He's filthy, dressed in stained jeans and a dirty white T-shirt that doesn't cover his paunch. His hair is long, combed over to hide his balding head. He's staring at me, his gaze dull and fixed. I stand there frozen, staring at him with a sense of morbid fascination. I feel as if I should recognize him.

I'm startled out of my paralysis when he reaches down and rubs himself vulgarly through his jeans, stroking his hardening length with the palm of his meaty hand. Then it dawns on me who he must be.

I never got a good look at him eighteen years ago. He covered my eyes as soon as he grabbed me off my bike in front of my house. And once I was in his cargo van, he tied an old bandana around my eyes.

I never once saw his face. The only things I remember are the gravel sound of his voice and his foul breath. I did see a mug shot of him once, years later. He looked just like what I'd expect a monster to look like.... like someone with no heart, no soul. His eyes were glassy and dull.

I turn to race up the stone steps to my front door, but I'm trapped at the top of the stoop because the door's locked, and I don't have my key. I pound my fist on the door, hoping Gabrielle's home.

"Open the door, Gabrielle! Open the door!"

But she doesn't come, and even without turning to look, I know he's behind me. I can hear his heavy footsteps as he comes up the stone steps.

I pound again, until my hand aches. "Gabrielle, open the door!"

"She's not home," he says, in that gruff voice that haunts my dreams. "No one's home. No one's coming to rescue you this time."

When he grabs me from behind, I scream, thrashing and kicking as I try to free myself.

He reaches around me and pokes his thick fingers between my legs.
"No!"

I kick at him, trying to dislodge him. But he's so much bigger and
stronger than I am. He lifts me off my feet with one arm and holds me
suspended above the ground as I struggle to get free. Then his fingers
are back between my legs, hurting me as he digs into me, pushing and
stabbing at my tender flesh.

"No!"

"Jesus, Beth, wake up!"

I come awake abruptly, my head fuzzy from sleep, and I flinch at
the outline of a man looming over me. My vision is blurred by tears,
and I can't make out his face in the semi-darkness. I struggle to get
out from under him, trying to scoot away, to escape, but he holds
me fast.

"Sweetheart, it's all right. You're safe."

Shane.

And just like that, I sink back down onto the mattress, gasping as
I try to catch my breath.

"Do you need your inhaler?" He's already reaching for the nightstand drawer on his side of the bed.

I shake my head and try to slow my breaths. "No. I think I'm okay."

He lies back down beside me and kisses my forehead. "That was a
bad one. I think I'm going to have a few bruises."

"I'm sorry." I'm groggy from sleep, but I have a dim recollection
of Shane crawling into bed with me earlier in the night. "What are
you doing here?"

"I missed you. I couldn't sleep without you."

My breath catches. "I missed you, too."

I realize he's naked, and I can't resist laying my hand on his chest.

I can feel the rapid beating of his heart beneath my palm, and it feels so good to be touching him. I want more. I skim my fingers down his hard abdomen, tracing the ridges of his muscles.

He captures my hand and brings it to his mouth for a kiss. "We need to talk. I've been an ass, Beth, and I'm sorry."

I swallow hard. "You've been holding yourself back from me."

"No, I haven't—"

"Yes, you have."

"Beth—"

I tug my hand free from his and reach down to his penis, which is already swelling and lengthening. I squeeze him.

He groans loudly. "Beth, no." He pulls my hand off of him and holds it captive in his.

"Have you changed your mind about us?" I'm determined to have it out with him. I have to know. "If you have, then you need to tell me."

"God, no!" He squeezes my hand so hard, it hurts.

"You won't even let me touch you. Why—"

He leans forward and kisses me, his lips prying mine open with a ferocity born of pent-up frustration. His mouth devours mine, sucking and nibbling on my lips, as he pushes up my T-shirt to bare my breasts. His lips trail along my jaw, kissing and nipping me as he moves toward my breasts. His hot, wet tongue lashes at one of my nipples, which puckers so quickly it hurts. I cry out, bowing off the mattress. His hand skims down my torso to my panties, and his fingers slip inside to stroke me. He zeroes in on my clitoris and teases me with firm little circles.

The pleasure is so sudden and so intense, I can hardly breathe. I'm so hungry for his touch, I'm already close to coming.

He raises himself up and kisses me again, drinking in my whimpers. "Don't ever think I don't want you, Beth." His voice is hoarse. "I want you all the God damned time. My body *aches* constantly from wanting you."

After shoving the bedding aside, he rises up over me on all fours and kisses his way down my body. He strips off my panties and opens my legs to kneel between them. He trails kisses past my quivering belly to the damp curls between my thighs. And when he presses his face to my crotch and breathes me in, I moan. I grab onto the only thing I can reach—his hair—and hold on for dear life, tugging hard on the short strands.

He grunts loudly—I'm probably hurting him—but I can't help it. I need something to hold onto in this maelstrom. He nudges my thighs farther apart and settles between them, using his shoulders to keep them pinned open. When his tongue touches my aching clit, I give a loud cry.

He practically growls as he licks and sucks me. His finger slips inside me, pushing through my wet flesh, searching until he finds what he's looking for, and then my thighs are shaking as he strokes me. He knows exactly how to drive me mad. He teases my clitoris mercilessly with his tongue, flicking and circling the little knot of nerves until I'm writhing beneath him, whimpering and gasping helplessly while his finger torments me deep inside.

When my climax hits, I buck my sex against his mouth, trying to dislodge him from my overly-sensitized flesh. But he continues tonguing me, easing me down with gentle licks and strokes. I finally collapse in a boneless heap, my fingers sifting through his hair.

As soon as I recover enough to catch my breath, I sit up, looming over him as he's still lying between my legs, kissing the tender, quivering skin of my inner thighs. I lean down and pull his face up to mine for a kiss. He tastes like me, smells like me. He opens his mouth and draws my tongue inside so he can suck on it. Then he comes up beside me and takes me into his arms.

I take his erection in my hand, wanting to guide him inside me. I'm desperate to have him filling me, stretching me with his iron-hard cock. But he removes my hand.

I make a face at him. "I need you inside me. I want you to come in me."

Breathing hard, he shakes his head. "Tonight is about you, not me. I'm fine."

But this time I don't want to take no for an answer, so I reach for him again and wrap my fingers as far as I can around his erection, which pulses fiercely against my hand. He groans, the sound loud and harsh, then begins thrusting helplessly into my palm, his velvety-soft skin slipping and sliding in my firm grasp. He leans his forehead against mine, his breath coming hard. My fingertips graze the crown of his erection, which is wet with pre-come. I know he's close.

I can't help smiling against his lips. "I'd say your body disagrees."

I'm bitterly disappointed when he pries my hand off him once more. "No."

I reach up to touch his face, my fingers brushing against his short beard, which is damp from my arousal. It's an intensely raw and emotional moment. How can this man be so giving to me, and yet so relentless in denying himself? He takes stubborn to a whole new level.

Shane wipes his face on the sheet, then takes hold of my chin, not hard enough to hurt, but hard enough to get my undivided attention. "Don't ever think I don't want you. I *always* want you. Every minute of every day, I want you. I love you, Beth. Do you understand me?"

I frown. "Then why won't you make love with me?"

"What was that I just did?" he says.

I reach up to trace his cheekbone and smile sadly. "As much as I love what you just did to me, it's not the same as having you inside me. I need you inside me, Shane. Or at least let me give you pleasure. It can't be all one-sided."

He frowns. "Just give me some time, okay? I made a vow, and I'm going to keep it."

The pain I see in his eyes hurts me to the quick. I cradle his beautiful face in my hands. "Listen carefully, Shane McIntyre. I don't blame you for what happened." I glare at him, as if daring him to contradict me.

He leans forward and kisses the tip of my nose. "I know you don't, sweetheart. But I do."

ℰ 9

I awake to a bright blue, cloudless sky. It feels like we're sleeping in a tree house, high up in the sky where nothing can touch us. Sunshine fills the room, so with a groan, I pull the sheet over my head.

I hear a deep chuckle. "Wake up, sleepy head."

When I peer out from under the sheet, I see Shane sitting on the side of the bed pulling on socks. His hair is damp from a shower, and I detect the faint whiff of his soap. He's dressed in jeans and a T-shirt instead of a suit. This is the first time in weeks that he's been around when I awake.

He leans back and kisses me, looking pleased with himself this morning. "Good morning. How do you feel?"

I groan as I stretch my entire body. "Fine."

As I recall the toe-tingling orgasm he gave me in the night, I'm not surprised that he's in a chipper mood. I wish I could say the same, but I'm still bothered by the fact that he's holding himself back.

I reach over to stroke his lower back. "I expected you to be gone already."

"I thought we'd have breakfast together, and then I'll take you to your doctor appointment this morning."

I frown because I've made other plans. I wasn't expecting him to be here. "Lia's taking me."

He starts to say something, and for a moment, I think he's going to pull rank on his sister, but then he stops himself. I know he wants me and Lia to become friends—and not just because Lia's my primary bodyguard. He truly wants us to be friends. He probably thinks I need all the friends I can get.

He smiles, looking resigned. "Okay. She can take you. How about breakfast, then? I'll make you pancakes."

Now he's playing unfairly, bribing me with my weakness.

"*You* will?" Shane does a lot of things very well, but cooking isn't one of them.

He gives me the charming grin I love so well. "With Cooper's help."

I sit up, suddenly feeling better than I have in days. I whip off the T-shirt I wore to bed, gratified by the flash of heat I see in his eyes as his gaze zeroes in on my bare breasts. I swallow, tamping down the typical insecurity I feel when I'm naked. Let's just say I'll never win a wet T-shirt contest. Fortunately for me, Shane doesn't seem to mind.

I feel my nipples tighten under his scrutiny, and my face heats up. His eyes scan my bare torso, growing hot and hungry. I let him look his fill, then I jump off the far side of the bed.

Naked, I walk backward toward the bathroom. "I'll just go take a quick shower."

I notice with satisfaction that his gaze follows my every step, and he never once looks away. I take comfort in the heat I see in his eyes. He certainly doesn't look like a man who's having second thoughts.

* * *

Fresh out of my shower and dressed in a short skirt and cotton blouse, I sit at the breakfast bar enjoying the sight of Shane and Cooper cooking together. They make a great team.

True to his word, Shane makes pancakes, with more than a little guidance from Cooper. Cooper watches over Shane's shoulder, offering the occasional suggestion to prevent disaster. I guess I shouldn't judge; I'm not much of a cook either. Rooming for several years with a professional chef ruined me for cooking.

"I went to Clancy's yesterday," I say to Shane, as he flips the first of the pancakes. I realize he probably already knows, but it's something I want to talk to him about.

He glances back. "How did it go?"

I frown, remembering my run-in with Vanessa. "Not very well, actually. Vanessa—the general manager—doesn't like me."

Lia walks into the kitchen, her eyes bleary and her blonde hair mussed from sleep. She's wearing a pair of workout shorts and a tank top, which leaves her muscled arms bare. She takes the seat at the breakfast bar next to me. "That's putting it mildly. The Dragon Lady was a total bitch to Beth. Beth should have fired her on the spot."

Shane chuckles at the dragon lady reference. "Vanessa Markham? Yeah, she's a little tightly wound."

"She said I'm unqualified to have any say in the running of the store."

Shane scoffs. "It's your business, sweetheart, to run as you see fit. If you don't like her, fire her."

"But she's right. I have no retail experience and no business experience, so I can't very well fault her observations. But I want to be involved in running the business. I'm thinking about going back to school. To UC to get an MBA."

Shane faces me and leans back against the stove. I think I actually managed to surprise him for once. "That's a great idea. The University of Chicago has one of the best business schools in the country. Go for it."

"I also met the new head of security. Mack Donovan. I didn't know you'd hired additional security."

Shane checks the dinner-plate sized pancake in the skillet and flips it over. "I assigned Mack to oversee and upgrade the store's security. It was too lax. Besides, I want additional security present whenever you're in the store."

The pancakes are soon done. Shane makes up a plate for me and one for Lia, and he and Cooper eat standing in the kitchen.

"I'm impressed," I tell him after taking my first bite. The pancakes are light and fluffy, perfectly golden brown, not a burnt edge anywhere. Finished off with butter and real maple syrup, each bite melts in my mouth.

After everyone has finished eating, I gather up all the dirty dishes and load them into the dishwasher, then clean up the kitchen while Shane disappears into his office to make a few work-related calls.

Shane comes out of his office just as Lia and I are ready to leave for my doctor's office. He pulls me close and kisses me. "I'm heading back to the house. Are you coming home after your doctor appointment?"

I look into blue eyes flecked with tiny bits of gold and nod. I could lose myself in those eyes.

"Don't be too long," he says.

* * *

The visit to Dr. Meyer is relatively quick and, fortunately, painless. After reviewing an x-ray of my arm, she declares the break well healed and has her assistant remove the cast. The skin on my left arm is tender and sensitive from two months of disuse, and my arm muscles are a little stiff, but otherwise it feels fine. She sends me on my way with instructions to avoid strenuous physical activity for a few weeks to give my arm bone additional time to mend.

We're out of the clinic in an hour.

"Where to now?" Lia says, popping on her sunglasses as we walk out of the medical building and into the morning sun. "Is there anything else you want to do? Shall we go terrorize Vanessa a little? That'd be fun."

As much as I've enjoyed getting out and getting away, I miss Shane. Waking up with him and having breakfast together just made me crave his company that much more. I smile, remembering how he'd watched me walk naked to the bathroom that morning. And now that my cast is finally off—the last visual reminder of my injuries—I think it's time to put an end to his self-imposed punishment.

"If you don't mind, can we go home?"

Lia grins as we head to her Jeep. "It's probably for the best. I don't think Shane can take much more of the strain."

* * *

When we arrive back at the estate late morning, I feel a sense of nervous anticipation. I'm excited about seeing Shane again. I keep picturing the heat in his eyes and the blatant hunger in his expression when he watched me walk naked to the bathroom that morning. I think he just needs a little more encouragement. And now that the last visual reminder of the attack is gone, it should be easier.

When Lia pulls up to the front door to let me out, Shane is waiting on the steps. At the sight of him, my heart rate picks up and I feel my body flush with excitement. Even dressed in jeans and a T-shirt, he makes me melt.

Shane opens my door and gives me a hand as I step down from the Jeep. And then I'm in his arms, right where I need to be.

He kisses the top of my head. "Welcome home. I missed you."

I wrap my arms around his waist. "I missed you, too."

He squeezes me gently. "Next time, please don't sneak off. Just tell me you're going, okay? This isn't a prison, Beth. It's your home. You can come and go as you see fit. I'm sorry if I made you feel otherwise."

I feel a fresh pang of guilt for sneaking off the way I did, but it was necessary at the time. Getting away—even for a short while—was very beneficial for both of us. I feel stronger now, more able to deal. And as for him... I think he missed me more than a little.

Shane pulls back to look at me, and he can't hide the censure in his pointed gaze. "You took two years off my life with that stunt. And I gave Cooper an hour-long lecture for distracting the guys in the security office while you two snuck out. Don't do it again."

Lia saunters up to the front steps with a cocky grin on her face, and Shane gives his sister a wry glance. "Thanks for bringing her home in one piece, Lia."

"Anytime, pal," she says, slapping her brother on the shoulder as she passes by. "At least we're making progress."

Shane releases me and takes hold of my left arm, examining it gently. "How does your arm feel?"

The skin on my arm is overly sensitive, and I shiver at his light touch. "It feels weird."

"What did your doctor say?"

"She said I'm fine. She told me to take it easy for a while. No strenuous physical activity for a few weeks."

Shane gets this *I-told-you-so* look on his face. "That means no martial arts training for a while. At least for a month. Got it?"

I smile in defeat. "Yes, I get it. But after that, I'm starting classes with Liam. Don't even think about trying to stop me."

For a moment, he doesn't say anything—he just looks at me—and I'm afraid he's going to renege on his promise. "Shane, I'm doing this. I want to learn how to protect myself."

"Fine. But give it a month, all right? Promise me. My heart won't be able to take it if you break your arm again."

"All right, I'll wait."

* * *

I leave Shane to his work and head up to our suite. I've been fantasizing about getting in the pool since the day I moved in, but the cast prevented me from doing that. Now, there's nothing standing in my way.

After a half-hour of preening in the bathroom—indulging in a long, hot shower and doing all those girlie tasks that someone would want to do before she parades around half-naked in a tiny string bikini—I head down to the lower level to the pool room.

I have a plan. There's no guarantee it will work, but knowing

Shane's predilection for spying on me, I'm pretty sure he'll catch an eyeful. In fact, I'm counting on it.

If this barely-there bikini doesn't give Shane ideas, then nothing will.

🌀 10

As I push open the glass door leading to the pool room, I'm immediately hit with an invisible wall of warm, chlorine-scented air, and that makes me smile. I've always loved the water. I probably spent the bulk of my free time as a child in a pool or at the lake. The smell of chlorine brings back a lot of happy childhood memories. I pull off my wrap and hang it on the row of hooks on the wall.

Lia's already in the pool, floating on a bright orange lounge chair. She gives me a thumbs up and a cat call. "Wow, Princess! You look hot!"

I glare at Lia when I notice we're not the only ones in the pool room. Jamie's in the water as well, swimming laps. He pauses mid-stroke and faces my direction, treading water. For a blind man, he has uncanny built-in radar. "Hi, Beth. How's the arm?"

Jamie's presence is a happy surprise. It's not unexpected, because Jamie spends a lot of time in the pool, as it's his preferred method of exercise. The water is one of the few places where Jamie's blindness isn't a hindrance. He swims like a fish and is perfectly at home in the water. Knowing Jamie's background, it doesn't surprise me in the least. He was a Navy SEAL until an explosion blinded him, and he's not the type to sit around feeling sorry for himself. Jamie's constantly pushing himself, testing his limits, just to prove to himself that he can still do it.

Of Shane's three brothers, it's Jamie I spend the most time with. Jamie lives here full time, so he's always around. Plus, he has the patience of a saint. There's just something about him—and it isn't his good looks. He's very empathetic, very kind. Maybe those qualities stem from the fact that he's blind.

Maybe his lack of sight has taught him to pay closer attention to those around him and read people better. Don't they say that when you lose one sense, you develop the others more fully? Maybe empathy is another human sense—like touch or sound or smell. Whatever the reason, he's a good guy, and I liked him from the first moment I met him.

Jamie's yellow Labrador puppy—Gus—runs up to me and drops into a sitting position at my side, patiently waiting for a pat on the head. I reach down and scratch the dog's ears and laugh as he squirms happily. Gus was supposed to have been Jamie's service dog, but because the puppy's afraid of water, he failed his training. But Jamie had already fallen in love with the dog after meeting him a few times, so he arranged to adopt him anyway as a pet. Now Jamie's training Gus himself to be a service dog.

"My arm feels good," I tell him. "Kind of sensitive, but otherwise good."

"Come on in then," he says, motioning me in. "The water's fine."

I walk to the zero entry end of the pool and step into the warm water, sighing with pleasure as it laps at my feet. Jamie swims toward the shallow end of the pool to join me.

I can't help watching the water sluice off his tall, muscular body—it's a sight any woman can appreciate. He has a handsome face with a square jaw and a perfect blade of a nose. He hasn't shaved in a few days, so there's a new beard on his face. His thick, auburn hair is cut short. I know his eyes are the color of fine whisky and framed by thick dark lashes, but I can't see them at the moment because they're covered by darkened swim goggles, which he wears to protect his eyes from the chemicals in the water. Normally, he doesn't cover his eyes in the house, and just looking at him, you'd never guess he's blind. There's no visible damage to his eyes, although he does have several scars at his temples.

Jamie reaches for my left arm—finding it unerringly, which amazes me—and examines it with deft, careful fingers. "What did your doctor say about physical activity?"

What is it with these overly-protective McIntyre men? It must be genetic. "She said nothing strenuous for a few weeks."

Jamie nods. "Sounds reasonable. A little low-impact swimming won't hurt you, but I guess we'll have to wait a while before we can start racing or diving. Shane tells me you were a swim-team champ in high school and college. I'd love to have a little competition when you're up for it."

The thought of swimming competitively really perks me up. "I would love to, Jamie."

Lia drifts toward us on her floating device and splashes Jamie full in the face. He growls and makes a show of lunging for her. She kicks water at him, then rolls off her floating couch and swims like crazy for deeper water. But she's no match for Jamie's speed. He catches his sister easily, snagging her ankle in mid-kick, and they wrestle beneath the water like a pair of frisky crocodiles. Gus prances at the edge of the pool barking frantically.

While those two are otherwise occupied, I move cautiously into water. It's been months since I've been able to get my arm wet, and the warm water feels heavenly.

I feel a little overly conspicuous in the scrap of fabric I'm wearing. The bottom piece barely covers my butt cheeks, and the top isn't much better. The two little triangles of fabric covering my breasts barely do more than obscure my nipples. For a moment, I feel guilty that I'm relieved Jamie can't see me. I already feel overly self-conscious about my body; being on display like this isn't easy for me. I'm way out of my comfort zone, but if this is what it takes to get Shane's attention, then I'm game.

My gaze flickers briefly up at the video surveillance cameras situated throughout the room, and I wonder if Shane is watching. If he is spying on me, then he deserves to get an eye full.

Once the bottom of the pool falls away from my feet, I begin taking slow strokes down the length of the pool.

Lia swims up beside me. "You doing okay?"

I give her a thumbs-up. "Fine."

Jamie swims up on my other side. I'm a good swimmer, but I doubt I could keep up with Jamie in a real competition. I just don't have his physical strength. If I'm a dolphin—as my mom and brother used to call me—then Jamie's an orca.

"I guess racing is out of the question right now," he says. "Shane told me you raced competitively in college. I'd like to see how fast you can go."

"Not nearly as fast as you, I'm sure." After all, the man was a SEAL.

He was trained to be at home in the water.

"You're the best competition I've had in a long time. I hope you'll train with me when you're cleared for physical activity."

"I'd love that," I say, absolutely meaning it.

I begin swimming laps, gliding through the water with minimal effort, taking it easy on my arm. I'm more interested in form than speed right now. Jamie keeps pace with me, taking things at my pace.

"Don't let me hold you back, Jamie." I know he can swim circles around me.

"It's okay," he says. "I like having the company."

As I watch his muscular arms slice cleanly through the water, it occurs to me that Jamie must be very lonely here on the estate. I've never seen anyone come visit him. I've never heard him talk about a woman, or any friends outside of his family. His former teammates keep in touch with him, but they're located all the way on the west coast, in California, and they're often deployed abroad. And when they're not deployed, they're busy training and spending quality time with their families.

He's a writer now, and I've read several of his military thrillers. But that's a pretty solitary job.

After accompanying me for a few laps, Jamie climbs out of the pool and heads for the high-dive platform that rises high overhead. My heart starts racing in anticipation as I gaze up at it. I love diving, especially the high dive. What I wouldn't give to dive right now.

Jamie climbs the ladder and walks out to the edge of the platform. He turns his back to the water, and I realize he's going to do a back flip off the platform. I have to admit, I'm seriously impressed. While I love diving, I doubt I'd be quite so sanguine about doing a back flip off a board twenty feet above the water when I can't see what's beneath me.

Jamie gets into position. "Clear?" he calls, his voice loud and clear. "Clear!" Lia yells up at him.

Obviously, this is something they've done before.

Jamie executes a picture-perfect back flip, his form straight and powerful as he slices cleanly into the water. I marvel at his courage, not to mention his technique. I don't think I'd have the guts to do that if I were in his shoes—not if I couldn't see what was beneath me. The guy has some serious balls to be able to trust what he *knows*, rather than what he *can't* see.

I climb out of the pool and step up onto the low diving board, which bounces and vibrates beneath my feet. It feels good to be on a diving board again.

Lia gives me a look. "I'm pretty sure diving would violate your doctor's orders."

I walk out to the end of the board and bounce a little. I have no intention of diving, but I enjoy the brief sense of weightlessness I feel bouncing on the board. Once I'm given the green light, I plan to give Jamie a run for his money on the high dive.

"Beth Jamison! Don't you dare jump off that diving board!"

I flinch at the booming voice coming over the loud speakers. Gus starts barking frantically as he races along the edge of the pool.

"I told you, Princess!" Lia yells at me. She lays her head back in the water and yells up toward the ceiling. "I told her not to do it, Shane!"

I glare down at Lia, the little traitor.

The dog's still racing around barking his head off, and Jamie tells him to be quiet.

I glance around the pool room searching for the source of the audio. "Shane, is that you? Can you hear me?"

"Of course it's me! Who the hell else would it be? Don't you dare jump, young lady!"

I roll my eyes. *Oh, my God, he did not just call me young lady.* "Shane, you're overreacting! I'm not going to—"

"I mean it, Beth! Don't you dare!" Shane's voice is little more than a growl over the speaker system.

I shake my head, exasperated. "Shane, would you relax!"

The audio falls silent then, and I linger on the diving board wondering why he's gone quiet all of a sudden.

Jamie's back up on the high dive, and Lia gives him the all-clear. I watch him as he executes another perfect dive, cutting cleanly through the water.

Just as Jamie surfaces, the glass doors to the pool room are thrown wide open as Shane storms in, his face flushed. His voice cracks like a gun. "Beth!"

"You're in trouble now, Princess," Lia says, enjoying herself way too much at my expense.

Shane scowls at his sister, and I seriously doubt he's fooled by her innocent act.

Determined not to be cowed by the expression on Shane's face, I paste a bright smile on mine. "Shane, hi!"

He's livid. "If you jump, I swear to God I'll paddle your ass!"

Gus runs up to Shane, barking excitedly as he nearly knocks Shane off balance. "Down, Gus!"

The dog drops down on his haunches, his tail wagging so vigorously I'm afraid he's going to topple over into the pool.

Shane looks completely exasperated, and I have to bite my lip to keep from laughing. He grabs the hem of his T-shirt and yanks the thing over his head and throws it to the ground. His eyes narrow on me, and my smile fades. He doesn't seem to think any of this is amusing. Maybe I've pushed him too far.

"Oh, for crying out loud," I mutter, placing my hands on my hips as I glare at him in return. "I wasn't even going to dive."

Now I'm mad, too. If he's going to be pissy, then so am I. I think we're both at the end of our ropes thanks to an overwhelming dose of sexual frustration.

Shane reaches down and pulls off his shoes and socks. "Get off that board, Beth! Right this minute!"

"Why are you undressing? Are you coming in?"

He stands there belligerently with his hands on his hips. "No, I am not coming in."

"Then what are you doing?"

"Get off that board and find out."

I start to turn, intending to walk back to the ladder and climb down. But the water looks too inviting, and I really want to go off the diving board. So at the last second, I head back to the end of the board and look down at the glassy, smooth water.

Shane gives me a black look as his voice drops an octave. "Don't you dare."

I'm tired of him telling me what to do, and I'm tired of him holding himself back from me. Purely to aggravate him, I step right off the board, my arms tucked protectively against my sides, and I slip down feet first into the water, barely making a splash.

When I come back up, I take in a big breath, feeling wonderfully energized. I push my wet hair out of my eyes and look around to find that I'm the only one left in the pool.

"Where did everybody go?"

Shane glowers at me. "Get out of the pool."

I've had just about enough of his attitude. "Excuse me?"

"You heard me. Get out of the fucking pool."

11

Everyone abandoned me—even the dog—and I'm looking at a Shane I barely recognize. He's standing with his hands on his hips, his expression tight and guarded. His eyes are narrowed and his jaw muscles are clenched. I'm not sure what to make of this Shane. He's never spoken to me like this before, his voice clipped and demanding. This isn't his master-of-the universe tone; it's something different.

It's edgy.

It's impatient.

He looks... pissed.

At me? Crap! This isn't how I saw this playing out. He was supposed to look at my half-naked body in this bikini and think about sex... not get mad at me.

When I swim to the side of the pool, Shane reaches down and

hauls me out of the water.

"What is your problem?" I demand when he sets me on my feet. I'm dripping wet and feel chilled. My bikini doesn't leave much to the imagination, and now I'm feeling seriously overexposed. I cross my arms over my breasts. I don't have much in the way of breasts, but what I do have is pretty much on display right now.

Shane's heated gaze scans me from head to toe. "Where did you get that swimsuit?"

Steeling myself, I drop my arms and let him look his fill, determined to brazen it out. After all, I wore the darn thing to catch his attention, and if the glittering heat in his eyes is any indication, it's working. "Do you like it?"

His eyes are blazing as they narrow on my chest. I look down and notice that my nipples are like tiny pebbles, pressing against the meager triangles of fabric covering them. He closes his eyes and takes a deep breath. I swear he's counting to ten.

I glance around, confirming my suspicions that we're the only ones left in the pool room. "Where did everybody go?"

"I kicked them out."

"Why? We were having fun."

"Because I didn't think you'd want an audience for this."

My heart rate kicks up, and I feel a fluttering of anticipation in my belly. "And audience for what?" Oh, dear. This could go either way.

Shane crosses his arms over his chest. "I told you I'd paddle you if you jumped off that diving board."

As his words sink in, I'm momentarily rendered speechless, and I think my heart skips a beat. Then I start laughing—I can't help it. He's not going to spank me, not really. Although I have to admit, deep in my twisted core, the idea of him taking me over his knees has more than just a little appeal. "Come on, Shane. I just stepped off the board. I didn't actually dive."

"That's not the point." He's frowning at me. "I told you not to do it. Besides, you could have hurt your arm."

I'm sick and tired of hearing about my stupid arm. "Shane, my arm is fine!"

I watch his jaw muscles flex as his patience continues to erode. "I'll decide when it's fine!"

"Since when do you get to call all the shots?" Now I'm yelling too. It feels exhilarating.

Without warning, Shane sweeps me up in his arms and heads toward the changing room.

I start squirming. "Put me down!"

He swats my butt cheek lightly. "No."

"Shane! I'm soaking wet! Put me down!"

"Don't care."

"You can't do this!"

"Sure I can."

When I start squirming in earnest, he gives me two more swats on my butt, considerably harder than the first one. "Ow! Stop that!"

My rear end starts to tingle. I'm not sure if I like it or not, but then I feel heat between my legs. I guess I do like it. Still, I don't think I should encourage him—not while he's in this kind of mood.

"Stop squirming before you hurt yourself!"

Shane uses his shoulder to push through a set of doors into the changing room and carries me to the leather sofa. He lays me down and takes hold of the waistband of my bikini bottom.

"Shane, I'm getting the furniture wet."

"Don't care."

He strips my bikini bottom off me and tosses it on the floor.

My hands automatically move to cover my sex, and I'm shaking now from a combination of the chilly air on my wet skin and excitement. All the steam has left me, leaving me a quivering mass.

The blatant heat in his gaze makes my belly clench in anticipation. "What are you doing?"

"What do you think?" He pulls me into a sitting position and reaches around me to untie the strings of my bikini top. My top lands in the floor as well, leaving me completely naked.

I can't help noticing his impressive erection trapped in his jeans. It's pretty obvious what he has on his mind. But we can't do that here. Anyone could walk in. Shivering, I draw my knees up and wrap my arms around myself strategically, trying to cover my mound and my breasts at the same time. It's a habit he's been trying to break me of—hiding my nakedness from him—but old habits die hard. I can't help feeling self-conscious.

Shane gives me a chastising look. "Beth."

Now *that* is his master-of-the universe tone that I know and love, the one that makes me go weak in the knees. That's *my* Shane talking now.

"What?" I say defensively. "I'm cold."

"Lower your arms, sweetheart." His voice drops an octave as he pops the button on his jeans. "I'll warm you."

Oh, my God, he's serious. Despite the butterflies flitting around in my belly, I shake my head. "Not here. Someone might come in."

He crouches in front of the sofa and cups the side of my face with one hand, his thumb brushing along my bottom lip. "No one's going to come in. Now lower your arms, sweetheart. Every inch of you is beautiful. You have nothing to hide."

The sudden softening in his demeanor takes me by surprise. "You're not mad?"

He smiles. "Of course not. Although you scared the hell out of me with that stunt. Jesus, I think my heart stopped beating when you jumped off the board. I was afraid you'd hurt your arm."

I smile with relief. "If you're not mad at me, then why did you chase everyone off?"

"Because I didn't think you'd want me to fuck you in front of an audience."

I can't help my grin. "Is that what we're going to do?"

He nods. "I figure if you're strong enough to jump off a diving board, you'll survive a little bit of fucking."

I glance nervously around the room, looking for surveillance cameras. "Are there cameras in here?"

He laughs. "No."

My face goes up in flames at the idea of having sex with him in here, where anyone could walk in on us. But the temptation is too great for me to pass up the opportunity. "All right, then, yes."

Shane smirks as he crawls onto the sofa and looms over me on his hands and knees, caging me. He's careful not to make me feel pinned down, and I love him for it. While we've made a lot of progress in that regard, we aren't out of the woods yet. The fear is still there, always lurking in my subconscious, but I've learned to manage it a little better. And I trust Shane. I know he'd never hurt me intentionally.

He leans down and kisses me, his warm lips coaxing mine to open. He doesn't have to work hard, though, because I'm way past ready for this. I'm starving for him. I open my mouth and welcome his tongue as it slips inside and strokes mine.

His kiss is slow and languorous, as if we have all the time in the world to get reacquainted with each other. My body heats up and a liquid warmth pools low in my belly. I can feel my sex swelling and tingling, and I'm aching for his touch.

I pull back to catch my breath. "I thought you were going to pad-dle me." He didn't, and I'm not sure if I'm relieved or disappointed.

He reaches down to swat my bare butt cheek. "There. Consider yourself paddled. Unless you want more?"

He seems serious, and I blush at his reminder of my penchant for spanking stories. But I don't want fantasy right now. I want the reality of him. It's been far too long since I've felt him there, surging inside me, filling me with his exquisite erection. I grab hold of his broad shoulders and pull him closer, licking the seam of his lips. I'm gratified when I feel a shiver ripple through him. "No, I just want you. You can spank me later."

His mouth covers mine as he kisses me hotly, drinking in my sighs and all the little sounds I can't help making. As usual, he's a master kisser, taking control as he licks his way into my mouth, find-ing my tongue with his own and stroking it. It's not long before we're both breathless and needing more.

He gazes down at me. "Top or bottom?"

It's not a casual question. Being pinned down can trigger all kinds of bad feelings in me. I'm doing better, but it's still unpredictable.

Still, I love having him over top of me. I love watching his body work, his beautiful muscles flex and ripple as he rocks into me. "Bottom."

"Are you sure?"

I can't blame Shane for being extra cautious. I know the last thing he wants right now is for me to have a panic attack. They aren't pretty, with all the ugly crying and screaming. I catch a momentary flash of something violent in his expression, something that looks like rage, but it's gone as quickly as it appeared. I know he has to be thinking about Howard Kline.

But I'm determined not to let old memories ruin this moment.

"Yes, I'm sure." I reach up and trace the top edge of his trim beard. "I want to try."

Shane stands and shucks off his jeans and boxers, and then he kneels on the sofa again, hovering over me. As he kisses me, gently coaxing me to lie back, he parts my legs and skims his hands slowly up the insides of my thighs. I close my eyes, reveling in the feel of his warm touch trailing along my sensitive skin.

When he reaches my sex, he touches me, lightly at first, to test my readiness. I can tell I'm already slick with arousal because his finger slips easily along my slit up to my clitoris, which he circles lazily, coating it in my body's juices. I groan and raise my hips, trying to increase the pressure of his touch, but he's not going to be hurried.

He sinks a finger partway into my opening and groans, his voice low and rough. "My God, you're tight."

I imagine he's thinking about putting his cock in there... *bare*. After moving in with him, I started taking birth control pills, so there's no need for anything to come between us. We haven't had sex without a condom yet—well, except for that one time in his apartment foyer when we both lost our heads. I think the thought of him being inside me bare is tantalizing for both of us... just his hot, velvety flesh against mine.

His next words confirm my suspicions. "Thank God for the pill."

He slowly withdraws his finger, letting it drag along my sensitive flesh, which does all kinds of wonderful things to me, and then he eases it back in, deeper this time. He makes a sound almost like a growl as my flesh clings to his finger, causing a delicious friction that makes me ache.

"You're going to kill me," he breathes.

He eases his finger in and out, each time pushing a little deeper, and my breath catches. It's been two months since we last had sex, and in some ways I feel like we're starting all over again.

As he slowly begins to thrust inside me with his finger, my hips start moving and my breath comes faster. I can't help the whimpers and moans I'm making—it's just too good.

He curls his long finger deep inside me and begins a methodical stroking that ratchets up my arousal. I know he won't stop until he teases an orgasm out of me, the kind that starts slowly and swells relentlessly, sneaking up on me until I suddenly explode. His finger focuses on a delicious spot inside me.

I gasp as the pleasure builds. "Shane!"

His gaze locks onto mine. "It's okay. Just relax and let it happen."

His thumb, slick with my arousal, starts rubbing firm little circles on my clitoris. The two-pronged attack is more than I can bear. My hips come off the sofa and I'm desperate to come. "Shane!"

"I know, baby." He leans down and kisses his way along my jaw-line, down my neck to the hollow of my throat, where he sucks my heated skin. "Mmm, chlorine," he murmurs, licking my frantic pulse point.

My belly clenches tightly and my thighs start to shake as I feel an orgasm looming. I'm so close! But suddenly, he withdraws his finger, leaving me hanging.

I glare at him as he sucks my juices off his finger. "Shane!"

"Patience, sweetheart. We've waited this long. Let's not rush it." He chuckles. "I have a feeling once I'm inside you, it'll be over way too soon."

He nudges my thighs wider apart and settles his shoulders between them. His breath is hot on my exposed sex as he parts my flushed folds with gentle fingers.

I practically growl at him in frustration. "You're trying to kill me, aren't you?"

"Nothing so dramatic. I just want a taste."

"At least let me come."

He shakes his head. "Not until I'm inside you."

He starts with light flicks of his tongue on my already oversensitized clit. I whimper, unable to help myself, and rock my hips shamelessly against his mouth. He moves in closer, nudging my thighs up over his shoulders, and uses his fingers to open me wide so that he has unobstructed access to my sex. His hot tongue takes one long swipe from my aching core up to my quivering bundle of nerves, and I shiver.

When he grasps my clit lightly between his lips and begins to suck, I nearly come out of my skin. My heels dig into his back. "Oh, God, Shane, please!"

He brings me right to the edge, again and again, tormenting and teasing me until I'm a shaking mess. Finally, he raises his head and wipes his mouth on his bicep, then rises up over me, settling his hips in the cradle of my thighs. As he slowly sinks down onto me, he's watching for signs of anxiety. "Doing okay?" His voice is low and hoarse, and I know he's reached the end of his patience, too. Thank God.

I nod, swallowing hard.

He positions the thick head of his cock at my opening and rubs himself in my wetness. He's a lot to take at first, and it's been a while.

When he wedges the crown inside me, I tense, my muscles going taut. Already he's stretching me, and this is just the beginning. I'm sure he can feel my limbs trembling, but I can't help it. He eases himself inside me a bit at a time, gently rocking forward and back, and the sensation of his firmness sinking inside me is exquisite.

My body stretches around his thick girth, and the slight burn makes me gasp. He distracts me by rubbing little circles on my clit with the slick pad of this thumb. Soon my impending orgasm is back with a vengeance.

Finally, his cock is seated fully inside me, and I can feel the weight of his balls pressing against my bottom. He's breathing hard now, his jaws clenched. His expression is strained, and I get the feeling he's holding himself back. He pulls slowly out, letting his cock drag against the sensitive tissues inside me. Then he rocks back inside in one slow, fluid stroke. I gasp.

"You okay?" he says, his voice hoarse.

I close my eyes and nod.

"Open your eyes, Beth. Look at me."

I lock my gaze on his as he starts to move, his thrusts slow and measured. Somehow he knows just how to angle his cock so that the head drags along the front wall of my passage hitting the sweet spot with every stroke. The pleasure inside me builds, stealing my breath, until I'm on the verge of coming. I'm so close, but then something changes, as if a switch has been thrown inside me. I feel my pulse pick up and my heart starts hammering—and not in a good way. As I begin to struggle for air, I recognize the beginnings of a panic attack. I grip his shoulders and push, my nails digging hard into his muscles. Immediately, he raises himself off me.

"Hey, it's okay." He leans down to kiss me lightly, and then he looks me in the eye and strokes my cheek. "It's just you and me, right?"

I nod, trying to remain rational. But it's not easy.

He studies my expression and frowns. "Sweetheart, if you're not ready—"

"I am ready!" And to prove it, I reach between his thighs and take hold of his erection.

He's hard as steel, his cock engorged and slick from my juices.

His balls hang heavy between his legs. When I squeeze his erection, he looks down to watch and groans. My hand slides easily along his length as I stroke him, and when my fingers slide over the sensitive crown, he grits his teeth.

"I'm not going to last much longer," he warns, giving me a self-deprecating look.

"That's all right. I just want to feel you inside me again. The rest is icing on the cake."

He smiles, and then he kisses me. "Come here, sweetheart." He maneuvers himself into a sitting position on the sofa and draws me onto his lap so that I'm straddling him, face to face. My thighs are spread wide over his, and my flushed sex hovers close to his erection.

His gaze burns into mine. "Put me inside you and ride me. Make yourself come." To help me along, he strokes my clit again, giving me something besides my anxiety to focus on.

My thighs tense as he rubs my clit, and I groan, dropping my forehead to his. "Shane."

His other hand settles on my hip, and he coaxes me closer. His voice is rough. "Put me inside you, honey."

I scoot forward, positioning myself right over him, and then I slowly sink down on the crown, biting my lip as the fat head of his cock pushes inside my swollen opening. My breath hitches in my throat as he fills me again, stretching me so perfectly. I raise up a bit, then sink down farther. With each rise and fall of my body, his cock slides deeper and deeper into me. When he's all the way in, I moan at the sweet feeling of fullness.

"Okay?" he says between gritted teeth.

I take in his tight expression. He's so determined to make this good for me. But it's been so long, and he's clearly on edge. I want this to be good for him, too. "You can let go, you know."

"Not until you've come."

I'm so close already, I'm pretty sure if he touches me again, I'll fall apart. "Touch me."

As he reaches between us and rubs my clit, I lean into him, my forehead against his, looking down to watch his thumb teasing me. I move up and down on his erection, and the combination of sensations sends me into orbit, and I come apart. Shane captures my mouth with his and swallows my cries, drinking them in and absorbing the sounds. My sex clamps down on his cock, squeezing him tightly. He throws his head back and cries out as he comes hard, grimacing as he shoots liquid heat into me, thrusting with each ejaculation.

"I love you," he says, breathing hard as he looks into my eyes. He cups the back of my head and draws me down to lay my head on his shoulder.

We hold each other for a long time, simply enjoying the physical connection as well as the intimacy of being joined together. The air is cool on my back, but my front is toasty warm against the searing heat of his body.

I snuggle into him. "Love you, too."

12

I must have zoned out for a while on Shane's lap, because when I try to move off him, my legs are stiff. He loosens his hold around my waist.

As I lift myself off his cock, semen trickles down the insides of my thighs. "Oh, my God, I'm leaking!"

Shane somehow manages to refrain from laughing, although I do detect a trace of humor in the curve of his lips. I'm not used to having sex without a condom, so I wasn't quite ready for the aftermath. He lifts me off the couch and sweeps me up into his arms. "That's just one of the joys of going bareback. Let's go clean you off."

He carries me into the shower stall and turns on the water, adjusting it to a comfortable temperature before setting me down beneath the warm spray. He steps inside the shower with me, and I stand on shaky legs, holding onto him for stability as he quickly rinses my body free of chlorine and his come. Then he washes himself quickly.

"Beth, are we okay?"

I look up at him and realize he's serious. He's actually concerned. My pulse speeds up. "Yes. Why?"

"I know I haven't been the easiest person to live with the past couple of months, and I'm sorry for that. I realized how bad it was when you felt the need to sneak off yesterday. You don't have to do that, you know."

"I just needed some space and a change of scenery. I've been cooped up here at the house for a while."

He nods. "Lia or I or Cooper will take you anywhere you want to go. You're not a prisoner. I want you to feel like this is your home. I want you to be happy here."

Now that he's opening up to me, I decide to come clean. "I miss my townhouse. I've given some thought to moving back there."

"Jesus, Beth, no." Shane turns off the water and pulls two large towels out of a cupboard. He hands one to me and begins drying himself with the other. "You can't go back to the townhouse. It's not safe."

While I'm towel drying my hair, Shane retrieves his clothes and comes back into the bathroom, holding out his T-shirt to me. "Your bikini is wet. Why don't you wear this?"

I slip his T-shirt over my head, grateful that it's long enough to cover my butt. I still feel ridiculously underdressed, but there's no way I'm putting my wet swimsuit back on.

Shane looks at me. "You're not happy here?"

I can tell he wants a straight answer. "This place is beautiful, Shane, really it is. I don't want to sound ungrateful, but I feel... isolated here. I guess I miss the city. I didn't realize how much until yesterday."

He frowns as he takes my hand. "Let's go upstairs and change, and then we'll talk. Whatever you need to be happy, we'll do it."

* * *

Back in our suite, I'm sitting on the bed wrapped in my fuzzy, pale blue robe, watching Shane dress. After donning black socks and boxers, he pulls on a pair of charcoal gray slacks and a white, button-down shirt. He looks a little over-dressed for being at home, and I can't help wondering what he's planning.

Still, I'm enjoying the show. I love watching him get dressed. He finishes buttoning his shirt and tucks it into the waistband of his trousers with brisk, precise movements. The man's gorgeous no matter what he's wearing, but when he dresses up, he takes my breath away.

"You look pretty hot for an older guy," I tell him, grinning. He's thirty-four, just ten years older than I am, but I like to tease him about the difference in our ages. And, he's got a birthday coming up soon, I remind myself. I need to plan something to celebrate.

"Thirty-four is not old," he says in mock indignation.

He disappears for a moment into the huge walk-in closet and returns wearing a black holster strapped to his chest and carrying a black handgun. Fascinated, I watch him check his ammunition and reset the safety, and then he slips the gun into the holster.

Now that I know Howard Kline is free, Shane doesn't have to hide the fact that he's armed when we go out. The gun scares me, I'll admit, because I know nothing about guns. I've never even touched one. But it also fascinates me.

Almost all of Shane's employees are armed, so I guess it's something I'll have to get used to.

Now that he's dressed and ready, Shane faces me, his hands on his hips. "Let's go out, on a date."

I'm still a little dazzled by his appearance, so it takes a moment for his words to sink in. "A date? Like, right now?"

"Yes, right now. What would you like to do? Name it."

The thought of going out with Shane—on a date!—is thrilling. We haven't been out on a date since before the assault, so I jump at the chance.

"There is one place I'd like to go. Clancy's."

I feel drawn to the place. It's always been my happy place, ever since I was a kid and my mom or brother would bring me downtown on the weekends to browse for books. Now that I own it—I still haven't been able to wrap my mind around that—I feel even more compelled to be there. And even though, as Vanessa pointed out, I don't have any retail experience, I have a legitimate and vested interest in the bookstore. I want to be part of it.

Shane nods. "All right. Let's go."

"Really? Right now?"

He smiles. "Just as soon as you get dressed."

I brighten as I hop off the bed and head into the closet to pick out something nice to wear.

* * *

As we head toward the city, I'm struck with a sense of déjà vu, as I remember the first time I rode in Shane's vintage silver Jaguar. That was the first night he took me back to his apartment—technically, that would have been our second date. That was the night I freaked out on him in the elevator and asked him to take me home. He'd taken me home without a single word of reproach.

He's never made me feel bad about my anxieties—that's one of the many things I love best about him. He kissed me for the first time that night, setting my body on fire. I glance over at him and smile, remembering our first real kiss. It had started out as a simple, hesitant meeting of our lips and quickly escalated into an inferno. He'd touched me, driving me crazy with a level of desire I'd never experienced before. I'd wanted him so badly, even from the beginning, that for the first time in my life I was willing to take a chance.

I think back to my only so-called boyfriend before Shane –Kevin Murphy—and cringe. What a disaster that was. We'd been so young, both of us just twenty years old, very young still, and very sheltered. We met in college in an American history class. We were both inexperienced, so we dated a couple of months before we got up the nerve to have sex. To this day, I can't think of that night without feeling sick. When he pressed me down into the mattress, I went into full-blown panic attack mode and ended up screaming at him to get off of me.

He didn't react well to my melt down. I can still hear him yelling as he hastily dragged on his clothes. *You're such a fucking headcase!*

He stormed out of my dorm room, and I never heard from him again. It gutted me. Shamed me.

I didn't try again after that. I'd had no intention of *ever* trying again... until I met Shane. Shane made it all okay. Shane, who comforted me the night I freaked out on *him* during our first attempt at sex.

Shane reaches over and lays his hand over mine, smiling. His blue eyes glitter, crinkling a little at the corners. "Tell me what you're thinking."

I guess I'm not very good at masking my emotions. My face burns under his scrutiny, and I shake my head and turn to look out the passenger window at the passing scenery.

"Beth."

I shake my head more vigorously as my throat tightens up. Some memories are better left forgotten.

He squeezes my hand gently. "I don't like the expression on your face. I want to know what put it there."

Surprised by the sudden edge in his voice, I turn to look at him.

"Talk to me, sweetheart."

I shrug. "I was just thinking about something that happened a long time ago. It's not important."

"Anything that puts that look on your face is important. Spill it."

I sigh because I know it's futile to fight him when he gets like this. "I was thinking about Kevin."

"The moron you dated in college?"

I nod, chuckling. Shane has a way of putting things into perspective.

"Don't take this the wrong way," he says, "but I'm glad your first boyfriend was a prick. If he hadn't been, I might not be sitting here with you right now. So, in a strange way, I guess I owe the guy."

I laugh, which I imagine was Shane's goal all along.

"I'm serious," he says, interlacing our fingers. "I owe the guy a huge debt. Maybe someday I'll have the chance to pay him back for what he did."

And if that isn't an implied threat, I don't know what is.

* * *

Traffic is light until we reach the outskirts of the city, and even though it isn't even close to rush hour yet, it's already bumper-to-bumper traffic—in other words, it's a typical Chicago afternoon. Shane heads toward The Gold Coast and pulls into a parking garage a few blocks from Clancy's. He hands his keys to an enthusiastic parking attendant who looks far too young to be driving, and we head on foot toward the bookstore.

As soon as we hit the sidewalk, I realize I'm a city girl at heart, because just being here amidst the noise and the bustle invigorates me. I even like the cars, the tour buses, and the constant stream of cabs of all shapes and sizes zipping in and out of traffic. The streets are filled with people from all around the world, and if I listen, I'll hear half-a-dozen languages spoken in the space of ten minutes.

Shane looks very *GQ* in his white shirt, dark slacks, and jacket. I still find myself catching my breath when I look at him. Since he was dressed nicely for our date, I decided to dress up a little too, with white sandals and a summer dress—a sleeveless, pale peach linen sheath dress. I even put on the pearl and diamond locket that Shane gave me the night of the hospital benefit. He takes my hand, and we walk along the crowded sidewalk to the bookstore, dodging baby strollers, shoppers, and the occasional panhandler.

The gun concealed underneath Shane's jacket seems unnecessary to me. After all, Howard Kline's not going to jump out at us from behind a trashcan on the streets of downtown Chicago. Shane has surveillance on Kline twenty-four-seven. They know where he is at all times and exactly what he's doing. So there's really no risk to us here. Besides, Kline lives in a suburb south of the city, at least twenty to thirty minutes away by bus on a good day, so it's not like he can sneak up on me, even if he knew where I was at any given moment.

I push thoughts of Kline out of my head. It's a beautiful, hot summer day, and I'm with Shane. I don't want to think about Kline. Glancing around, I take in the sights and the sounds of the city I love so well. We walk past a bakery, and the sweet scent of pastries wafts out the open door. Even though I've lived here all of my life, it still feels like a magical place to me.

We pass a Starbucks, and of course we have to stop for coffee. Shane orders his black, but I have to indulge my sweet tooth with my favorite iced caramel macchiato. We take our beverages outside and sit at a little patio table situated beneath the shade of a dark green awning. I watch the flow of people and traffic with a growing sense of contentment.

Shane reaches across the table and holds my hand, giving it a light squeeze. "You love being in the city, don't you?"

I nod, smiling.

"Would you rather we live in the penthouse, instead of the estate?"

My eyes widen in surprise. "Can we?"

"Sure. I used to spend most of my time at the penthouse. I mostly stayed at the house only on the weekends. I thought you'd be more comfortable there while you were recuperating. But if you'd rather we live downtown, we can relocate to the penthouse."

"Oh, my gosh, yes."

Shane pulls out his phone and sends a quick message. "I'll have your clothes and personal possessions moved to the apartment today."

"You don't mind?"

"No, of course not," he says, putting his phone away. "I want you to be happy, Beth."

When we reach the entrance to Clancy's, I pause outside the glass doors and peer inside.

Shane squeezes my hand. "What is it?"

I might as well tell him—he'll find out soon enough. "Vanessa hates me."

He chuckles. "Sweetheart, it's your signature on her paycheck. She doesn't hate you."

"Yes she does. Just wait. You'll see."

Shane opens the door and follows me inside, his hand a reassuring warmth on my lower back. The cool air indoors feels good after our walk outside in the August heat.

The first thing I notice is that there's an armed security guard standing inside the front entrance. I hadn't noticed a guard at the entrance before. I glance up at Shane, who greets the guard with a nod. They know each other. This must be part of Shane's security upgrades.

There's a good crowd in the store this afternoon. Shoppers are bustling around the displays of new merchandise at the front of the store. I glance over at the customer service counter where employees are busy ringing up purchases at the check-out stations.

There are at least a dozen people in the queue that feeds into the check-out lines. The employees behind the sales counter look slightly harried as they ring up customers as quickly as they can to keep the line moving. I'm wondering if we shouldn't expand the checkout capacity. If it's busy on a normal weekday, I can't imagine what it will be like during the weekends and holidays. It'll be an absolute madhouse then, and I really don't like the idea of people having to stand in line for a long time.

I turn to Shane. "The last time I was here, Vanessa pointed out that I have no retail experience. She's right, of course. I have no business experience whatsoever. But I love this place, and I want to be involved. That's why I want to go back to school."

He nods. "That sounds like a good plan. But going back to school for an MBA is a big commitment. Are you sure you want to take that on right now? You don't have to, you know. The store is yours, period."

I watch an employee push a cart of hardback books up to the New Releases table and begin making room for a stack of books. He sets the first few books on the table, and I notice it's a new release by JD Robb—a new Eve and Roarke novel. I love those books, and they're right here, in my store. I feel like a kid in a candy store. I want to be part of this place more than I've ever wanted anything. I just never dreamed that something like this could be possible for me.

I walk over to the cart and pull off one of the new Robb books and crack open the front cover. I fan through the crisp pages, loving the pristine sight and smell of a new book. I close the book and tuck it securely in the crook of my arm. This book is coming home with me.

I look up at Shane with a huge smile on my face. "I'm sure. I'm absolutely sure."

"Then do it. You know I'll always support you. You never need to ask."

ᨦ 13

S hane shadows me as I walk through Clancy's, just meandering through the front tables stacked with books and other merchandise. We breeze through the newspapers and magazines and calendars, and around to the other side of the store where the fiction books are shelved.

"Miss Jamison, I didn't expect to see you back here so soon."

I jump, startled to find Vanessa standing right behind us, a scowl on her perfectly made-up face. Good grief, the woman has built-in radar.

I can't help noticing that her gaze is focused primarily on Shane, and she gives him an appreciative scan from head to toe. Is it my imagination, or does she look flushed all of a sudden? She smiles at him a little longer than I think is necessary.

When her gaze finally turns to me, her expression sours, as if she's looking at something distasteful. Her coolly assessing gaze dwells momentarily on my attire and her lips flatten in disapproval.

Of course Vanessa looks like something right off the cover of *Vogue*. She's stunning in a form-fitting sheath dress with a sleeveless black bodice that hugs every inch of her perfect body attached to a black-and-white houndstooth skirt. I have no doubt that the diamond studs in her lobes are the real thing, as is the dainty gold chain around her neck. On her feet are slim, black stilettos—and I'll bet they're one of those brands that cost an arm and a leg. I might not like the woman's demeanor, but I certainly can't fault her sense of style.

I feel painfully underdressed. I just don't spend a lot of money on clothes and accessories. I'm perfectly happy scouring the department store clearance racks or shopping in nice second-hand shops. Vanessa makes me feel positively gauche. I sigh and put on a smile. "Hi, Vanessa."

After giving me a fleeting half-smile, she directs her attention back to Shane and extends her delicate hand to him. "Shane, it's lovely to see you again."

He nods, giving her a brief handshake. "Vanessa."

Vanessa's gaze cools when it returns to me. "What can I do for you, Miss Jamison?"

I really wish she'd stop calling me that. It sounds condescending the way she says it. "Call me Beth, please." I take a deep breath, steeling myself. "Vanessa, I would like to take an active role here at Clancy's. I know I don't have any retail experience—"

"Miss Jamison—"

"Beth, please."

"*Beth*." She releases a long, suffering sigh. "I—"

"I'll start at the bottom and work my way up. I could start with learning how to run a cash register."

Vanessa arches a slender eyebrow. "You mean a *point-of-sale terminal*?"

"Yes." *Bitch.* Why does she feel the need to embarrass me?

Vanessa crosses her arms, displaying beautifully manicured nails. "Do you really think that's a good idea?"

"Yes. I do."

"Well, I'll keep you in mind the next time we have an opening for an entry-level position. Right now, I'm afraid we don't have any."

"It would just be part time. I'm sure you can fit me in."

"Beth, have you even filled out an application?"

"Well, no. I didn't think I—"

"And did you bring a resume with you?"

My face heats up. I haven't updated my resume since I started working at the medical school library. "No."

"Well, then. I guess that settles that."

I glance at Shane, who's standing at my side uncharacteristically silent. He has an impassive expression on his face, as if he's not paying any attention to our exchange. I expected him to jump into this uncomfortable conversation, but he hasn't said a word. In fact, his expression gives absolutely nothing away. I realize he isn't going to be any help, which is so not like him.

Vanessa sighs. "I run a business here, Beth. A successful business relies on the execution of standard policies and procedures. You can't just waltz in off the street and start demanding things."

Technically, since I own the place, I'm pretty sure I can waltz in and start demanding things. And honestly, Shane's silence confounds me. Why doesn't he say something?

"Fine," I say, after deciding I'll have to take the bull by the horns. "I'll come back tomorrow with a copy of my resume, and I'll fill out an application. Anything else?"

"Well, then there's the interview—but I guess we'll dispense with that, since we already know you have no experience whatsoever. But there is the background check and the drug testing. Those are mandatory—it's company policy."

"Drug testing? Are you serious?"

"Of course I'm serious, Beth. I don't hire drug users."

"I don't use drugs! I've never—okay, fine. I'll pee in a cup." Now it's my turn to raise an eyebrow, daring her to throw up more road blocks. "Is there anything else?"

Vanessa's lips flatten. "I guess that's it. If you pass those hurdles, I guess I can put you on the schedule as a part-time entry-level employee. You can start with the POS terminals."

I force a smile. "Thank you. I'll be back tomorrow to fill out an application and give you my resume."

"You can do all of that online, so there's no need for you to come in. If you'd spent any time at all on our website, you'd know that. When can you work? How about mornings? Ten to two?"

I feel my face burning as I realize I've never once looked at the company website. Oh, great. One more thing for Vanessa to rub my nose in. I mentally shake myself and try to recall what she just said. "Um, ten to two? Sure. That sounds fine, thanks."

As she walks away, I wonder what I did to make her dislike me so much. I've tried to be nice to her. And I've never done anything to make her feel that her position in the store is in jeopardy due to the change in ownership. I haven't come into the store demanding changes in personnel or policies.

After Vanessa's out of earshot, I turn to Shane. "I told you she hates me."

Shane bites back a grin. "She doesn't hate you, Beth. She resents you because you own the store that she considers hers, and she feels intimidated by you because she knows you could boot her out the door at any moment, if you were so inclined. I suspect Clancy gave Vanessa tremendous leeway in the running of the business, and she doesn't like that she has someone to answer to."

"Why didn't you say something?"

"Because this is your fight, sweetheart. I can't fight it for you. You may be the owner, but the employees don't know you yet. You have to earn their respect, from Vanessa all the way down through the chain of command, from the assistant managers to the staff to the janitors. I have all the confidence in the world that you'll succeed in doing just that." He pauses, fighting a grin. "Or, you could simply fire her and bring in your own general manager. I admit the idea has some appeal."

I frown. "I may not like the woman personally, but she's good at her job. The store's well run and very profitable. I can't just fire her, no matter how much I might want to. Still, she drives me crazy. She's so patronizing!"

Shane puts his hand on my back and propels me in the direction of the romance books. "Stop thinking about Vanessa and go look at books. Relax and enjoy yourself. I'll stand guard against The Dragon Lady."

Shane leaves me to myself in the romance section so I can spend some quality time browsing. He grabs a copy of *The Chicago Tribune* and claims an armchair in a nearby seating area. I go about my business browsing the new romance releases and am thrilled to discover a new paranormal romance by Kresley Cole. I add it to my stash.

The next time I glance Shane's way, he's on his feet, deep in conversation with two men. One of them is the man I met here yesterday—Mack Donovan, the new head of security. The other guy I've never seen before. He's a striking redhead and seriously hot. His hair is short on the sides and long on the top, pulled back and gathered into a man-bun. He also has that ex-military look that I've learned to recognize.

I assume the new guy is one of Shane's security employees too. He's fit and muscular, although a little on the lean side. His black T-shirt molds itself nicely to his torso and arms, but he isn't bulky like Mack, who's built like a tank—a solid wall of muscle. I'd put him in his early 30s. He catches me looking at him and smiles, giving me a friendly wave. He's definitely one of Shane's guys. He has to be. I can't help smiling back as I return the gesture.

The redhead says something to Shane and Mack, and then he heads my way.

"Hey, boss," he says, extending his fist.

Holding my two books in the crook of my arm, I stick out my own fist and bump him back, grinning. I like this guy already. He certainly doesn't take himself too seriously.

I can feel the energy radiating off of him. With small black plugs in each earlobe and small gold hoops through the cartilage in his ears, he strikes me as a young, cocky pirate. Definitely a hipster. The black tattoos covering his arms reinforce the image.

I smile. "Hello."

"Sam Harrison, ma'am," he says. "I'm your security detail here at Clancy's. It's a pleasure to meet you."

Ma'am? Yes, he's definitely ex-military. "Just Beth, please. Which branch?"

He chuckles. "US Army, ma'am—I mean Beth. Former Ranger, like Mack. I broke both legs in a parachute drop gone bad, so now I'm a civilian. When you're here on the premises, I'm your shadow, unless Lia's here. Shane says you're going to be working here part-time."

Shane doesn't waste any time. "That's the plan."

Sam nods. "Don't worry about The Dragon Lady. She's a real bitch, but I've got your back."

"Thanks, Sam."

He nods. "All right then. Carry on, boss. I'll be close by if you need me."

Sam disappears from sight as I move to the next aisle, where the erotica books are shelved. While I can no longer see him, I don't doubt for a second that he's somewhere close by. Ever since I started dating Shane, I've experienced a definite loss of privacy in my life. It seems everywhere I go, I'm under scrutiny of one sort or another. Is it too much for me to want some privacy while I'm browsing erotica? It's embarrassing enough without having an audience.

The erotica section is mostly BDSM these days, ever since *Fifty Shades* exploded onto the market. I'm not into people tying each other up and hurting each other, but I do love alpha males. I guess that's a good thing since I seem to be surrounded by them now. I skim the shelves looking for new books, passing over women stripped and gagged and tied up, looking for something more my style. Surely there are some good old-fashioned, over-the-knee spanking stories to be found.

"Beth? Holy shit, is that you? Beth Jamison?"

I flinch at that sound of that familiar voice, that smooth-as-melted-dark-chocolate voice. My heart rate kicks painfully into overdrive, sending my pulse through the roof. Immediately my chest tightens, and the bottom of my stomach drops making me instantly queasy. He's the absolute last person on Earth I want to talk to.

I keep my eyes glued to the shelf of books in front of me, hoping desperately he'll take the hint and walk away. I can't even bear to look at him, let alone talk to him.

"Hey, Beth. It's me. How are you?"

I feel a warm a hand on my bare arm, and I glance down, recognizing the many rings on those long, tapering fingers—the fingers of a pianist. A jazz pianist, to be precise.

"Beth? Aren't you even going to look at me?"

Turning my head, I look up into a pair of large, puppy dog eyes the color of fine chocolate. At one time, I loved looking into those eyes. Was it just four years ago? It seems like a lifetime.

"Hi, Kevin."

14

Kevin Murphy is taller than I remember—of course, he was still young then, so he probably kept growing. Other than that, he looks pretty much the same. His light brown hair is still long and streaked with blond highlights, tucked up inside a slouchy gray knit hat. He's wearing faded, ripped blue jeans and a form-fitting T-shirt featuring his jazz band's logo. I wonder if the band is still together, playing nights and weekends at restaurants and coffee shops across Chicagoland. Like a dutiful girlfriend, I spent many nights sitting in those venues, watching him play, fetching and carrying for the band members like a good little fan girl. God, I was such an idiot. I was so grateful for his attention, I'd have done anything for him.

I stopped following them the night he walked out on me.

Automatically, I look for Shane, but the chair he'd been sitting in is empty, and there's no sign of Mack or Sam either. I glance around hoping to spot Shane, but he's nowhere to be seen. It shocks me to realize how much I've grown to depend on him coming to my rescue.

Kevin's long fingers slip down my bare arm and clasp hand, and he gives my fingers a light squeeze. The contact makes me shudder, and I abruptly pull my hand away.

"Hey, what's wrong, babe?" he says, dipping his face toward mine. He smiles at me with perfect, unnaturally-white teeth surrounded by full, sensuous lips and a goatee. "Aren't you going to say something? Jeez, it's been, what? Three years? Four? I can't believe it."

"Four." That's all I can manage. He's acting as if we're long lost friends, but in the back of my mind, all I can remember is Kevin yelling at me.

You're such a fucking headcase!

As if I didn't already know.

I remember with shame how I'd cowered in my college dorm room bed, naked and shaking as he stormed out, slamming the door behind him. That night was utterly mortifying. A disaster of epic proportions.

I feel a wave of hot nausea sweep through me and my insides are churning. I turn to leave.

"Beth, wait!" Kevin grabs my wrist and pulls me up short. "Don't run off. I wanna talk."

Talk? Is he crazy? That's the absolute last thing I want to do. My breathing falters as the vise around my chest tightens, squeezing my lungs and stealing my breath. I try to free my arm, but he tightens his hold. Then I remember what Lia showed me the day before. I tuck my elbow in to my side and twist my wrist, and just like that his hand pops off my wrist. It worked!

When I look up, I see Shane standing at the end of the aisle, not four feet from us, his steely gaze locked on the back of Kevin's head. His expression is tight, his jaws clenched. When his eyes meet mine, I see they're hot with suppressed anger. But why is he just standing there? When the new guy, Sam, comes up beside him, Shane gives him a curt hand signal, and Sam falls back.

"I just wanna talk, babe," Kevin says in a cajoling voice, completely unaware of the rapt audience behind him.

Knowing Shane is nearby gives me the courage I need to look Kevin in the eye. I take a steadying breath. "There's nothing for us to talk about, Kevin."

As soon as I mention Kevin's name, Shane's expression darkens. He knows exactly who I'm talking to, and I recall the veiled threat Shane made in the car just this afternoon on our drive in to the city.

Kevin reaches for my cheek, but I dodge his hand before he makes contact.

He frowns. "I owe you an apology for the way things ended between us. I was young and stupid. I regret what happened, what I did." He smiles and rubs his goatee. "I've thought about you a lot over the years. I shouldn't have bailed on you like that. I totally fucked up, and I'm sorry. I'm sorry if I hurt you."

If he hurt me? Is he kidding?

Seeing Kevin again brings it all back. The initial excitement, the trepidation I'd felt taking off my clothes for the first time in front of a guy. It had started off okay, as we'd snuggled naked under the covers of my twin bed in my dorm room. We'd lain together, facing each other, shivering as we kissed and worked up the courage to touch each other's body.

But then, in his eagerness, he'd lunged on top of me, his weight pushing me down into the mattress, and I panicked. I'd pushed at his skinny chest, trying to dislodge him, but he was lost in a hormonal rush, oblivious to my signals.

So I'd started screaming. *"Get off me! Get off!"*

Afterward, his face had been beet red, his breaths coming harsh and fast. *"You're such a fucking headcase!"* And then he'd dashed out the door of my dorm room, slamming it behind him, leaving me alone with my shame.

Afterwards, whenever we crossed paths on campus, he'd look the other way and pretend not to see me.

I think back to the first time Shane and I actually managed to have sex and smile. He took my panic attacks—there'd been a couple—in stride. He taught me that I could have a healthy sexual relationship. He taught me how to *cope*.

And that's when I realize why Shane's just standing there watching my exchange with Kevin. He's doing it again—he's helping me learn how to cope. He's showing his support, and yet giving me the space to work it out on my own. My gaze flickers briefly to Shane's, and he simply nods.

"There's no need to apologize, Kevin," I say, managing to sound calm. I swallow past the lump in my throat and take a deep breath. I speak the words I know I should say, the mature, responsible words. "That was a long time ago. We were both young and inexperienced. Don't worry about it."

Kevin smiles with obvious relief. "I'm so glad you don't hate me." He glances at his watch. "I don't have to be at our gig tonight until nine o'clock. Let me buy you a coffee. We can catch up."

I smile politely. "Thanks for the offer, but I don't think so."

"Come on, Beth." Kevin reaches for my hand again, his grasp more gentle this time. His voice is low, seductively smooth and warm, as he puts on all his considerable charm. "I'd really like to see you again, babe."

Kevin suddenly lifts his gaze above my head, and a moment later I feel the solid weight of Shane's hands on my shoulders, squeezing gently. I can't help smiling. I guess he'd reached his limit.

Shane draws me back against him and kisses the back of my head. "Who's your friend, sweetheart?"

The feel of him at my back is both soothing and seductive. "This is Kevin Murphy. We... um, we met in college."

"Actually, we *dated* in college," Kevin clarifies, frowning as he watches Shane's thumb stroke my shoulder.

"Kevin." Shane reaches around me and deftly removes Kevin's hand from mine. Then he offers his hand for a handshake. "Shane McIntyre. I'm Beth's boyfriend."

Shane turns me to face him, effectively dismissing Kevin. "Ready to go, sweetheart? It's time for dinner."

I nod, only too happy to get away from Kevin, who's now scowling at Shane. I have to bite my lip not to laugh. If Kevin's smart, he'll just walk away.

Shane glances at Kevin. "If you'll excuse us."

Shane takes my free hand, and we start to walk away until Kevin reaches out and catches my elbow, pulling me up short. I almost drop the books I'm holding.

"Beth, wait! Can we meet up another time? We need to talk."

Shane's eyes narrow on Kevin's hand. "Let go of her." His voice is deceptively quiet.

Kevin releases my hand instantly, but he glares at Shane. "Back off, buddy. We're old friends."

Shane tucks me under his arm, and I can feel the energy and heat radiating off him. His voice is so tightly leashed I almost don't recognize it. "First of all, I'm not your *buddy*. And secondly, I never back off. If you lay a finger on her again, I'll break it. Is that clear?"

Out of my peripheral vision, I catch movement at the far end of the aisle. It's Sam. He's standing silently on alert, watching. His easy-going, energetic manner has suddenly morphed into something very different.

Kevin shifts his gaze back to me, seeming determined not to take no for an answer. "Look, is there somewhere we can talk alone? Without your guard dog?"

I smile and shake my head, thinking Kevin has absolutely no sense of self-preservation. "There's nothing to talk about, Kevin."

* * *

Despite my bravado, I'm shaking as we walk away. I'd never expected to see Kevin again, and running into him here at Clancy's is surreal. As Shane leads me toward the exit, Sam joins us, falling into step on the other side of me, so that I'm sandwiched between the two men.

Shane looks over my head at Sam. "I want that asshole removed from the premises immediately and banned from the store. If he steps one foot inside this place again, detain him and have him charged with criminal trespassing."

Sam nods. Then he looks at me and his expression softens. "Hey, I'll see you next time you're in, okay? I'll get a copy of your work schedule."

I smile gratefully at him. "Thanks, Sam."

As we reach the main doors, I come to an abrupt stop as I realize I'm still holding two books in my arms. "Wait! I need to pay for these."

Shane shakes his head as he opens one of the large glass doors and ushers me outside into the August heat. "No, you don't. It's your store. They're your books."

I feel like a shoplifter. "I doubt Vanessa would agree."

He chuckles. "That's her problem."

15

As we head to the penthouse, Shane calls in an order for Chinese food—a little bit of everything—eggrolls and fried wontons, crab rangoon, fried rice, and several entrees. Shane can really pack away a lot of food. I don't know how he manages to stay so trim—I guess it's because of all the physical training he does. I'd better start getting more exercise, too, with all the food I've been eating lately. It's all going to go straight to my belly.

Speaking of training, that little maneuver Lia taught me for breaking free of a wrist-hold actually worked on Kevin. Granted, he wasn't actually trying to hurt me, but still, it worked, and no one was more surprised by that than I was. I'm even more committed now to having self-defense training.

As we ride up in the private elevator to the penthouse, I can't help thinking that a girl could get spoiled living here. I'm sure Gabrielle's loving it. She's at work by this time, or I'd invite her to come up and have dinner with us. I'll have to make plans to see her soon. It was great seeing her yesterday, but that just made me realize how much I miss her and how much we have to catch up on. Now that we'll be living in the same building, we'll be able to see each other more often.

I'm pleasantly surprised to find Cooper waiting for us as we step out of the elevator into the apartment foyer. He's got a backpack slung over one shoulder, and he's carrying a black duffle bag.

He gives us a little salute and steps into the elevator. "Have a nice evening, kids. Don't wait up."

"Where are you off to?" I say.

"The shooting range."

As the elevator doors close, I can't help suspecting that Cooper timed his departure to give us a little privacy in the apartment this evening.

Shane opens the door to the apartment for me and I walk inside. "Did you see what I did at the bookstore? When Kevin grabbed my wrist?"

He nods. "Yes, I did."

"Lia taught me that yesterday, right before you went all ballistic on her and Liam. This is why I want self-defense training."

"All in good time, sweetheart. Rome wasn't built in a day."

"Hey! I did okay back there." I'm actually kind of proud of myself. I managed to keep it together, and I didn't go into panic mode.

"You handled the situation very well, and I'm proud of you."

Shane leads me into the kitchen and shrugs off his jacket and drapes it over the back of a chair at the breakfast bar. He removes his gun holster as well and lays it on the countertop, along with my new books and purse.

He lifts me up and sets me down on the counter. Pushing my dress up, he spreads my legs and steps between them so that he's standing right in front of me.

He doesn't look happy.

"What's wrong?" I ask him, reaching up to run my fingers through his hair.

"I wanted to beat the hell out of that little prick for touching you."

"Who? Kevin?"

Shane nods as he skims his hands up my arms, past my shoulders, to cup my face. He looks pensive.

"What is it?" I say.

His expression turns tender, and he leans forward to place a gentle kiss on my lips. "If you see that guy again, I want you to call me. No matter what, no matter where, you call me. All right?"

I nod. "Sure."

"Promise me," he says.

"I promise."

He kisses me again, just a quick, gentle meeting of our lips, and brushes my cheeks with this thumbs. "The idea of someone hurting you makes me go a little crazy." He frowns at me. "You are so fucking vulnerable."

"I'm tougher than you think, Shane. I did okay with Kevin today. And once I've had self-defense training—"

Shane captures my wrists and pulls them swiftly behind my back, securing them with one hand. I try to pull free, but he holds my wrists fast. His expression is tight, and he's angry, but I'm not sure why.

My heart starts hammering in my chest at the sudden change in his demeanor. "What are you doing?" I try once more to pull my arms free, but I can't budge them. "Shane, let go."

He's not hurting me, but I don't like this. I don't like the look on his face. Suddenly my lungs feel like they're being compressed, squeezed tight by an invisible force, and I can't breathe. "Stop it, Shane!"

"Let's see you get free of that." His voice is hard.

I try again, getting pissed off, and of course I can't break free. He's far too strong for me, and we both know it. I force myself to relax, and he immediately releases my wrists.

"Your little college boyfriend is a pansy, Beth. Just because you broke his hold doesn't mean you can break the hold of someone who knows what he's doing. Yes, I want you to have self-defense training, but never underestimate your opponent. Not if he's someone who really wants to do you harm."

Shane pulls my hands around in front of me and gently examines my wrists. "Did I hurt you?"

"No. But you scared me."

He sighs. "I'm sorry." He cups my face. "It's just that the thought of someone hurting you again—I can't handle that." He shakes his head. "If it were up to me, I'd keep you locked up safe twenty-four-seven, so no one could ever hurt you again."

I pull his face toward mine and kiss him, my lips soft and gentle on his as I coax him out of that dark place he's gone to. I run the tip of my tongue along the seam of his lips, and his entire body shudders.

"Come with me," he says, sweeping me off the countertop and into his arms. "I want to hold you."

* * *

Shane lights a fire in the great room hearth, and we relax on the sofa while we wait for the food to arrive. We're the only ones in the apartment right now, so it's unusually quiet. I wonder if everyone's keeping away intentionally this evening, because it's rarely this empty.

Shane turns down the lighting to a cozy level and turns on the sound system. We're soon being serenaded by Adele's newest album. He must have recently purchased it, because it only just came out. He knows how much I love Adele.

"Can I get you a drink?" he says as he walks to the bar.

"Yes, thanks. A Coke or Pepsi, please."

He pours my drink into a glass with ice. "You did well this evening, with Murphy. That must have been difficult."

"It was."

He pours himself whisky in a tumbler and carries our drinks to the sofa.

"Can I have some of that?" I say, holding my glass out to his.

He raises an eyebrow. "You hate whisky."

"I know, but I want some. Just a little of the fire water."

He tips his glass into mine, giving me about half of his whisky. Then he retrieves the bottle from the bar and brings it back to the couch to resupply his own. "I think I created a monster."

I take a sip of my drink, loving the icy sweetness but grimacing at the pungent aroma and burn of the whisky. But I like the warmth as it settles in my empty belly. "I kind of expected you to intervene with Kevin, but you didn't. At least not at first."

He sips his whisky neat, savoring it. "I wanted to, believe me. It was difficult to stand there and watch, but I knew it was something you needed to do on your own. Security will keep him out of the store. You won't have to worry about seeing him there again."

"Good. I'm going back to Clancy's in the morning. I'll e-mail my resume to Vanessa ahead of time, and then I'll arrive at the store at ten. She can't stop me from working there."

"She can't stop you from doing a damn thing, Beth. Remember that." He gazes down at me. "You'll be running that place in no time."

"I wouldn't go that far. But I'll do whatever it takes to fit in there and prove to them that I'm not a liability."

He grins at me. "You're hardly a liability."

Shane sets my glass on the coffee table, next to his empty one, and pulls me onto his lap. I kick off my sandals and tuck my bare feet up on the couch. His body radiates heat like a furnace, and I curl into him, soaking up his warmth. He smells delicious, and naturally my body responds.

Shane caresses my bottom lip with the pad of his thumb. "You will never be a liability, sweetheart."

His lips are warm and gentle, and he tastes like whisky as he kisses me. The gentle suction of his mouth generates an aching heat between my legs, and my belly quivers in anticipation. I swear, he could make me come just from kissing me.

His mouth molds itself to mine, his lips somehow both soft and firm at the same time. His breath is warm and spicy from the liquor, and soon I feel an answering tug deep in my core.

I moan when his hand snakes up underneath my dress, his fingers slipping between my bare thighs and easing upward. When he reaches the apex of my thighs, he nudges my legs apart and skims his fingertips up and down the crotch of my panties. My face flushes, because I'm sure they're damp.

I'm trembling now, in anticipation of him touching me *there.* The lips of my sex are tingling as if they have a mind of their own and they know what's coming. His fingers brush aside the damp material, exposing my heated core to the cool air, and I shiver. I'm starving for him. Even though we made love earlier that day, we've had such a long dry spell I think it'll take a while for my hunger to be sated.

Right now I just can't seem to get enough of him. I cup the back of his head, my fingers tunneling into his hair to massage his scalp. When I grasp a fistful of his hair and tug, he groans, releasing my mouth with an indrawn breath and pressing his forehead to the crook of my shoulder.

It still amazes me that I have such an effect on this man.

I feel his lips on the pulse point in my throat as he presses a gentle, open-mouthed kiss there. His tongue darts out to wet my skin, and then he starts sucking. I'm sure he's going to leave a mark on me in a rather obvious place, but right now I don't care. I want him to mark me. He inhales deeply, breathing me in, and then he makes a sound that's awfully close to a growl.

When his finger slips between the lips of my overheated sex, I moan and open my legs wider. He rims my opening with his finger, teasing me as he collects my silky arousal, and then he swipes his finger up to my clitoris, the movement slow and delicious. Just as he begins to torment my clitoris with lazy circles, his phone chimes, breaking the spell.

I groan when his finger abandons me.

Shane sucks my arousal off his finger as he checks his phone. "Our food's here. Someone from the front desk will bring it up." He punches a code into an app on his phone, sending the private elevator car down to the main lobby to pick up the guard.

I press my hot face against his shoulder, lamenting the interruption and the loss of his touch. My body is primed for sex now, thanks to him, and all I can think about is having Shane inside me again. Who needs food? But instead, he's lifting me off his lap and setting me down on the sofa cushions.

"No!" I plead, as he rises to his feet, abandoning me.

He checks his phone. He has this insanely useful app that tells him exactly where the elevator is on its way up, as well as multiple camera feeds that show him who's in the elevator.

He reaches down and touches my face, grinning. "We have about five seconds until we have company. Five, four, three, two...."

Right on cue, the elevator pings in the foyer to announce the arrival of our dinner, and I throw my head back against the sofa cushions and growl with frustration.

Shane pats my hip. "Hold that thought, sweetheart. I'll be right back."

16

This smells delicious," I say, as we spread out our feast on the coffee table in front of us. My stomach growls.

We sit on the sofa and eat our dinner by firelight. There's a roaring fire in the wood-burning fireplace, and Shane changes the music to a playlist of old-time blues—Muddy Waters, and one of my new favorites, The Black Keys. I share bites of my food with him, and he shares his with me. It feels good, just being here with him like this, just the two of us. He seems so much more relaxed now than he has in weeks. I hope he's finally starting to get over the trauma of what Andrew did to me.

And that leads me to wonder what's happening with Andrew. The last I heard, he's being held in a psychiatric hospital undergoing evaluation. A psychiatrist will make a recommendation to the judge as to whether Andrew should stand trial for assault and battery or go into an in-patient treatment center. Honestly, I don't care either way as long as I don't have to see him again.

Toward the end of our meal, I realize Shane's pretty quiet, and I sneak a glance at him. He's watching me intently as I bite into an eggroll.

I chew and swallow, all of a sudden feeling rather self-conscious. "What?"

He smiles, shaking his head. "Nothing. I just like looking at you."

I lay down my half-eaten eggroll, my appetite gone. Immediately butterflies take flight inside me, careening around like tiny drunken fairies. How does he do this to me with just a look? He makes me fairly dizzy with wanting him. "I like looking at you, too," I tell him. As if that's not the understatement of the year.

His gaze darkens. "I want you. Right here, in front of the fire."

My eyes widen. We're out in the open here. Anyone walking into the apartment would practically trip over us with very little warning. I glance back toward the foyer door. "What if someone comes in?"

Shane shrugs. "I'll disable the elevator and put a Do not disturb sign on the foyer door. Besides, Cooper won't be home anytime soon."

I blush at the idea of having sex out here in the open. It would be so easy for someone to walk in on us... and why does that thought make me shiver?

Shane picks up the remote control to the sound system and suddenly the plaintive strains of Adele fill the air once more. He stands up and holds his hand out to me, his long fingers beckoning. "Come dance with me."

"That's cheating!" He knows I love Adele, and he knows that when I'm in his arms, I turn to putty.

"It's not cheating." He pulls me up off the sofa. "It's a sound tactical move."

I'm barefoot as Shane leads me to the wide open center of the great room and pulls me close. The warm glow from the fireplace, coupled with the darkening night sky outside the apartment windows, creates the illusion that we're hidden away from the rest of the world. He slips his arms around my waist and pulls me flush against his much taller body. I wrap my arms around his waist and stroke his lower back, which elicits a deep groan out of him. We're barely moving, just swaying to the melody.

My knees go weak when his hand slips into my hair at the back of my head. He kneads my neck muscles with strong fingers. When he kisses me, I moan into his mouth.

"All right, that's it," he says, sweeping me up into his arms and carrying me back to the sofa. He sets me on my feet and takes my face in his hands and leans down to kiss me, his lips molding themselves to mine.

My whole world narrows to this man. I feel giddy all of a sudden. Just yesterday morning, everything was all doom and gloom, and now less than a day later, I'm exactly where I want to be.

I shiver when his hands steal around to my back and he begins to pull down my zipper. My dress slips off my shoulders and down my arms, baring me to the evening air and Shane's hot gaze. A moment later, it slides to the floor and pools at my feet.

His fingers are warm as they deftly unfasten my bra, and it too falls to the floor, leaving me standing there practically naked, while he's still fully dressed in his shirt and slacks. When he drops to his knees in front of me and slips his hands around to the back of my thighs, my head starts swimming and I fear my knees will give way.

He presses his open mouth to my belly and begins kissing his way down, stopping briefly to tease my belly button. His hot breath sets me on fire, and I grab his shoulders to steady myself. I'm pretty sure I'm at risk of melting into a puddle on the floor.

He continues to kiss his way down my torso, pausing when he reaches my panties. He presses his face against my mound, breathing my scent in through the silk fabric. *Oh, my God.* He's such a raw, sexual animal, so blatantly male and unabashed about his needs.

He takes hold of the waistband of my panties and tugs them down to my ankles. At his silent coaxing, I step free of my panties and he tosses them aside. Then his hands are on my buttocks, holding me in place as he presses his face to me, breathing me in. When his tongue slips between the folds of my sex, I sway on unsteady feet. He catches me and holds me securely.

"Shane." My voice isn't much more than a whimper.

I'm shaking now, and I don't know how much longer I can stand on my own two feet. When I feel the warm heat of his tongue circling my clitoris, I cry out and reach down to cup his head. I'm torn between pulling him closer and pushing him away. I'm standing stark naked in the living room, terrified that someone will walk in on us. But at the same time, I relish the way he pushes me past my comfort zone, ratcheting up my desire in the process.

He nudges my legs farther apart, and I'm pushed to the limit when one of his long fingers dips into my wetness, then slips back between my butt cheeks to tease me. I flinch when his finger presses against my tightly clenched hole.

I pull back from him, dislodging his inquisitive finger. "Shane, no." But the truth is, even though I'm afraid of this, I want it.

He glances up at me, and his solemn, heated expression steals my breath. "You know I would never hurt you."

"I know." I shake my head, afraid to take that step. "But I can't."

I've read plenty about this. Anal play seems to be more and more popular in romance books these days, but reading about it and actually doing it are two very different things. I just can't bring myself to go there.

I breathe a sigh of relief when his hand withdraws from my backside. He stands and unbuttons his shirt. Then he unbuckles his belt and opens his slacks, shoving his boxers down just far enough that his erection springs free. He's fully erect, his long ruddy cock defying gravity as it lifts. He drops down onto the sofa and pulls me onto his lap, so that I'm straddling him face to face. It feels shocking to me, that he's still mostly dressed while I'm completely naked, my thighs spread wide open on his lap.

He looks at me, and when he speaks, his voice is low, rough. "I fantasize about having you like this in my office, while I'm sitting at my desk. I want you there, with your gorgeous body open to me, just like this."

His words make my belly quiver, and I find myself squeezing my sex tightly. I feel empty there, and I realize how badly I need him to fill me.

He must be reading my mind, because he fists his erection with one hand and pulls me close with the other. "Put me inside you."

Eager to feel him filling me, and I wrap my fingers around him and direct him to my opening. I'm already wet and aching, so when I lower myself on him, the broad head of his cock pushes right through my lush opening. He's a big man, and I revel in the feel of him sinking inside me, invading my body. The sudden feeling of fullness as he stretches me makes me gasp.

He tightens his hands on my hips. "All right?"

I nod, not trusting myself to speak. Our gazes are locked together in silent communication as I work myself down on him. His cock is soon coated in my body's slick juices, making it easier for me to take him in. He's patient as I squirm and fidget on him until I'm fully seated. His hands cradle my butt, and he lifts me up and down on his erection.

I love being on top like this, because it doesn't trigger my anxiety, but even better, I can control the angle, and I know just how to put him exactly where I want him. I adjust my angle until the head of his cock is dragging along that tender spot inside me that feels so damn good. The pleasure is climbing, and I'm soon panting in anticipation. He pulls my face to his, and our mouths meet, open and hungry. I close my eyes and allow myself to let go, riding him shamelessly, rocking my hips on him, stoking the fire deep inside me.

Both of us are breathing hard now, our gasping breaths intermingling. I'm so close I can feel my orgasm swelling like a wave that's just about to crest. Without warning, his slick finger is between my butt cheeks again, seeking entrance into my back hole.

"Relax and push out. I promise you, there's nothing to be afraid of."

I'm so close to coming, I force myself to focus on the aching pleasure deep inside me and try to ignore what he's doing back there. *I trust him.* He knows far more about this than I do, so I let him have his way while I lose myself in my impending orgasm.

As I relax my muscles, his finger slips inside me back there, and I gasp at the strange feeling of fullness. It doesn't hurt, but it makes me nervous because I don't know what he's going to do. I try not to think about what he's doing, and soon he's slowly thrusting his finger in and out of me. It feels oddly... good. Really good in fact, and that surprises me. And then the most intense orgasm I've ever felt blindsides me, sweeping through me like a wildfire. The pleasure is so exquisite, I throw my head back and cry out, arching my body in his arms. He draws one of my nipples into his hot mouth and gently sucks on it as his cock erupts inside me, filling me with spurt after spurt of his hot come. He growls against my breasts as he bucks his hips into me over and over.

* * *

I am slain.

We're lying in Shane's big bed, although I have absolutely no recollection of how we got here. I must have passed out after experiencing the most intense orgasm I've ever had, and he must have carried me to bed. All I know is that we're in his bed, both of us naked, our limbs intertwined. My muscles have turned to mush, and I don't have the energy to move.

At least he's taken his clothes off. I smile at my memory of him sitting on the sofa, looking sexy as hell still dressed with me sprawled naked on his lap like a submissive sex slave. If I'm not mistaken, I think he fulfilled a bit of a fantasy tonight. He did mention that he'd been fantasizing about us having sex in his office. I'll have to keep that little tidbit of information tucked away for future reference.

I'm lying on my belly, my head turned toward him, and he's rubbing my back with long, gentle strokes. It feels heavenly. My eyelids are so heavy I can barely keep them open. He's watching me closely with a hint of a smile on his face.

"Feeling good?" he murmurs, reaching up to tuck my hair behind my ear.

I nod, too tired to manage more than mm-hmm.

"I'm sorry for the way I've been acting," he says in a low, quiet voice, his expression serious. "I realize now that I wasn't just punishing myself. I was punishing you, too."

"You don't have to apologize. I know it's been a difficult time for you."

He shakes his head. "Beth, you have no idea. When I saw you in the hospital, I think something died in me. If Andrew had killed you—God, I don't think I would have survived it. All I could think was that it was my fault. I underestimated him. I thought he was just an overindulged, spoiled brat. He's just a kid, for Christ's sake! It never occurred to me he had the capacity for so much violence."

"I don't think it occurred to anyone, Shane. You can't blame yourself. You have to stop."

I swear he looks downright ashamed. I can't bear to see that defeated look on his face, so I lift my face toward his and kiss him lightly, just a feather-soft meeting of our lips. He makes a sound deep in his throat, and when I meet his gaze, I'm shocked by the level of pain I see. Unshed tears sparkle in his eyes like glitter.

"It's okay, Shane."

He draws me close, wrapping his arms around me. I lay my head against his chest and listen to the rapid beating of his heart. His chest hair tickles my nose as I nuzzle him.

He chuckles, but it's a harsh, self-deprecating sound. "You should have seen Cooper yesterday morning, after you and Lia ran off. My God, he ripped me a new one. I've never seen him so angry."

Now it's my turn to chuckle. I can just picture Cooper doing that.

"I was in the control room ripping into the guys on duty for allowing themselves to be distracted when he let me have it."

"I wondered why no one stopped us at the gates."

"Cooper sent them off to the kitchen and opened the gates for you. When I realized what had happened, I chewed out the guys on duty for getting suckered. But then Cooper laid into me for being an asshole. God, he was pissed. I've seen him mad before, but never like this, and never directed at me. For a moment, I thought he was going to get physical."

Cooper's always so calm and steady, it's hard for me to imagine him losing his cool like that. "Why was he so mad?"

"Cooper has apparently appointed himself your protector. I think he sees himself as some kind of father figure to you. He said, 'You realize she just ran away from her own home because she's so fucking miserable. *You've* made her fucking miserable.' That's when I came to my senses."

I reach out and touch his face gently. "I was feeling pretty lonely. I mean, you were there every day, but you weren't really *there with me*, if you know what I mean."

He nods. "I had to keep my distance, otherwise I would have caved. It killed me to hold myself back from you."

"Are we okay now?"

He nods, then kisses me. "When you ran off, I lost it. I can't lose you, Beth. You have no idea—"

Abruptly, he stops talking, and I can see the muscles in his throat working as he swallows hard. I close my eyes to give him a moment and press my lips to his chest, right over his thundering heart.

"I need you," he says, his voice rough. "I'm not talking about sex—although I need you for that, too. But I need you in my life. You make me feel things I've never felt before. You give me purpose. You make me imagine a future I never thought I'd have."

I pull him close for another kiss and close my eyes, losing myself in him. "I need you, too."

"Good, because I can't do this without you."

17

It's just the two of this morning in the penthouse, so we make a simple breakfast of toast, jam, and coffee and carry it out onto the balcony to eat. The sky's clear this morning, so we have an unimpeded view of the lake as far as the eye can see.

I spoon some jam onto my toast. "Where's Cooper?"

Shane sips his coffee, then sets his cup down. "I don't think he came home last night."

"Where did he go? Back to the house?"

"I doubt it. If I had to guess, I'd say he had a sleepover of his own."

My eyes widen. "Cooper has a girlfriend? Why didn't anyone tell me?"

Shane looks at me, his expression guarded.

"What?"

"Not a girlfriend, exactly," he says, oddly hesitant.

"A friend with benefits?"

"Sort of. Although he's definitely not with a girl. I mean a woman."

As his words sink in, my eyes widen even more. "Cooper's gay?"

Shane picks up his coffee and takes a sip, watching me intently. "Yes."

I sit there stunned into silence. It's not that I have anything against gays, because I don't. It's just that... well, I had no idea. I can tell Shane's waiting for me to say something. "Oh. I see."

He peers at me over the rim of his steaming coffee mug. "Are you okay with that?"

"Sure. It's just... I didn't see that coming. I had no idea."

Shane shrugs. "Cooper's a very private person. He doesn't advertise his sexual orientation."

"Does everyone else know? I mean, Lia? Jake? The rest of your family?"

"Yes, they all know."

"So, I'm the only one who didn't know."

Shane sighs. "He was afraid of what you might think. Don't forget, Cooper was in the military for thirty years. He's used to keeping his private life private. Please don't take it personally. Honestly, I think he'll be relieved to find out you know. He really cares a lot about you, sweetheart. It matters to him what you think."

I feel tears forming in my eyes as Shane's words sink in. My heart aches for Cooper. And I hate that he was afraid to tell me who he is. I care about him too. I more than care about him. "Cooper's like family to me now. He's like... if I had a father, I'd want it to be Cooper."

Shane nods. "Good choice."

* * *

Shane goes back to our room to get dressed while I use the computer in his office to retrieve my resume from my Internet e-mail account. I make a few updates to my resume—like listing the penthouse as my new address—and submit it on the bookstore's website.

The only remaining hurdles to my new employment are facing Vanessa once more later this morning and peeing in a cup. I can't believe she's going to make me do that, but I think she enjoys making this hard for me.

I head to the bedroom to change into something a little more appropriate for work and find Shane getting ready. He's dressing for the office.

"You're going to the office today?" I say, as I head into the enormous walk-in closet to select an outfit.

He pops his head in the closet doorway. "Yes. Since you're abandoning me for the world of retail, I thought I might as well put in an honest day's work at the office."

I smile, realizing that he was hanging around the penthouse this morning just for me. Normally, he would have left for work hours ago, before I even woke up.

He lounges in the doorway, watching me flip through my meager wardrobe for something suitable to wear. Even after my clothes back at the house were delivered here, there's still not much to choose from.

I pull a sleeveless, pale linen blue dress off its hanger and hold it up to him. "Is this appropriate attire for peeing in a cup?"

He chuckles. "She's not really going to make you do that, is she?"

"Probably. Out of spite, if for no other reason."

"I'd like to see her take a drug test. After all, fair's fair. I'm sure it's in the employee handbook."

I exchange my shorts and top for a slip and the dress, then stick my feet into a pair of flat sandals.

"You don't have many clothes, do you?" he says, scanning my rather bare side of the closet.

I shrug. "I have enough."

"I know women who could fill this closet several times over."

I scoff. "You mean you've dated women who could fill this closet several times over. And by dated, I mean slept with."

He chuckles, and if I'm not mistaken, he blushes. Shane has a well-deserved reputation as a ladies' man. I don't even want to know how many women he's been with over the years. I'm sure the number would stagger me.

"They weren't all women I dated," he says. "Sophie has an extensive wardrobe."

"Yes, but your sister is a hot-shot interior designer. She needs a lot of clothes. I don't. Lia doesn't, and I would imagine Hannah doesn't either."

He laughs. "I'd be surprised if Hannah owns more than two pairs of jeans and a couple of sweatshirts. What more does she need roughing it in the Montana wilderness, spying on wolf packs? The wolves don't care how she's dressed." He crosses his arms over his chest and leans into the door jamb. "Would you like to go shopping? I'll take you. Anywhere you want to go."

"Shopping for what?"

"Clothes. I thought women like to shop."

"Maybe all your other women like to shop. I'd rather go out on the lake. Can we do that instead?"

"Of course we can." He comes away from the doorway and takes me into his arms. "But only if you kiss me first."

In the parking garage, we pass Cooper as he's coming in from his night out. He's got his backpack slung over his shoulder, and he's carrying that black duffle bag, which I think has guns in it.

"Cooper, hi!" I run to meet him halfway and give him a hug, squeezing him tightly. "I'm glad you're home. I missed you at breakfast this morning."

"That's quite a greeting," he says, as he hugs me back. "Thank you. Good luck on your first day of work, kiddo. Knock 'em dead."

* * *

Shane drops me off at Clancy's on his way to the office, saving Lia a trip. She'll come pick me up at two, after my half-day shift ends. He pulls up to the curb in front of the store—in a spot clearly marked "ABSOLUTELY NO PARKING."

I don't remember seeing that sign before. "Where did that come from?"

"I had it installed last night. It'll be easier for Lia to drop you off and pick you up."

Sam is standing just outside the doors.

"Is this really necessary?" I ask Shane, as I wave at Sam. "I don't think I need security in the bookstore." It's not like Kline can get within five miles of me without the surveillance team raising an alarm.

"Yes, it's necessary. And not just because of Kline. As my girlfriend, you automatically become a target. I'm sorry about that, but it's unavoidable."

I think back to the woman who cornered me in the ladies' room at the hospital charity ball a couple of months ago. I can still remember the vile, hateful things she said to me. Just thinking about Luciana Morelli makes my skin crawl. She definitely falls under the category of disgruntled ex-girlfriend.

"If you don't like Sam—"

"No, it's not that," I say. "He's really nice."

"I'm sorry it has to be this way, sweetheart. You're just going to have to get used to it."

"It's all right. I'll deal with it." I lean over and kiss him. As I walk to the front door, I think bodyguards are a small price to pay for having Shane in my life.

* * *

"Hiya, boss," Sam says when I step through the front doors. He's wearing baggy gray cargo pants and a form-fitting camo T-shirt that hugs his muscular torso nicely, along with a pair of chunky combat boots. I don't see a gun on him anywhere, but I'm sure he's carrying one. It must be in an ankle holster, or perhaps it's in one of the pockets of his cargo pants.

"Hi, Sam." I smile at him.

He shoves his hands in his front pockets. "So, what's on the agenda this morning?"

I glance up the wide, curving staircase to the second floor, where the administrative offices are located. "I should probably go upstairs and find Vanessa."

He grimaces. "Do we have to?"

I can't help smiling at Sam's reluctance. He obviously doesn't like her any better than I do.

He shudders. "That woman scares me."

"Me, too. Come on, chicken. Let's brazen it out."

We enter the administrative area on the second floor marked "staff" and find a mostly empty room. The door marked PRIVATE is closed. There's a young man wearing earbuds attached to his smart phone who's busy tapping away on his computer keyboard. He glances up once to look at us, then returns to his work, paying us no mind.

A young woman my age walks into the office right behind us and smiles. "Hi. Are you Ms. Jamison?"

I nod. "Yes. I'm Beth."

She offers me her hand. "Erin O'Connor. I'm one of the assistant managers. Ms. Markham told me to expect you this morning. I'm supposed to show you around and get you started working at the check-out counter."

Erin's definitely a refreshing alternative to Vanessa. Her sweet and guileless face is dominated by a pair of large, light blue eyes. Shoulder-length black hair is parted on the side and held back from her face by small, gold barrettes. With her pale complexion and the dusting of freckles across her nose and cheeks, she's absolutely darling.

Erin picks up a nametag off her desk and hands it to me. It's an oval tag, hunter green, with the words "HI, I'M BETH" engraved on it. Vanessa was prepared for me after all.

Erin looks over my shoulder at Sam, who's standing quietly behind me, trying to look unobtrusive. She smiles at Sam, and I detect a pink tint to her cheeks that I don't think was there before.

Erin smiles at him. "You must be one of the new security guys."

Sam nods, smiling back at her. "Don't mind me, ma'am. I'll just blend into the scenery."

I barely manage to refrain from chuckling when Sam calls Erin ma'am as she's at least five years younger than he is.

Our first stop is the employee lounge, which is located next door to the administrative office. We step inside a dreary, utilitarian space. On one side of the room is a wall of vintage, green metal lockers. On the other side is a kitchenette with a full-size refrigerator, a double sink, and a microwave oven. There are three small round tables with chairs for seating. In the center of the room are two sofas and a couple of armchairs, all of which look like thriftshop hand-me-downs. Pretty much the only nice thing about the employee lounge is the view. It's a corner room, so two of the walls offer large window views overlooking N. Michigan Avenue and let in lots of natural light.

Erin shows me my locker, and I put my purse inside. Then she shows me the time clock, which I missed when we first came in.

"I have to clock in?" I say, studying the machine. It's mint green and looks like something right out of the 1950s.

"Yes." She pulls a card with my name printed at the top from a rack on the wall and shows me how to punch it. "Each day you'll clock in when you first arrive, and clock out when you leave."

"Is this really necessary?"

She shrugs. "Vanessa says we have to do it."

"What happens if people are late for work?"

"She docks their pay, a dollar per minute."

I'm still processing the idea of clocking in when Erin leads me downstairs to show me the check-out system.

She's wearing a gray pencil skirt, a white blouse, and tiny, three-inch black stiletto heels. She's so wobbly on the heels I'm afraid she's going to topple over any minute. She even reaches out to the wall once catch her balance, and I have to wonder why she's wearing shoes like that when she's obviously not comfortable in them. I glance at Sam, who's walking beside me, and notice he's watching Erin like a hawk, as if he too expects her to topple over any moment. At one point, she does stumble and Sam extends a hand as if to catch her, but she rights herself in time.

"Sorry," Erin says, her face flushing pink. "I just can't get the hang of these stupid shoes."

Those shoes are perfect for a Saturday night out on the town, not for someone in retail who's on her feet eight hours a day. It makes no sense. "Shouldn't you be wearing something a little more practical?"

She makes a face, wrinkling her little nose. "They're required."

I can't help my expression, which I'm sure is purely incredulous. "What do you mean, they're required?" I'm sure not going to be wearing heels to work. I'd fall and break my neck the first day.

Erin shrugs. "All of the female assistant managers have to wear dresses or skirts and heels. The heels have to be at least three inches high. But I just can't seem to get the hang of them."

I can just imagine who instituted the dress code. Ms. Walking-Fashion-Magazine herself. But it's silly. No one who works on her feet all day should be forced to wear high heels if she doesn't want to.

I'm surprised when Erin passes right by the bank of elevators and heads for the grand staircase. Surely she's not going to attempt the stairs in those shoes. She'd be putting her life in jeopardy. And based on the look on Sam's face, he shares my concern.

I stop her at the top of the stairs. "Erin? Why don't we take the elevator?" I'm seriously afraid she's going to go head-first down the steps.

"Employees aren't allowed to use the elevators."

"Why?"

She shrugs. "Company policy. Vanessa said it's lazy."

"So, you're going to risk breaking your neck going down the stairs in those heels because someone thinks using the elevator is lazy?"

"Yes." She says it like it's a question.

I shake my head and glance at Sam, who gives me a WTF look. He casually steps in front of Erin and precedes her down the stairs, and

I'm sure it's so he can break her fall.

It looks like I'm going to have to rock the boat after all.

The check-out counter is bustling with activity which, from a business standpoint, is a really good thing. All four *point-of-sale terminals*—I will never make the mistake of calling them cash registers again—are busy beeping and blinking as they total up customer purchases. There's still a line, though, of about a half-dozen customers queued up for their turn at the check-out, and that can't be good. People are busy; they shouldn't have to stand around waiting, especially if they're just popping in from work during their lunch break.

Erin takes over one of the terminals from one another employee and shows me how it's done. It's a brand new retail system, she tells me, top of the line, and honestly it's pretty intuitive. They're—I mean, *we're*—set up to take smart cards and mobile phone payments, and all the new technological innovations. I watch her for a while, and then she hands the reins over to me, and I start checking out my very first customers.

There's a huge smile on my face as I greet each customer.... a young woman with a newborn in a stroller is buying the new JR Ward—definitely a paranormal/urban fantasy romance fan. An elderly man in a plaid, polyester suit—I didn't know anyone still wore those—is buying a copy of *The Chicago Scoop*, a pack of spearmint gum, and a pair of thick cheater glasses. A harried mom with three rambunctious young boys is purchasing a stack of beginning readers on spiders, snakes, and sharks. I certainly wish her luck in trying to get those energetic kids to sit down and read.

Sam lurks behind me with his hands behind his back, as if he's standing at attention, ready for anything. I'm seriously worried about him. The poor guy will be bored out of his mind before the morning's over.

I turn back to him. "You don't have to hover, Sam. Go do something. Walk around, take a break. Read a book—we have plenty."

He gives me a suffering look, as if I have no idea what I'm talking about. "I'm fine, boss."

"Beth."

"Beth," he repeats.

A couple of times, I see glimpses of Mack Donovan moving through the store, talking with employees and looking as inconspicuous as a tank. Fortunately, there's no sign of Vanessa. I think if I had to deal with her condescending attitude right now, I'd lose my happy.

My shift is half over before I know it, and I realize I'm having fun. It doesn't feel like work. I also didn't screw anything up, which is a definite plus. But my feet are killing me—and I'm wearing comfortable sandals. I don't know how Erin can stand being on her feet for hours in those unforgiving heels. I'm really going to have to do something about that.

I also desperately need to pee. The two cups of coffee I had that morning with Shane have caught up with me, and there's no way I'll make it until two without making a visit to the ladies' room.

When there's a rare lull in the customer line, I lean over to whisper in Erin's ear. "I need to use the ladies' room."

She looks at me and sighs, smiling apologetically. "I'm sorry, you can't."

"Why not?"

"You're only scheduled to work four hours, so you'll have to wait until your shift is over."

I sigh. "Let me guess. Another company policy?"

She nods, and her nose wrinkles as she smiles apologetically. "It's in the employee handbook."

"So, what if someone has to pee really badly? They just have to stand here and hold it?"

"I'm afraid so."

I look at my watch. It's just a little after noon. I suppose I can try to hang on for another hour-and-a-half. I had no idea from the outside looking in that this place was run by an anal-retentive taskmaster. People should be allowed to pee if they need to. I'm definitely going to have to rock the boat.

18

After my shift is over, Erin takes me back upstairs to the employee lounge so I can clock out and grab my purse. There are a few employees in the lounge, one sitting on a sofa doing a crossword puzzle from a newspaper and another pouring a cup of coffee. They smile politely at me, and I smile back.

"So, I'll see you tomorrow morning at the same time?" Erin says.

"Yes. Erin, can I have a copy of the employee handbook?"

"Sure. I'll e-mail you a copy. Come with me to the office, and I'll show you your desk."

I didn't realize I warranted having a desk. Surprised, I follow Erin into the business office next door. She points at a beige metal desk and a small black office chair on wheels crammed into the far corner of the room. That's it—just the desk and a chair. There's no computer, no phone, not even a stapler. I guess Vanessa doesn't want me to get too comfortable.

"There's a supply cabinet over there, with pens and pads of paper and stuff like that," Erin says, wrinkling her nose in apology. "And you can bring things in to accessorize it, if you like."

"Are you sure that's allowed?"

She flushes. "I know, I'm sorry. Vanessa's a little... territorial. And I think she sees you as encroaching on her territory."

"But I'm not here to encroach. I'm here because I want to fit in. I want to be part of this place."

Erin smiles. "Don't worry. I'm sure she'll ease up over time."

Erin takes me around the office and introduces me to the staff. It's all a blur of names and faces I'm sure I won't remember this first time.

Charlie stands out, though, the guy I noticed earlier listening to music through earbuds. Charlie handles payroll and accounting. He's about my age, with Harry Potter glasses and a lock of dark, curly hair hanging over his wide forehead. He puts me on the company books as an employee at minimum wage, and I complete all the tax and employment paperwork to make it legal. I am officially employed again.

"Minimum wage?" I ask Charlie. I'll certainly be making a lot less money than I was at the medical school library, especially since I'll only be working part time. I do a quick mental calculation to determine if I'll be able to cover my car payment and graduate school loan payment. Just barely.

"Yes." He gives me a *duh* look.

I know how profitable this business is—I've seen the financial records for the past ten years. And the profits have grown year-over-year, even during the worst of the recession—which I guess is a testament to Vanessa's business acumen. But surely we can afford to pay the employees more than minimum wage. It's a privately owned company, so it's not like there are stockholders to appease. There's just the owner to appease, and now that's me.

This is a nice establishment, and we want to attract talented workers. Can't we offer them more? Shoot, the indie grocery store I used to shop at in Hyde Park pays their employees more than minimum wage.

I feel a headache coming on.

It's two-thirty now, and I'm starving since I haven't eaten anything since breakfast. I remind myself to start packing my lunch. Lia stalks into the business office, and I could faint in relief.

She hops up onto the corner of my barren, utilitarian desk. "Hey, Princess. I like what you've done with the place—very industrial chic."

I smile at her. "I'm starving. Please feed me."

She grins. "I was hoping you'd say that."

Sam and Erin walk us down to the front entrance, and I thank them both for helping me muddle through my first day.

"You did great!" Erin says, throwing her arms around me in an impromptu hug. I hug her back, laughing at her enthusiasm. When she releases me and steps back, she has a huge smile on her face, and the corners of her light blue eyes crinkle. I think I have a new friend.

Sam gives me a gentle fist bump. "See you tomorrow, boss."

"Thanks, guys. I'll see you both tomorrow."

"Bye, Beth!" Erin calls, giving me a little wave as I follow Lia out onto the bustling sidewalk.

* * *

Lia talks me into walking over to Hub 51 for lunch. I've heard of it, but I've never been there. We're both starving, so we order an appetizer—a sushi sampler platter. I have the chicken tacos, which are melt-in-your-mouth delicious, and Lia has a burger and steak fries. After we finish our meals, she orders a slice of carrot cake for us to share. Apparently, their carrot cake is to die for, and after I take my first sinfully-good bite, my sweet tooth definitely agrees. It's so good, I actually moan.

Lia forks a big bite of her half of the cake into her mouth and licks the cream cheese frosting from her lip. "So, what's on the agenda for this afternoon?"

I shrug. "I guess I'm done for the day. My primary goal was to start working at Clancy's today, and that's done." I take a sip of my iced tea and check my phone to see where Shane is at present—I'm really starting to love GPS tracking. He's right where I expected him to be—at his office.

I wonder if I have the nerve to do something I've been thinking about. He did mention he had a fantasy involving me and his office. The only problem is, the one and only time I've been in his office is when I had a total meltdown and broke up with him after I found out my brother was paying him to protect me. When I realized he'd been deceiving me, I freaked. And just a few days later was when the incident with Andrew Morton occurred.

There are some bad memories tied up with his office, but I can't live in fear of visiting him there again. That's just stupid. I need to get over this and go see him. We need to make new memories in his office—wonderful memories—because I'm sure he remembers what happened the last time I was there just as keenly as I do.

I take a deep breath and step off that ledge. "Let's go surprise Shane at his office."

"Surprise him, or *surprise him*?" Lia says, giving me a pointed look as she finishes off her half of the cake.

I blush. Ever since Shane told me of his fantasy of us having sex in his office, I've been having one of my own. I want to show up unexpected at Shane's office and seduce him at his desk. Maybe I could give him a blow job while he's working.

Of course I don't think I could ever do something that outrageous in reality. But it's hot to contemplate. But, maybe I could manage a little seduction. After all, he does have that apartment attached to his office. We could sneak in there for an afternoon quickie. Just the thought of that makes me tingle.

My face heats up, and I know it must be beet red. "Yes, I want to *surprise him* at work."

Lia's eyes widen. "Oh, my god, you're serious! Princess is going to make a booty call!"

She gives me this mock scandalous look, and I ball up my cloth napkin and throw it at her. But she easily bats it aside before it makes contact.

When our server arrives with the check, Lia hands the young woman several bills. "Keep the change." Then she grins at me as she stands. "Let's go, Princess. This I gotta see."

⸻ 19

Shane's building isn't that far from the center of the shopping district, so we walk, and that gives me time to plan my seduction—assuming I have the nerve to go through with it.

When we arrive at The McIntyre Building, it's nearly five o'clock, but I know Shane's still here. We take the elevator up to his floor and step out into a well-appointed lobby. As the owner and CEO, he rates some pretty fancy digs. We walk through the glass doors etched with his name and title, and there is Shane's administrative assistant, Diane, seated at her desk outside Shane's office.

Diane is the nurturing grandmother type. She's soft spoken and petite, barely five feet tall, with boyishly short white hair and a softly wrinkled face. Her eyes are a pale blue, surrounded by tiny laugh lines. She adores Shane, like a grandmother adores her handsome, successful grandson.

I haven't really had a chance to get to know Diane very well yet. The few times I've seen her, she's always been very cordial to me. But the last time she saw me here in this building was when I had my melt-down in Shane's office. I'm sure she could hear me screaming at him, even from her desk.

After leaving Shane's office that day, I collapsed in the ladies' room in a puddle of hysterical tears, and I know she witnessed Shane comforting me in the bathroom floor. I try not to contemplate what she must think of me, but Shane told me she was the first one to bring me flowers in the hospital, so she must not hate me too much.

"Beth! Hello!" Diane cries, brightening as I approach her desk. She jumps to her feet and hurries around her desk to grab me and hold me at arm's length to get a good look. "What a wonderful surprise! How are you? You look wonderful, dear. Are you feeling better?"

Based on her enthusiastic welcome, I realize she's not holding a grudge against me.

"Hi, Diane. I'm fine, thank you." I glance at Shane's office door, which is closed. "Is Shane in?"

"Yes, he is, dear." Then she frowns. "But I'm afraid he has some people in there with him." Diane's voice drops to a whisper as she glances at Shane's door, as if she's imparting some top-secret information to us. "He's meeting with a new client, and I take it he's famous! I don't know who he is, but the girls down the hall were practically squealing when he walked in."

"Oh." Well, there goes my seduction plan. I guess I should have called ahead to see if he was free, but that would have ruined the surprise. "Would you tell him we stopped by?"

"Of course, dear. Do you want to wait? I'm not sure how long they'll be—"

The door to Shane's office opens, and Shane is standing in the doorway, smiling at me. "Hello, sweetheart. What a pleasant surprise." But he doesn't look very surprised.

"Did you know I was here?"

"I knew the minute you entered the building."

"Well, you're hard to surprise then. I guess I should have called ahead. I didn't know you had a meeting."

Shane's gaze flickers over to Lia, and he smiles. "Actually, I'm glad you're here. Both of you." He opens his door wide. "There's someone I want you to meet."

I glance past Shane and see two men seated in front of Shane's desk. One of them is short and slender with a receding blond hairline, dressed in a gray pinstriped suit. The other one—oh my God! The other one glances back at us through the open doorway and smiles.

I look at Shane. "Is that who I think it is?"

Shane smiles, nodding. "Yes. Come say hello."

"What's all the fuss?" Lia says, as she sidles up next to me. She peers through the doorway and catches a glimpse of the two men seated in Shane's office. It's sure not the skinny guy in the suit she's staring at. It's the other one. "Holy fuck," she breathes.

My thoughts exactly.

Shane grins. "Come inside, ladies."

It's not unusual to see celebrities in Chicago—after all, it's a pretty sizable city. It's not Manhattan or L.A., but it will do. Right now I'm looking at a *very* familiar face—and body—seated in front of Shane's desk. I saw this guy on television recently when he hosted one of the big music award shows on cable. Jonah Locke is the lead singer of the four-member rock band known simply as *Locke*. They're a relatively new band on the scene, but since their debut hit single, they've been dominating the charts and the radio airwaves.

My first thought is that he's even hotter in person than he appears on television—if that's even possible. I try not to gawk, but it's hard. He's... gorgeous.

As Shane ushers us into his office, Jonah rises to his feet. He's about Shane's height—six-two—and he looks to be in his late twenties. His hair is the color of dark chocolate with rich, burnished highlights. It's long, and right now, he's got it pulled back into a messy man-bun. His beard is the same rich color as the rest of his hair, trimmed close to his chiseled face. His eyes are dark, his brows dark slashes against a tanned complexion. The guy's just stunning.

He's wearing a pair of worn, ripped jeans and a faded gray graphic T-shirt that lovingly hugs his muscles. Both arms are covered to his wrists in intricate, black tattoos. I think those are Celtic knots. And he's smiling expectantly at me and Lia, patiently waiting to be introduced.

I risk a glance at Lia, who's being uncharacteristically quiet all of a sudden. She looks shell-shocked, and that has to be a first for her. I don't think I've ever seen Lia speechless.

Jonah's companion stands, too, clutching a leather portfolio in his arms. He's a slight man, much shorter than Jonah, and probably in his mid-40s. He has a pale complexion and not much left of his thinning blond hair. His suit is ill-fitting, and he seems antsy, fidgeting on his feet as if there's somewhere else he needs to be.

Shane shuts the door behind us. "Gentlemen, this is my girlfriend, Beth Jamison. And this is Lia McIntyre. She's one of our undercover bodyguards—and my sister."

"Ladies, it's a pleasure," Jonah says, his voice deep and resonant. He talks just like he sings. When he sings, females swoon. Probably some men do, too.

There's a flash of heat in Jonah's dark eyes as his gaze lights on

Lia. The man is intense, and he's staring at Lia like he's a hungry man and she's his next meal. I sneak another glance at her, and now she's looking anywhere except at Jonah.

"Ladies, this is Jonah Locke and his manager, Dave Peterson. Jonah's in town for a few months to write and record a new album. And, he's our newest client."

"Hello," I say, feeling a little tongue-tied. I clear my throat, trying not to sound like a total fan girl—because who doesn't love this band? I've got all their hits in my favorite rock playlist.

I notice Shane fighting a grin as he looks at me.

"It's nice to meet you, Mr. Locke," I say, managing a cool, polite tone. "Mr. Peterson."

Jonah smiles back and, surprisingly, it looks like a genuine smile. So many big-name celebrities have egos a mile wide, but this guy seems like... just a regular guy. "It's a pleasure, Beth. Call me Jonah, please."

"Hello, Lia," Jonah says, turning his gaze to Shane's sister.

Lia glances at him and nods her head dismissively, saying nothing. Where is the snarky comment, I wonder.

"Jonah, we'd better get going," the manager says, checking his wrist watch—a huge diamond-encrusted Rolex. "We have to be at the recording studio at six to meet the leasing agent."

Jonah nods, sparing just a quick glance at his manager. He steps forward and shakes Shane's hand. "Thanks, Shane. I'll see you tomorrow."

Shane nods. "I'm looking forward to it."

Jonah smiles at me and then once more at Lia. "Ladies." I feel the reverberation of his deep voice all the way down to my toes. I sneak another peek at Lia, and I swear she looks flushed.

Lia and I watch, fascinated, as Jonah and his manager walk past us and out the door.

As soon as Shane closes his door, Lia finds her voice. "Holy fuck."

I can't help laughing—she pretty much hit the nail on the head. "No kidding."

Shane grins at his sister. "Jonah's relocating to Chicago for a while because he's had some stalker issues back in L.A. It's too soon to know if the problem will follow him here. He's going to keep a low media profile while he's here, and we're providing him close personal protection while he's in town, just as a precaution."

Lia shakes her head. "That man is sex on a stick." She looks at Shane. "So, who's the lucky stiff who gets to guard that fine ass?"

Shane smiles enigmatically as he studies his sister. "I haven't made up my mind yet."

"Damn." Lia shakes her head as she turns and walks out the door, muttering to herself.

When Lia's out of sight, I shut and lock Shane's office door. "I've never seen Lia act like that. She seemed almost... I don't know, nervous or something."

"Yes, that was interesting, to say the least."

Shane looks edible in his trademark charcoal gray suit and white shirt. He's not wearing a tie, though, and the top two buttons of his shirt are undone, showing a little bit of tanned throat and a smidgen of dark chest hair—and that just makes him look a little bit rakish and a whole lot sexy. His blue eyes look bright and amused.

"What are you smiling about?" I say as I walk toward him.

He props his hands on his hips and eyes me with a good measure of curiosity. When I reach him, I slip my hands inside his jacket and smooth his shirt over his chest. He's fighting a grin, as if he's already in on the game. Am I that obvious?

"I'm smiling because you look like trouble," he says, pulling me into his arms. "What can I do for you, Miss Jamison?"

I take a deep breath, determined to go through with this. "It's not about what you can do for me."

He arches a brow. "Oh, really?"

I nod, running my hands slowly up his chest to his shoulders, and when I squeeze his shoulder muscles, he groans, and that makes me smile. Maybe this won't be so hard after all.

I gaze into those beautiful eyes of his. "Are you done for the day?"

"I certainly can be."

"Good. Then we won't be interrupted."

"Well, that I can't promise. What did you have in mind?"

Reassuring myself that I'd already locked the door to his office, I channel my inner seductress and slowly release the next two buttons of his shirt. I spread the material wide, exposing a good deal of his firm chest to my appreciative gaze.

I lean forward and lick one of his tiny, flat nipples, my tongue catching on the firm little tip. His big body tenses as a shudder rips through him, and he groans, his voice loud in the quiet hush of his office. How unprofessional of him. Inwardly I chuckle.

His hands come up to grip my arms, not to push me away, but to pull me closer. I smile. I've dreamed about doing this so many times, and now I have him right where I want him. The knowledge is heady, and when I flick my fingernail lightly over the nipple I just licked, his body jerks.

I push his jacket off his shoulders and let it fall to the floor. Then my hands return to his remaining buttons, and I start slowly releasing them. His gaze is glued to my fingers.

"I just thought you could use a little relaxation," I say. "I'm sure you've had a long day, what with hobnobbing with rock stars and electronically stalking your girlfriend."

"And you think undressing me in my office will *relax* me? Think again."

His shirt is completely unbuttoned now, so I push it off his broad shoulders and it slips to the floor to join his jacket. The view of Shane's bare chest—his chiseled muscles and well-defined abs—is mouthwatering. My eyes follow the path of his chest hair as it converges into a dark happy trail that leads beneath his belt buckle. I lean into him, pleased to feel the hard ridge of his erection through his slacks.

I put my mouth on his chest and kiss him from his sternum down to his belly button, moving slowly, mixing sensuous kisses with a little bit of licking and sucking and tasting. His entire body is thrumming now with barely restrained energy.

Since Shane has a corner office, there are two walls of windows overlooking busy N. Michigan Avenue and the cross street. We're on the twentieth floor, so no one can really see into his office unless they're in the building directly across from this one and holding a pair of binoculars. But still, there's an air of exhibitionism going on. As I run my fingers along the outline of his erection, his gaze darkens and his eyes narrow with a sudden ferocity.

There's no going back now.

"Is this for me?" I say, stroking his erection through his clothing. I swear he grows even harder, longer right before my eyes.

"You know it is." His hands slide up to cradle my face, his thumbs brushing my cheeks, and he leans down to kiss me, pressing his warm lips gently against mine. He makes a noise deep in his chest and then his kiss grows firmer as his lips nudge mine open.

Out of the blue, I have a flashback to the last time I was in his office. I remember screaming at him at the top of my lungs. I remember the agony of feeling betrayed. I start shaking, and Shane pulls back, still holding my face in his hands. "What's wrong?"

My eyes shoot over to the door that leads to his apartment, and then he knows. I can tell by the sudden change in his demeanor.

"Beth." He pulls me against his chest and holds me close, his warm hand stroking my back. "It's all right."

But I can't stop thinking about it. The last time I was here was the morning my life unraveled before my eyes. I was devastated. I felt so betrayed and utterly gutted.

It all comes back to me now, like a film reel playing in my head. I remember yelling at him here in this office with my then-bodyguard, Miguel Rodriquez, looking on. When Gabrielle told me the truth that morning—that my new boyfriend had in fact been paid to protect me—I stormed out of the townhouse and confronted Miguel in his car parked out in the street. I demanded to be taken to Shane, and I had it out with him right here in his office.

I can still remember the choking panic and anxiety. It wasn't until I nearly passed out during a full-blown panic attack that Shane picked me up and carried me into the small apartment attached to his office. I haven't been back here since.

"I didn't think being back here again would affect me this badly," I say, my voice quiet and strained. "I'm sorry."

"It's different this time, sweetheart. Everything's different. Let's replace the old memories with new ones, all right?"

I nod because I know he's right. It is different this time. *I'm* different this time.

↜ **20**

The last time I was in Shane's office apartment, I never made it past the sofa where I collapsed. This time, I'm a lot more clear headed and able to observe more.

The apartment is small, but well appointed and very comfortable. It's a perfect little hide-a-way for him to escape to on long days at the office—even some overnights at the office. It's very tastefully decorated in Shane's favorite blues and browns—definitely a comfortable, yet masculine space.

There's a small sitting area with a taupe-colored sofa, two side tables with lamps, and a big screen TV on a console. Across the way is a dining table and a small galley kitchen. This time, I notice a short hallway that leads presumably to a bedroom.

He takes me in his arms. "I have to admit I've had more than a few fantasies about bringing you in here." He nods down the hallway. "There's a perfectly good bed in there we have yet to christen."

Shane swings me up in his arms and carries me down the hallway. The bedroom, like the rest of the apartment, is a masculine, modern space. There's a large bed with two nightstands and a beautiful mahogany dresser. The floors are dark hardwood and the bed sits on a plush gray rug. The only other furniture in the room is an upholstered armchair and a coffee table situated by the large window.

He sets me down on the rug at the foot of the bed and takes me in his arms. This quiet, restful hideaway is like a private little retreat, high above the city. Outside the window is all blue skies and puffy white clouds and sunshine. We're alone here, where no one will disturb us. As if reading my mind, Shane removes his phone from the holder attached to his belt, silences it, then tosses it onto a nightstand, where it makes a loud thud.

"Do you stay here often?" I ask him.

"I used to stay here quite often. But since I met you, no." He pulls back and cradles my face in his hands. "It's always too far from where you are."

The heat in his gaze makes me feel weak in the knees. I think we're definitely going to christen this big bed. His lips cover mine, and he kisses me tenderly, almost reverently. I suck in a shaky breath as my body starts to tingle.

"Are you hungry?" he says.

It is close to dinner time, but food is the last thing on my mind right now. I just want to feel the heat of his naked skin against mine. I shake my head. "What about you?"

"I'm hungry, but not for food."

When I reach between us to unfasten his belt, he drops his arms, holding them to his sides as if offering himself to me. The thought that this kind, caring, sexy-as-hell man willingly surrenders himself to me is both humbling and thrilling.

I unhook the fastener on his slacks and lower the zipper slowly. I have him all to myself for a while, and I want to take my time. I want to tease him and torture him. I want to make him hard and impatient. I reach inside his slacks and stroke him through the silky fabric of his boxers. Already he's enormous and hard, his erection pushing insistently against my palm. I look up at him, and the intensity of his expression takes my breath away.

He reaches for the hem of my dress and pulls it up and over my head in one fluid motion, leaving me in just my panties and bra. At least this time they match. I'm wearing a pale blue silk bra and panty set I bought at Sylvia's Boutique. Since I've acquired a boyfriend who likes to see me half-undressed as much as he likes to see me naked, I've started taking a little more care with my undergarments.

I think Shane approves. He runs the tip of his index finger along the top edge of my left bra cup, stroking the slight swell of my breast as it rises above the silky material. He cups my left breast and his thumb brushes my nipple through the sheer material. Immediately, my nipple hardens to a tight little point, and I moan. I feel a corresponding response between my legs.

He unclasps my bra and lets it slide to the rug at my feet. His hands are warm when they cover both my breasts, and he molds them to his palms. He leans down to suck one of my nipples into the wet heat of his mouth, his tongue lashing the hypersensitive bud, and my knees go weak.

As I sink to my knees on the soft, my eyes travel down the hard, flat ridges of his abdomen to the sight of his erection, which is engorged and thick and defying gravity as it lifts upward from the patch of dark hair. I wrap the fingers of one hand around his cock, and I'm amazed at the girth of him. My fingers come nowhere close to meeting. No wonder he stretches me so exquisitely. My other hand gently cups his testicles, which hang heavy and warm beneath his cock.

I glance up at him as I wet my lips, and I'm stunned by the stark look of arousal on his face. I smile, wanting to make this good for him. When my tongue darts out to lick the blunt head of his cock, he groans, fisting his hands at his sides.

"Beth." His voice is low, rough. "Sweetheart, I should shower first."

"Shh." He shudders when I lick a path upwards along the iron-hard stalk of his erection, from the root to the tip, sliding back his smooth foreskin with my fingers to expose the crown. My tongue swirls around the exposed head of his cock, stroking and tasting the warm, salty earthiness of him. Out of my peripheral vision, I can see his hands opening and closing as he flexes his fingers, fighting the urge to grab hold of my head.

I bathe the head of his cock with my tongue, teasing him as I run the tip of my tongue beneath the rim and over the crest.

"Fuck , Beth!"

The tortured sound of his voice tells me I must be doing something right. I lick the glistening pre-come at the tip of his cock, then swirl my tongue around the plush head. My hands grasp him, working in tandem to stroke the entire length of him as I suck the head of him into my mouth. His breath is coming hard and fast now. When I suck harder, my lips and tongue teasing him without mercy, he gives up the battle and grips my head, kneading my scalp.

"Jesus, sweetheart," he gasps. "Fuck!"

My hands and lips and tongue work in concert to drive him wild, and soon he's thrusting into my tight mouth, gasping and grunting with pleasure as he strokes his cock between my lips.

"I can't—Beth, I can't—"

On the verge of coming, he tries to pull out, but I don't want him to. I want this. I want him, all of him. I tighten my hold on the base of his cock and swallow him down as far as I can.

When the head of his cock hits the back of my throat, he cries out, his voice loud and sharp as he comes in a hot rush. He's struggling for breath, his hands caressing my hair as he tries to extricate himself from my hold. But I want it all. I want every bit of him, every silky, salty drop of him.

When the tumult has passed, he withdrawals from my mouth and sweeps me up into his arms.

I smile at him. "Take me to bed."

As he carries me to the bed, he kisses me with a gentle reverence that takes my breath away.

* * *

I awake to the sound of running water and realize Shane's in the shower. It's dark outside and I've lost all track of time. I don't even know if it's morning or night. I check the time on my phone and groan. It's a little before six a.m. Shane's such an early bird, ready to hop out of bed and tackle the world's problems before the sun's even up. I guess that's why he's the CEO of a billion-dollar global corporation and I'm not.

After making love the night before, Shane made a trip to the deli down the block and brought back sandwiches and soup, and we ate in bed while watching a movie on the flat screen television mounted on the wall. After taking a shower together, we ended up back in bed and made love a second time, then laid in bed talking until we eventually fell asleep.

I stretch, feeling the delicious, lingering sensation of his mouth on me, of him surging inside me. It's sweet of him to let me sleep, but honestly, I wish he'd wake me up when he's awake so we could cuddle for a few minutes before we have to go our separate ways, maybe even have some early morning sex, the kind that's warm and sleepy and slow. Just thinking about it makes me tingle. I reach between my legs and feel how wet I am still from what we did last night.

I throw off the covers and walk naked into the bathroom, where it's hot and steamy as a sauna.

I pull back one end of the curtain to peek in on him. "Hey."

He's lathering his hair. "Hey yourself. You're up early."

"I missed you."

He shoves his head under the hot spray to rinse off. "Join me."

I take his hand and step inside the shower stall, and he pulls me into his arms. His skin is hot and wet, and there are rivulets of shampoo running down his chest. I reach up and brush aside the residual shampoo and run my hands along his chest. I like the smell of his shampoo—it's a masculine scent, so different from my minty, tea tree oil shampoo.

He kisses me. "Good morning. Did you sleep well?"

His breath is minty fresh, and I realize he's already brushed his teeth.

I pull back. "You brushed your teeth. I should, too."

He gives me an impatient scowl and pulls me back into his arms. "Don't you dare move one inch."

His mouth devours mine, until I'm breathless and my knees are weak. Pretty soon we both taste minty. When my fingers brush over his nipples, he moans, the sound low and rough. I'm enjoying learning where his most sensitive spots are.

He turns me so that the water hits my hair, then reaches for a bottle of shampoo, squirting some into the palm of his hand.

I recognize the scent of my own shampoo. "How did that get here?"

He smiles. "What can I say? I'm an optimistic man."

I laugh, picturing him sending Diane out to buy girly products just in case I sleep over here one night.

Now it's my turn to groan as Shane's strong fingers massage my scalp. Then he tips my head back into the water and rinses out the suds. I think he has an ulterior motive when he squirts body wash— my favorite vanilla scent—into his hands and starts washing my body.

After stepping out of the shower, we towel ourselves dry. I towel my hair to get out most of the water. When I'm done, he pulls a clean towel out of the cupboard and wraps me in it, then sweeps me up in his arms and carries me back into the bedroom.

He lays me on the bed and crawls in beside me, leaning down to kiss me. "Top or bottom?"

The man's insatiable. I grin, thinking I'm going to have morning sex after all. "My hair's a tangled mess. If I don't brush it out, it'll dry like this and I'll look like a freak all day."

"You'll figure something out later," he says, palming my breast. His hand is warm on my damp, chilly skin, and the contrast makes me shiver. "I'm not about to waste an opportunity to start my day off right. How about we compromise?" With that, he pulls me up onto my hands and knees, then moves behind me, reaching between my legs to tease my clitoris.

I can't help laughing. "How is this a compromise?"

I can't stop giggling, and Shane swats me lightly on my butt. "Hold still and be prepared to be amazed."

I am indeed amazed when he pushes the thick head of his cock into my soft, wet opening. I moan loudly and my head sinks down onto one of the pillows as my arms give way. My bottom is up in the air, and he's clutching my hips, holding me in place.

He rocks against me, coating himself in my wetness, thrusting deeper each time. When I squeeze my vaginal muscles tightly, he growls. "God, sweetheart. Fuck!"

I turn my heated face to the side and grip the bed sheets with both hands. Once he's in as far as he can go, we both groan loudly.

"Okay?" he says, his voice little more than a rasp as he rocks himself inside me.

A nod and a whimper is all I can manage right now, because I'm panting already from the exquisite feeling of fullness. He so big from this angle, it takes my breath away.

He pulls out slowly, then presses forward, sinking deep into my body. "Oh, fuck."

His voice is low and rough, and that makes me even wetter.

My entire body feels overheated and swollen and aching. My breasts feel heavy, and my nipples are tightly puckered and sensitive. I grab the pillow beneath me and press my cheek into it and hold on for dear life.

When Shane reaches between my legs and strokes my clit, I cry out and grip the pillow even tighter. His finger slides over that little bundle of nerves easily, slick with my arousal, and he begins to thrust, slowly and steadily. I can feel the head of his cock dragging along the sensitive tissues inside my body, hitting my sweet spot over and over with careful deliberation. He knows exactly what he's doing to me.

The incredible sensations swell and coalesce deep in my core, and I feel my release building. There's a high-pitched keening sound in the room. My face heats and I close my eyes tightly when I realize it's coming from me. I can't help it. I can't be quiet, not when he's driving into me like this, relentless and insatiable.

I cry out when my orgasm hits, and my sex clamps down tightly on his burrowing cock, triggering his violent release. He falls forward, covering my back with his body, and grips my hips hard as his cock erupts, filling me spurt after spurt with liquid heat.

I collapse on the mattress, and he follows me down, both of us spent. He rolls to the side, taking me along with him so that we're lying side by side, still joined together. His cock is still firm enough that he can gently rock in and out of my slick passage.

He brushes my hair back from my heated face, then leans forward to press a kiss on the nape of my neck. I shiver.

"You drive me insane," he says, sounding winded, as if he's just run a marathon.

I smile. I'm just as winded, my breathing hard and fast.

He pulls out and presses up against my back, wrapping his arm around my waist and tucking me in close. I turn my head back toward him, and his lips meet mine, our kiss gentle and unhurried.

He puts his lips to my temple and murmurs, "I love you."

Shane disappears back into the bathroom to finish washing up, and then he returns to the bedroom to get dressed for work. I lay in bed, reveling in the delicious sensations lingering in my body.

I watch him dress, and the final product—Shane in a dark gray suit and white shirt—sets the butterflies in my stomach loose. He's an incredibly attractive man no matter what he's wearing, but when he puts on a suit—holy cow. He's sex incarnate. And those beautiful blue eyes—they're so unexpected on such a ruggedly handsome man.

"So, what's on your agenda today?" he says, sitting on the side of the bed to pull on his black socks.

"I work at the bookstore from ten until two, and then I'm going to UC to meet with an admissions counselor and get signed up for fall classes."

Shane stands and leans down to kiss me. "Lia's going with you?"

"Yes."

"Good. It's still early. Stay in bed and relax. I'll have some breakfast brought in for you."

I smile, realizing that Shane's office is just on the other side of the apartment door. I'll get to see him again before I leave for work.

"How many places do you have, anyway?" I say, shaking my head. I know of three—the Kenilworth house, the penthouse apartment, and this place.

"In Chicago, just the three you know of."

"You mean there are others places outside of Chicago?"

"Yes." He tucks me in, then brushes back my damp hair, which is a tangled mess, I'm sure. "Now, go back to sleep. You don't need to be up this early."

"My hair is a rat's nest." I'll have to take another shower.

He grins. "You look beautiful and well fucked."

I realize I have no clean clothes with me. "Oh, crap."

"What it is?"

"I didn't bring a change of clothes." Apparently, I didn't think this office seduction plan through very well.

"You'll find some of your clothes hanging in the closet, and some of your undergarments are in the dresser, in the top drawer on the right."

"Thank you."

He thinks of everything.

21

I'm up, showered again, and dressed by eight-thirty. When I open the door that adjoins the apartment to Shane's office, I see him seated at his desk. His brother Jake is sitting in one of the chairs in front of the desk. They're deep into a quiet, tense conversation. Neither one of them looks happy.

I poke my head through the doorway, and both men turn to look at me. "Sorry. Am I interrupting?"

Shane smiles as he beckons me into the office. "Of course not. Come in."

He points me to a credenza along one wall, where I find a bag containing a still-warm breakfast sandwich and a cup of coffee from my favorite coffee shop just a few blocks from Shane's office building. I pick up the coffee and inhale the fragrant steam—it's a caramel, espresso, and steamed milk concoction with whipped cream and caramel drizzle—my addiction.

I take a sip and moan in delight. "Thanks for breakfast."

Shane tips his head at his brother. "You can thank this guy. He played delivery driver this morning. Come join us while you eat. Lia's on her way to pick you up."

I take the empty chair beside Jake and dig into my food, suddenly aware of how hungry I am. We burned a lot of calories last night and this morning having sex—it's no wonder I'm starving.

Shane and Jake sit quietly watching me eat, their previous conversation abandoned. I realize I must have interrupted something sensitive, because now they're suspiciously quiet.

"I did interrupt something," I say, cradling my coffee cup in my hands. "I can take this back into the apartment and give you some privacy."

"No, don't be silly," Shane says. "I'd much rather talk to you than to this guy."

"Ditto," Jake says. "Stay. You're doing us both a favor."

Shane is the oldest McIntyre sibling, and Jake's the third oldest. In a lot of ways, they're probably the closest of the brothers. They make a good pair... Shane's good cop to Jake's bad cop. I don't think it's a coincidence that Jake's nickname in the company is *the enforcer*.

To look at him, Jake is rather intimidating. His hair is jet black, as are his irises are so dark they almost look black. He's also ex-military, as well as a former professional, heavyweight boxer. I've seen him in the martial arts studio before, pummeling the hell out of a punching bag. His body looks like it's carved from stone, his muscles sharply defined and well honed. There's not a soft edge on him.

And those tattoos. Jake's arms and shoulders are covered in dark, tribal tattoos. There's a date—a month, day and year—inked down the left side of his torso: March 5, 2005. I don't know what the date signifies, and no one will tell me. I've never had the courage to ask Jake myself.

I have to admit Jake intimidates me. He's always been very nice to me, and he's never given me a reason to fear him, but still, I wouldn't want to run into him in a dark alley. I've seen the wickedly sharp knife he wears in a calf harness. Not to mention the fact that he never goes anywhere without his gun holstered to his chest. He's wearing it even now. In a lot of ways, he is Shane's muscle. The CEO can't get his hands dirty, but Jake can—and does.

Jake challenges Shane a lot, and I think Shane values that. Shane doesn't want to be surrounded by yes men. He wants honesty, and he's guaranteed to get that and more from his brothers and Lia and Cooper. But especially from Jake. Jakes always gives it to him straight.

I have to ask. "Before I came in, you were talking about Howard Kline, weren't you?"

Jake frowns, but he answers honestly. That's what I like best about him; he's always upfront with me. He doesn't try to sugar-coat things, the way Shane does. "Yeah."

Shane shoots his brother a recriminating look. "It's nothing to worry about, sweetheart."

I look at Jake, because I know he'll give it to me straight. "Tell me."

"Kline's getting more and more out of control," Jake says. "He's drinking and using drugs at alarming rates, buying the cheap stuff from low-level dealers. And lately, he's taken a few late-night forays into Hyde Park. That's what concerns me the most. I don't care what he does to himself, but when he starts making moves in your direction, I start to worry."

My townhouse is in Hyde Park—and there's no other reason on Earth for Kline to go there. My heart starts hammering in my chest, and I set my food down on Shane's desk, my appetite gone. "He's checking out my house."

Jake nods. "I'm afraid so."

"That's enough, Jake," Shane says.

Jake looks at Shane. "What? You want me to lie to her?" He shakes his head. "I'm not going to do it. She needs to know."

I turn to Jake. "Know what?"

Shane gives his brother a warning glance. "Jake."

But I want to know. "No, Shane. I have a right to know."

Jake eyes me directly. "He's been casing your townhouse. I think he's working up the courage to break in."

I swear I can feel the blood drain from my face because my cheeks grow ice cold.

"It's okay, Beth," Jake says, reaching out to cover my hand with his. "We want him to break in. The sooner he does, the sooner this ends."

"I said that's enough, Jake," Shane says, his voice sharp.

I glance at Shane. "Are you planning something?"

Shane shrugs. "I told you, sweetheart, it's nothing for you to worry about."

A rap at the door has us all turning our heads. It's Lia.

"Hey, Princess," she says, walking into Shane's office with a cocky grin on her elfin face. She's wearing faded jeans, a ninja T-shirt, and hiking boots. "Your chariot has arrived."

Shane's watching me intently, as if he expects me to have a meltdown any minute. "Don't worry about Kline, Beth. I promise, he can't get to you. He still thinks you're living in the townhouse."

If Shane had his way, I'd never know anything about Kline. But it's my life. I have a right to know. I know Shane just wants to protect me, but I don't want to be kept in the dark.

Lia walks up behind my chair and puts her hands on my shoulders and squeezes. "What's with all the drama faces? What'd I miss?"

I stand and grab my coffee. Even though I don't feel like finishing my breakfast sandwich, I do need my caffeine. "I'm ready. Let's go."

Shane intercepts me halfway to the door and pulls me into his arms. "Don't worry. Have a good day. I'll see you at dinner, okay?"

I nod. I should be back from UC well before then.

Shane looks over my head at Lia. "Bring her to the penthouse when she's done for the day."

"Will do," Lia says, saluting.

22

Lia and I are seated in the rear seat of an SUV, and our cab driver is engrossed in a phone conversation and not paying us any attention. I catch Lia's attention and whisper to her. "What do you know about Howard Kline's actions lately?"

Lia shrugs. "Not a lot. Jake's folks are keeping tabs on him. Why?"

I can't help wondering if Lia's telling me everything, or if Shane's warned her not to say anything. "Jake says he's casing my townhouse."

Lia shrugs. "Yeah."

"But why would he do that, when the place is empty? Gabrielle and I both moved out."

"Kline doesn't know that."

"But surely he'd catch on when the place is dark all the time. No mail delivery, no trash pick-up. No car in the garage."

Why would Kline keep coming back to my townhouse if it was

dark all the time? It would be obvious to anyone paying attention that the place was vacant. Unless.... "It is still vacant, right?"

Lia just looks at me, saying nothing.

But I can see it in her eyes. She's hiding something. "My townhouse isn't dark, is it?"

She frowns. "I'm not at liberty to discuss this."

"Someone's in my townhouse? Are you kidding me?"

The cab pulls up in front of Clancy's. Lia hops out on the curb side and holds the door for me as I scoot out after her.

I grab her arm. "Spill it, Lia!"

She looks me in the eye. "What part of 'I'm not at liberty to discuss this' did you not understand?"

Oh, my God. Someone's living in my townhouse without my knowledge. That doesn't make any sense. Shane wouldn't sublet my townhouse—it wouldn't be safe. And it's not like money is an issue, at least not for him. "Don't you dare hold out on me, Lia McIntyre. Tell me what's going on. I swear, if Shane is hiding something from me—"

Lia ushers me through the bookstore doors and practically throws me at Sam, who's waiting inside. "She's all yours, red. I'll be back at two."

"Lia, wait!" I say.

"Sorry, Princess. Gotta run."

"Hey, boss," Sam says.

"Hi, Beth!" Erin calls, as she wobbles over in her three-inch, royal blue heels. "Let's go clock you in."

Lia's long gone, so I have no choice but to go upstairs to the employee lounge and start my day. Sam follows us upstairs and loiters around while I stick my timecard in the machine and stow my purse in my locker.

I'm irritated at Lia for running off like a coward. Something's up, and she knows what it is, and she's not telling. I probably have Shane to thank for that. Sometimes I want to ring his stubborn, controlling, over-protective neck.

As we're heading out of the employee lounge, I pause and look at the time clock. "Is it really necessary for employees to punch a timecard?"

Sam looks at me and shrugs, while Erin smiles apologetically.

Great. It's just one more reason for me to be at odds with Vanessa. I don't like punching a time card, so I'm sure the others don't like it either.

* * *

It's wonderful to see Erin again, even if she's making me a nervous wreck as she teeters precariously on her shoes. And she wastes no time reminding me how much she hates them. This time she does stumble on the stairs, and Sam and I both reach out to steady her.

I take my place at one of the four check-out terminals as Erin hovers over my shoulder, giving me pointers and watching me work. It doesn't take me long to figure out how to run the point-of-sale terminal, and then it becomes fun. I'm actually enjoying myself.

I love talking to customers. I ask them how they're doing and if they have any feedback about the store and their experience shopping here. The most common response I get is that the check-out lines are too long, which is no surprise. That's got to be one of the first things to be fixed. That, and the dress code for the assistant managers.

I'm ringing up a young man who just bought several video gaming magazines when I realize someone's standing right behind me. I turn to see Vanessa looming over me, watching my every move. The smile on my face dies when I see her scowl. Undoubtedly, I'm in for another lecture.

I sigh. "Hello, Vanessa."

She leans closer and hisses in my ear. "What's *he* doing here?"

"Who?" It takes me a minute to realize whom she's referring to. Sam's standing a few feet behind me, casually leaning against a shelving unit reading a motocross magazine. "Oh, you mean Sam? Well, he's working."

She crosses her arms. "Employees aren't permitted behind the sales counter unless they're ringing up customers. He'll have to move."

I finish with the video gamer guy and hand him his magazines and his receipt with a smile and a "come back soon."

As the customer walks away, I spare a quick glance at Vanessa. "I'm sorry, but you'll have to take that up with Mack. Or better yet, take it up with Shane." The thought of her doing that makes me smile, because I know what Shane's answer will be.

Vanessa glares at me and approaches Sam. She lowers her voice. "Can you make yourself a little less conspicuous, please?"

Sam doesn't even glance up from his magazine. "No, ma'am. I'm being as inconspicuous as I can."

"You shouldn't be behind the sales counter," she hisses. "Go stand somewhere else."

"That's not possible, ma'am."

Erin's gaze is bouncing back and forth between Vanessa and Sam, her eyes wide.

Vanessa walks off in a huff. "We'll just see about that!"

I glance back at Sam, who rolls his eyes at me. Erin, who's working the terminal next to mine, tries valiantly not to laugh as she waits on the next customer.

* * *

Lia shows up right on schedule. "Hey, Sam," she says, giving him a nod. Then she turns to me. "You ready?"

"Yes. I just need to run upstairs to clock out."

After I turn my station over to another employee, Sam gives me a fist bump. "See you tomorrow, boss," he says.

Lia follows me upstairs, and I pop into the employee lounge to clock out and collect my purse. On the way out, as we're passing the administrative office, we hear loud voices inside. I pause by the door for a moment just as Vanessa starts yelling at someone. The yelling stops abruptly, and a moment later the door opens and Erin storms out into the hallway, her face flushed bright red.

Erin's so upset, she doesn't seem to notice us. As she makes a bee-line for the ladies' room, I stare after her.

Lia shrugs. "Sounds like The Dragon Lady ripped her a new one."

Erin is a total sweetheart, and for Vanessa to yell at her like that is unacceptable.

"Wait here." I follow Erin into the ladies' room where I find her dabbing her face with a wet paper towel. She's shaking.

I lay my hand on her back and give her a sympathetic pat. "Hey, are you okay? What happened?"

Erin's expression morphs instantly as she pastes a bright smile on her face. "Oh! Hey, Beth. Hi."

"Are you okay?"

"Sure. I'm fine. Why?"

I don't mention the obvious—that her eyes are red and her cheeks are wet with tears. "I heard Vanessa yelling."

Her fake smile falls, and she gives me a sheepish look. "Oh, that. It's nothing. Don't worry about it."

"Why was she yelling at you?"

She shrugs her soft, round shoulders. "I messed up. It's nothing serious."

"No manager should yell at an employee like that, whether you messed up or not. Even I know that, despite my egregious lack of..."—and I'm air quoting here—"*retail experience*."

Erin laughs at my air quotes, and that puts a genuine smile on her face. She's finished wiping her cheeks, and she tosses the paper towel in the trash can. "Thanks, Beth. But it's okay, really."

Erin doesn't seem inclined to say more on the subject, so I decide to let it drop. Vanessa's always been a bitch to me, but I thought it was because I own the store, and she resents my intrusion into what she sees as her territory. But maybe it's more than that. Maybe she's a bitch to everyone. And if so, that's not going to fly. Not if I have any say about it. And apparently, I do.

* * *

Lia and I grab a cab and head to The University of Chicago so I can meet with an admissions counselor. I've already applied online to their graduate business program and been accepted for fall term, but I need to meet with an advisor to sign up for classes. Since I'm going to be working part time, I'll go to school part-time, taking two classes each semester.

After my meeting with the admissions counselor is over and I'm registered for my first two classes—*Introduction to Management* and *Introduction to Marketing*—Lia and I walk across campus to a main road where we can hail a cab.

It's only four-thirty, and I have some time to kill before I'm supposed to meet Shane at the penthouse for dinner. We're just fifteen minutes from my townhouse, which I haven't seen in over two months. I miss the place. Plus I worry that since the house is supposed to be vacant, it's vulnerable to a break-in.

I glance at Lia. "I want to make a quick stop at my townhouse before heading home."

She gives me this withering expression as if I just suggested we run naked through the center of campus.

"Come on, Lia! We have plenty of time."

She shakes her head. "Sorry, Princess. That's not on the approved agenda."

Approved agenda? "Since when do I have to have my agenda approved?"

It's my house. Well, technically, it's my brother's house, but I'd been living in it with Gabrielle for the past two years until a couple of months ago. If I want to go see my townhouse, I should be able to.

"Okay, fine," I say, deciding to call her bluff. "I'll go by myself."

I head toward the main thoroughfare, where I know I can find a cab. Lia follows along behind me, muttering under her breath. When I flag down a cab, she slips into the rear seat right after me.

"You are such a pain in the ass!" she mutters as she buckles her seatbelt. "If we get busted, I'm telling Shane this was your idea."

"Don't worry. If we get in trouble, I'll take the blame."

It feels odd driving through my neighborhood for the first time in a couple of months. On nice days, I walked to work at the medical school library, so these streets are very familiar to me. I feel a sudden pang of homesickness—I miss the days when Gabrielle and I lived here. Life was so simple then. We worked, we watched movies during our free time, and Gabrielle made great food for us. Everything was so simple then—before I found out that Howard Kline had been paroled early.

I shudder at the thought that he's a free man now, walking the streets of Chicago and doing God knows what. The thought that he might try to hurt another child makes me sick. I was one of the lucky ones—I was rescued quickly, before Kline had a chance to do real damage. But not every child who disappears is so lucky. I try not to think about what might have happened if the police hadn't tracked me down so quickly—just thinking about it leads to a deep dark hole of anxiety.

When the cab turns onto my street, I shake myself out of my painful reverie and look around, noting that not much has changed. I ask the driver to park in the open spot across the street from my house and wait.

He shuts off the engine and immediately picks up his phone and starts texting. I sit quietly, observing my house. It's a beautiful two-story, red brick townhouse from the 1940s. My paternal grandparents were the first—and only—owners of this building until they both passed. When my grandmother died, she left the house to Tyler. I was just a baby then.

By the time I finished graduate school and started working at the medical school library, Tyler had purchased a condo in Lincoln Park for himself, and he let me and Gabrielle stay here in the townhouse. This townhouse has a lot of sentimental value to me, and I hate the fact that Gabrielle and I had to abandon it because of Kline.

Just as I decide I want to go inside and have a look around—just to make sure everything's okay—a woman walking down the sidewalk turns up my front walk and uses a key to let herself in my front door. Call me crazy, but I don't think it's a coincidence that this woman looks *exactly* like me. And I do mean exactly. She's the same height I am—five-eight. She's slender, with pale blond hair hanging just past her shoulders, just like me.

I glance at Lia. She's watching the woman too, with a guarded expression.

I poke Lia in the ribs with my elbow. "Who is that?"

She grimaces. "I told you this was a bad idea, Beth."

"Never mind that. Just tell me who she is."

When Lia doesn't answer me, I reach for my door handle, fully intending to confront this woman to find out why she's in my house.

But Lia lays her hand over mine, stopping me. "Calm your jets, Beth. Her name is Caroline Palmer. She works for McIntyre Security."

"What is she doing in my house?"

Lia shrugs. "She's living there at the moment."

"Since when?"

"Since Shane moved her in right after you got out of the hospital. She's your stand-in."

"My what? Why do I need a stand-in?" I'm not even sure I know what that means.

"Your stand-in. So Kline thinks you're still living there. We don't want him to know you've moved out. As long as he thinks you're living here, he won't go looking for you elsewhere."

Oh, my God. Some poor woman who happens to look like me has put herself in danger because of me. "This is crazy."

Lia doesn't look happy either. But apparently, she's got other problems on her mind. "Shane's not going to be happy about this. He didn't want you to know."

"Well, that's too bad."

I give the driver Shane's office building address, and we head downtown. I've had enough of Shane doing things without telling me. I know he's just trying to protect me, but I'm not a child who needs protecting.

23

When the cab pulls up to the front of Shane's office building, I jump out and head inside at a good clip, leaving Lia to settle the fare. As the elevator takes me up to Shane's floor, I contemplate what I'm going to say to him. I'm not mad really, because I know he's just trying to protect me. But I don't like being kept in the dark about things that pertain directly to my life. He has to start letting me in on the decision-making. He has to stop sheltering me like this.

I smile at Diane as I reach her desk. The door to Shane's office is closed. "Hi, Diane."

"Hello, Beth," she says, smiling. "What can I do for you?"

I glance at Shane's door. "Is he in?"

"Yes, he is. He's in a meeting, though." She frowns, as she's not sure what to do.

I blow out a frustrated breath, because I'm anxious to talk to him. "Who's he meeting with? Is it a client?"

"No. Cooper and Jake."

Perfect! Just the people I need to talk to. "Then I'm sure he won't mind if I interrupt."

With that, I walk up to his door, knock twice, then open it. Shane is seated at his desk, and Cooper and Jake are sitting in the chairs facing him. Shane freezes mid-sentence, and Cooper and Jake turn to see who's interrupting their meeting.

I step inside the room and shut the door behind me. "Hello, gentlemen."

Shane rises, straightening his jacket. "Hi, sweetheart. Come on in."

There's a sharp rap on the door just before Lia pushes it open and jogs into the room, a little short of breath. "Sorry, Shane. I tried to stop her, but in case you haven't noticed, she's a little pigheaded. Short of sitting on her, there wasn't much I could do." Lia points an accusing finger at me. "And *you*—don't run off like that again, or I will sit on you."

I hear Jake chuckling as Shane eyes his sister. "Stop her from doing what?"

"This should be good," Jake says, and Shane shoots him a quelling glance.

I'm losing patience with all of them. "From visiting my own house, that's what!"

Shane's expression is carefully neutral, giving absolutely nothing away.

"I saw her, Shane. Why didn't you tell me there's a woman—a woman who looks *just like me*—living in my house?"

"Sweetheart—"

"No. Don't *sweetheart* me. Just answer the question."

"Guys, do you mind?" Shane nods pointedly at the door.

"That's my cue," Lia says, heading for the door. "I'm off duty now. She's all yours, pal."

Jake and Cooper stand.

"No, wait!" I know they all have information about Kline and my house and the woman who looks like me. "You guys, stay."

Shane crosses his arms. "Beth—"

"No! Listen, all of you. I'm done with being left in the dark. I want some answers, starting now. Who's the woman living in my townhouse?"

Shane lets out a sigh. "Her name's Caroline Palmer. She works for me."

"I know her name. What I want to know is why she's living in my house." I can't bear the thought of that woman being in danger because of me.

"She's a decoy, Beth," Jake says, crossing his arms as he leans back against Shane's desk. "She's staying in your townhouse because we don't want Kline to know you moved out."

"That's dangerous," I say. "She could get hurt living there, because of me."

Cooper shakes his head. "Caroline knows how to take care of herself. Besides, she's not there alone. She has backup with her in the townhouse at all times. The risk is minimal."

"I don't like people putting themselves at risk for me."

"Sweetheart." Shane walks up to me and pulls me into his arms. "There's nothing to worry about. Besides, it won't be for much longer."

"Why is that?"

"Because Kline's getting bold," Jake says. "He's casing your townhouse, and it's only a matter of time before he makes his move. And when he does, we'll be ready for him."

"What's the plan?" I say that because I know there's a plan. There has to be. These guys always have a plan.

Jake looks to Shane, and Shane shakes his head.

"She should know," Jake says. "We'll have a team in place, inside the townhouse. When Kline breaks in, assuming he's armed, which I'm sure he will be, we'll neutralize the problem, once and for all."

"You mean kill him. Can you do that?" I look from Jake to Shane for confirmation of my suspicions.

Shane nods. "If he breaks into your home, armed, then whoever's in that house has the legal right to defend himself."

"Or herself," I say, thinking of the woman living there now.

Shane nods. "Or herself, yes."

"Kline's actively casing the townhouse, Beth," Jake says. "He's been checking out the front of the building during the daytime, as well as the garage in the alley. We think he's getting ready to make a move. When he does, we'll have a team in place to respond."

I nod. "So, who's this team going to be?"

"Jake and I, plus a couple other guys," Shane says. "Plus, Caroline will likely be there since Kline would only break in if he thinks she's there."

"What about me?" I say. "I want to be there, too."

Shane shakes his head. "Absolutely out of the question. When this goes down, you'll either be in the penthouse or at the estate. You will not be at the townhouse."

I recognize the look on Shane's face—it's his adamant face. I could argue with him until I'm blue in the face, and it wouldn't do a bit of good. So I back off, for now. But this conversation's not over, as far as I'm concerned.

Shane checks his watch. "It's getting late, guys. Time to call it a day."

* * *

I wake up in the middle of the night and wander into the kitchen. It's terribly cold, and my skin is covered with goose bumps. I rub my bare arms in an attempt to warm myself.

When I look down, I'm surprised to see I'm naked. That's odd. I'd never walk through the penthouse naked—there are usually other people staying here, too.

I hear a sound behind me and turn.

At first, I just stare at the man standing in our kitchen—a stranger in our apartment. I shake my head. "This is Shane's apartment. You shouldn't be here."

He's a big man. Not tall, but stocky, broad in the chest and hips, and his belly is so huge his filthy white T-shirt can't cover it completely. He's wearing stained jeans and ratty old sneakers. How in the world did this guy get past Shane's security measures?

I glance at his face, thinking I should recognize him, but I don't. His face is round, his jowls heavy. His eyes are blood-shot and watery, with heavy bags underneath. Thin gray hair hangs dankly to the side of his head, and his face is covered with gray stubble.

My heart starts hammering in my chest, and I look around for Shane, but I don't see him.

"You shouldn't be here," I repeat, shaking my head at the stranger.

When he speaks, his voice sounds like crushed gravel. "I've waited a long time for you."

I may not recognize his face, but I certainly recognize the voice. That awful, grating voice has been haunting my dreams for eighteen years.

I tell myself it's just a dream, to relax. He can't hurt me. But my natural inclination for self-preservation kicks in, and I take a couple of steps back. I stumble when he lunges forward to grab me. He has a roll of black electrical tape in his hand, just like before.

"Shane!" I scream as loudly as I can and back out of the kitchen. "Shane!"

I turn and run, but he's right behind me. He grabs my neck and pushes me face down on the dining room table. He yanks my hands behind my back and wraps them with the electrical tape. The table top is ice cold against my bare breasts and belly. He kicks my legs apart, and I feel cold air brushing against my hot core.

"No!"

"Yes!" he shouts. "I've waited a God-damned long time for this!"

I scream with everything I have.

I feel thick, calloused fingers prodding between my legs, poking at me and hurting me. He kicks my legs farther apart. I hear the hiss of his zipper going down, and my entire body shudders in revulsion when his hairy thighs press up against my naked backside. I can feel the blunt head of his cock searching for my opening.

I scream and thrash, fighting to free myself, but then he grabs my hair and lifts my head off the table, then slams it back down on the hard surface, stunning me senseless.

I start crying.

24

"God damn it, Beth, wake up!"

Someone grabs my shoulders and shakes me hard. I fight back, unsure if I'm dreaming or awake. My throat feels shredded and my head is throbbing. It's never been this bad before.

"Look at me, Beth!"

I open my eyes and bolt upright into a sitting position, gasping for air. Shane leans over to the nightstand and grabs my inhaler from out of the top drawer. He gives it a quick shake before shoving it between my parted lips. "Here! Inhale!"

My hands are shaking as I hold the inhaler to my mouth and suck in a deep breath. I sit there trembling as the medicine begins to take effect and I feel the vise gripping my chest begin to relax. When I'm done, Shane takes the inhaler from me, and I fall back weakly onto the bed and close my eyes. I take a hesitant breath.

He lies down beside me and draws me into his arms and holds me tight. I'm shivering, cold as ice, and I gravitate toward the heat of his body.

"Sweetheart, talk to me." His voice is low, and he sounds as shaken as I feel.

I shake my head and press my face against his bare chest, holding onto him for dear life. I'm so sick of this. I'm sick of these nightmares, of being terrorized in my sleep. I'm embarrassed and ashamed that he sees me like this. The poor man can't ever get a solid night's sleep.

He rubs my back, warming me and comforting me at the same time. "It's all right. You're safe. Now tell me about it. You know that helps."

My voice is muffled against his chest as I reluctantly tell him. "He was here, in our apartment."

Shane tightens his arms on me. "He can't get in here, I promise."

"He tried to rape me."

"Ah, fuck."

"I could feel him trying to push inside me." I shudder, feeling sick at the memory. Then I pull back and look up into his face, frantic. "Where is he, Shane? Right now, where is he?"

Shane grabs his phone from the top of the nightstand and pulls up a company app. After pressing a couple buttons, he shows me the screen and a real-time report provided by the surveillance team. I see a red push pin symbol on a map indicating Kline's current location.

"Where is that?" My voice is so hoarse from screaming that I don't even recognize it.

Shane zooms in on the map, switching to a street-side view. The pin hovers over a run-down, single-story business in a strip mall. "It's a hole-in-the-wall bar, on the south side," he says. "He's nowhere near us."

"Are you sure?"

"Yes, honey, I'm sure."

The tension seeps out of me, and I wilt. We both jump when there's a quiet knock on our bedroom door.

"Shit." Shane clears his throat. "Come in."

The door opens slowly, and Cooper steps inside our room. He looks half asleep. "She okay? I heard her all the way down the hall."

Shane nods, pulling me closer. "She's just a little shaken. It was a bad one. She dreamt Kline was here in the apartment."

Cooper frowns as he approaches the bed. I realize I'm naked, and the sheet's down around my waist. Shane pulls it up to cover my breasts. Cooper sits on Shane's side of the bed and reaches over Shane to pat my leg through the blanket. "It's okay, kiddo. You know we won't let him get to you."

Shane and Cooper eye each other, neither saying a word. They don't have to.

Cooper pats my leg again. "Try to get some sleep, Beth." Then he rises and heads out of our room, closing the door quietly behind him.

Shane settles down beside me and kisses my temple. "You heard the man. Try to get some sleep."

But I'm afraid if I close my eyes, I'll see that monster in my dreams again. "I can't."

"Look at me, Beth."

When I do what Shane asks, I'm stunned by what I see in his expression. He leans forward and kisses me gently on my lips.

"I won't let him hurt you. I won't let *anyone* hurt you."

"It's not that easy. I can still feel him, touching me, trying to push inside me." I shudder. "I can't shut it off."

He contemplates me for a moment, then he rolls me over onto my belly and draws the sheet down to my waist. His fingers are warm as they drift over my back, gently caressing my skin. Then he sits up and begins massaging my back, his hands firm, yet gentle as he coaxes my muscles to loosen up. "Just relax, and let your mind go."

I groan with pleasure as his hands stroke my back and shoulders and neck, sending waves of warmth flowing through my body.

I feel his warm breath stirring my hair as he leans down to whisper in my ear. "Close your eyes and relax. I'll watch over you."

I do close my eyes, knowing I'm safe with Shane standing guard. He talks to me, his voice low and soothing. My eye lids are heavy from exhaustion, and I can't quite make out the words, but that's okay. His voice will keep the demons away, at least for tonight.

I'll worry about tomorrow when the time comes.

* * *

Surprisingly, Shane's still asleep when I awake. The sun is out in full force, lighting our room, so I know we both overslept. I reach for my phone on my nightstand and glance at the time. Nine o'clock! I'm supposed to be at the bookstore in an hour, but the thought of getting up right now is more than I want to contemplate.

Shane and I are wrapped in each other's arms, and he has a tight hold on me, as if he's afraid I might slip away in the night.

Bits and pieces of my nightmare return to me slowly, as if my brain is shielding me from remembering too much too quickly.

I lay quietly, watching the rise and fall of Shane's broad chest. His body really is beautiful, and I could lie here and gaze at him for hours. His warm, golden skin stretches tautly over chiseled muscles and lovely bones. He's such a strong man, both physically and emotionally, and I think about how much I've come to rely on him. How much I need him. The love I feel for him makes my chest ache.

I run my fingertips through the crinkly brown hair on his chest, following the path where it converges over his abdomen and trails down to his groin, where there's a patch of thick, dark wiry hair at the root of his penis. As I study him, his penis twitches and lengthens right before my eyes. Good grief, the man wakes up primed for sex.

"Good morning." His voice is a quiet, low rumble close to my ear.

I place a gentle kiss on the curve of his shoulder. "Thank you for last night."

He lifts my hand and kisses my fingertips. "I'll always be here when you need me."

I can't help smiling at his gallantry. He always seems to know the right thing to say. "Shane?"

"Hmm?"

Now he's kissing the pads of my fingertips, and I'm having trouble following my own train of thought. "What if the nightmares never stop?"

He shrugs. "Maybe once he's gone for good, they'll stop."

"Maybe." But as much as I want Kline gone, I'm afraid for Shane. I know he's planning something, but what if it goes wrong? What if Shane gets hurt? Or what if he's charged with a crime and ends up in prison? I couldn't bear that. "I don't want you to do anything risky. Please, Shane, promise me."

He kisses my forehead. "Don't worry. I know what I'm doing."

But I can't shake a premonition that something might go wrong. "I want to be there when it happens. I've lived my entire life hostage to this monster, and I want to see with my own eyes that he's no longer a threat."

He's pensive for a moment, and then he looks me in the eye.

"I can understand your need to be there, Beth, but I can't let you. Please, I'm asking you to trust me. Let me handle this for you. This is what I do. I eliminate threats. And I will eliminate Kline. You have my word on it."

I don't want to disrupt our quiet moment by arguing with him, so I let it go for now. But I'm not giving up so easily. I want to be there when it happens. I can't sit back and let Shane take all the risk on my behalf.

"Come on," he says, sitting up. "I'm pretty sure I hear Cooper rattling around in the kitchen. Knowing his predilection for spoiling you, I'm sure there will be pancakes this morning. Let's go see."

* * *

As it turns out, Cooper is making pancakes, this time with fresh blueberries and whipped cream. The tall, stoic man with close-cropped gray hair has no other family that I'm aware of, so I think he needs us as much as we need him.

Cooper's the designated cook in this household. Shane can't cook worth a darn, and I've never learned how. When I was at home, my mom insisted on doing all the cooking. The kitchen was her private domain. She loves to cook, and food is love, and all of that, so she kept me well fed. And during college, I moved in with Gabrielle, who was in training to be a chef, and she insisted on doing all the cooking. So, if Shane and I were left to our own devices, we'd starve if not for take-out.

I sidle up next to Cooper, who's standing at the stove wearing a white apron with black lettering that says *World's Greatest Cook*. "Would you teach me how to cook?"

"You want to learn how to cook?" He sounds more than a little skeptical.

"I figure one of us should know how to do it, and I don't think it's going to be Shane."

Cooper laughs. "Good point. Of course I'll teach you how to cook. Why didn't your mom teach you?"

I shrug. "Cooking is Mom's thing. She loves cooking."

"You can start by keeping an eye on the pancakes while I whip the cream." He hands me a spatula and chuckles. "Just don't let them burn, kiddo. It's not rocket science."

As I tend to the pancakes that are as big as dinner plates, I watch Cooper whisk the cream. Like Gabrielle and my mom, he doesn't do things by half-measures. He goes all out.

I happen to glance across the kitchen and notice his gun and holster lying on a counter. I find myself staring at the big black gun.

Cooper is the lead shooting instructor for McIntyre Security, Inc. When he was in the military, he did a lot of gun training, sniper training even. Now he supervises gun training for Shane's employees at a private shooting range outside of the city.

I've always been afraid of guns. I've never even seen one up close except for Tyler's, and he usually keeps his gun concealed when he's around me. But since meeting Shane, I've gotten accustomed to seeing people around me armed. The guns still make me nervous, but maybe if I learned how to shoot, I'd grow more comfortable with them. If I was armed, Howard Kline couldn't hurt me again—no one could.

"Cooper, will you teach me how to shoot?"

He stops whisking the cream and looks at me, his expression neutral. He's studying me as if he's not sure he heard me correctly.

"I want to learn how to shoot."

He frowns. "Beth, honey, why do you want to learn how to shoot?"

I don't remember much of the aftermath of my nightmare last night, but I do remember Cooper coming into our bedroom and laying his hand on my leg, patting me. He must have heard me screaming. "You know why."

He shakes his head. "You don't need to carry a gun. You're surrounded by people who are armed—and professionally trained. Guns are dangerous, honey. A gun in an untrained hand often leads to tragedy."

"I know that. But if I was trained—"

Shane strolls into the kitchen holding a folded-up copy of *The Chicago Tribune* under his arm and reading something on his phone. "Trained to do what?"

"She wants gun training," Cooper says, scowling as he resumes whipping the cream with a little more force than necessary.

Shane drops the newspaper on the breakfast counter and looks at me like I've sprouted a second head. "Hell no. No way."

I roll my eyes at his reaction. "Shane. All of your employees are armed. They all have concealed carry permits. Why can't I?"

Shane walks over to me, takes the spatula out of my hand and sets it down, then pulls me into his arms. "For starters, you aren't one of my employees. You're my girlfriend. Besides, you don't need to defend yourself. We'll do that for you."

For a split second, I'm tempted to bring up Andrew Morton and how badly that went, but that would be unfair. Shane had argued with my brother until he was blue in the face to have Lia in my office with me at the library, but Tyler—who was Shane's client at the time—had refused to allow it because he didn't want me to know what was going on. If Shane had gotten his way, Andrew never would've had a chance to hurt me. I can't blame Shane. But I'm not giving up. "I may be your girlfriend, but that doesn't preclude me from learning how to shoot a gun. It's a free country, Shane. If Cooper won't do it, then I'll find someone— "

"Food's ready!" Cooper says, whipping off his apron, essentially putting an end to the conversation. "Eat while it's hot."

* * *

The three of us eat a wonderful spread at the breakfast bar. In addition to the pancakes with blueberries and whipped cream, Cooper went all out this morning and made bacon and hash browns. And, of course, there's always freshly ground coffee. I suspect I'm getting the special treatment this morning because of the rough night I had.

Cooper really should get married, because he'd make some lucky... guy's... dreams come true. He's handsome and amazingly fit for an older guy. But more than that, he's smart, kind, loyal, funny, and obviously a great cook. Yeah, he needs someone special in his life.

Shane's phone chimes as he's sipping his coffee, and he peers at the screen. "Lia's on her way up."

I swallow my last bite of breakfast, wash it down with the little bit of coffee left in my cup, and hop off my barstool. I check the time. "Oh, my god, I'm so late! Vanessa's going to kill me!"

I race back to our bedroom to finish washing up and get dressed for the bookstore. When I emerge, Lia's sitting at the breakfast bar eating. As soon as she sees me, she finishes off her coffee and stands. "Princess, you're late."

"I know!" Breathless from rushing around, I slip on my sandals and grab my purse. "Let's go."

Shane walks us into the foyer and kisses me before I step into the elevator. "I'll see you at dinner," he says. "Have a good day, sweetheart."

"Thanks. You too." I gather my hair up into an impromptu twist and secure it with a scrunchie. "Do I look okay?"

Shane smiles as the elevator doors begin to close. "You look perfect."

Lia rolls her eyes at me and shakes her head. "You guys make me sick."

꩜ 25

I'm already ten minutes late, and it will take us at least ten more minutes to get to the bookstore. "Maybe she won't notice me coming in late."

Lia chuckles. "You have to clock in, remember? She'll know."

"Oh, right. Crap." There's no avoiding the wrath of Vanessa now.

Lia gives me a sardonic look. "You do recall that you're the owner of this fine establishment, right? Why do you care what Vanessa thinks?"

Lia has a point. I suppose being the owner does give me a certain degree of latitude. But still, I want to set a good example, and I don't want to rock the boat, not even where Vanessa is concerned. After all, she was there first.

* * *

Lia hands me off to Sam at the entrance to Clancy's, and Sam follows me upstairs to the employee lounge so I can clock-in and put my purse away. After that, we head back downstairs to the sales counter, where I find Erin filling in for me at my station.

"I'm sorry I'm late," I tell her, breathless as I take over in the middle of a transaction.

She smiles at me. "No problem. I covered for you. I don't think Vanessa noticed."

Sam steps back out of the way, trying to be inconspicuous, which is tough to do when you're six feet tall and as strikingly good looking as he is. With his lean, muscular torso and gorgeous chocolate-brown eyes—not to mention that amazing, wild hair pulled back in a ponytail—it's kind of hard for him to simply blend in to the background. His jeans have so many rips in them I'm afraid they'll disintegrate. And his grunge T-shirt says PUNK.

"Hi, Sam," Erin says, and I swear she's blushing. Oh, my. I think Sam has an admirer.

"Hi, Erin," he replies, smiling politely before turning his attention to a book on military history.

Sam doesn't seem to have the same interest in Erin that she has in him, and I have to wonder why. Erin's a darling girl, with a sweet face as well as a sweet disposition. And she's got all the right curves in all the right places. But Sam seems oblivious to her charms.

When I wonder if he already has a girlfriend, I realize I know nothing about him. "Sam, are you married?"

He glances up from his book. "No."

"Got a girlfriend?"

He shakes his head. "Nope."

I turn to smile at my next customer and about have a heart attack. Vanessa is standing in front of my register, her arms crossed over her gray pinstriped suit.

"Ms. Jamison, how nice of you to join us."

I paste what I hope is a contrite smile on my face. "Good morning, Vanessa. I'm sorry I was late this morning."

"Don't let it happen again." Then her amber eyes drift over to Sam, who's seemly engrossed in his book and paying her no mind. "Please don't handle the merchandise, Mr. Harrison. This isn't a public library."

Good grief, could the woman make him feel any more unwanted here? Sam's just doing his job, and he's making the best of it. I'm sure there are a million things he'd rather be doing than babysitting me. I'm tired of Vanessa giving him a hard time.

I look pointedly at Vanessa. "Can I speak with you? In private."

"I'll be in my office when your shift is over. Come see me then."

As Vanessa walks away, Erin and I both look at Sam. He rolls his eyes at us, perfectly unfazed by Vanessa's hostility. We both start laughing.

* * *

I'm in the middle of ringing up another customer when Erin brings me a message. "Beth, there's someone here from *The Chicago Scoop* to see you."

That takes me by surprise. Why would someone from the newspaper want to talk to me? I follow the line of Erin's gaze and see a stocky man in jeans and a button-down shirt standing a few feet away, a digital camera slung around his neck. He lifts the camera with a smile on his face and takes several shots of me standing behind the sales counter.

I look at Erin. "What does he want with me?"

Erin shrugs. "He said he wants to ask you some questions about Clancy's. He said he's doing a piece on local women business owners."

"All right. I'll talk to him." I finish ringing up a customer and ask Erin to take over for me. As she steps into my place, I walk out from behind the sales counter and head toward the reporter.

"Hold up, Beth," Sam says, falling in step with me. "Do you know this guy?"

I shake my head. "I've never seen him before."

Sam frowns. "I'm coming with you."

I approach the reporter and introduce myself. "You wanted to talk to me?"

He nods, extending his hand for a brisk handshake. He gives Sam a quick visual once-over, then turns his attention back to me. "Derek Sanderson, *Chicago Scoop*. Can I have a few minutes of your time?"

I take a deep breath. "Sure. Why don't we sit down in the cafe?"

The reporter follows me to the cafe, and we grab one of the available tables. Sam takes a seat at the table next to ours and sits so that he has his eyes on both of us.

"So, what can I do for you, Mr. Sanderson?" I say, folding my hands on the table in front of me. I'm still at a complete loss as to why he'd want to talk to me. I focus on my breathing, trying to remain calm. Strangers make me nervous, let alone one who specifically asks to talk to me.

"Derek, please." He removes the camera from around his neck and sets it on the table, along with his phone. "I only recently learned that ownership of Clancy's changed hands a couple of months ago. I didn't realize the old guy had sold the place."

I nod. "That's right. Mr. Clancy sold the store and retired to Florida." I can't help wondering how Sanderson found out about the sale. Shane didn't publicize it. In fact, he went out of his way to keep it quiet.

Derek shakes his head in disbelief. "I thought that old relic would die here before he'd ever agree to sell."

I smile. I only met Mr. Clancy a few times before he relocated south. In his 90s, Mr. Clancy was surprisingly still a spry man, with a mind as sharp as a tack.

Derek takes out a small digital recorder and sets it on the table between us. "Do you mind?"

I shake my head. "Go right ahead."

"Thanks." He presses the record button. "So, Beth Jamison, you bought Clancy's Bookshop."

"Well, my boyfriend bought it, actually."

"But it's in your name. You're listed as the sole owner."

"Yes, that's right." Those aren't questions, those are statements. Derek must have looked into the sale already.

"Your boyfriend is Shane McIntyre, the CEO of McIntyre Security."

"Yes." Again, not a question.

"Are you and McIntyre serious? You haven't been dating that long. Three months or so, according to my sources. Buying this store for you seems like a pretty big move on his part."

"Mr. Sanderson, why exactly do you want to talk to me? Erin said you're doing a story on local women business owners."

He grins. "Yes, that's right. I was just curious. Shane McIntyre is a big name in Chicago. When he does something, it makes news. And the fact that he bought something this big for a woman—well, that's news. I had to check it out for myself. You're awfully young to own a business like this, and the fact that your boyfriend bought it for you seems, well, unusual. I write a business column for the paper. I think my readers would be fascinated to read more about you and

McIntyre."

I smile. "Well, there's not much to tell, really."

"Are you engaged to McIntyre?"

I suddenly don't like Derek Sanderson's interest in my personal life. He's digging, but for what, I'm not sure. "That's private information, Mr. Sanderson."

He nods. "Do you mind if I ask you this… you were assaulted by a young man named Andrew Morton just a little over two months ago at the Kingston Medical School library, where you worked."

"That isn't a question, Mr. Sanderson." He's not interviewing me, he's digging for dirt—either on me or on Shane, and that makes me very uncomfortable.

"I understand that Shane McIntyre assaulted Andrew Morton at a hospital fundraiser just a few days prior to the assault on you. Do you think there's a connection?"

My face flushes, and I've had enough. I don't know what he's looking for, but he's definitely looking for something. I glance at Sam, who has his fingertips up to a listening device in his ear.

I rise to my feet, pushing my chair back. "I'd better get back to work now, Mr. Sanderson."

He picks up his camera. "Wait. Do you mind if I take some more photos?"

Sam snatches the guy's camera right out of his hands.

"Hey!" Sanderson yells, grabbing for his camera. "You can't do that!"

"Yes, I can," Sam says, easily holding the camera out of Sanderson's reach. "This is private property."

Sam removes the data card from the camera and slips it into his jeans pocket. Then he hands the camera back to Derek. "You'll get your data card back after we've deleted the images of Ms. Jamison."

"That's my personal property! You can't just take it!"

"Yes, I can," Sam says. "Don't worry, I'll have it delivered to your office by four o'clock this afternoon."

Sanderson looks at me accusingly, obviously put out by Sam's actions. "Is this really necessary? It's just an article in the local interest section of the paper."

"There won't be any article," Sam says. He stares hard at Sanderson. "You got that? No article, no photos. Ms. Jamison is completely off limits to you."

Angry, Derek picks up his digital recorder, turns it off, and slips it in his shirt pocket. Then he slings his camera strap over his neck and glares at Sam. "We'll see about that, asshole! Ever heard of freedom of the press?" And then he storms off.

Sam and I watch Derek as he marches toward the exit and storms out.

I took at Sam. "What was that all about? He only took a couple shots of me at the sales counter."

"Mack saw the whole thing from upstairs." Then Sam points at his earpiece. "Mack called Shane to tell him a reporter was here talking to you, and Shane said to shut it down. He doesn't want you talking to reporters. Shane said absolutely no publicity."

* * *

The rest of my shift passes without incident, and I think I have the hang of checking out customers. I'm glad, because I'm anxious to work my way through the store and learn everything I need to learn as quickly as possible.

I head up the staircase to the administrative offices to have a word with Vanessa. Sam's with me, of course, and Erin joins us. She's teetering dangerously on the stairs in her stilettos—the employee dress code is yet another thing I need to talk to Vanessa about.

Sam opens the office door for us and we file in. Vanessa's talking to the guy with the Harry Potter glasses who's seated at a computer—the payroll guy, Charlie.

I don't relish the idea of having an audience for my conversation with Vanessa. I want to tell her to back off Sam, and I really don't want him to hear this. I turn back to face Sam. "I'd like to speak to Vanessa alone. Would you mind waiting out in the hall?"

"Yes, I'd mind."

"Sam—"

He shakes his head. "My job is to shadow you. I can't do that from out in the hallway."

"But I'm just going to have a brief talk with Vanessa."

"Save your breath, boss."

I sigh. I don't want to do this in front of Sam, but it looks like he's not going to give me a choice. "Fine. Suit yourself."

"I plan to," he says.

Vanessa turns to look at the three of us and scowls, and I can't wait to hear what she's going to say next.

"What?" I say to her, because my patience is wearing thin. Vanessa needs to get over herself and start acting like a decent human being instead of the manager from hell.

She crosses her arms over her chest and taps a long, manicured fingernail on her sleeve. "What can I do for you, Miss Jamison?"

"For starters, you can call me *Beth*."

"If you insist."

"I do. And secondly, you need to stop harassing Sam. He's just doing his job. I'm sure there are other things he'd rather be doing than shadowing me, but this is his assignment right now, so just leave him alone."

Vanessa's lips thin. "Is that it?"

"No." Actually, I'm just getting warmed up. "I want you to relax the dress code for the assistant managers. Erin shouldn't be wearing three-inch heels if she doesn't feel comfortable in them. She's going to fall and break her neck."

Vanessa bristles at my request. "We have standards to uphold here, *Beth*. I expect my assistant managers to act like professionals, and they should dress like them too."

"Shoes don't define the person, Vanessa. All I'm asking is that Erin be able to wear whatever shoe she feels comfortable in. She can be *professional* in a different style of shoe."

Vanessa glares at Erin as if this is all Erin's fault.

"Don't blame Erin," I say. "This is my idea, not hers. And honestly, it's not a request."

Vanessa's jaw tightens and she swallows hard. "Very well. Anything else?"

"No, that's all." Actually there is more, but I don't dare press Vanessa more than I have right now.

"Then if you'll excuse me, I have work to do." And with that, Vanessa turns on her stylish, four-inch pointy-toed heels and disappears into her private office.

My shoulders slump and I frown. "That woman's never going to like me."

"Thanks, Beth," Erin says, putting her arm around my shoulders and giving me a little squeeze.

Erin's staring at Vanessa's closed office door and looking a little pale.

"Are you worried?" I say.

"About Vanessa?" Erin laughs half-heartedly. "Well, maybe a

little."

"If she retaliates against you, let me know."

Erin nods, but she doesn't look very reassured.

"I mean it. You tell me if she does. It'll be fine. Don't worry."

But I'm not as confident as I'd like to be. I'm afraid one of these days Vanessa's going to go too far, and when she does, I'll have no choice but to fire her.

* * *

When I go back downstairs, I find Lia waiting for me at the front entrance to the store. "Where to, Princess?"

Where to? There are so many things I want to do. Self-defense training, gun training. But first things first. I find Liam in the contact list on my phone and hit the call button.

He answers right away. "Hey, Beth. What's up?"

"Do you have any free time this afternoon? I want to start self-defense training."

"Did Shane okay this?"

Not exactly, but I'm not about to tell Liam that. "I got my cast off, yeah, so I'm cleared for action."

"I've got some free time this afternoon. Can you be here at three?"

That gives me nearly an hour to pick up some proper workout clothes and shoes and head over to Shane's building. "Sure. I'll see you then." I end the call and look at Lia. "I need workout clothes."

She narrows her eyes at me. "Shane didn't okay this."

I shrug. "I'm doing it."

She shakes her head. "It's your funeral. You'll need proper outfitting, then. I know the place. Let's go."

Fortunately, Clancy's is located right in the middle of shopping central. Lia and I head out from the bookstore on foot, and she takes me to the Nike store just down the street, which is the holy grail of athletic wear—three full glorious floors of it. I quickly pick out what I need—a few sets of workout shorts and tanks, a couple of sports bras, an awesome pair of sneakers, and a gym bag to carry it all in.

We take a cab to the McIntyre Security building. When we arrive, Lia walks me up to the third floor where the martial arts studio is located, then heads off to God knows where, leaving me in Liam's more than capable hands.

The studio is impressive by any standard. Glossy wooden floors are covered with numerous black workout mats. There's a boxing ring, a half-dozen black punching bags suspended from the ceiling by chains, kick bags, and dummy torsos hanging from the ceiling just waiting to be kicked and pummeled and otherwise abused.

The interior walls are all mirrored and the external wall is mostly windows, so it's a bright, airy space. The studio is empty at the moment and eerily quiet. I can hear a radio coming from somewhere off in the distance, perhaps from the locker room?

I walk inside, looking around, feeling my heart rate pick up with excitement. I'm finally going to do this. I don't want to get Liam in trouble with Shane, but I'm tired of putting off my training. I need this.

Liam walks out of the locker room dressed in a martial arts uniform—black trousers with a black jacket and a matching black belt. His hair is damp, but whether from sweat or a recent shower, I'm not sure. When he draws near, I detect a hint of soap, so I'm guessing it was a shower.

He glances at the shopping bags in my hand. "I see you've got your gear. Good. Go through those doors there to the locker room and change. Then meet me back here."

When I come back out, he's waiting for me, his arms crossed. He has a skeptical look on his face. "Shane okayed this?"

My smile falters. "My cast is off, Liam." I flex my left arm. "So I'm good to go." I didn't actually lie to him, but I omitted a key fact, such as the fact that Shane didn't okay this. He wants me to wait at least a month. But I don't want to wait.

Liam mouth curves in a knowing smile, and for a moment, I'm afraid he's going to change his mind. But then he shrugs and heads over to one of the mats muttering, "It's your funeral."

We warm up with some basic calisthenics, and then he has me following along with him as he does some very basic, repetitive movements that seem pretty pointless to me, but I'm not about to question him. He's the expert here. I know he's competed and won several MMA championships, so I have no doubt he knows what he's doing. As a mixed martial arts teacher, he's mastered many forms of fighting.

He teaches me a little routine with steps and lunges and turns that I'm supposed to practice until I can do it without thinking. He gives me some explanation about muscle memory and the importance of repetition so that the movements become second nature.

Before I know it, nearly an hour has passed, and he still hasn't taught me anything useful, like how to fight off an assailant, which is what I really want to learn. Or better yet, how to gouge out someone's eyes or stab someone in their carotid artery—those would be useful skills to have.

"That's it for today," Liam says, walking off the mat. He grabs a white hand towel from a cart and tosses it to me.

He's not even breathing hard and I, on the other hand, am panting and sweating like a pig. I definitely need to start exercising more.

"That's it?" I say, unable to mask my disappointment.

"You have to learn to walk before you can run, Beth."

"Can't we do a little more?"

He shakes his head, looking at the clock on the wall. "I'm sorry, but I teach a self-defense class for employees in ten minutes."

Just as he says that, two women carrying gym bags walk into the studio and wave to Liam before heading to the locker rooms.

"Can I join the class?" A real class with real students—that sounds like exactly what I need.

"It's fine with me, if Shane okays it. We meet Mondays, Wednesdays, and Fridays from four to five. Now you'd better go out into the hallway and placate my big brother, because he looks like he's about to have an aneurism."

I glance out the viewing window, but I don't see anyone.

"Oh, he's out there, trust me," Liam says, grinning. "He's been pacing out there like a tiger with a thorn in his paw the entire time. He didn't clear you for working out, did he?"

"Well, not in so many words, no. But I did get the cast off. That was his main concern."

After a quick trip back to the locker room to change into my own clothes, I walk out into the hallway and find Shane leaning against the far wall, his arms crossed over his chest. Liam was right—he doesn't look happy. My stomach gives a little lurch, but I'm determined not to let him intimidate me. I know he's just trying to protect me, but sometimes he goes too far.

"Don't even start!" I tell him, trying to head off the inevitable lecture. "My cast is off, and my arm feels fine. *I'm* fine. I'm joining Liam's self-defense class, so just deal with it."

I can see the muscles in his jaw flexing as he mulls over what I said. Then his expression eases up and he smiles at me and takes my hand without a word. He leads me to the bank of elevators down the hall and steers me inside one of the cars when the doors open.

"Where are we going?"

Inside the elevator car, Shane pushes the button for his floor. Then he pushes me gently up against the wall and closes in on me, his hands braced on both sides of my head, caging me in.

"You might not want to get too close," I tell him. "I'm sweaty, and I'm pretty sure I need a shower."

He ignores my warning as he leans in and bends down to whisper in my ear. His warm breath ruffles my hair, which makes me shiver. "What happened to taking it easy for *four weeks*? You didn't even make it one week."

I flex my left arm and look up into his impassive gaze. I can't tell if he's really mad or just playing with me. "My arm's fine, Shane."

"I swear to God, Beth, if you get hurt—"

"I'm not going to get hurt. All we did was warm up and do repetitious little lunges. A five-year-old could have done it."

Shane's hands come up to frame my face. "What's going on, sweetheart? Why are you pushing yourself like this? Why are you pushing *me*? You have nothing to prove."

But he's wrong. I have everything to prove.

When we arrive at his floor, Shane leads me into the executive suite. We pass through the glass doors into the inner sanctum, and he marches me right past Diane's desk.

Diane glances up at the two of us with a surprised expression. "Oh, hello, dear," she says, smiling kindly at me. "Shane, honey, Jack Elliot's on the phone for you—"

Shane shakes his head. "I'll call him back later."

Once we're inside his office, Shane shuts the door, then turns me to face him, holding me by my upper arms. "Listen, Beth—"

I pull out of his hold. "No. You listen. I'm perfectly capable of having self-defense training. And gun training, for that matter."

He frowns and crosses his arms, contemplating me for several long moments. "Self-defense, fine. Gun training, no. I don't want you anywhere near a gun."

I'm getting tired of his paternal attitude. "You have no right –"

"Why are you so dead set on all this training?"

"Because I'm tired of being afraid! Howard Kline's been a shadow hanging over me for my entire life. I want it to stop!"

"It will stop! But you've got to let me handle it. "

My eyes prickle with unshed tears, which only aggravates me more. "I can't even sleep through the night because of him! I want him gone. He never should have been released—that monster has no right to be loose on the streets."

There's a quiet knock on the door, and I flinch.

"Not now!" Shane growls.

The door opens anyway, just far enough for Diane to poke her head through the opening. "You might want to keep it down in here, kids. We can hear you out here."

Hearing Diane refer to Shane as a kid makes me laugh. Shane scowls at me as he walks to the door and eases Diane back through the doorway. "Thank you," he says to her. "We'll try to keep it down." Then he closes the door and locks it.

When he stalks to me, I retreat a few steps. Without warning, he leans down and hauls me over his shoulder in a fireman's hold.

I squirm in his arms. "Put me down!"

"No."

Shane carries me into the attached apartment and kicks the door closed. He heads straight for the bedroom, where he dumps me on the bed. As he loosens his tie and whips it off, I sit up.

"Um, Shane, what are you doing?"

Then he starts to unbutton his white shirt. "Isn't it kind of obvious?"

I'm mesmerized by the fact that he's undressing during work hours. "You want to have sex? Right now?"

"That's the idea, yes. You come into my office, half-dressed, and yeah, it's going to occur to me."

"I thought we were arguing about Kline."

"No, you're arguing, Beth. I'm stating facts. If you insist on taking self-defense training, fine. But I draw the line at guns and Howard Kline. I don't want you anywhere near either of them, and that's not up for debate."

Whatever I was going to say next flies right out of my head when he shrugs off his shirt and drops it on the floor. As always, the sight of his naked torso robs me of speech. I've never seen a more beautiful sight than Shane's chest, with his broad shoulders and well-defined musculature. My mouth goes dry and the blood in my body begins to pool between my legs. The effect he has on me isn't fair.

He unbuckles his belt, then pauses to look at me. "Well? What are you waiting for? Get undressed."

He's still mad, and he expects me to strip for him? Just like that? "No."

Shane crawls on the bed toward me, half undressed, looming over me like a grouchy, sexed-up bear, and I fall back on the bed trying not to laugh. He leans down to nuzzle the side of my neck and behind my ear where he knows damn well I'm incredibly sensitive and ticklish.

My violent shiver is followed by giggles. "You don't fight fair."

He grins. "I know. Now take off your clothes." His voice is little more than a low growl. "Please."

My entire body responds to his deep, raspy voice, and I realize how much I like this side of Shane. How he can be sexy and playful at the same time, I don't know. Not only am I throbbing between my legs, but my nipples are tingling, tightening almost to the point of pain. He's distracting me with sex, and I'm okay with that. I want this Shane, this aggressive, overbearing, growling Shane.

My face heats up as I grin back at him, wanting to taunt the bear a little. "You want me to take my clothes off? Then make me."

His blue eyes glitter in the face of my challenge, the corners crinkling. I could get lost in those eyes.

His hands go to the waistband of my skirt and he pulls it right down my legs, taking my panties along with it. I can't help squealing when my body is suddenly bare from the waist down. He pulls my sandals off next and tosses them unceremoniously to the floor. Then he sits me up and pulls off my top, leaving me in just a white satin and lace bra.

He gazes down at me, his eyes burning, and brushes his thumb against my nipple through the lacey fabric, making the tip tighten into a hard, tiny nub. My breasts are tingling, and I shiver.

"Are you cold?" he says.

"Yes."

"I can fix that," he says, reaching around my back to unfasten my bra and pull it off me.

He bends down, his mouth warm on my breast as he sucks on one of my nipples. His tongue dances over the sensitized little tip, and I go from cold to hot in an instant.

He pulls back, a little more serious now as he studies me. "Are you okay?"

I nod. Leave it to him to take a time-out in the midst of seduction to make sure I'm okay with this before he proceeds to ravish me. But as much as I appreciate the care he takes with me, I want the growling bear back. I reach out to cup his erection through his slacks, rubbing him firmly with my palm. I'm rewarded with a deep grunt, and then he lunges back on his feet so he can strip out of the rest of his clothing.

Finally naked, he crawls back onto the bed, looming over me. I lie back and reach up to cup his head, threading my fingers through his hair. I bring his mouth down to mine, and we devour each other until we're both breathing hard.

My breath catches on a hitch. "I thought you were mad at me."

He shakes his head. "Not mad. Just frustrated, and a little jealous."

"Jealous? Why?"

"Watching you with Liam. Watching you with any man makes me jealous."

"But he's your brother!"

He shrugs. "He's still a guy."

I shake my head, perplexed. "And why frustrated?"

"Because you keep wanting to do things I consider risky. That frustrates the hell out of me. Trying to keep you safe is turning into a full-time job."

His kisses me hungrily, his mouth swallowing my reply. His lips nudge mine open, and when his tongue slips between my lips to caress mine, he moans.

He slips his hands between my legs and pushes them open. One finger sinks into my wet opening, while his thumb rubs tiny circles on my clitoris. Already I'm achy and desperate to come.

He rolls over onto his back and pulls me over him so that I'm straddling his lap. His hands go to my hips and he positions me over his cock. "Ride me. Put me inside you and ride me. I want to watch you come on me."

He knows how much I like this—being on top. Not only does it help with my anxiety, but I can control the angle of his penis and direct the head of his erection right where I need it. Plus, I love to torture him by setting a nice, slow pace—a slow burn—and drawing out both our orgasms.

His hand is wrapped around the base of his erection, angling it at me. I position myself so that the blunt head of his cock brushes against the lips of my sex, and I tease him, rubbing myself on him.

"Put me inside you," he growls, his voice rough now with demand.

I wrap my fingers around his length and continue to brush the head of him against me, coating him with my slickness. Beneath my fingertips, his erection is thick and hot, pulsing with excitement. His skin is like smooth velvet stretched over a hot steel core. The ropey vein that runs the length of him is throbbing in time with the rapid beat of his heart.

His eyes narrow. "Damn it, Beth. No teasing."

He's gripping my waist now with his strong hands, encouraging me to sink down onto him. But the build-up is too sweet to rush, so I take my time. I steal some of the silky wetness from my sex and stroke his erection from root to tip.

His hips are rocking now as he tries to nudge himself closer to his destination.

I smile as I dip down to leisurely brush the head of his cock with my sex. "I thought you said patience is a virtue." He's always telling me to be patient, now it's my turn.

He closes his eyes and groans, his fingers flexing restlessly on my hips. "If I have to exercise any more patience, I'm likely to die of a heart attack."

My teasing has backfired on me, because now I'm aching to have him inside me. I reach down with my free hand to stroke my clitoris, and that only makes the ache worse. When I groan with pleasure, he opens his eyes and watches me touch myself, his nostrils flaring. To spare us both further torment, I lower myself on his cock and gasp as the broad head pushes into me, pressing through wet, swollen tissues as he opens me wide and stretches me. Slowly I work myself down onto him, wriggling and rocking my body as I sink an inch at a time.

When I'm seated as far as I can go, I lean forward, bracing my hands on his chest and angling myself so that the head of his cock drags against a tender spot deep inside me, one that steals my breath and ratchets up my release. Pleasure blooms inside me as I begin to rock myself on him at my own sweet pace. I'm not going to rush this, despite his growling and groaning, because the feel of him stroking inside me is exquisite.

I revel in the myriad sensations bombarding me. The sound of his heavy breathing; the scent of his warm, male body, which tantalizes me to no end; the pressure of his erection deep inside me, hot and hard and thick. I can feel his heart hammering beneath my palms as I brace my hands on his chest.

When the inevitable explosion hits me, I cry out, a shameless keening sound. Shane throws his head back in the pillow, gritting his teeth as my sex squeezes him like a fist. When I brush my thumbs over his flat, beaded nipples, he bucks into me with a loud, guttural cry and explodes in a forceful rush of liquid heat. I collapse on his chest, and he wraps his arms around me, stroking my back gently as we both come down from the high.

He nuzzles my temple and breathes "I love you" against my heated skin.

Shane rolls us to the side, his cock still semi-erect inside me, and he gently thrusts in and out, gliding easily through our combined juices. His movements are unhurried and tender, as if there is nowhere more important he needs to be right now than lazing in bed with me. My chest aches with emotion as I watch his face.

Warm and satiated, and comforted by the proximity of Shane's heat and scent, I feel my eyelids grow heavy. Sex always makes me sleepy. It also shuts my brain off for a while so I can find some peace. It doesn't hurt that we're tucked away safe and sound in his little office hideaway. I want to stay hidden here forever.

A huge yawn slips out before I can stifle it.

"You're sleepy," he murmurs, as he trails gentle kisses across my forehead. "It's okay. You can sleep."

I feel bad because I must be interfering with his work. "You can go back to work if you need to. Don't let me keep you."

Shane grabs his phone from off the nightstand and makes a call. "Diane, I'm done for the rest of day," he says in a low voice, as he strokes my bare back. "No interruptions, please."

He turns to me. "Get some rest. I'll grab my laptop and work here in bed for a while. Then we'll have dinner."

* * *

I must have dozed off, because the next thing I know, I open my eyes to a dimly lit room. Shane is sitting beside me in bed, working on his laptop. He's wearing a pair of faded jeans and a T-shirt. His feet are bare.

"What time is it?" I mumble, trying to rouse myself from a drowsy fog.

He glances at the laptop screen. "Seven-thirty."

I sit up in bed, and the sheet falls to my lap. "I slept three hours! Why didn't you wake me?"

He shrugs. "You must have needed it. It's okay. I got a lot of work done, and I enjoyed watching you sleep."

I run my fingers through my hair and I can tell it's a tangled rat's nest. I'm also wet between my legs—a very obvious reminder of what we did in this bed.

I groan. "I've got to get cleaned up." I crawl as gracefully as possible off the foot of the bed, pretty sure he's staring at my ass.

He chuckles. "Need any help?"

I glance back at him, and he *is* looking at my butt, that bastard. "I think I can manage on my own."

"Hurry, I'm hungry. After you get cleaned up, let's go eat."

We leave the apartment and walk through his office, which is eerily silent. Diane must have come in here and shut everything down, including Shane's PC, because everything is off. Her desk is vacated for the evening—in fact, we don't see anyone around the executive suite.

We head down to the parking garage.

"Where to?" he says, taking my hand as we exit the elevator. "What sounds good?"

I feel a little disoriented from my impromptu nap, and I just want to go back to the penthouse and snuggle with Shane on the couch in front of a fire. "Can we go home and order something in? Maybe watch a movie?"

He reaches into the car to fasten my seatbelt for me, and I smile. Some habits are hard to break.

"Sure," he says. "That sounds good."

❧ 26

We pick up carry-out from our favorite Thai restaurant near Shane's office building and bring it home with us. As soon as we arrive home, we change into comfy clothes, Shane in a pair of sweats and a T-shirt, and I in pajama bottoms and a cami—sans bra.

With our feast spread out on the coffee table before us, we eat sitting on the sofa in front of a blazing fire. There's something soothing and romantic about the crackle and scent of burning wood in a big stone hearth. We're the only ones home at the moment, so it's quiet and cozy, just the two of us.

Shane opens a bottle of red wine, and we each have a glass with our meal. I'm feeling pretty lazy and sated from the impromptu afternoon sex, following by a nap and now a glass of wine, which warms my belly nicely, along with the deliciously spicy Thai food.

After we finish eating, we sprawl comfortably on the couch and watch the fire and sip more wine. Shane's arms are around me, and his warm hand slips beneath my top and palms one of my breasts. When his thumb and finger start playing with my nipple, causing it to tighten and tingle, shooting off all kinds of fireworks inside me, I'm thinking we should take the party to our bedroom.

I know we should when he begins to press light kisses along the curve of my throat, working his way to the back of my ear. I shiver in his arms, and he chuckles. But then the elevator dings and we find ourselves suddenly with company.

Cooper walks into the great room—that's not a surprise as he lives here—but he's accompanied by Lia, Jake, and Jamie—half of the McIntyre siblings. I have to admit I'm surprised to see Jamie here. I've never seen him anywhere other than the Kenilworth estate. And Jamie's not alone. He brought Gus, who's looking very smart in his service dog harness.

"Hey, guys," Shane says, casually withdrawing his hand from underneath my top as we sit up.

Jake makes a beeline for the bar and grabs bottles of beer from the fridge and hands them out.

Lia plops down on the couch, inserting herself between me and Shane, and inspects our food cartons on the coffee table. "Aw, they're empty. Why didn't you save me some?"

"Because we weren't expecting you," Shane says, giving her a wry look. "Next time, call ahead."

"That's okay," Lia says. "We ate. But I would never turn down ... what is it anyway? Thai? Right. I'd never turn down Thai food."

"So, to what do we owe this unexpected pleasure?" Shane says, not bothering to mask his annoyance at the interruption. "We're kind of busy here."

"Busy making out, you mean," Lia says, scoffing as she twists the cap off her beer bottle.

"We came to spar," Jake says. He takes a long drink of his beer. "You up for a few rounds? Jamie even said he might get in the ring."

Shane looks at me and shakes his head. "Sorry, guys. Beth and I have plans to watch a movie tonight."

"I don't mind," I say, looking from Shane to the others. I love watching Shane and his sibling spar.

Shane looks at me. "Are you sure? I'd be happy to kick them all out and watch a movie with you."

"Really, I don't mind. I'd like to see what Jamie can do in the ring." I've seen Jamie do some amazing things, but I've never seen him in the boxing ring. I have a hard time picturing a blind man sparring.

"Yeah, Shane," Lia says. "Princess doesn't mind. Let's do it. I feel like kicking ass tonight."

"Anyone's ass in particular?" Jake says, smirking at her as he reaches out and musses her short blond hair.

She swats at his hand. "Yeah. Yours, asshole."

Jake chuckles. "In your dreams, little girl."

And the trash talk begins.

We head into the 'fight club'—that's their nickname for the martial arts studio in the penthouse. And yes, no one's allowed to talk about it, rule number one and all—apparently that joke never gets old. It's a big room, very industrial chic with exposed red brick walls, a high ceiling painted black to camouflage the air ducts and the electrical conduits, and chrome lighting fixtures that hang from the ceiling like pendulums.

There's a boxing ring in the center of the room, as well as workout areas with weight-lifting equipment and floor mats. There are also several leather sofas positioned strategically around the room for optimal viewing of the action.

Shane flips a series of light switches near the entrance to the room and the overhead lights come on. He claps Jamie on the shoulder. "You coming into the ring?"

"Maybe later," Jamie says. "I'll sit this first round out. I don't feel like showing off just yet."

"That's pretty tough talk for a blind guy," Jake says, lightly smacking Jamie on the back of the head as he passes him on the way to the locker room.

Shane gives me a quick kiss, and then he and Lia follow Jake to get changed into their workout clothes. Gus leads Jamie to a long sofa which offers a front-row view of the action. This is the first time I've seen Gus wearing a service-dog harness.

Gus failed service dog training because he's afraid of water—rain, bodies of water like ponds or lakes, even puddles on the ground. Whoever heard of a Labrador Retriever that's afraid of water? But Jamie had already met the dog a few times during his early training and had bonded with Gus, so he arranged to adopt the dog after he flunked out of service dog school. Jamie's been continuing Gus' training on his own, and apparently the pup is doing all right... as long as it's not raining, that is.

I take a seat on the sofa beside Jamie. Gus lies down at Jamie's feet and lays his big, boxy head on Jamie's boots.

I pat the dog on the head. "Gus seems to be doing well with his training."

"Yeah, he is," Jamie says.

We can hear the others in the locker room, talking trash and psyching themselves up for a big match. I try to imagine Jamie in the boxing ring and have a hard time picturing any scenario where he comes out on top. Shane and Jake and Lia are all very skilled fighters.

I just don't see how Jamie can hold his own against them. Not when he can't see what's coming.

"How are you doing?" I ask him.

I know that Jamie's been struggling with his circumstances for a while. He told me he loves living at Shane's estate, but he feels that they—Shane and Elly especially—coddle him too much.

"All right, I guess. I just finished the first draft of my new book and sent it off to my editor. While she's reviewing it, I'm taking a couple weeks off to do some serious thinking."

Jamie writes military thrillers. Thanks to his distinguished career as a Navy SEAL, he has an endless supply of harrowing stories to tell. After the explosion that destroyed his retinas and left him completely blind, Jamie turned to his other love, which is storytelling. His military experience gives him the perfect fodder for writing thrilling military action novels, all of which I've read and enjoyed.

Gus jumps to his feet and lays his head on Jamie's thigh, and Jamie absently strokes the dog's ears.

"I'm thinking about moving out," he says, his voice low. "I need to know that I can handle it on my own. Elly's wonderful—she does so much for me. Too much, actually. She can't just sit back and let me fend for myself, and that's what I need."

I hate the idea of Jamie moving out of the house, but I guess I can understand how difficult it might be for someone with his background and training to be dependent on others.

"Have you mentioned this to Shane?"

"No, not yet."

"Where would you go?"

He shrugs. "I'm thinking about getting an apartment in either Old Town or Wicker Park. I'm not going too far away. I just need to be on my own for a while, to sink or swim on my own merit."

I feel a sharp pang in my chest, and I realize how much I've grown to care about Jamie. I'd miss him terribly if he moved out. I swallow hard as I feel tears prick my eyes.

Jamie, who has an uncanny ability to read people's emotions, puts his arm around me and pulls me close. "Don't worry, I'm not going far. I'll still be around."

"Why don't you move in here with us? There's plenty of room. Or move into one of the apartments in this building?"

Jamie shakes his head. "No. That's still too close. I need to be truly on my own. I was hoping you would do me a favor."

"Of course. Anything."

"Will you come apartment hunting with me? It's hard for me to accurately judge the character of a neighborhood if I can't see it. I could use a pair of working eyes."

I chuckle and lean into him. "Of course I will."

I know Jamie's capable—very capable. But the idea of him living completely on his own scares me. He's stubborn and out to prove something to himself. I'm afraid he won't ask for help when he needs it.

"Stop worrying," he says, tightening his hold. "I'll be fine."

For a blind man, he sure sees a lot.

Dressed in workout gear, Shane and the others come out of the locker room ready and eager for action. They guys are wearing long shorts and gloves—nothing else. Lia has on shorts and a black sports bra. This is going to be fun. I love watching them go at each other. They're pretty blood thirsty.

Jake and Shane climb into the ring, padding barefoot across the floor, stretching their shoulders and arms. They fight dirty, and they fight hard. And Lia, even though she's small compared to her brothers, gives as good as she gets.

Jake and Shane take positions in opposite corners of the ring as they wait for Lia to give them the signal to begin.

Lia's the referee, and I'm going to play the role of sportscaster for Jamie, giving him a blow-by-blow recap of everything that happens in the ring. At first there's not much to tell. Shane and Jake are just dancing around each other, taking little jabs as they test the waters. But before long, the hits start coming. They're pretty evenly matched, but Shane manages to get a kick in that nearly knocks Jake off his feet.

"I thought this was boxing. Are they allowed to kick?" I say.

Jamie chuckles. "We don't play by any rules."

"If there are no rules, then why is Lia refereeing?"

"She's just there to make sure no one gets seriously hurt. She can call an end to it at any time. Sometimes they get a little too serious and a little too competitive, and don't know when to call it quits. Especially those two. Jake's a former heavyweight boxing champion, and he likes to rub it in Shane's face."

Both of them manage to score some direct hits, and they each take a fall to the mat. They fight for a good ten minutes, pretty evenly matched. They both takes hard hits and kicks, and they each end up on the floor a time or two. Lia finally calls it, not because either of the guys is hurt, but because, as she says, she's bored as hell watching and wants her turn.

So Shane steps out of the ring, and Lia pulls on her gloves. Then Shane takes over the referee job. Lia has a slight advantage over Jake, because he's been working hard for a while, and he's already a bit winded, and she's just getting started. She comes at him hard, pushing him back and keeping him on the defense as she hammers away at him.

"Wow, she's good," I say. I've seen her spar before, but I've never seen her this focused. She's relentless.

Jamie nods. "She's small, but feisty as hell. She uses her size to her advantage. She's well trained in Aikido, and that gives her an advantage over the big guys. She uses their size against them, wears them out, and then sneaks under their guard."

Lia rules the ring by keeping Jake constantly on the defensive. He's already tiring when Lia manages to trip him, sending him crashing to the floor. He just lays there, breathing heavily, while Lia dances circles around him, taunting him. He finally cries uncle, conceding the second round to Lia. Although, secretly, I think he let her win. Jake may be tough, but Lia's still his little sister.

After helping Jake and Lia out of their gloves, Shane comes over to the sofa and steps in front of Jamie, nudging his brother's black boot with his bare foot. "All right, hot shot. It's your turn. Stop flirting and show Beth what you can do."

Jamie shakes his head, grinning. "That's all right, I'm good. Listening to Jake take a beating from his baby sister was enough fun for one night."

But Shane doesn't take no for an answer. He kicks Jamie's boot, harder this time, jarring his brother's leg. The dog jumps to his feet, startled. "On your feet, soldier. You and me. I wouldn't want you to lose your edge."

Jamie sighs. "Are you sure you want Beth to see this? Her estimation of you might take a dive when she sees you pleading like a baby for mercy, because I won't let you up until you beg."

Shane winks at me. "Those are pretty tough words coming from a blind guy."

I gasp in shock, unable to believe Shane said that. I glare daggers at him. How could he say that to his own brother? But Shane smiles at me and shakes his head.

"Suit yourself," Jamie says. "It's your neck."

Jamie rises from the sofa and instructs Gus to lie down. Then he walks to the ring, holding out his hand until he comes in contact with the ropes.

Lia comes to sit beside me, drenched in sweat and practically vibrating with excitement. She squeezes my hand. "This is going to be so good."

"Are you kidding?" I hiss at her. "This is hardly a fair contest."

"Just watch and learn, grasshopper."

Jamie unlaces his boots and pulls them off, along with his socks. Then he bends down to climb through the ropes. Shane follows behind.

I shoot a quick glance at Lia. "Aren't they going to use gloves?"

She shakes her head. "They're not going to box. This will be more Krav Maga—close contact. Once Jamie gets a hand on Shane, Shane's done. Watch."

Jamie walks to the center of the ring and stands motionless, his arms hanging loosely at his sides. Shane walks in circles around his brother, as if examining him for a weak spot.

"This is ridiculous!" I hiss at Lia. "Jamie can't possibly fight Shane."

She raises her hand. "Shh. Watch."

Shane stops at Jamie's back. Suddenly, the room is quiet. Everyone holds their breath as Shane and Jamie stand there perfectly still.

Suddenly Shane explodes into motion, striking out lightning fast at Jamie. It happens so quickly, I can't even track their movements, but suddenly Shane's on his back, and Jamie's kneeling on top of him, pinning him down with a knee to his chest. Jamie has his hands around Shane's throat, his thumbs pressing hard into the sides of Shane's neck. Neither man says a word until Shane finally slaps the floor with his palm, and Jamie jumps back, putting several feet between himself and his brother.

I'm shaking my head, still not sure what just happened. "What the hell?"

Lia's grinning from ear to ear. "You know how they say a Navy SEAL can kill a man with his pinky? Well, it's true. Whether he can see or not is irrelevant."

Shane comes to his feet, rubbing his throat. Even from here I can see red marks on his neck. "Again," he says, his voice faintly raspy.

"Christ, Shane," Jamie says, shaking his head. He takes a few steps around the ring, feeling out with his right arm for the ropes.

"Maybe you just got lucky," Shane says, taunting his younger brother.

Jamie smiles. "You'd like to think so, wouldn't you?"

Jake walks up to the ring and pulls a switchblade out of his pocket. "Let's raise the stakes, gentlemen."

Jake tosses the knife to Shane, who catches it and flicks it open.

"Try not to hurt yourself, Shane," Jamie says.

Shane walks lightly on bare feet, crossing the ring toward Jamie. "If I draw blood, you lose."

Jamie shakes his head. "You are such a drama queen."

But Shane ignores the taunt and lunges, aiming the knife at Jamie's forearm.

I gasp. "My God, he's really going to cut him!"

But before Lia can even shush me, Jamie turns to meet Shane's attack, and after a flash of swift, sudden movement, Jamie has hold of Shane's arm and has Shane's wrist bent at an awkward angle. Jamie extracts the knife from Shane's hand, flips it closed and sticks it in the back pocket of his jeans.

"Hey, that's my knife!" Jake says.

"Too bad." Jamie climbs out of the ring. "To the victor go the spoils."

I glance at Lia, shaking my head in disbelief. She just grins at me. "Blind or not, Jamie knows his shit."

Barking, Gus runs to his master and jumps up on Jamie's legs.

Jamie gives the dog a hand signal, and Gus drops down on all fours. "Whose turn is it next?"

⟫ 27

Monday morning, Erin brings a copy of *The Chicago Scoop* to me at the check-out counter. She's got the paper folded open to the lifestyle section, and there's a huge picture of me standing at the check-out counter ringing up a customer.

I stare at the photo. "How did he get this picture?" I glance up at Sam. "You took the data card out of his camera."

Sam peers over my shoulder at the newspaper article. "Fuck. He must have taken this with his phone. I didn't think to confiscate his damn phone."

I read the caption under the photo.

"Beth Jamison lucks out as Chicago millionaire playboy Shane McIntyre's new arm candy. McIntyre gifted Jamison with Clancy's Bookshop on N. Michigan Avenue as an engagement gift, just weeks after she was sexually assaulted by college student Andrew Morton at her place of

work. Is this a guilty conscience at work? Sources indicate Jamison was assaulted in retaliation against McIntyre, after he assaulted the young college student at a hospital fundraising event earlier in the summer. Morton's parents are reportedly contemplating pressing assault charges against McIntyre."

My knees buckle, and Sam catches me as I stumble.

"Here, sit down," he says, pulling a chair close. Erin takes over my register for me, her attention divided between ringing up customers and trying to read the article over my shoulder.

"I wasn't sexually assaulted," I say woodenly, staring at the caption printed in black and white. I go on to read the rest of the article, growing sicker by the moment. The reporter, Derek Sanderson, implies that Shane bought Clancy for me as some kind of bribe, to prevent me from pressing charges against *him*, although Sanderson never states what these charges might be.

Exasperated, I cover my face with my hands and concentrate on regulating my breathing.

Sam lays his hand on my shoulder. "Are you all right?"

"Yeah, I just need a minute." I look at the article and shake my head in disbelief as I continue to read.

Beth Jamison is one in a long line of beautiful romantic partners for the millionaire business owner who's dated some of the most beautiful women in Chicago. But is Jamison, who is ten years younger than the business mogul, old enough and experienced enough to realize what she's getting into with McIntyre? And how long will it be before McIntyre tires of monogamy and returns to his philandering ways?

I stare at the hateful article, shaking my head. Why would someone print this garbage?

* * *

I fold the newspaper and drop it in a trash can behind the service counter, out of sight, out of mind, and try in vain to forget about it. It's impossible, of course. The article makes me sound like some kind of gold digger who's in over her head. And it makes Shane sound like a womanizer, practically accusing him of using his wealth and position to coerce and bribe people—namely me.

Erin doesn't say anything, but she keeps giving me these sympathetic, soulful looks, and that's not really helping. I can't help wondering if Shane has seen the article yet, and more importantly, how he's going to react. Oh, God, and then there's Tyler to worry about. I have no idea how he'll react if he sees it. He already doesn't trust Shane.

Abruptly, Sam grabs my upper arm and leans close to whisper in my ear. "Come with me now!"

His voice is so clipped, so tense, I don't even recognize it. He hauls me to my feet, and his grasp on my arm is bordering on painful. I try to pull away, but he tightens his hold.

"Now, Beth!" He steers me away from the check-out counter and marches me toward the stairs.

"What are you doing?" I hiss at him, surprised and slightly alarmed by the sudden change in his easy-going demeanor. I look back at Erin, who's staring after us in confusion, flustered as she rings up a customer.

"Just move," Sam says, practically pushing me up the steps.

Mack is waiting at the top to the stairs, his expression dark and calculating.

"What's going on?" I say when we reach the upper floor.

Mack looks at Sam. "Take her to the bunker and lock up. I'll watch the entrance and wait for Shane and Jake to arrive."

"Shane?" I say, more confused than ever. "Why's he—"

But Sam walks me across the upper floor toward the hallway that leads to the administrative office. We pass right by the office and the employee lounge to an unmarked door that I've never paid any attention to. There's an electronic keypad on the wall beside the door, and Sam enters a code, then presses a button. The door to the room unlocks with a loud snick, and Sam opens the door and shoves me inside.

For a moment, it's pitch black in the room and I try to back out, but Sam's in my way. My heart starts hammering in my chest, until Sam flips a light switch. I look around in surprise. It's a control room of some sort, much like the one back at the Kenilworth estate, with a bank of computers and monitors and closed-circuit television viewing screens. There are probably ten different screens aimed at different areas of the store.

"What is this place?" I feel like I've just stepped into the Twilight Zone. I didn't even know this room existed.

Sam ignores me as he punches a code into a keypad on the wall just inside the room, sealing us in.

"Have a seat," he says, nodding at a sofa across the room. There's a small seating area, with a sofa, a couple of armchairs, and a low table. Beside the seating area is a credenza with a single-serve coffee maker. "Make yourself comfortable."

"Sam, what's going on?"

I glance over at the bank of monitors and see one of the screens that's focused on the front entrance to the bookstore. I recognize the two plain-clothed security guards standing near the doors, surreptitiously watching everyone coming into the store.

"Sam, I want to know what's going on. Right now!"

Sam takes a seat at the control desk and glances back at me. "Howard Kline is on his way here. The surveillance team raised the alarm. Shane and Jake are both on their way. Shane instructed us to bring you here to the bunker and secure you."

The blood drains from my face, leaving me cold. "Kline's coming here?" My stomach drops, and I feel nauseous. "Are you sure?"

Sam nods. "The surveillance team reported him getting on a bus headed to this part of downtown. Shane thinks he might have seen the article about you in the Scoop, and if he did, he knows where you work now."

The article. "Oh, my God."

I join Sam at the control station and scan the monitors myself, watching the flow of customers in and out of the store. Suddenly, I see Shane storm inside, followed closely by Jake. Shane speaks to the undercover security guards monitoring the doors. Then, he and Jake head toward the stairs.

I lose them on the surveillance feed. "Where are they?"

Sam shakes his head as he quickly checks the other camera feeds. "I don't see Jake, but there's Shane on the stairs."

I just happen to glance again at the feed pointed at the main entrance and notice Lia walking into the building, making a beeline for the stairs.

Sam's hand goes to the communication device in his ear. He presses a button on the tiny insert and says, "She's in the bunker, with me." Then he looks at me. "That was Shane. He's coming."

I hear a buzzing sound and a click, and then the door opens. Shane walks in, and I'm so happy to see him, my knees go weak.

"Sit down, sweetheart," he says, taking my hand and leading me to the sofa.

The door opens again, and Lia walks in and secures the door behind her.

"Did you see Jake?" Shane asks her.

"He's monitoring the stairs and the elevator." Lia comes to me and drops down on the sofa beside me, nudging me with her elbow. "Well, you caused quite a commotion today, Princess, with your juicy newspaper interview!"

I shudder. "Did you read the story? It's awful."

Lia leans back on the sofa and props her boots on the coffee table. "Kline must have seen it, because he crawled out from under his rock this morning with an apparent hangover and hopped a bus downtown. He didn't even bother to shave."

Shane's talking to Jake through their wireless communication devices. Finally, Shane relays the information he's getting from his brother. "Kline's ETA is six minutes. He's off the bus and walking this way."

I'm sick to my stomach, but at the same time, I feel morbidly compelled to catch a glimpse of the man who's been haunting my nightmares for so long.

"I'm going down there," Lia says, hopping to her feet. "No fair that Jake gets to have all the fun."

Shane walks over to the bank of monitors, and I join him.

"Go sit down, honey," Shane says. His eyes are glued to the monitors.

"No. I want to see him."

Five minutes later, Howard Kline walks through the front doors of Clancy's Bookshop, under the close scrutiny of the plain-clothed security at the entrance. I can't believe his audacity. He's actually here, polluting the air inside my happy place.

My skin crawls at the sight of him. I've seen his police mug shot from before, right after he was apprehended for kidnapping me. I'm struck by how much the man has aged in the past eighteen years. He's in his mid-sixties now, but he looks like an old man—far, far older than his actual years. Prison must have taken its toll on him. That and the drugs and alcohol he's been using steadily since he was paroled.

Dressed in dirty, ill-fitting clothes, Kline walks toward the sales counter. I catch a glimpse of Jake as he moves in behind Kline.

"What's Jake doing?" I say.

"Nothing right now," Shane says. "We want to see what Kline does. And Jake will try to determine if he's armed."

Kline walks out of range of the cameras at the entrance, but soon he appears on the monitor covering the check-out counter. He's loitering around the sales counter, pretending to peruse a selection of reading glasses.

Acting casual, he scans the employees behind the counter, his gaze going from one to the next. I realize he's looking for me. I'm not there, of course, but Erin is.

"Erin's down there," I say, watching her smile at a customer, completely oblivious to the fact there's a dangerous ex-con standing not ten feet from her.

"Don't worry," Shane says. "She's fine. We've got four people down there monitoring Kline."

Then Kline moves on, again out of range of the surveillance camera.

Shane checks the other monitors for a sight of Kline. He runs the fingers of his free hand through his hair, and I smile at the familiar restless habit.

Shane touches the communication device in his ear. "Jake, can you tell if he's armed? Stay on him. If he goes for a gun, take him out. No hesitation. I don't want any bystanders getting hurt."

The thought of Kline down there with a concealed weapon scares me to death. There are scores of innocent people down there who have no idea that a monster is walking amongst them, possibly carrying a gun. "Shane, there are children down there."

"1 know, sweetheart. It's okay. We have the situation under control."

Shane tenses immediately and looks at Sam. "He's heading upstairs. Which monitor—"

"This one," Sam says, indicating one of the screens. "This one covers the hallway leading to the administrative office and this bunker."

Watching that monitor, we notice Mack standing near the entrance to the business hallway. We watch Kline walk right past the hallway to this office, right past Mack, seemingly paying him no mind. When 1 realize how close Kline is, 1 shudder.

Almost as if he can sense my agitation, Shane draws me close and brushes his lips against my temple. "He can't get in here, sweetheart. The door and walls to this room are reinforced. They're bullet proof."

"It's not me I'm worried about," 1 say. "What about the people out there? They have no idea—"

Shane shakes his head. "He's looking for you. He's not here to cause trouble if you're not here. He won't want to blow his chances of coming into contact with you here sooner or later."

Kline walks around the store for another half-hour, presumably searching for me. When he comes up empty-handed, he heads out the door onto the sidewalk and walks away.

Shane pushes the mic button on his communication device. "Jake, stay with him until the surveillance team picks him back up again outside."

Once the coast is clear, and the surveillance team reports back that they have Kline in their sights and that he has boarded the bus bound for his neighborhood, everyone stands down.

"Let's go, sweetheart," Shane says, grabbing my hand. "I'm taking you home. You've had enough excitement for one day." Then he hits the mic button on his earpiece. "Jake, Lia, Mack, come back to the penthouse with us. We need to review security protocols at the bookstore."

Then Shane extends his hand to Sam for a handshake. "Thanks for taking care of Beth. Why don't you come, too?"

28

Despite that tumultuous day, I settle quickly into a new routine. Lia drops me off at Clancy's each morning, where I work half a day. Kline returns to Clancy's several more times, apparently looking for me, and each time I end up in the bunker with Sam for company, while Mack and the rest of the security team keep a tight lid on the situation in the store. Each time, Kline eventually tires of looking for me and leaves. It's a stalemate situation, and it's completely unnerving. Even if I'm safe in the bunker room, I can't help worrying about the employees and the customers who are clueless about the risk Kline presents.

Three afternoons a week, I go to Shane's building after my shift to participate in the self-defense class. The class is made up of what they call "noncombat" employees—the folks who work in support roles like accounting and IT and marketing. There are four other women in the class, besides me, and three men. This class soon becomes the highlight of my week.

By the second week of class, I'm starting to get the hang of things. We begin each session with calisthenics to warm up, and I find my physical endurance is increasing. I make a mental note to start working out more often, to increase my stamina. Shane has workout equipment at the penthouse, and there's a gym in the building as well. Maybe Lia would be willing to work out with me.

After the calisthenics, we get into the good stuff. First Liam demonstrates a move for us, and then we pair off and practice it. I'm usually paired up with either Marilyn from accounting or Kara from IT. I don't think it's a coincidence that I'm *never* paired up with a male partner. That's not true for either Marilyn or Kara, or the other women in the class.

Marilyn is in her mid-fifties, a little heavy set and very much out of shape. Kara is not much older than me, and as she's a long-distance runner, she has no trouble keeping up with Liam's instructions.

We're practicing holds and evasive maneuvers, taking turns acting as the 'bad guy.' We grab each other and hold on for dear life while the 'victim' tries to escape. After a while it's pretty obvious to me that the others are treating me differently, treating me with kid gloves, careful not to grab me too hard or get too physical with me. They're not nearly so careful with each other.

In the locker room after class, I ask Marilyn about it after the others have left. She seems a little flustered.

"What's going on?" I ask her. "Why is everyone being so careful with me? They're not that way with each other."

She looks nervously around the locker room. "We were told to take it easy with you—to be careful not to hurt you. Especially your left arm."

"Who told you this?"

"Mr. McIntyre."

"*Which* Mr. McIntyre? There are several of them."

She grimaces. "Shane?"

Oh, my God, I'm going to kill him! How can I learn self-defense if I don't have anything to defend against? There's no point in taking it out on my classmates. They're innocent bystanders, just following the boss's orders. So I head upstairs to confront the source of the problem. I'm so irritated I don't even bother showering or changing out of my workout clothes.

When I get up to Shane's floor, I storm past Diane's desk. Fortunately, she's not there at the moment, and Shane's door is wide open.

I walk into his office and find him standing beside the credenza, pouring a cup of coffee. He looks so damned good standing there in his suit, handsome and polished and urbane, and that makes me even madder. "What did you do!"

He turns to me, his lips curving into a welcoming smile. "Hi, sweetheart. What do you mean, what did I do? I do a lot of things. Can you be more specific?" He's got an innocent smile on his face, which irritates me even more.

"Did you tell the people in my self-defense class to be *careful* with me?"

Fighting a grin—that smug bastard!—he takes a sip of his coffee. "I might have reminded them that you're just getting over some pretty serious physical injuries. And I might have suggested that they be careful with you. So, yes."

At least he doesn't try to deny it. "They're practically afraid to touch me, let alone to attack me! How can I learn what I'm supposed to learn if no one will attack me?"

"Sweetheart, I'm just trying to—"

"Stop babying me, Shane! You've got to stop."

Shane loses his smile. "Close the door."

The sudden change in his demeanor throws me off balance. "What?"

"You heard me. Close the door."

I ignore the flash of anxiety that courses through me at the tone of his voice. This is Shane, after all. He would never hurt me. Still, he doesn't look happy. I reach behind me and shove his door closed, perhaps a little bit too hard. He sets down his coffee and stalks over to me. I find myself backing up until my back hits the door, and I'm trapped.

"I'm not *babying* you," he says, getting in my face. His voice is tight. "I'm *protecting* you. There's a difference."

I swallow, determined not to be cowed. "Not the way I see it."

He leans closer and I can smell his delicious scent as it washes over me. He has me at a distinct disadvantage, because I'm a hot, sweaty mess. Crap! Why didn't I stop to shower and change my clothes first?

His eyes narrow on me and his words are clipped. "Beth, if I were babying you, you'd be back at the estate playing in the pool or watching movies on the big screen. But you're not, are you? You wanted to come back to the city, so we did. You're working at Clancy's—which, for the record, I think is a good idea—and you're taking a self-defense class. Hell, you're even going back to graduate school soon. I'm not *babying* you. I'm giving you what you asked for, while managing the risks."

He moves like lightning, grabbing my wrists and pinning them to the door above my head, making my pulse kick up into overdrive. "I'm giving you what I can, sweetheart. But you have to cut me some slack here. Howard Kline isn't the only risk out there. As my girlfriend, you're a target."

"A target? What are you talking about?"

"Because of the nature of my business, I've made a lot of ene-mies, Beth. And because of my wealth, I'm naturally a target, and that makes you a target, too. If anyone wanted to get to *me*, all they'd have to do is go through you. You're my weak link. If you're going to be in my life, then precautions need to be taken, and you have to ac-cept that."

"What kind of precautions?"

"Bodyguards, for one thing. Surveillance. Protection."

"I thought the bodyguards were because of Howard Kline."

"They are, for the most in part. But even if Kline were no longer a threat, you'd still have to have a bodyguard."

He grips my chin firmly and looks me in the eye. "Don't ask me to stop protecting you, Beth, because it's not going to happen. I'll bend over backward to make you happy, but I won't compromise your safety."

My heart is hammering now. I've never seen him like this.

He tips my chin up. "You were assaulted by Andrew because I wasn't on my guard. I made the mistake of letting Tyler call the shots, and you paid the fucking price for it. Now *I'm* calling the shots where you're concerned, and I will not slack off on your protection. Don't ask me to, sweetheart, because I won't do it."

I'm breathing hard, and there must be signs of an impending pan-ic-attack written all over my face, because Shane's expression soft-ens. "Just breathe, honey." His thumb brushes gently along my lower lip.

His gaze drops to my lips. I know he's about two seconds away from kissing me, but I feel at such a disadvantage right now. He looks all *GQ*, and I'm a hot mess—literally. He doesn't seem to mind, though, as he lays his mouth on mine and uses his lips to nudge mine open. His tongue steals inside and strokes mine with slow, velvet licks.

My knees go weak, and I attempt to push him back. "Shane, no. I'm a mess. I need to shower."

"Don't care."

"But, Shane—"

"Don't. Fucking. Care. I don't care if you just came from wallowing in a barn yard."

He reaches around me and locks the door, then swings me up in his arms and carries me to his desk. After pushing aside a small stack of files, he sits me down on the top, then presses an intercom button on his high-tech desk phone.

When Diane responds, he says, "Hold all calls. I don't want any interruptions until further notice."

Shane spreads my legs wide and slips his hand down inside my workout shorts, his fingers slipping between the lips of my sex. I'm hot and damp there already, and I'm mortified when I smell myself. But he doesn't seem to mind in the least. The heat in his gaze makes me shiver, and when his fingertip rims my opening with a gentle, teasing motion, my head falls back and I groan in surrender. "This is so not fair."

"This is one of my fantasies," he says, his voice low. "Fucking you on my desk."

"Actually, it's one of mine, too," I say, breathless.

I glance out the windows at the high rise buildings across the street, and I can't help wondering if the occupants can see inside Shane's office. It's a bright day, and lots of sunlight is streaming through the uncovered windows.

"Don't worry, they can't see you," he says dismissively, following the direction of my thoughts.

"Are you sure? How do you know?"

"Because the windows in my office are specially tinted to prevent anyone from seeing inside."

He pulls off my sports bra, freeing my hot, sweaty breasts. The fresh air feels so good against my damp, heated skin.

His hands come up to cover my breasts, and he leans in for a kiss, stealing my breath in the process. "No one can see us. Relax."

"That's easier said than done."

He chuckles, then bends down to suck one of my tightly puckered nipples into his mouth. My nipples are so sensitive, they almost hurt, and I whimper. He bathes the taut little peak with his hot tongue, and a shiver racks my body.

I moan as he practically swallows my nipple, drawing it deep into his mouth and sucking. "Shane."

"Shh."

I can't look away from the window, at the stream of cars I can see off in the distance, at the buildings looming tall directly across the street from us. It's as if we're exposed to the entire city. It's broad daylight, and I can't just block it out.

Shane pushes me back on the desk and reaches for the waistband of my shorts. He pulls them off, along with my panties, and drops them on the desk. I'm sitting bare butt naked on his desk, while he's standing there dressed in a suit and tie. It's wickedly arousing, and I'm so hot I think I'm going to combust.

"I'm going to fuck you right here on my desk," he says, his hands going to his belt buckle. "Do you have a problem with that? If you do, speak up now."

I can't help but notice the huge erection tenting his slacks. Just the thought of that thick, hard length of him buried inside me makes me tremble with need.

His hands still as he waits for my answer. If I say yes—that I do have a problem with it—he'll stop. He might not be happy about it, but he'll stop. He likes to push me. And the thing is, I like it. I want this. I want to do this right here, right now. And my concern that someone might see us—or that someone will come knocking on his door—ratchets up my arousal even higher. I am such a twisted individual.

No, I don't have a problem with it. I shake my head.

"Beth, you have to say it, out loud. No misunderstandings."

"No, I don't have a problem with it!" I gasp. "I want this, you."

"Right here, right now?"

"Yes!"

That's all the permission he needs. He pulls my bottom to the edge of his desk and touches me, opening me and testing my readiness. I must be soaking wet, because he groans loudly, a pained expression on his face. He pulls his belt free and drops it to the floor where it lands with a loud thud. Then he unfastens his slacks and lowers the zipper. Shoving his clothing down to mid-thigh, he frees his erection, which is straining eagerly upward, and fists his ready cock.

He grabs one of my legs and pins it high on his hip, opening me wide. His chest vibrates with what I can only describe as a growl.

He steps closer, and when I glance down, I see the glistening pre-come seeping from the slit in the head of his cock. He feeds himself into me one inch at a time, pressing slowly and relentlessly into my body. He's so thick and full right now, his flushed cock stretches me deliciously, making me gasp.

He leans into me, sinking into my aching, wet body in a slow, steady motion. I bite my bottom lip as he fills me, trying not to make a sound as my body softens to accommodate him.

"Let me hear you, Beth," he says, catching my gaze.

He likes the feminine sounds I can't help making when he's inside me, the whimpering and the cries. God, it's embarrassing. I shake my head. "Someone might hear."

"The walls are soundproofed."

"No they're not. You're lying." But I can't help smiling. And then, when his cock finally comes to rest balls-deep inside me, I can't help the moan that escapes me. "Shane! Oh, God!"

He grins at me. "I'm not lying. They are soundproofed."

I fall back onto my elbows on the desktop, reduced to a quivering puddle as he starts to move. At first he's careful, making slow, steady thrusts. But as my body softens, sucking him deeper into my lush, wet channel, his pace picks up.

His hands grip my thighs hard, pinning me in place so he can thrust hard and deep. I turn my head toward the window, looking outside at a perfect, cloudless day. I can hear the drone of distant traffic, the squeal of brakes, an emergency response siren in the background. The city goes about its business, oblivious to the fact that the man I'm crazy about is about to make me come—hard—on his desk.

"Shane!" I cry out, overcome with almost unbearable pleasure. Every thrust of his cock sends shafts of pleasure shooting through me. The friction is so exquisite, I can barely catch my breath.

His jaw clenches as he tunnels in and out of me in a steady, hard rhythm. This man is everything to me. He's kind and loving and sweet. He's also controlling, overly protective, and stubborn as hell. I guess it's a package deal.

His chest is heaving, and I know he's holding himself in check until I come first, gritting his teeth so hard the muscles in his jaw twitch and flex. He's always taking care of me, even when he's half out of his mind with pleasure. I look up at him, and he's gazing down at me as if he can see right into my soul. Even now, he's protecting me.

Shane reaches down and rubs tiny circles over my hyper-sensitive clitoris with just enough pressure to push me over the edge. I come in a blinding rush of pleasure, wailing and whimpering as I fall apart. He throws his head back and joins me, grimacing as he erupts inside me, filling me with spurt after spurt of his thick, scalding seed.

This man owns me, body and soul. But that's all right, because I own him, too.

$\text{\textit{29}}$ 29

Friday is Shane's birthday, and I think I'm more excited about it than he is. Whenever I bring it up and suggest we plan a celebration, he shrugs it off. I told him you only turn thirty-five once, but he didn't seem moved by my observation. Still, I'm determined to do something for his birthday.

He's already up and gone to work Wednesday morning when I amble into the kitchen and find Cooper putting on a pot of coffee.

"Morning, kiddo," he says. "You sleep well?"

I take a seat at the breakfast counter. I'm not firing on all cylinders yet, and I desperately need some caffeine. "Yeah."

Cooper pours a cup of freshly-ground coffee and sets it on the counter in front of me, along with a tiny pitcher of cream and the sugar bowl.

"I want to do something for Shane's birthday," I tell him, as I spoon sugar into my coffee.

Cooper smiles. "Good luck with that."

"I mentioned it to him last night, but he didn't seem very interested."

Cooper shakes his head. "Celebrating his birthday really isn't his thing. He doesn't like the attention."

"I want to do something for him, though. You know him better than anyone. What would you suggest?"

"Knowing Shane... if you're going to do anything, I think he'd prefer to get together for drinks after work with family and a few friends. Nothing extravagant. No hoopla, no fanfare. Just good food, good liquor, and maybe some good music."

"Got any suggestions where?"

"Call Rowdy's. They've got a party room. They play blues, and the food's great. He'd like that."

I've heard of the place, but I've never been there. "All right. I'll make some calls."

I sip my coffee as I make a mental list of what I'll need for Shane's birthday celebration. Cake, invitations, reserve the party room.

"What do you want for breakfast?" Cooper says.

"I can make some toast." I hate to make more work for him. He does so much for me already.

He looks at me, raising his brow. "You need protein. How about eggs to go with that toast?"

I watch Cooper scramble two eggs. Sometimes he reminds me of my mom. He's always trying to feed me. He's such an amazing guy, and he needs someone besides me to fuss over. He needs someone special in his life.

We're the only ones in the apartment at the moment, so I figure now is a good time to have this conversation. "Cooper, can I ask you a question?"

"Sure."

"It's sort of personal. If you don't want to answer—"

"Beth. Just ask it."

"Okay. Why don't you have a boyfriend?"

He stares at me, looking completely shell-shocked. For a moment, I think I must have heard Shane wrong. Maybe Cooper's not gay.

"Shane told you?"

I smile apologetically, wishing now I hadn't said anything. He looks painfully uncomfortable. "Yeah. I was trying to think of a woman to set you up with, and he told me. Are you mad?"

He gives me a guarded smile. "No, honey. I'm not mad."

"Why didn't you tell me yourself?"

He shrugs it off. "I was in the military for 30 years, and 'Don't Ask, Don't Tell' was in force for a good part of that time. It's not something I speak about openly."

"Do you mind that I know?"

"No, you're family. Everyone in Shane's family knows."

"Does this mean you're in the closet?"

He shrugs. "I don't go around publicizing my sex life. If that means I'm in the closet, then yeah, I guess I am. Is that a crime?"

"No, of course not! I'm sorry, I didn't mean to offend you."

"You didn't, honey. It's just, I'm old school. I'm not comfortable discussing this with folks, that's all."

"Things have changed, you know. Same-sex marriage is legal—"

"That's fine for the younger generation. But how I grew up—and where—it just wasn't talked about, you know?"

My heart is breaking for this man, this proud, amazing man. I jump down from my barstool and walk around the counter to hug him. "I love you, Cooper. You're family to me."

He hugs me back, wrapping me tightly in his strong arms. "I love you too, Beth. And yeah, you're family to me too."

I had no idea how closed off he was from his own identity, how alone he must feel sometimes. "You still need a boyfriend, Cooper."

"It's just not that easy, kiddo, especially for someone like me. Where I was raised, if someone came out of the closet, he was tarred and feathered and run out of town, and that's if he was lucky. Other times he ended up face-down in a ditch."

My heart aches for him. "It's different now, Cooper. It is."

* * *

Two days later, on a Friday afternoon at four-thirty, I surprise Shane in his office at five o'clock. He looks up when I knock on his open door and waves me in. He does a swift double-take when he sees what I'm wearing... a gorgeous, flirty little swing dress I found on the clearance rack at Sylvia's Boutique.

The dress falls to mid-thigh on me, and it's sleeveless with a high neckline. There's a sheer black, sequined layer floating over a black silk shell. I'm wearing sheer black stockings and mini-boots with a tiny heel. Shane will get one of his presents once we're home tonight—I'm wearing a matching silk garter belt with stocking clips, which I know he'll appreciate. The man does have an avid appreciation for fine lingerie.

He leans back in his chair and grins, his gaze following me as I sashay toward him. When I come around to his side of the desk, he turns his chair to face me, his expression appreciative.

He opens his legs and I step between them, bringing my hands up to cup his beautiful face.

"Hello, sweetheart," he says. "To what do I owe this unexpected pleasure?"

Cradling his face in my hands, I lean forward and kiss him sweetly on the lips. "Happy birthday, darling."

His hands come around to the backs of my thighs, and he draws me closer. "Thank you. You look gorgeous, honey."

His hands slip beneath my dress, running up the backs of my thighs, and when he encounters the garter clips, his gaze darkens. He tries to pull my dress up for a peak at my garter belt, but I swat his hands away.

He pouts. "You're my present, right? When do I get to unwrap you? Now?"

"No, later. Do you like my dress?"

He has a wry grin on his face. "I think you already know the answer to that." He cocks his head toward the door to his private apartment. "Let's duck inside the apartment so I can show you how much I like it."

Now it's my turn to grin. "Not so fast, mister." I grab his hand and pull him out of his chair. "Come with me. I have a surprise for you."

He chuckles. "I thought you gave me my surprise this morning."

I woke up early this morning—at the same time he awoke—and gave him a birthday blowjob. I sent him off to work a very happy man. "Well, that was your first present. I have more. But you have to come with me. Are you done here for the day?"

"I can be. Just let me save this file and shut down my computer."

When we leave his office, Diane is already gone for the day, which is unusual for her. She usually leaves when Shane does. Of course, I happen to know why she's gone already—she left early to organize everything at the pub. I rented their private party room, which is plenty big enough to hold our group.

Shane accompanies me down to the front lobby and out the main doors where a cab is already waiting for us at the curb. I'm sure Shane will have a few drinks this evening, so we'll leave his Jaguar parked here in the company garage and take a cab home tonight.

Once we're seated in the cab, Shane reaches for my hand, cradling it between his. "So, where are we going?"

He's got a grin on his face, and I think he likes the fact that I've kidnapped him. I smile back, doing my best to appear enigmatic. I'll just let him wonder where we're going. The cab driver already knows our destination, so I don't have to say a word.

It's five-thirty when we arrive, but the bar isn't overly crowded yet. Diane greets us at the door, giving Shane a hug, and telling me that everything's ready. I lead Shane to the private party room and pull him through the open doorway into the darkened room. As we enter, someone flips on the lights, and a small crowd of boisterous well-wishers scream "Happy birthday!" at the tops of their lungs. I see his brothers and two sisters standing near the front of the crowd, along with Cooper, Miguel, Mack, Sam, and a few other familiar faces.

On a table in the center of the room is a birthday cake that resembles Wrigley Field—in honor of Shane's love of Chicago baseball. There's also a table covered with a small mountain of brightly-colored packages of new toys.

"The toys are to be donated to Children's Hospital," I tell him. Shane serves on the board of directors for the hospital and is very much involved with fundraising for the hospital.

Shane takes in the cake and the toys. "This is absolutely perfect, Beth. Thank you."

When he takes me in his arms and bends me back to kiss me senseless, my face heats up amidst all the hooting and hollering that ensues.

After enjoying hot appetizers and free drinks, our guests spill out into the main bar area, which is crowded now with customers. A dozen television screens are positioned around the pub, broadcasting a variety of sports programs, including a baseball game at Wrigley Field. Shane drags me with him to the bar so he can check the score, and he orders a whisky for himself and a Strawberry Daiquiri for me.

When I see Miguel Rodriquez walking my way, I jump down from my barstool to give him a huge hug. I haven't seen much of Miguel since right before the assault. He was my daytime bodyguard when Tyler first hired McIntyre Security to protect me from Howard Kline—although I never knew it. He protected me covertly—at least until the day Gabrielle spilled the beans and told me what was going on around me. That was the day I discovered that Shane—my then brand-new boyfriend—had been hired by my brother to watch over me. When I confronted Miguel in his car, which was parked outside my townhouse, he ended up driving me to Shane's office, where I confronted Shane and had a total meltdown.

Miguel witnessed it all, the ugly crying and the glorious panic attack—all of it. He was a good friend to me that day. He was also a good friend to me the day Andrew Morton attacked me—Miguel was the first one from McIntyre Security on the scene, and apparently, he rode with me in the ambulance to the emergency room. I don't remember because I was unconscious.

Shane leaves me with Miguel and goes to the end of the bar to talk to a couple of coworkers I don't recognize. Mack and Sam stop by to say hi, and we chat for a while. The place is bustling and noisy, and everyone seems to be having a good time. A stream of people stop by to congratulate Shane and wish him well. Even Gabrielle shows up for a few minutes on her way to work, dressed in her pristine, white sous chef uniform.

I glance over at Shane, who's still at the far end of the bar. He's standing with Lia, and I can tell instantly that something's wrong. Lia looks... gutted. Absolutely gutted. Her expression is bleak—her eyes radiating pain—I can see it even from where I'm standing. She looks like she's just barely holding herself together.

Shane lays his hands on his sister's shoulders and leans down to get right in her face. This Lia is nothing like the snarky, opinionated girl I know. I've never seen her like this. She's always so energized, so... indestructible. With a sick feeling in my gut, I start to walk toward them, but Jake catches my arm and stops me.

He shakes his head. "Let Shane deal with her. He's the only one she'll listen to."

I'm totally confused, having no idea what's going on. I've never seen her like this. Her expression is tense and her eyes are burning... with hatred? Or is that pain? I look up at Jake, hoping he'll shed some light on the situation, but he just shakes his head.

Lia glances over at me and catches me watching her, and immediately her expression changes, as if a mask has dropped into place, concealing her raw emotions. She pulls out of Shane's grasp and stalks off toward the ladies' room. Shane calls after her, but she flips him the bird as she keeps walking. I start to go after her, but Jake stops me.

"Let her go," he says.

"What's wrong?"

Shane heads our way, and he looks like he's ready to kill something or someone.

When he reaches us, I grab his forearm, feeling how tense he is. "What's wrong with Lia?" I say.

Shane looks at Jake, his expression hard. "You want to deal with that?"

"My pleasure." Jake nods and steps away from us, heading toward a table of boisterous young men across the room who are well into an alcohol-fueled celebration of some sort.

Shane watches Jake for a moment, then redirects his attention to me. "Lia's fine, don't worry." He pulls me into his arms.

"I've never seen Lia like that. What happened?"

He shakes his head, exhaling hard. "I'm sorry, Beth. I can't go into it. You'll have to ask Lia."

I'm still haunted by the bleak expression I saw on her face. "I'm going to go talk to her." I pull away from Shane and head to the ladies' room.

"Beth, wait!"

But I shake my head and keep walking. Lia may be their sister, but she's also my friend. And just now, Lia sure looked like she could use a friend. As I reach the ladies' room door, it swings open and Lia walks out looking perfectly normal, with one glaring exception. Her eyes are bloodshot, and it's obvious she's been crying.

"Are you okay?" I say, grabbing her arms.

"I'm fine. Why?"

She's looking at me like she has absolutely no idea what I'm talking about. But I know what I saw. She was far from all right. She'd looked devastated. "I saw you talking to Shane. You looked... upset."

Lia shrugs. "It's nothing. Don't worry." And then she pulls away from me and heads to the bar.

I know what I saw, but now's apparently not the time or place to pry. She's such a guarded person—I get that. I step up beside her at the bar, but don't say anything. The bartender hands her a shot glass with someone clear in it, and I notice that her hand is shaking slight-ly when she knocks it back. Her eyes are focused on the mirror be-hind the bartender's head, her gaze hard and unflinching. It's almost like she's watching someone. I turn to see a group of college guys around our age clustered around a table. Then I notice Jake there, talking to one of them. Jake's face is set in a rigid mask, and I can tell he's restraining himself. The young man he's talking to is half drunk and openly belligerent. Jake says something that angers the guy, who then turns and walks out of the pub without looking back.

The bar tender hands Lia another shot glass filled with some-thing clear, and she swallows it, grimacing.

I've never seen her drink anything harder than beer. "What are you drinking?"

She gives me a scornful look. "Water."

"Lia, come on. Don't do this."

She sets the shot glass upside down on the bar, a little harder than necessary, and walks away from me without a word. I swallow hard, trying not to feel hurt by her dismissal.

Before I can go after her, Tyler arrives, looking like he's come straight from work. He's wearing his typical black suit with a white shirt and black tie. My brother—bless his heart. My over-protective, control-freak brother. He doesn't know how to cut loose or relax. He's wound so tightly, I'm afraid someday he'll just snap. But I love him dearly.

Tyler opens his arms and I walk right into them, hugging him tightly around his waist. He kisses the top of my head. "Hey, kiddo. How are you?"

"I'm fine." I miss my brother. Since the assault, I haven't seen much of him. We haven't had our weekly Saturday lunch outing in two months. But now that Shane and I are living in the penthouse,

I hope that will change.

Shane walks up and offers Tyler his hand, and they shake.

"Happy birthday, Shane," my brother says, giving Shane a curt nod.

"Glad you could make it. Let me buy you a drink."

"I'll have a beer." Tyler gives his order to the bartender.

Tyler and I receive a lot of curious stares from Shane's co-workers. Tyler's dark, like our father was, with midnight black hair and lightly bronzed skin. I take after our mother, with my pale blond hair and light complexion. Some people have trouble believing we're siblings, especially since Tyler, who's 44, is old enough to be my father. Our blue-green eyes are the only physical trait we share.

Jake comes up and slaps Tyler on the back. "Detective, how's it going? You arrest any murderers today?"

"Hello, Jake," Tyler says, not rising to the bait.

My brother is a homicide detective in Chicago. Naturally, he takes his job very seriously. I guess you'd have to, when you deal with death and tragedy day in and day out. It takes a toll on a person, no doubt.

The bartender hands Tyler his bottle of beer.

After a little polite talk with Shane and Jake, Tyler asks me to join him—*alone*—at a table in the corner of the room, away from the distraction of the television screens and the McIntyres. Shane remains at the bar with Jake, but I notice him glancing my way periodically as if keeping tabs on me.

Tyler is less than thrilled with my relationship with Shane, to say the least, and Shane knows it. Tyler's main complaint is that Shane's too old for me. But I don't think ten years difference in our ages is that big of a deal. My parents had an even bigger age gap between them, and they were very happily married for twenty-two years before my father was killed in the line of duty.

Tyler and Shane are cordial around each other, but I suspect they're both putting on a show for my sake. I know Tyler wants me to move in with him, at least while Kline's a free man.

"How are you, really?" Tyler says, drawing my attention away from Shane.

"I'm fine. Really."

He nods at my newly-liberated arm. "I see you got the cast off."

"Yes, finally. How are *you*?"

He shrugs. "I can't complain. Work is busy, as usual. Tell me what you've been up to. Have you decided when you're going back to work?"

I nod, taking a sip of my daiquiri. "I've started working at the bookstore. And I signed up for classes at UC starting fall semester. I'm going for an MBA. Wish me luck."

Tyler raises his brows, and if I'm not mistaken, I think he's surprised. Or maybe even impressed? Deep down in his heart, my brother still thinks I'm twelve years old. I think I'll always be a kid in his eyes. He nods in approval. "You always do well in school. I'm sure you'll do fine. How are things with you and Shane? Is he treating you well?"

"Of course he is, Tyler."

Tyler asks me that question every time we see each other.

"Why don't you come stay with me for a while?" he says, and then he takes a long swig of his beer. "I've got plenty of room. You know you're always welcome—my home is your home. It's a well-secured building."

I lay my hand over his and squeeze it. "Tyler, I love you. But I'm not coming to live with you. I'm an adult, and I'm in a committed relationship with a man I love."

He nods, as if he expected my answer. "As long as he's treating you right. If he's not—"

"Tyler, don't worry. Shane and I are fine."

He frowns. "Beth, the man had a reputation as a serial dater long before he met you. And the type of women he's always dated... well, they're... let's just say you're not his usual type. Tigers don't change their stripes overnight, you know."

Tyler takes another long draw on his beer and scrutinizes me. I know my face is flushed, because I can feel the rising heat. "All right," he says. "I'll shut up now. I just stopped by to say hi—not to give you a hard time." He sets his half-finished bottle on the table. "I need to get back to work."

"This late?" By now, it's well after seven. "Stay and eat. Have some cake."

He shakes his head. "Can't, kiddo, sorry. I'm working a time-sensitive case." He stands and inconspicuously adjusts his gun holster beneath his suit jacket. "Since you're out and about again, how about having lunch with me tomorrow?"

I stand and hug him goodbye. "That sounds great."

"I'll pick you up at eleven—where? At the Lake Shore apartment building?"

"Yes." I walk Tyler to the exit and wave as he heads off to his car.

Shane comes up behind me, slipping his arms around my waist. "Everything okay?"

"Yeah. It was nice to see him. We're having lunch tomorrow."

"I'm sure he misses you. Now come with me, young lady, and help me cut my birthday cake."

* * *

The party goes on for a couple more hours, until everyone has eaten and drunk their fill. A couple of Shane's employees collect all the donated toys and pack them up to be sent to The Children's Hospital. At nine-thirty, I go looking for Shane and spot him at the bar with Mack and Cooper.

I'm heading their way when a woman I've never seen before walks up to Shane, leans into him and kisses him on the cheek. I stop dead in my tracks and watch them, feeling flushed all of a sudden. She's smiling at him as she fingers the lapel of his suit jacket. Mack and Cooper make their excuses and walk away, leaving Shane and the woman alone.

She's beautiful, a tall brunette, maybe in her early thirties. She's wearing a nicely cut gray skirt suit with a cream-colored silk shell and a pearl choker. Her dark hair is long and wavy, falling well past her shoulders, pulled back in a loose ponytail. With her stiletto heels, she looks tall and regal, definitely professional.

Shane casually removes her hand from the lapel of his jacket. Seeing him with another woman—it bothers me. My heart starts racing, and I feel hot. When she says something to him, he shakes his head no. Then she reaches out and runs a manicured fingernail painted a deep red down the center of his chest, following the path of his dark tie. From the way she's touching him, stroking him, it's obvious she knows him very well. Intimately. I'm sure of it. And she's practically undressing him with her eyes. Is this one of his former... what? Dates? Girlfriends? Lovers? She's so polished and urbane, just looking at her makes me feel gauche. If she's typical of the women he's dated, then Tyler was right. I'm not his usual type at all.

Shane glances my way, and our gazes lock across the room. For a moment, I see a flare of some strong emotion on his face, and my stomach drops. What was that? Panic? He starts to move in my direction, but the brunette grabs his arm and pulls him back to her. She's talking to him, but his attention is on me. When he turns back to face her, and I feel sick.

Tyler's words come back to me in a rush. *Tigers don't change their stripes overnight, you know.*

I turn, needing to get away, and run smack into Cooper.

He reaches out to steady me. "Where are you off to, honey?"

Not trusting myself to speak, I shake my head and try to pull away from him. He tightens his hold on me and looks over my head in Shane's direction.

"I need to go." My heart is racing, and I need to get out of here before I implode.

"Oh, no you don't," Cooper says, holding onto me. His gaze is still on Shane and that woman.

"Who is she?" I can't help asking.

"Beth—"

"Just tell me, who is she? Do you know?"

"Her name is Alanna Cox. She's an assistant district attorney here in Chicago."

"They were an item, weren't they? I can tell by the way she's touching him."

Cooper frowns. "Honey—"

"Please, just let me go. I need to get out of here, Cooper. Now."

"Beth." I freeze when I feel Shane's hands on my shoulders, squeezing them. "Time to go."

That's not a request. I swallow hard and glance up at Cooper because I'm just not ready to face Shane.

Shane turns me toward him, but he's looking over my head at Cooper. "Wrap this thing up, will you? I'm taking Beth home."

Cooper nods. "Go on. I'll handle things here."

"We can't just leave," I say. "We have guests. We have to say good-bye."

"We're leaving, Beth," Shane says, steering me toward the exit.

It's dark outside the pub, and the night air is cool on my bare arms. I look down at my beautiful dress, and the anticipation I'd felt earlier about Shane undressing me after the party dissipates in a flash. I shiver.

Instead of immediately hailing a cab, as I'd expected him to, Shane backs me up against the brick wall and leans into me so we're face to face. "Her name is Alanna Cox." His breath is warm and spiced with fine whisky.

I'm shaking now, and I chalk my reaction up to the night air, even though I know that's not the real reason. "I know what her name is." I sound sullen and sulky, but I can't help it. My ego took a crushing blow when I watched Shane with that woman. Why would he want to be with me, when he could have a woman like that? Someone worldly and sophisticated.

"You dated her."

He nods. "Yes."

"You slept with her."

For a split second, the corner of his mouth curls in amusement, but he wisely loses his grin fast. "Yes."

At least he's honest.

"She's very beautiful," I say.

"Yes, she is."

At his ready admission, my heart feels like it's being squeezed in a vice. My chest aches.

"Breathe." His hands cradle my hot face, and he strokes my jaw-line with this thumbs. "I've dated a lot of women, Beth. I can't change the past."

I know I'm being melodramatic. It would be stupid of me to think he'd lived the life of a monk before we met.

His eyes narrow. "You think I wasn't burning up with jealousy when we encountered your ex-boyfriend at Clancy's? You think I didn't want to beat the living shit out of him right then and there, for the simple fact that he'd once touched your body? That he'd almost had you? Because I did. I wanted to beat the hell out of him. You think I don't understand jealousy? I do. I know firsthand because I choke on it when I think of you with someone else."

I'm mortified when hot tears spill down my cheeks. My throat tightens painfully. "I don't want anyone else."

"Neither do I. You're stuck with me."

Shane pulls me against his chest and wraps me in his strong arms, one hand rubbing my back. "God, I want you so badly I can't think straight sometimes. Beth, honey, I can't change my past, but I can promise you my future, because you are my future. The past doesn't matter. Even if I'd dated a thousand women in the past, it doesn't matter. Only you matter."

He takes off his suit jacket and drapes it over my shoulders. Then he leads me to the curb and opens the rear passenger door of an available cab. He follows me into the cab and buckles my seatbelt as he gives the driver our address.

We don't talk in the cab, neither one of us wanting to share our personal, and very private, business with a complete stranger. He has hold of my right hand and refuses to relinquish it even for a second. Not even when we arrive at his apartment building, and he pulls his wallet out of his pocket one-handed and swipes his credit card to pay the fare.

We walk in through the front lobby, and Shane uses a key to summon the private penthouse elevator.

Inside the elevator, he pulls me into his arms and kisses my fore-head. "Thank you for a wonderful birthday party. The location, the cake, the toys for the hospital... it was perfect."

I smile at him, but don't say anything as we ride up to the our floor. I'm still too shaky.

"Do I get to unwrap my best present now?" he whispers in my ear.

He slips his jacket off my shoulders and slings it over his own shoulder. Then he turns me to face the mirrored wall of the elevator car. Surprised at his turn of mind, I meet his very heated expression in the mirror.

His hands come around my waist, and he interlocks his fingers over my belly. "This is a very pretty little dress you're wearing, but I'm curious to see what's beneath it."

I chuckle. "You already know what's beneath it."

He grins. "That's why I'm curious."

When his hand slips underneath the hem of my dress, I feel flushed for the second time that evening, although this time it's for a completely different reason.

$\backsim$ 30

S hane, are you sure about this?" There's a very sizeable and insistent erection poking me in my lower back. "What if someone comes up?"

Shane consults an app on his phone and starts tapping buttons. "No one's home. And I disabled the cameras in the elevator and the foyer."

I'm torn. I would die of mortification if someone walked in on us... but maybe that's why I'm also so excited. Maybe I'm a bit of an exhibitionist deep down inside. "But what if someone does try to come up?"

"I'll disable the elevator once we're upstairs. No one can override my command—except for Cooper, and he knows better." Shane leans down, and I feel his lips in my hair. His warm breath caresses my ear as he whispers to me. "Earlier you said I could unwrap my gift when we got home, and we're home. Besides, you're wearing a garter belt. You know what that does to me."

I do know. The last time I wore one, the night of the hospital benefit, he was insatiable. A shiver wracks my body.

I watch the mirrored wall as his hands slowly skim down the sides of my torso, pausing to linger at the sides of my breasts. His hands reach around me to cover my breasts, and he leans down to press his warm lips to the side of my neck. He knows how sensitive I am there. His tongue darts out to taste my skin.

"Watch us," he says, his gaze meeting mine in the mirror.

His hands continue their downward journey, following the curve of my torso, past my waist, over my hips, to the hemline of my dress. He begins lifting my dress, very slowly, exposing inch after inch of my stockinged thighs, until the stocking clips are visible. I swear he growls.

He continues, lifting my dress achingly slowly, until it's bunched up at my waist, exposing my black silk panties and the matching garter belt.

"Oh, fuck," he groans, his gaze locked on our reflections in the mirror. "Those panties need to come off."

At his words, an arrow of desire shoots through my body, hitting that aching spot between my legs. I start trembling, and he tightens his hold.

He kisses my neck, just below my ear. "Do you want me?"

My voice is little more than a breath. "Yes."

"Do you trust me?"

I nod, stunned by the hunger I see in his eyes.

"Say it."

"Yes, I trust you."

Shane reaches between my legs and takes hold of my panties.

Gripping them tightly, he rips them open along both side seams, then tugs them off and sticks the torn material in his pocket. Holding up my dress with one hand, he snakes his other hand around to my front and covers my quivering belly. The air feels cool on my body, but his hand on my belly is like a brand, hot and scorching.

"I don't know what I did to deserve you," he breathes into my ear.

I melt back into him, and he catches me, chuckling softly.

I do trust Shane. He has a way of making things all right for me. I know he'll be there to catch me when I fall, and to help me cope when I panic, like I did tonight at the tavern. So, when he says the cameras are off and no one can walk in on us, I believe him. Still, the thought that someone *might* walk in on us is oddly tantalizing.

My knees almost give out when Shane slips his index finger between the puffy lips of my sex and dips the tip of it into my opening. He nudges my legs apart with his hand, and then his finger is there again, teasing my opening, rimming me and sliding through my slick arousal. When his finger migrates north to my clitoris, the torment begins in earnest. My legs are shaking now, and I don't know how much longer I can stay upright. I just want to sink to the lush, burgundy carpet at our feet and open my legs for him.

I startle when the elevator pings and the doors open. Shane sweeps me up into his arms and steps into the dimly-lit foyer.

"Lights twenty-five percent," he says, and the ornate, crystal chandelier hanging overhead brightens a little, casting soft, fractured rays of golden light on the foyer walls.

Shane kisses me, his mouth hot and hungry, as he crosses the foyer to the mahogany table along the wall. Without breaking our kiss, he shoves a vase of fresh flowers aside and sits me down, bare bottomed, on the cold marble tabletop. He pulls my bottom to the edge of the table and spreads my thighs wide, then drops down onto his knees. I cry out when he flicks my clitoris with the tip of his tongue.

He proceeds to feast on me. There's no other way to describe it. He's like a starving man let loose on a banquet. Greedy and demanding, he licks and tastes and sucks every inch of me. My thighs tremble and my hips rock against his firm tongue, savoring every lick, every lash. I know I'm wailing like a wildcat now, but I can't help it. The pleasure is so sharp, so intense. I gasp when he pushes a finger inside me. He finds the tender spot unerringly and strokes me methodically, until only moments later my belly is contracting and I'm panting and whimpering through an orgasm.

Shane shoots to his feet and unfastens his belt and his slacks. He shoves down his clothing and steps between my thighs, guiding his erect penis to my opening. I'm mesmerized by the sight of his erection in his hand, thick and flushed. A thick vein ridges his length, from the base of his cock to the fat crown, which is already leaking fluid in anticipation. He pulls me closer and presses inside me. I gasp as the head of his cock pushes inside, stretching me. We both watch as he sinks into me.

His chest heaving, he catches my gaze. "Okay?"

I nod, then close my eyes as I wallow in the feel of him penetrating me, stretching me almost to the point of pain. His cock is big, and it always takes a bit of getting used to at the beginning. I exhale as he continues to sink slowly and steadily inside me, withdrawing, then sinking back in, continuing this retreat and surge until he's fully seated, until I can feel the dark, wiry hairs at the root of his cock brushing against with my pale curls.

I open my eyes and realize he's still wearing his shirt. I want to see his chest, to put my hands on him, so I start unbuttoning it, and it lands in the floor at his feet.

Running my hands along his broad shoulders and down his arms, I stroke the contours of his muscles and caress his tanned skin. My fingers skate down his forearms to his wrists. He's gripping both of my thighs, holding them open so he can get closer, and I clutch his wrists.

He begins moving in earnest, thrusting hard and deep as he takes his pleasure. His expression is tense, his jaw muscles clenched and his nostrils flaring wide from exertion. He reaches for my clitoris and rubs tiny, firm circles, determined to make me come again.

"I can't!" I gasp, trying to pull his finger away. "I already—"

"Again," he grunts, as he pistons in and out of me. "I want to feel your body clamp down on mine."

I'm so overly-sensitized right now, I don't think I could possibly come again. Shane growls, then reaches for the hem of my dress and pulls it up over my head and tosses it aside. He strips off my bra and then his mouth is on my breast, hot and wet as he tongues the tip of my nipple, making it draw up tight as a little pebble. Pleasure shoots from my breast down to my womb, exploding in a bright burst of exquisite pleasure. When I come, he's there to drink in my high-pitched cries. It takes me a moment to realize he's coming with me, shoving himself deep inside me as he releases into me.

I fall forward and lay my head on his shoulder as his thrusting slows, becoming gentle and coaxing. I'm barely coherent when he pulls up his clothing and carries me into the apartment.

I'm drifting, half asleep, when I feel a warm, wet cloth between my legs. Utterly exhausted, I groan and try to roll over in bed to cuddle with my pillow.

I'm met with a low chuckle as firm hands roll me back. "Hold still for just a minute longer."

Soon the cleansing cloth is gone, and the sheets and blanket are pulled up to cover me. Sometime later, I feel the mattress dip as Shane slides into bed beside me. His skin is warm and damp, and he smells of soap.

"You showered," I groan, feeling sticky. "That's not fair."

He chuckles. "You could have joined me in the shower."

"Too tired. You wiped me out."

Shane spoons behind me, wrapping his arm around my waist. "Go to sleep. I'll give you a bubble bath in the morning. How's that?"

The last thing I remember is the feel of his lips in my hair. "Best birthday ever. Thank you, sweetheart."

It's his birthday, but I feel like I'm the one who got the best present. I smile. "You're welcome."

31

"Hey, you!" Lia says, stepping out onto the penthouse balcony, where I'm sitting with my late morning cup of coffee and my new J.D. Robb novel that I technically stole from Clancy's. "Thought you should know... *my* brother is giving *your* brother the third degree."

I'm happy to see Lia this morning. She seems in a good mood—her typical happy self. I can't help wondering what was wrong with her last night at the pub, but I don't want to pry. She'll confide in me when she's ready. "Tyler's here?"

"Yeah, he's been here for a while."

I close my book and lay it on the patio table. "Why didn't someone tell me?" I check the time on my phone and realize that Tyler came a little early.

Lia smirks. "Probably because Shane's interrogating him in his office."

I jump up from my chair and head inside, afraid to leave the two of them alone in a room for too long. I don't know why Shane and Tyler can't get along. I love them both, and I need for them to make peace with each other, at least for my sake. Is that too much to ask?

I pass Cooper, who's in the kitchen making himself a sandwich. "Why didn't you tell me my brother was here?"

Cooper shrugs. "Shane wanted to talk to him first."

Even from here, I can hear the yelling in Shane's office. "You call that *talking*?"

I don't even bother knocking on Shane's home office door. I open the door and walk inside, ready to knock their heads together if I have to. "Stop it, both of you!"

I think that got their attention, because they both stop yelling mid-sentence. Shane's standing behind his desk, and Tyler's standing in front of the desk, and they're squaring off face-to-face like two grizzly bears ready to fight to the death.

"Just stop it!"

Shane glares at me, apparently not appreciating the interruption. "Beth—"

I jab my finger in his direction. "Don't. He's my brother, Shane. You need to cut him some slack."

I know Tyler can be hard to deal with. Yes, he's opinionated and stubborn and controlling. But he's also loving and loyal to a fault. He would give me his last nickel if I needed it. He's been more like a father to me than a brother my entire life, and it's hard for him to share me with Shane.

"And you!" I glare at Tyler. "We talked about this last night. I told you I'm happy, and I asked you to back off. You need to respect my wishes."

Tyler crosses his arms over his chest, his jaws clenched so tightly I'm afraid he's going to crack his teeth. His eyes are as dark and hard as flint as he glares at Shane.

I turn back to Shane. "Why didn't you tell me he was here?"

Shane shrugs, not looking the least bit repentant. "I wanted to have a chat with him first."

"You call this chatting? Really? Are you done now?"

Shane has the decency to look sheepish. "I guess we're done. For now."

I shake my head in dismay and grab Tyler's hand, pulling him from the room. "Let's go. I'm hungry."

Outside, we hail a cab.

Tyler's still tense. "Where do you want to eat?"

"We aren't going to Mario's?" Tyler and I have been having pizza at Mario's in Hyde Park near my townhouse every Saturday for eons.

Tyler gives me an incredulous look. "We're not going anywhere near the townhouse."

Oh, right. Kline. "Okay. Then where do you want to go?"

"How about my place? I'll make lunch."

"Sure. That sounds good." I haven't been to Tyler's Lincoln Park condo in ages, and surprisingly, my brother's a pretty good cook. Unlike me, he did spend time learning how to cook with our mother when he was young.

On the drive to Tyler's condo, I sneak a peek at him. He's wearing black jeans and a button-down white shirt—his version of casual. He's a very good looking guy, physically very fit, short dark hair, bronzed skin, and blue-green eyes. He's a contradiction. Hot as hell, even if I do say so myself, and yet he's far too serious, too straight-laced. Someday, he'll make some woman very happy. But she'd better be just as opinionated and stubborn and controlling as he is, or else he'll smother her to death.

Once we reach his condo, up on the 38th floor of his upscale building, Tyler suggests that we grill burgers on the balcony. He has a spacious condo in a nice building, which he's decorated himself in dark woods with a natural palette of browns and other Earth tones. It's a masculine space, very bachelor, and a little sparse—but it's also cozy and tidy. I've spent plenty of nights here in the guest bedroom sleeping under a quilt our grandmother made long before I was even born.

While Tyler puts burgers on the grill, I make us two salads and steam some mixed fresh veggies on the stove. We settle in at a little wrought iron bistro table for two out on the balcony to eat. The food is simple and delicious, and we eat in companionable silence, relaxing as we gaze out over his gorgeous view of a lush, green park. Park goers are walking, jogging, and pushing baby strollers. There's a playground filled with children, and the buzzing drone of their chatter wafts up to us faintly on the breeze.

"You're a good cook," I tell him, after having taken a bite of my burger. "You need a girlfriend to cook for."

He shoots me a wary glance. "My life is complicated enough as it is, Beth. I don't have the time or the patience for a girlfriend."

I shake my head at him, thinking he's in for a rude awakening someday. "You're not getting any younger, Tyler. You need to make time." Tyler's forty-four years old. It's not too late for him to have a family of his own, but he's got to make an effort. For starters, he's got to actually get out there and meet someone. And then, he's got to convince her to put up with him. The thought makes me chuckle, and he looks suspiciously at me.

I decide to change the subject. "Tell me what you and Shane were fighting about."

Tyler shrugs, then pushes up his sunglasses and pinches the bridge of his nose. I can't tell if he's exasperated or bashful. Most likely exasperated.

He sighs, as if resigning himself to answering the question. "I asked him what his intentions are in regards to you."

I sputter, nearly choking on a mouthful of my soft drink. "You what?"

He shrugs again. "I asked him what his intentions are. I have every right to know. Is he going to marry you or not?"

I roll my eyes. Not only is Tyler acting like a father, but he's acting like a father from the previous century. "I've only known him a few months, Tyler. It's way too premature for us to start thinking about marriage. We're still getting to know each other. Besides, I'm an adult. Is my relationship with Shane really any of your business?"

Tyler's gaze is locked on the scenery. "He's *cohabitating* with you, Beth. He's having *sex* with you. Yes, his intentions are my business. If Dad were alive, he'd be asking Shane these questions. You can bet on it."

"Well, it's premature for all that, anyway." I take a sip of my drink, and I can't help wondering how Shane responded to Tyler's questions—all the yelling aside. I doubt Shane took well to being interrogated. Still, I am curious. "So, what did he say?"

"He told me to mind my own fucking business."

I snort with laughter. I can't help it. That sounds like Shane.

Tyler scowls as he rises from his chair. "Do you want ice cream? I have a brand new carton of mint chocolate chip."

My favorite flavor. "I'd love some, thank you."

While Tyler gets the ice cream, I sit on the balcony and gaze off into the distance. I meant it when I said it's too soon for Shane and me to even think of marriage. We're in a committed relationship, yes—of that I have no doubt. And I trust Shane. I know he had a reputation as a love-'em-and-leave-'em guy, and he's left behind a trail of broken hearts, but I don't worry that he'll cheat on me. But marriage? Is marriage even on his radar screen? He could have any woman he wanted—like the assistant district attorney I saw him with at the pub last night. Would he really want to settle down to just one woman, presumably for the rest of his life?

Tyler carries two bowls of ice cream out onto the balcony, and we watch the kids playing in the park as we eat.

"I'll try to be civil where Shane's concerned," Tyler says after a long, companionable silence.

I glance at him. "Thanks. It's important to me that you two get along. I love you both, and I can't live without either one of you."

His expression is somber. "As long as he takes good care of you and keeps you safe, I'll give him a chance."

I think that's the best I'm going to get out of Tyler.

32

Monday morning arrives all too soon, and I'm back at Clancy's learning the ropes. When I graduate from running the check-out counter, Erin reassigns me to straightening and restocking the shelves. I'm pretty much in bibliophile heaven. She gives me the coveted fiction sections (and yes, maybe I did pull a few strings to make that happen), so I'm pretty much spending half a day playing with books and getting paid for it!

Shane's been paying my bills since I left my job at the medical school library—he refused to let me use any of my small nest egg of savings. So, I really need to start making some money again so I can take over paying my own bills and figure out a plan to pay him back.

Having worked in a library for two years, I'm a pro at alphabetizing and shelving books. And I've been known to get a little anal retentive about it, making sure the books are in the proper order, all lined up neatly and evenly on the shelves. And sometimes, if I'm feeling particularly obsessive, I'll even alphabetize an author's individual titles.

Sam is always lurking nearby, usually entertaining himself with a book or with merchandise from the toy section. Honestly, sometimes I think he's just a big kid. Apparently, he's a huge sci-fi fan, liking everything from Dr. Who to Star Trek to Firefly. Fortunately, there's plenty here in the store to keep him entertained.

I'm in the Westerns section, straightening up the Zane Greys which got mixed in up with a ton of James Griffin novels. I still can't believe I'm getting paid to do this. I could shelve and organize books all day. I feel like a kid who's been let loose in a candy store and told to have fun.

After I finish straightening the shelves, I spend some time at the front of the store straightening up the tables displaying newly released hardbacks and paperbacks. A table of Dr. Who merchandise is looking a little worse for wear, so I straighten that up as well. It's very satisfying to be here, working to keep the merchandise organized and neat, and helping customers find what they're looking for.

Every few minutes a customer asks me where to find something. One young woman asks me where she can find the *Outlander* books, and a young boy and his father ask me where they can find *Diary of a Wimpy Kid*. I've been coming to this store my entire life, so of course I know where every genre is shelved. I take customers around the store and help them find what they're looking for, and it all feels so right.

I'm having so much fun, I pull out my phone—even though it's against company policy—and send Shane a text message.

I love working in the bookstore. I know this is the right decision. Thank you, Shane! <3

A couple minutes later, he sends a reply.

I'm glad, sweetheart. Enjoy it.

"You'd better put that thing away before The Dragon Lady sees you."

I jump, not realizing Sam's standing right behind me. "Don't do that! You scared the crap out of me."

He chuckles. "In case you haven't noticed, your shift ended fifteen minutes ago. Lia's here, looking at porn magazines."

"We don't carry porn magazines, Sam."

"If you don't believe me, go look for yourself."

He leads me to the magazine section, and I find Lia mulling over a fitness magazine. On the cover is a beefy guy with well-oiled muscles, posing in a pair of tiny swim trunks.

Sam looks at me, gloating. "See? I told you."

"Told her what?" Lia returns the magazine to the shelf. "Hey, Princess. Ready to roll?"

I can't believe my half-day's over already. Time flies when you're having fun. And to make a great day even better, I didn't see Vanessa once during my entire shift.

Lia follows Sam and me upstairs to the employee lounge so I can grab my purse and clock out. As we're heading back toward the staircase, we pass the administrative office. I hear what sounds like muffled yelling coming through the closed door. I stop and try to make out what's being said—or rather screamed—but it's difficult.

The three of us stand eavesdropping outside the administrative office door, and it doesn't take us long to realize it's Vanessa doing the yelling. I open the office door, and we all file in, but the front office is empty. The yelling is coming through the closed door of Vanessa's private, inner office. She sure is giving someone hell.

"You idiot! How hard is it to follow instructions? I told you not to get friendly with her! I don't want her here. I sure as hell don't want her working here. What did you think you were doing?"

"Vanessa, you've misjudged her. She's really very nice. If you'd just get to know her—"

"That's Erin!" I say.

Lia glares at me. "Shh!"

"Don't tell me what to think, Erin. Just shut the fuck up and follow instructions, or I'll find someone who can. Stop being bud-dy-buddy with her, or I'll fire you."

"Vanessa, please—"

"Just do what I tell you. That's all you need to worry about."

I've had enough. I really don't care what Vanessa thinks of me, but she has no right to yell at employees like this, especially Erin, who wouldn't hurt a fly. I won't tolerate it. I march toward Vanessa's door, Lia and Sam both on my heels, and push it wide open. Erin turns to look, and her face pales when she sees me.

Vanessa's face turns beet red. For a moment, I see a flash of what looks like panic in her eyes, but it's gone just as quickly.

"Do you mind?" she says to me, propping her hands on her hips. "This is a private conversation in a private office. You have no right to waltz in here—"

"Actually I do," I say, fed up with her attitude. "I have every right, because this is my company. You're the one who's overstepped her bounds, Vanessa. You have no right to speak to an employee that way." I glance at Erin, who has tears streaming down her cheeks. Then I glance back at Vanessa. My heart is pounding, and I swear I can hear the blood rushing in my head. I take a deep breath and try to rein in my anxiety before it spirals out of control. "Vanessa, your services are no longer needed here. I'm sorry, but I'm going to have to let you go."

Her face turns an even deeper shade of red and her jaw drops. She looks incredulous. "You can't fire me."

"I'm pretty sure she can," Lia says, crossing her arms over her chest, as if daring Vanessa to contradict her. "And it's long overdue, if you ask me."

Vanessa glares at Lia. "No one asked you, so butt out." Then she looks at me. "If you fire me, I will sue you for wrongful termination so fast your head will spin. How would you like that?"

I honestly don't know if that's an empty threat or not, because I'm not up to speed on Illinois employment laws—something else I need to brush up on. But I do know one thing—Vanessa needs to go. She's a bully, and I don't want her here.

I feel a sense of calm settle over me because I know it's the right decision. This is my store. The people who work here are my employees. I have a responsibility to see to their welfare. "Go ahead and sue me, Vanessa. I don't care. I'll give you three months of severance pay—which is more than generous—but I want you out of the building. Now." I turn to Sam. "Please help Vanessa gather her personal belongings and escort her out of the building."

Sam grins. "Sure thing, boss. It would be my pleasure."

I look at Erin, who's literally shaking in her stilettos. "Are you all right?"

She nods, but she looks far from all right. Her bright blue eyes look huge in her face. She looks like she's about to collapse. "Come with me, Erin. Let's go down to the cafe and get something to drink."

"Damn, girl," Lia says to me as she and I and Erin walk out of the office, leaving Sam to supervise Vanessa's packing and departure. "That was downright impressive. I'm so proud of you. My protégé is growing up."

* * *

I need to talk to Shane, soon, and tell him what's happened. And I need to find out if Vanessa really can sue me for wrongful termination. But first, I need to deal with Erin. She's a complete wreck.

"But I can't be the general manager!" Erin says, clutching a cup of mocha-caramel-something coffee with whipped cream and chocolate shavings. Her eyes are wide with panic, and she stares at me like I've lost my mind.

"Why not? Somebody has to take over for Vanessa. You'd be perfect. Everyone likes you."

"Beth, no! This is my first management job, and I've only worked here for six months. I don't know how to run a business. You should do it. It's your store. You be the general manager."

"Erin, that's crazy. I've only been here a week. Your six months outrank my one week easily. Besides, I don't know anything about running a retail store. At least you have retail experience."

Lia looks at me and shrugs. "Need I remind you that your boyfriend runs a billion-dollar company? If you need any help, Beth, just ask him."

"You'd be great, Beth," Erin says, warming up to the idea. She reaches across the table and grabs my hand. "You care about the people who work here. Vanessa didn't. You're a natural with customers—I watched you with them today. Honestly, I think you'd do an excellent job."

I want to be involved in running the business, but I never contemplated acting as the general manager. I have so much to learn—and I haven't even started my MBA program yet. "I don't know, Erin. I'll have to think about it."

Mack Donovan comes up to our table and lays his hands on the back of my chair. "Sam filled me in. I can't say I'll lose any sleep over the departure of The Dragon Lady. It's probably the best thing that's happened here in ages. So, who's the new general manager now?"

I glance up at Mack, but don't say anything. I'm not sure what to say.

"I think you're looking at her Mack," Lia says, giving me a soft punch to the shoulder. "Beth is the new head honcho around here. How about we call her The Dragon Princess?"

* * *

After Sam escorts an irate Vanessa out of the store, I go back upstairs to her office—which is apparently now my office—and sit down at the desk to contemplate what I've gotten myself into. The office is a mess, with papers strewn everywhere, covering every flat surface as well as the floor. It looks like a tornado swept through here—a very angry tornado.

I call Shane.

"Hi, sweetheart," he says. "How did work go today?"

I take a deep breath and come clean. "Not very well. I fired Vanessa."

I can hear Shane chuckling over the phone. "Really?" He sounds almost... pleased. Certainly amused.

"Yes, really. I had to. She was being awful to Erin."

"Good for you. Mack says she's a real terror."

"Yeah, well, she threatened to sue me for wrongful termination. Can she do that? Am I in trouble?"

Shane sighs over the phone. "No, sweetheart. You're not in trouble. Don't worry. If she does sue, which I doubt she will, Troy will take care of it."

This might be the second time Shane's lawyer has had to come to my aid. He's also handling the assault and battery case against Andrew Morton.

"So, who's going to take Vanessa's place?" Shane says.

I just sit here for a moment, because I'm not sure what I've gotten myself into. "I guess I am."

* * *

It looks like my part-time job has suddenly morphed into a full-time job, and that's a good thing. At least now I'll be earning a living wage, and I can pay back Shane for what I owe him.

Fortunately, we have an IT staff member on-site—Megan. She sets up a network ID and password for me on the computer in Vanessa's office. In *my* office. I guess I need to get used to saying that. Charlie in payroll changes my status in the system from part-time employee to full time, general manager.

"So what's my salary?" I ask him, looking over his shoulder as he keys in my information.

He looks at me like I'm nuts and shrugs. "What do you want it to be?"

"Let's go with whatever Vanessa was getting. That'll be fine." When he keys in the amount, I'm shocked. "Are you kidding? Doesn't that seem a little high to you for a bookstore manager? I mean, I know this is Chicago and all, but I'll bet there are some medical doctors who make less than that." Now I'm doubly glad I fired Vanessa.

He shrugs. "Vanessa gave herself a hefty raise right after Mr. Clancy retired."

"What was her salary before the raise?"

When he tells me, I nod. "That sounds more reasonable. I'll go with that."

After I'm done with Charlie, I send my first e-mail from my official company account.

To: Shane McIntyre
From: Beth Jamison

I've got e-mail now. This is all so surreal. Any minute now, I'm going to wake up and find out it's all a dream. Wish me luck.

Love u,
Beth

* * *

I'm sitting at my desk reviewing the employee handbook, making a list of the changes I want to make, when there's a knock on my open door. I smile when I see Shane lounging in the doorway, looking very debonair in his suit and tie. I practically melt at the sight.

A grin steals over my face at his unexpected—and very welcome—appearance. "Can I help you, sir?"

He smiles, and those gorgeous blue eyes glitter with amusement. "I'd like to see the manager, please."

"Oh?" I lean back in my chair, trying to look managerial. "Is there a problem, sir?"

Nodding, he straightens and walks into the office and takes a seat on the corner on my desk. "Yes, there's a problem. I was so busy today I skipped lunch, and now I'm starving. I'd like to take Clancy's new general manager out to dinner to celebrate her sudden promotion, if she'll let me."

"She'd be delighted, thank you. Where did you have in mind?"

"I think I'll let the new general manager choose."

I quickly run through some options, and then I know what I want. "You know what I'm craving? Sal's Bar-B-Q. Remember, that little barbecue place we ate at in Hyde Park?"

Shane loves barbecue and old-time blues music, and Sal's one of the best places in Chicagoland to get both. It's a tiny hole-in-the-wall restaurant-slash-pub where I took Shane a few months ago on one of our first official dates.

But the restaurant is located in my old neighborhood—Hyde Park—just a five-minute walk from my townhouse. At first I think he'll veto the idea, but then he surprises me. "Sure. That sounds fine."

* * *

We drive to the little business district where the restaurant is located, and Shane parks on a side street just a few blocks from our destination. We walk hand-in-hand past the small independent grocer I used to frequent, past the florist and a Chinese restaurant. There's even a small used bookstore. When we reach Sal's, Shane opens their battered wooden door for me, and we walk inside, hit immediately with the mouth-watering aroma of slow-cooked meats and barbecue sauce.

We seat ourselves at a small booth in the back corner of the restaurant, choosing to sit together on one side of the table, rather than across from each other. A middle-aged woman brings us two glasses of ice water and asks what we'd like to drink.

An old mahogany bar accented with brass fittings and vintage lighting runs along one side of the small restaurant, and the rest of the place is filled with small tables covered with red-and-white checkered tablecloths that have certainly seen better days. The place may look a bit run down, but I know for a fact that the food here is superb.

The sound system is playing a classic Muddy Waters song. You can't grow up in Chicago and not know who Muddy Waters is—he's the acknowledged father of Chicago blues. This place has a wonderful vibe all its own.

Our server brings Shane a tall glass of dark ale and me a Coke, and then she takes our food order. While we're waiting for our food, Shane lays his arm across my shoulders. His free hand snags my right hand, and he rubs his thumb across the back of my knuckles. Sitting this close to him, tucked under his shoulder, I'm warmed by the heat of his body. I lean into him and inhale his scent, male skin and fresh laundry and the barest hint of cologne. I turn my hand in his so that I'm the one doing the caressing now. I stroke each of his long fingers one at a time, from the base to the tip, mimicking how I might like to stroke another part of his anatomy.

He groans when I begin to knead the center of his palm, pressing my thumbs into his flesh.

"You're asking for trouble," he says, his voice low as he shifts on the bench seat, trying to adjust himself in his slacks.

I think my little hand massage is having a definite effect on him. I let go of his hand and turn to him, slipping my arm inside his jack and around his waist, feeling his firm abdominal muscles flex with every breath. My hand brushes against the gun holster strapped to his chest, and I pull back, momentarily startled when I realize he's armed. It shouldn't really surprise me. He's usually armed now when we go out, especially if it's just the two of us. And we are just a few minutes from my townhouse, where Kline has recently been known to loiter.

"It's okay," he says, wrapping his arms around me to draw me back to him. "It's just a precaution. It's nothing to worry about."

Our food arrives, and we eat in comfortable silence, each one of us aware of the other, sharing glances and small touches throughout our meal. Shane steals a few of my fries, and he gives me a bite of his brisket. As much as I'm enjoying having dinner with him here, I can't wait until we get home.

We've both just about finished with our meals when his phone chimes with an incoming call. It's a ring tone I don't recognize.

Shane reaches into his jacket and pulls out his phone. "Report." His voice is uncharacteristically sharp.

I look at him, wondering what's wrong.

He listens for a moment, and I can just barely make out a male voice coming over the phone, although I can't distinguish who it is or what he's saying.

"God damn it!" Shane says. "You're sure?"

He's silent for a moment as he listens to the caller. "She's here with me. We're at a restaurant in Hyde Park. Fuck! I can't believe the timing. How soon can we get someone here to pick her up?"

Another pause.

"No! I can't wait that long, Jake. Damn it! I don't believe this."

Another pause as Shane glances at me. "No, I'm not bringing her. It's too risky. I'll call you back."

Shane ends the call and sits there, staring straight ahead. I can practically see the wheels turning in his head. He types something quickly into his phone, then he pulls two twenties out of his wallet and lays them on the table.

He turns to me, garnering my full attention. "Listen to me carefully, Beth. Lia's on her way here," he says, rising from the booth. "She'll take you to the penthouse. Stay right here at this table until she gets here."

Something's seriously wrong for Shane to abandon me in a

restaurant. My heart starts thundering painfully, and I grab his wrist. "You're leaving me here? Why? What's wrong?"

Leaning down, he pins me with a hard gaze. His voice is strained. "You stay right here—don't leave this table, do you hear me? Lia will be here soon. She'll take you home."

"Where are you going?" But I have a sinking suspicion I already know.

He shakes his head, gritting his teeth. "Do not leave this table."

As he turns and walks away, I jump up and run after him. I'm not about to stay here when I know what he's walking into. "Shane!"

He stops and turns, and I nearly run right into him. He grabs my shoulders and steadies me. "Sit back down and wait for Lia."

"No. This is about Kline, isn't it?"

Shane looks away, his chest lifting as he draws in a big breath, then exhales.

"I'm going with you."

He glares at me. "The hell you are!"

Everyone in the restaurant is staring at us now. Shane lowers his voice. "You are not coming with me, Beth. Stay here and do what I said. Don't worry, you'll be perfectly safe until Lia gets here."

"If you walk out of here, so will I. You're going to my townhouse, aren't you? Kline's heading there right now, isn't he?"

Shane closes his eyes and blows out a heavy breath. "That was Jake on the phone. Kline just boarded a bus headed this way, and he's armed. This may be it. This may be our chance—*my* chance—to put a stop to this. I can't miss this opportunity, Beth. I have to be inside your house before he arrives. You need to listen to me and wait here."

"No. I'm coming with you."

"Damn it, we talked about this!"

"No, *you* talked about it! I want to be there. If something happens—if something goes wrong and you get hurt, I could never live with myself. This isn't your decision to make, Shane. This is my life. It's me he's coming after me. I—"

Shane runs his fingers through his hair. "Beth, please don't do this to me."

He sounds agonized, and I hate cornering him like this, but I'm not going to sit here while he risks his life for me. I can be just as stubborn as he is. "I'm not staying here, Shane. I'll follow you."

I know I'm being a brat, but I don't care. If this is the only way I can get him to take me seriously, then so be it.

"Fuck!" He grabs me by the arm and marches me toward the door. "I don't have time to fucking argue with you. Fine, I'll bring you with me, but you will do exactly as I say, do you hear me? If not, I swear to God I'll lock you in a closet."

I nod, struggling to keep up with his long, determined strides. He shoves the restaurant door open, and we head for the Jaguar.

33

My street is just minutes away. Shane parks in the alley behind my house, about a block away. He's talking on his phone to Jake as we hustle down the narrow alley toward my house. The sun's setting, and it'll be dark soon.

Jake meets us at the side door to my garage, ushering us inside quickly and shutting the door behind us. "What the God damned fuck is she doing here?" he growls, glaring at me.

"Deal with it!" Shane hisses. "I need to get her somewhere safe inside."

Shane and Jake both march me across the backyard and through the French doors into the kitchen. There are two men I don't recognize standing at the kitchen table, plus the blonde woman who looks like me. They're all clustered around the table, where weapons are laid out, plus some other electronic devices I don't recognize.

They all stop what they're doing to stare at me.

"Change in plans," Jake says, his voice brisk. "We have a fucking bystander. Where do we put her?"

At first, there's dead silence as everyone stares at me. Then one of the men I don't recognize steps forward. "Put her in—shit! Beth's bedroom is the last room upstairs. He'll look in every upstairs room first, before he gets to her room. You can't leave her downstairs, so you have no choice but to take her upstairs with you and hide her in her bedroom."

"There's a small walk-in closet in the bedroom," the blonde woman—Caroline—says. "We can hide her in there. It's out of the line of fire, so she should be okay if she hunkers down and has protective gear on."

Jake comes forward with a heavy black vest, which he shoves into Shane's waiting hands. Shane draws the vest over my torso and secures it tightly with thick Velcro straps. The vest is huge and it weighs a ton, hanging on me and weighing me down. All of the others have similar protective gear on, except for Shane. Jake hands Shane a vest, and he slips it onto himself and secures it.

Jake's phone vibrates, and he checks it. "ETA bus stop in seven minutes. Everyone into position."

Two of the men slip out the back through the French doors and disappear into the night. Caroline, Jake, Shane and I head up the back staircase to the second floor. I notice then that Jake and the woman both have communication devices in their ears. Jake hands a similar device to Shane, who quickly inserts it into his ear.

Shane has a painfully tight hold on my arm as he walks me down the hallway to my bedroom. I can tell he's angry at me, really angry, but I can't worry about that right now. It's too late for me to back out now.

All of the lights downstairs are off, but there are two lights on upstairs—one in the hallway bathroom and one in my bedroom. Shane directs me down the hall to my bedroom, and once inside, he opens the closet door and thrusts me inside, following me into the small, dark room. He jerks the pull-chain to turn on the closet light, then grabs my shoulders and turns me to face him. His voice is hard. "You stay in here and don't make a sound, do you hear me?"

As he double-checks that my vest is secured, I nod. My heart's beating so fast I can hear the blood rushing through my skull.

His hands frame my face, and he pulls me in close as he leans down so that we're practically nose to nose. His eyes are as cold and hard as blue diamonds as he stares at me. "Do not make a sound. Do not come out of this closet, no matter what you hear. Do you understand me?"

"Yes." My voice is little more than a croak.

His eyes close briefly, and when he reopens them, his gaze is surprisingly tender. "There's no time." He pulls me close, despite the awkwardness of our armored vests, and wraps his arms tightly around me. He presses his mouth to the top of my head, his hot breath ruffling my hair, sending chills down my spine. He walks me backward, deeper into the closet, into the farthest corner where some clothes are hanging on the rod. He pushes me down into a sitting position and crouches down in front of me. "I swear to God, Beth, if you move from this spot, I'll blister your hide, do you hear me? This time I'm not kidding."

Nervously, I chuckle—it's an inside joke with us. We met while I was reading an anthology of spanking stories, and he teases me with the threat of spanking. He's never done it, of course, but this time I think he might be serious. He's so tightly-wound right now that if he was pushed far enough, he might actually carry through with his threat.

Even though he's so on edge, his thumb is gentle when it brushes the curve of my cheek. "Be safe, Beth," he murmurs, leaning forward to bring his lips to mine. He kisses me gently, almost reverently, and that makes me choke up.

"Now listen to me," he says. "I'm going to turn off the closet light and shut the door. You will remain frozen in place until I—or one of my people—come to get you. Do you understand?"

"Yes." My voice is thick with unshed tears.

"You're going to have to be okay here in the dark, sweetheart. I can't let you have any light on. All right?"

I nod. "It's not me I'm worried about." I almost choke on the words as hot tears burn my cheeks. I know perfectly well it's Shane who'll be in the line of fire. He's going to be the one to confront Howard Kline and risk getting himself shot—or even killed. Because of me.

I clutch Shane's arms. "Be careful." My voice is barely audible, and I can't seem to catch my breath.

Shane reaches inside his armored vest and pulls one of my rescue inhalers out of his suit pocket and shoves it into my hands. "In case you need it."

I swallow against a painful lump in my throat. "I love you." I try hard not to wonder if this could be the last time I can say that to him.

Jake pokes his head inside the closet and growls at Shane. "ETA two minutes! Get into place!"

Shane nods at his brother, then turns back to me with a smile, suddenly looking calm and unhurried as he brushes my cheek with his fingers. It's as if he simply flipped a switch, shutting off his emotions. "I love you, sweetheart. Wait here. I'll see you soon."

Shane turns off the light, and I hear a quiet snick as he gently closes the door. I'm left huddling in the back corner of my old closet, sitting under the few clothes I'd left behind. It's pitch black in here. I can see a thin ribbon of golden light underneath the closet door as the light in the bedroom is still on. I keep my gaze locked at that little bit of light as I bring my knees up and rest my arms on them. I slow my breathing, counting with each regulated breath, and try not to hyperventilate. None of us can afford for me to have a panic attack right now.

I count as I inhale through my nose and exhale through my mouth. I hear muffled voices in the bedroom, both male and female, as final arrangements are made.

I can't believe this is happening. Shane and Jake and the three others are calmly waiting for Howard Kline to break into my house, come up the stairs to my bedroom with the intention of... what? Kidnapping me again? Raping me? Killing me? I don't think any of them know what Kline's intentions are. But if he's willing to break into my house, it can't be good.

No matter how unnerved I am by the thought of Howard Kline's proximity, it's Shane's safety that I'm most worried about. I couldn't bear for anything to happen to him. And I'm terrified by the idea that he could be arrested for killing Kline.

34

At first, everything's quiet. I don't hear a single sound coming from the bedroom. My own breathing sounds overly loud to me in the tiny closet. I'm trying not to dwell on the fact that it's almost pitch black in here—it's as if I'm locked in a tomb, far removed from light and sound and air. The air thins and time slows to a crawl. Then I hear quiet sounds coming from my bedroom, a few whispered words that I can't make out.

What's happening out there? The last I saw, Jake and Caroline were in the bedroom, too. That makes me feel marginally better. At least Shane's not alone. If something goes wrong, Jake and Caroline will be there to give Shane some back-up.

Time seems to crawl as the seconds pass, long agonizing seconds. I hate being locked in here, because I have no idea what's going on out there. I wish I'd thought to ask for one of those communication devices—at least then I'd be able to hear what's being said. I wrap my arms around my knees and try to still my shaking. I'm hot underneath the heavy armored vest, and I can feel sweat soaking through my blouse and trickling down my back.

I nearly jump out of my skin when I hear the sound of the toilet flushing in the upstairs hall bathroom. I hear soft footfalls entering my bedroom. And then the light in the bedroom switches off, and I'm left in utter darkness. Caroline must be going through the motions of preparing for bed. I hear the antique bed frame creak as someone climbs into the bed, and then it's silent again.

After an interminable period of waiting, I think I hear someone on the stairs. The old wooden boards creak like crazy, and I hear the tell-tale sound of someone walking up the stairs. My heart is practically in my throat now. Then I hear the familiar sound of my old mahogany bedroom door swinging slowly open on squeaky hinges.

Even though I can't see what's happening in my bedroom, I can imagine Caroline lying in my bed beneath the covers, pretending to be me, putting herself in harm's way on my account. I don't even know this woman, and she's risking her life for me.

Suddenly, the silence is broken by the sound of a man chuckling. It's a horrible, gravelly sound—the same one that's haunted my dreams for years. Oh, my God, he's really here. He's really coming after me. I feel sick as a shudder wracks my body, and then I hear that awful voice, low and grating. It sounds like it's coming from just outside the closet door.

"You stupid little cunt," he rasps, his voice dripping with hatred. "I spent eighteen years in hell because of you! You owe me!"

I hear a single popping sound, faint and muffled, followed by a heavy thud and the sound of something metal hitting the bare wood floors. Did Shane have a silencer on his gun? I don't know. My heart rockets up into my throat, choking me to the point I can barely breathe. I gasp for air, feeling hot and stifled in the small, dark room. I need to use my inhaler, but I'm afraid it will make too much noise. I don't want to do anything to distract Shane.

Then all hell breaks loose as I hear Jake yell, "He's down!"

Who's down? Where's Shane?

I hear shouting—men's deep voices, loud and urgent—and shuffling feet. The bedroom light comes on, and I hear heavy boots pounding on the wooden stairs.

Then I hear Shane's voice right outside the closet door, steady and calm. "He's dead, Jake. Make the call."

I'm blinded by a flood of light when the closet door opens. I throw up my hands to block out the light. Shane's standing in the open doorway, holstering his gun. His protective vest is gone.

"Beth, honey, it's me. I'm coming in." He steps into the closet, closing the door halfway behind him, whether to block some of the light or give us privacy, I'm not sure. "It's done, sweetheart. It's over."

I scramble awkwardly to my feet and rush to him, and he catches me in his arms. I'm shaking from head to toe, and my face is wet with tears. He takes my inhaler from my trembling hand and shoves it into his suit pocket.

He kisses my forehead. "It's all right now. Everything's all right."

"Was that Kline? Is he dead?"

Shane nods as he unstraps my body armor and pulls it off me. "He's dead. He'll never threaten you again."

I look at Shane, studying his expression, and I'm surprised he's so calm. Almost too calm. "Is everything okay?"

He nods. "Fine. I'm going to take you downstairs now. You can wait with me until the police arrive."

"I want to see Kline. I want to see his body."

I start for the doorway, but Shane stops me. "Beth, there's no need—"

"I need to see his body. I need to see with my own eyes that he's dead."

"Beth—"

I push past him, and this time he lets me go, although I don't get very far. Not three feet from the closet there's a body lying on the floor, a thick pool of dark blood spreading out from beneath the man's head. Jake is standing over the body, his gun in his hand, as if on guard.

I look at the dead man's face and feel a wave a nausea sweep through me. He has a fleshy face, wrinkled with heavy jowls. He's mostly bald now, and his face looks a sickly shade of gray. There's a hole in his forehead, dead center, just above his eyes.

I walk closer to the body and stare at the spreading puddle of blood on my bedroom floor. I can't help wondering if it will leave a stain. Kline's wearing black clothing, filthy, stained trousers and a black T-shirt with holes in it that doesn't quite cover his massive belly. On his feet are old black sneakers, ripped and torn.

What's most frightening is what he's holding in his clenched fists. He's holding a gun in one hand, and a roll of black electrical tape in the other. He didn't just want to kill me. He wanted to *hurt* me, just like in my dreams. He wanted to tie me up again and finish what he started eighteen years ago. I feel sick.

"He could have been a free man," I say, staring down at him. My voice sounds distant, even to my own ears. "He could have just walked away."

Shane comes up behind me and puts his hands on my arms, pulling me back against him. "He made his choice. Now let's go downstairs and wait for the police. You don't need to see this."

I shudder at his reminder that the police will be here soon. That's my biggest fear—that Shane will be charged with murder, that he'll be arrested and taken away from me. I start shaking violently.

"Don't worry," he says, rubbing my arms. "Everything's going to be fine. Please don't cry."

I'm shocked to realize I am crying, my shoulders shaking with messy sobs. Shane says everything will be okay, so why don't I believe him? Why is there a gaping hole in the pit of my stomach that tells me my nightmare is just beginning?

35

S hane sits beside me on the sofa in the front parlor, and neither of us says a word. I'm in shock. As for Shane, I'm not sure how he's feeling at the moment. He seems rather subdued. I can sense he's physically and emotionally exhausted, but he's putting up a strong front for my sake. He just killed a man, for God's sake! That has to take a toll on him. He puts his arm around my shoulders, but I can't stop shaking.

He leans close, his lips in my hair. "It'll be all right, sweetheart. Don't worry."

But I can't help worrying. What if the police arrest Shane for the shooting? What if he's charged with a crime? What if he's charged with murder? The thought sends me into a panic, and my heart thunders in my chest.

Cooper walks through the front door and glances up the stairs, listening to the muted voices coming from the second floor. Then he glances at Shane through the open doorway into the parlor. "Do you want me to call Troy?"

Shane shakes his head. "Not yet. Let's see how this plays out. If there's a complication, call him."

A complication. As in Shane getting arrested.

At the mention of Troy Spencer's name, my stomach cramps painfully. The thought of Shane needing his attorney terrifies me. What if the police charge him? I know he has a license to carry a gun, but what if something goes wrong? I can't shake the fear that this could all explode in our faces. If something happened to Shane, I'd never forgive myself.

It's only been about five minutes since Jake made the nine-one-one call, but it seems like a lifetime.

Shane takes hold of my trembling hands. "Relax, honey."

"Don't worry, Beth," Cooper says, peering out the narrow sidelite beside the front door as he watches for the police to arrive. "What Shane did is perfectly lawful. Kline committed a felony by breaking into your home, armed. Shane faced the threat of imminent death or great bodily injury. He's in the clear. They'll question him, but they won't arrest him."

The front of the townhouse is suddenly awash in flashing blue lights.

Cooper confirms what we already know. "Shane, they're here."

Shane kisses my temple, then stands. "Cooper, come sit with Beth."

Cooper opens the front door to let in three uniformed officers. Shane meets them in the foyer and says a few words. One of the officers goes directly upstairs, and the other two remain downstairs talking to Shane.

Cooper joins me on the sofa and puts his arm around my shoulders to give me a reassuring squeeze.

My ears are ringing and I can barely hear as Shane recites the events of this evening to the officers. Kline, an armed and known felon, broke into our house. He came upstairs to our bedroom and pulled a gun on Shane. Shane shot and killed Kline before Kline could pull the trigger. End of story. Self-defense.

While the officers are taking down Shane's story and asking him questions, a black pick-up truck pulls to an erratic stop in front of my house. Tyler races up to the front door and pushes inside, flashing his detective badge to the officers. The officers must at least recognize Tyler, because they wave him in.

It's late, and Tyler's dressed down in gray sweats and a T-shirt. I'm so glad he's here, but I wonder who called him.

I must have said that aloud, because Cooper says, "I did."

Tyler's up in Shane's face, demanding answers. "Is she here? Where is she?"

Shane tips his head in my direction as he answers an officer's question.

Tyler looks my way, assessing me with a quick glance, and then he lunges at Shane, grabbing him by the shirt front and slamming him hard against the foyer wall. "What the fuck were you thinking!"

Tyler wraps his hands around Shane's throat and squeezes, cutting off Shane's air as he holds him pinned to the wall. "You God damned son of a bitch! She could have been killed!"

I jump up from the sofa, swaying on my feet as the blood rushes from my head. "Tyler, stop!"

Cooper grabs me and hauls me back down beside him, wrapping his arms around me and holding me fast.

Shane grabs Tyler's wrists and forcibly pries them off his throat.

Tyler pulls free and slams his fist hard into Shane's face, knocking Shane's head against the wall with a sickening thunk. I scream as Shane staggers from the blow, shaking his head to clear it. Bright red blood is streaming from his nose and down his chin. Growling, he barrels into Tyler, pushing him across the hall and slamming him into the opposite wall.

Both officers jump in, the two of them hauling Shane off of Tyler. One of the officers—a big, muscular guy—slams Shane face first into the wall, pinning him in place while the other officer grabs Shane's right arm and twists it up high behind his back, locking a handcuff around his wrist. Shane stops fighting and leans into the wall, his chest heaving, as they bring his other wrist behind his back and cuff him.

I strain against Cooper's hold.

Jake comes thundering down the staircase and stops abruptly when he sees Shane held face first against the wall by both officers, handcuffed, his face bloody.

"Fuck," Jake says, looking peeved as he takes in my brother, who's bent at the waist, breathing hard from the exertion.

"Stay with the body!" Shane barks at his brother.

Tyler's face is flushed, and he looks livid. "What the fuck were you thinking, Shane?"

Shane's eyes are hard as they lock on Tyler. His nose is bleeding profusely now, and there's blood at the corner of his mouth. "I did what had to be done."

I finally manage to pull free from Cooper and run to Shane's side, grabbing hold of his arm. I can barely see through the tears in my eyes.

One of the officers grabs hold of me and pulls me away from Shane. "Miss—"

"Get her back, Cooper!" Shane shouts, his voice hoarse.

"Arrest him," Tyler says to the officers.

The officer holding Shane against the wall starts reading him his rights. "You have the right to remain silent," the man says. "Anything you say can and will be used against you in a court of law."

"No!" *Oh, my God, no!* It wasn't supposed to happen like this. Shane said it would be okay!

As the officer continues reading Shane his rights, I can hardly hear over the loud ringing in my ears, and I'm gasping for breath now, suddenly feeling light headed. My vision starts to grow dark around the edges as my knees go weak. Strong arms catch me.

"Get her inhaler!" Shane says. "It's in my jacket pocket."

Tyler reaches inside Shane's jacket and pulls out my inhaler, shakes it, and puts it to my mouth. "Breathe in, Beth," he says, as I suck in the medication. "It's okay, kiddo. Just breathe."

"Beth—" Shane's voice sounds agonized. "Jesus, sweetheart, I'm sorry."

I meet my brother's gaze, feeling heartbroken. "Tyler, please. Don't let them take him." Surely he can do something. They're arresting Shane. They're going to take him away.

Tyler looks away. "Take him to the local precinct," he tells the officers. "I'll be along shortly, after I see to my sister."

Tyler walks me to the parlor sofa and sits me down. I lunge back to my feet, wanting to go to Shane, but Tyler pulls me back down. "Sit down, Beth, before you fall down."

Shane cranes his head back so he can see me. "Don't worry, sweetheart. Everything will be fine." He sounds utterly confident. Then he looks at Cooper. "I guess you'd better call Troy."

* * *

Two officers lead Shane out the front door, and I watch through the front window as they put him in the backseat of one of the patrol cars and shut the door. The flashing police car lights bathe everything and everyone in a surreal shade of bright blue, making the whole situation feel unreal.

One of the officers drives away with Shane, and the other one comes back inside and heads upstairs.

I think I'm going to be sick. I'm not even sure what just happened—it all happened so fast. Cooper's on his phone, talking to someone in a low voice, presumably to Shane's attorney.

It's all too much. Not just what happened tonight, and my fear Shane would be arrested over this, but the past eighteen years of my life. It's countless nightmares and panic attacks and a constant underlying sense of fear. And now this. My biggest fear—Shane's been arrested. It's all my fault! I've reached a breaking point, and the damn is blown wide open and all the fear and heartache come pouring out.

I glare at my brother, choking on my own tears. "Why did they arrest him? What are the charges?"

Tyler ignores me and looks up at Cooper, who has just ended his call. "Shane shot Kline? He's dead?"

Cooper nods. "Kline broke into this house, armed. Shane was waiting for him."

Tyler nods, his expression pensive. "Where's the body?"

"Upstairs. On the floor in Beth's bedroom."

"Her bedroom? Jesus! Where was Beth when all this went down?"

"In the closet," I say. "I had on a protective vest and I was never in any danger. Shane made sure of it."

Tyler ignores me, his eyes still on Cooper. "What were they doing here in the first place?"

Tyler's not stupid. He knows I've been living at Shane's place for the past two months, far from the townhouse. He has to wonder what we were doing here tonight.

"You'll have to ask Shane that," Cooper says.

Tyler eyes narrow as he tries to work out the events of this evening. "He planned this, damn it," he says. I don't know if he's referring to Shane or to Howard Kline.

Tyler turns to me and hugs me tightly. "Take her home, Cooper. I have to go to the precinct to deal with Shane."

Cooper's arms are crossed over his chest, his expression tight. "What exactly is he being charged with, detective?"

Tyler scowls. "That remains to be seen."

I try one more time. "Tyler, please. Get him out of there. He didn't do anything wrong."

Tyler looks at me, but says nothing. He's furious at Shane, that much is clear.

"Tyler, please!"

Just as Cooper and I are leaving, the coroner and the crime scene investigators arrive and head upstairs to the survey the body and the crime scene.

Cooper takes me back to the penthouse in his Jeep. Lia's waiting for us in the foyer, and when the elevator doors open and I see her wan expression, I burst into fresh tears.

"Shit, Princess," she murmurs as she hugs me tightly. "What the hell has my big brother done this time?"

My voice is thick with tears. "He shot Kline, and Tyler came, and he fought with Shane, and the police arrested Shane."

But of course Lia already knows all of this. She'd changed course and come straight to the penthouse as soon as she was alerted to the change in plans.

Numb, I follow them both inside the apartment. Lia leads me to the great room, and we both crash on the sofa. I grab the blanket over the back of the sofa and a throw pillow and wrap myself up in a protective cocoon, shutting everyone and everything out. I just need to be alone with my pain.

Cooper brings me a tumbler with an inch of what I assume is whisky. "Here. Drink this."

I swallow it down, gasping as it burns a path down my aching throat. I don't care. I demand a refill, and that one follows the first, leaving me coughing and teary-eyed.

Someone must have sent out an alert to the whole family, because it isn't long before Liam and Jamie and Gus arrive at the penthouse, followed soon after by their sister Sophie, the buxom brunette beauty who lives nearby in a Lincoln Park condo. Of the McIntyre siblings, only Jake and Hannah are missing. Jake's likely still at the townhouse, dealing with the coroner and monitoring the crime scene investigation. Their sister Hannah is away at college, living in Denver, Colorado.

Sophie takes a seat in one of the chairs by the fire and smiles at me. "Hello, Beth. It's good to see you again, although I wish it were under happier circumstances."

I smile at her, although I don't know what to say. What can I say? *I'm sorry your brother is in jail because of me?*

Jamie crouches down in front of me and takes hold of my hands, warming them in his. Jamie's life has thrown him some difficult challenges, and yet he's the one comforting me. "Don't worry, Beth. Shane always lands on his feet. He'll be okay."

I sit huddled beneath my blanket, feeling sick, my mind racing. I peer up at Cooper. "Have you heard anything from Troy yet?"

"Just that he's on his way to the police precinct where Shane's being held."

Liam steps forward. "Do we know what he's been charged with?"

Cooper shakes his head. "Not yet. Hopefully we'll know once Troy arrives."

If Shane is charged with murder... I don't know what I'll do. He did what he did to protect me. This is my fault.

Liam starts a fire in the fireplace, and the warm, crackling glow of the flames is comforting. The lights are turned down low—it's well after midnight now—and everyone's seated near the fireplace, either on the sofa or on one of the several upholstered chairs, waiting for news.

The whisky warms my belly, lulling me into a coma as I listen to the quiet murmurs of Shane's family all around me. Lia's seated beside me, and every once in a while she reaches over and pats my hip and tells me not to worry. How can I not worry when Shane's in police custody?

Cooper's phone chimes, and I jump. *Please, God, let it be news from Troy.*

After a brief and cryptic conversation, Cooper ends the call. But he doesn't look very pleased. Everyone waits for an update.

"That was Troy," Cooper says. "Shane's been booked, and they've moved him to the county jail."

My stomach plummets like a stone at the news.

"On what charges?" Liam says.

"Assaulting a police officer."

That shakes me out of my daze, making me sit up. "Tyler's the one who started the fight! Shane was only defending himself!"

Lia pats my knee. "Look at the bright side, Princess. They haven't charged him with murder. An assault charge is nothing in comparison to that."

"Not yet, they haven't," Cooper says. "Give them time. The night's still young." He rises to his feet. "I need another beer."

Sitting here waiting and worrying is driving me nuts. "I want to go to the jail." I have this burning desire to see Shane with my own eyes. To tell him I love him, and that I'm sorry for dragging him into my sordid life drama.

Cooper shakes his head as he returns to his chair. "Shane would want you to remain here. Jake's at the jail now, and so is Troy. That's enough."

* * *

I must have dozed off on the couch. When I awake, I'm in Shane's bed. *Our bed.* It's still dark outside, so I haven't slept for long. I get out of bed and walk in my rumpled clothing back into the great room. Lia is stretched out asleep on the sofa, and Cooper is seated in one of the upholstered chairs by the fire. The fire is nothing more than glowing embers now. Liam and Jamie and Sophie are gone.

Cooper peers at me through tired, blood-shot eyes. "You should go back to bed, Beth. Staying up all night's not going to help Shane. He'd want you to sleep."

"I can't sleep. Every time I close my eyes, I see Kline's dead eyes staring up at me from a pool of blood." I shudder. "Have you heard any more about Shane?"

"Troy called a couple of times. They're dragging their feet on filing the charges. I think Tyler's just jerking his chain."

"How's Shane?"

Cooper shrugs. "He's worried."

"About the charges?"

"No. About you."

I need to call Tyler and ask him to put an end to this, but I have no idea where my phone is. In all the chaos, I must have left my purse in my bedroom closet at the townhouse. That was the last time I remember having it. "Can I use your phone?"

Cooper hands me his phone, and I dial Tyler's number. He answers on the second ring. Apparently, no one's sleeping tonight. "Jamison." His voice sounds rough. "Who is this?"

"Tyler? It's me."

"Beth? Are you okay? Where are you?"

"I'm at the penthouse. And no, I'm not okay. Shane's been moved to the county jail."

"Yeah, I know. I'm there now."

"Isn't there anything you can do to get him released? Shane didn't assault you, Tyler, and you know it. You started it. You attacked him. He was just defending himself."

There's a long pause, and then I hear Tyler exhale heavily. "Beth—"

"Get him out of there, Tyler. Please! I'm begging you!"

Another long pause. "All right. But I'm still mad as hell at him. He should never have brought you there."

"He didn't have a choice, Tyler. We were at a restaurant nearby when Jake called to say Kline was on his way to the townhouse. Shane didn't want me there tonight, but I insisted. I really didn't give him any choice. Don't blame him."

Tyler exhales heavily, sounding tired. "I'll see what I can do. Now try to get some sleep. It's late."

* * *

I don't want to be alone in our suite, so I stay in the great room with Cooper and Lia—my adopted family. I grab my pillow from our bed and an extra blanket and crash on the sofa, at the opposite end from where Lia lies. As I settle in, trying to find space for my legs, she grumbles in her sleep but shifts to make room for me.

My eyes are heavy, and even though I'm worried sick about Shane, I can't keep sleep at bay for long. I close my eyes—just to rest them—and don't open them again until I'm awakened by the ding of the elevator doors opening in the foyer.

I'm still trying to get my bearings, groggy from an unsound sleep, when a dark shadow looms over the back of the sofa and bends down to kiss me gently on my forehead.

I'm barely half-awake and still more than a little disoriented. "Shane?"

"Yeah," he mutters, his voice hoarse. "I'm home, just a little worse for wear."

I wrap my arms around his neck and pull him down for a proper kiss.

He chuckles, attempting to pull back. "I'm also a little ripe, honey. I need a shower."

"Don't care," I say, happily stealing his line. Yes, he does need a shower, but I honestly don't care. I'm just so happy he's home. I pull him back down for another kiss. He's home, and that's all that matters.

After ending our kiss, Shane scoops me up in his arms. He glances at Cooper. "Thanks, man." He sounds utterly exhausted.

Cooper nods. "Anytime, son."

"For crying out loud, can you guys keep it down?" Lia mutters, pulling a blank over her head. "I'm trying to sleep here. Jesus, it's like Grand Central Station."

"Nice to see you, too," Shane says to his sister, reaching down to muss her hair through the blanket.

She slaps his hand away. "Cut it out, will ya? Princess has been a basket case all night. Take her to bed, pal."

* * *

Shane deposits me in his bed, then heads to the bathroom for a quick shower. I'd go with him, but I don't think my legs will hold me upright. Now that he's home, I'm finally able to relax for the first time in what feels like days, although really it's only been about nine hours since he was arrested. I'll have to wait for him to get out of the shower and come to bed before I can find out what happened. I look out the windows and see the sun's just starting to rise.

It's not long before Shane climbs naked into our bed, his skin warm and damp from his shower. He sighs as he pulls me against him and holds me close.

I press my cheek to his chest, taking comfort from the solid thud of his heartbeat against my ear. "Tell me."

"Tyler dropped the charges."

I flinch, feeling guilty that my own brother was behind this. "You should never have been charged in the first place. He assaulted you. I'm so sorry, Shane."

He squeezes me. "It's not your fault, sweetheart. Tyler had a right to be pissed at me—I never should have let you come with me last night. But, short of handcuffing you to the table at Sal's, I really didn't have much choice."

I chuckle, feeling some of the tension seep out of me, which is what I think Shane wanted in the first place.

"This is between me and your brother, Beth. He and I need to come to terms with each other. We're both stubborn, and we both have a claim on you. It's just that my claim trumps his now, and he hates that."

"He's my brother, Shane. I love him." I feel guilty, as if loving my brother is somehow a betrayal of Shane. I shudder when I think back to the day when Tyler, as a uniformed police offer just beginning his career, broke down the door to the cellar where Kline was holding me. After my eyes adjusted to the bright light of a half dozen flashlights, the first thing I saw was my brother's face, crumpled in agony as he cut me free and wrapped my freezing, naked child's body in his police jacket.

"Of course you love him," Shane says. "Don't worry, sweetheart. Since he and I both love you, and neither one of us appears to be willing to give you up, we'll just have to learn to get along. It would help, though, if he'd stop trying to strangle me."

"Is the danger passed, then?" I ask. "There won't be any more charges? Of any kind?" Of course I'm thinking about Howard Kline's death.

"There's an ongoing investigation, but that's routine. It's nothing to worry about. Don't worry, honey. What I did was justified self-defense. Now close your eyes and try to relax. I just want to hold you and sleep for a week."

❧ 36

W hen I awake the next morning, I check the time on my
phone, surprised to see it's already eight-thirty.

Shane wasn't kidding when he said he wanted to
sleep for a week. He's still sound asleep, with his head turned on his
pillow to face me. It's not often that I get a chance to observe him
sleeping, so I take full advantage of the opportunity.

His hair is a tousled mess, with bits of it sticking up. It doesn't
look like he bothered to comb it after his shower last night. His forehead is smooth in sleep, free of tension, free of the Herculean weight
of responsibility that he carries on his shoulders. His brown lashes
are thick and curved, and I never realized before how long they are.
My beautiful man.

My gaze travels down the straight bridge of his nose to the lower
half of his face, which is covered in a trim beard, the same rich brown

as his hair. His lips are smooth and soft in sleep, and I find myself staring longingly at them, wanting to taste them. I blush hotly when they curl up in a knowing grin.

"Good morning," he says, his voice rough from sleep and perhaps from lingering exhaustion. He reaches out and brushes the tips of his fingers across my cheek in a gentle caress.

"Good morning. You slept a long time." I touch his face too, brushing the pad of my thumb along his lower lip.

He kisses my thumb. "It was a long night last night. How are you holding up? I was worried about you."

"That should be my line. I was worried about *you.*"

"Honey, I pay Troy good money to keep me out of trouble. There was never anything to worry about. I just had to wait out Tyler's little temper tantrum."

I chuckle, relieved that Shane doesn't appear to hold a grudge against my brother.

"It's eight-thirty," I say. "We'll both be late for work." But the truth is, I don't want to go anywhere. I don't want him to go anywhere either.

As if reading my mind, Shane shakes his head. "We're not going to work today—neither of us. We're going to play hooky and spend the day together."

That makes me smile. There's nothing I need more than that.

He leans forward and kisses me. "So, what do you want to do today? You name it, we'll do it."

"Can we go to the lake? I've hardly spent any time there all summer."

He smiles. "Absolutely." He kisses me again, then sits up in bed. "Let's get cleaned up and dressed, then we'll have some breakfast. After that, we'll walk down to the beach and play tourist all afternoon."

While Shane calls Diane to tell her he won't be in today and asks her to reschedule his appointments, I send Erin a similar message and ask her to take over for me as acting general manager for the day. She freaks out a bit at first, but after a few more texts and a quick phone call to give her some words of encouragement, she agrees to stand in for me. I also send Lia and Sam messages informing them they both have the day off.

After a quick joint shower, which quickly turns into a soapy, slippery make-out session, we dress in beach attire. I don a one-piece swimsuit underneath my cotton shorts and tank top. Shane puts on a pair of khaki cargo shorts and a T-shirt that hugs torso nicely.

We find Cooper in the kitchen, seated at the breakfast bar drinking coffee and reading on his tablet.

"It's about time," he says, glancing up at us when we make an entrance. "I was about to send out a search party." He points out the two plates of food warming on the stove top. "There's your breakfast."

Shane claps him on the shoulder. "Thanks, man."

We help ourselves to plates of scrambled eggs and bacon and pour some freshly-ground coffee. Cooper really does spoil us.

After finishing my breakfast, I hug him fiercely. "Thank you, Cooper. For last night and for breakfast. For everything. I love you."

He blushes and rubs the top of my head, messing up my freshly-washed hair. "You're welcome, kiddo. Let's just hope Shane doesn't make a habit of spending the night in jail."

I run off to brush my teeth and put my hair up in a ponytail. When I return, Shane is wearing a plaid shirt over his T-shirt, and I know what that means. He's wearing his gun holster. He holds out his hand, and I take it.

We take the elevator downstairs to the main lobby. The beach is just a few hundred yards from the apartment building, so we walk across the parking lot and head down the street. Oak Beach is packed with people, so we head north along the Lakeshore Trail to enjoy a long, leisurely walk along the shoreline. We dodge the occasional bikers and people pushing baby strollers. It's a beautiful late August day, still warm and sunny, although summer is beginning to wind down as we get closer to fall.

We walk hand-in-hand, stopping occasionally to admire the view and watch the yachts cruising along the shoreline. We finally reach North Avenue Beach and stop for iced coffee drinks at a cafe. We wade into the surf to cool off, standing knee-deep in chilly water. I wouldn't mind going for a swim, but I didn't bother to bring a towel, so I pass. I don't want to spend the rest of the afternoon wearing wet clothes.

"Come sit down with me for a bit," Shane says, taking my hand and leading me to a wooden park bench situated beneath a large shade tree.

We sit and watch the passers-by for a while, Shane's arm resting across my shoulders. I'm tucked under his arm and pressed up against him, just enjoying the heat of his body and the scent of his skin.

"I have something for you," he says, gazing out over the water.

"Oh?" I look at his profile, and he seems... nervous. Even the tone of his voice sounds odd, almost as if he's unsure of himself. "What is it?"

He reaches into his baggy front pocket and pulls out a small, black velvet jewelry box. *A ring box.* My heart immediately begins hammering in my chest as he holds it out to me. When I reach for it, his warm hands envelop mine, cupping both my hands and the velvet box. He holds my hands for a long moment, his warm gaze locking with mine. He looks... wary.

He clears his throat. "I love you, Beth." Then he lets go of my hands, leaving the ring box in mine. "Go ahead. Open it."

Carefully, I open the box and stare at the diamond solitaire ring nestled inside. It's a lovely ring, a perfect diamond perched inside prongs of rose gold. The band is rose gold too, slim and dainty. I swallow hard. "It's beautiful." Then I look up at him, stunned. "What is this?" I'm afraid of jumping to a premature conclusion.

"It's whatever you want it to be, sweetheart. Whatever you're ready for. A friendship ring, a promise ring. An engagement ring. You tell me."

I stare down at the gorgeous ring cradled in my hands, my eyes filling with hot tears.

His hand comes up to lift my chin, so that we're looking eye to eye. He leans forward and kisses me gently on the lips. "There is no wrong answer, honey," he says, smiling. "It's whatever you want it to be."

I know what I want it to be. I have to stop and clear my throat. "It's an engagement ring."

He smiles then, and I swear I see relief in his eyes. How could he doubt what I feel for him? How could he ever doubt, even for a minute?

"In that case..." He gets down on one knee on the sand in front of me and takes my left hand in both of his. "Elizabeth Marie Jamison, will you marry me? Will you allow me the honor of becoming your husband?"

Tears spill unchecked down my cheeks, but I pay them no mind. These are tears of joy. I'm not the only one moved. His beautiful blue eyes are glittering with a little extra moisture too.

"Yes," I say, my voice not much more than a shaky whisper.

Shane pulls me off the bench onto his lap, and we sit on the sand, holding each other.

He kisses my temple. "I promise to love, honor, cherish, and protect you for the rest of your life, and that includes vanquishing all your monsters."

"That sounds like a vow, Shane."

"Yes, it does. And you know I keep my vows."

Neither of us can know what the future brings, but I know that as long as we have each other, we'll get through it... together. Just like we've done since we met one Friday evening in a bookstore.

~ *The End* ~

NEID IN THE SERIES...
Broken, book 3, features Lia McIntyre's story.

Lia McIntyre experienced the worst kind of betrayal a young woman can face at an age when she was very vulnerable. She survived to tell the tale. But the impact on her life has been devastating. When she's assigned as rock star Jonah Locke's personal bodyguard, she finds herself feeling things she'd rather not feel. Can Jonah teach her to trust again? Can Lia help Jonah vanquish memories of his dark past, as well as the threat facing him now?

Thank You!

Thank you for reading *Fearless*. I hope you enjoyed the continuing journey of Shane and Beth.

Please, if you would be so kind, take a moment to leave a quick review on Amazon for me. Amazon reviews are vitally important for authors. Every review helps a lot!

To find out about new releases and to receive free and exclusive bonus content featuring Shane, Beth, and other characters from this series, sign up for my New Release Mailing List at:

www.aprilwilsonauthor.com

This mailing list will be used only to announce new releases, giveaways, and to send out periodic free bonus content. The names on the mailing list will never be shared or sold. And you can unsubscribe at any time.

About the Author

April Wilson has been writing fiction since the age of 10, when she wrote and illustrated (in Crayon) her first children's book. With the explosion of the indie publishing market, she knew it was time to make her dream come true. Her first published novel, *Vulnerable*, was a great success, far surpassing her hopes and dreams. *Fearless* is her second novel. But stayed tuned, because she has many more novels in the pipeline.

April lives in Ohio with her teenage daughter and more than a few dogs and cats. When she's not writing, this die-hard romantic is reading romance novels, watching *The Walking Dead* and *Outlander*, and eating dark chocolate.

April adores receiving reader feedback! You can reach her here:

Email: aprilwilsonwrites@outlook.com

Website: www.aprilwilsonauthor.com

Facebook Reader Group:
Author April Wilson's Fan Group

Acknowledgements

I'd like to thank the following people who've been so helpful to me on my journey to realizing my lifelong dream to be an author:

A huge thank you to my darling daughter, Chloe, for patiently listening to me prattle on and on about writing and for kindly reading all of my books. I love you, sweetheart!

Without the unwavering support of my sister and BFF, Lori, I wouldn't be where I am today. She's my steadfast cheerleader, manager, sounding board, and therapist.

I want to thank my parents, Herb and Barb, and my brother, Matthew, for always being there for me and believing in me. Your support and patience are very much appreciated.

Thank you to my friend Ssamantha Christy. A mutual love of writing brought us together, and friendship keeps us together.

Thank you, Becky Morean, for sharing your love of writing and your authoring experience with me.